Blood Ties

Three Strand Cord Book 2

by

Tracy Krauss

Fictitious Ink Publishing
Tumbler Ridge, BC

Blood Ties

ISBN:978-1988447-44-5 (ebook), 978-1988447-45-2 (kindle), 978-1988447-46-9 (paperback),

Published by Fictitious Ink Publishing

Tumbler Ridge, BC, Canada

V0C 2W0

DEDICATION & ACKNOWLEDGMENTS

Of all my novels so far, I think this one went through the most changes from its inception to the finished product. I simultaneously loved the characters and hated some of the things they would do. Sometimes this led to lazy writing. It was easier to skim by certain scenes or even leave them out rather than try to weave the complexities of their lives together. Thankfully, I had a very discerning group of beta readers who picked up on some of these inconsistencies and I was able to go back and persevere through the difficult bits. The rewrites took much longer than anticipated, but good things often take time and are worth the wait. In the end, I am so grateful for their honesty and encouragement, since I believe this story now sings with authenticity while still presenting a powerful message about the gospel's life changing truth. Like the characters in this book, I am grateful for God's grace in my life. He accepted me despite my past, and calls me His beloved.

Tracy Krauss

I am my beloved's and my beloved is mine

Song of Solomon 6: 3a

PROLOGUE

*H*ot light exploded, deafening and sulphuric, as the bullet found its mark. The detective sank into a slow motion death spiral in time to a hollow scream. Her own.

"You killed him." A thick, dark puddle formed beside the his body.

"You'll be joining him in the afterlife soon enough. Now get moving." Her abductor grabbed her roughly by the arm and pushed her forward through the door, the pistol cocked and ready at her back.

Cherise stumbled forward, almost falling down the flight of stairs as Alistair Montgomery, once someone she trusted, pushed her from behind. Garneault - her gallant rescuer - was dead.

"You know, we could have had this over and done with a lot sooner, except your brother went and showed up."

Cherise turned her head. "Dirk is here?"

Alistair jerked her back into a forward position. "Yes, Dirk is here. Now, shut up. Nobody said you could talk." He laughed. "You know, I won't say that I'm not going to enjoy this. Seeing your poor family's faces when they get the news that your boyfriend, that beast Roberto, had you murdered. Your father's reaction will be stoic, of course. Maybe he'll take up drinking full time, so your mother won't have to do it alone."

They reached the main floor and the dimly lit garage where Alistair's car was waiting. He gave her a shove toward it but the sound of tires rolling to a stop outside the closed garage doors brought them both to a halt as he jerked her arm. "If you so much as make a peep, I'll blow your brains out."

He maneuvered them both to the grimy window that was high up in the garage door and stood on tiptoe to peer out. He gave a snort and then hit the automatic door opener. Cherise's eyes widened in shock as the door whirred open. There on the other side stood her brother Dirk, and her two best friends, Stella and Tempest.

"Here for the final act? I can't say I'm surprised." Alistair pressed the revolver into Cherise's temple. The distinct click as he cocked it in readiness made her jump.

"Don't do it, man." Dirk's voice was calm. Steady.

"Shut up!" Alistair barked, tightening his grip. "Why couldn't you leave well enough alone? Unfortunately, I like you, Dirk. We've always been good pals. I wasn't planning on hurting you. But you've gone and made things complicated. Now I'm going to have to make it look like Roberto killed all four of you rather than just one."

"Not today."

Roberto. Cherise would recognize that voice anywhere. A whimper escaped her lips.

Roberto Percelli approached from the outside, his gun trained on Alistair. He stepped forward steadily, both hands holding his revolver at the ready. "Get back," he instructed. Dirk, Tempest and Stella obeyed, sliding slowly out of her line of vision.

"Well," Alistair said conversationally. "Isn't this an interesting reunion? So nice of you to join our little party, Roberto."

"Let her go." Roberto's voice was calm and full of steel.

"Stop right there or I blast her." Alistair tightened the wrestling hold he had around her neck.

"Shut up and let her go," Roberto repeated.

"Why? You were done with her, weren't you? Although you might like to know that it didn't take her long to find another gigolo. Isn't that right, Cherise? A French cop. Rather old, in my view, but beggars can't be choosers."

"You will stop talking now and you will let her go. Or I shoot."

"The moment your gun goes off I'll squeeze my trigger. You might kill me, but Cherise will be dead, too. We could strike a deal, I suppose. You help me eliminate all of them and I won't try to pin it on you. How does that sound?"

"You are a sick man," Roberto replied.

"Really? So maybe you'd like to die instead?" Alistair whipped his gun arm forward and aimed at Roberto, still holding Cherise around the neck.

Suddenly, Alistair was stumbling forward, his arm slackening around her neck. Simultaneously, she saw Dirk diving sideways, knocking Roberto off balance as gun shots sounded.

She spun to see Jean Yvres Garneault, the detective she thought was dead, kneeling on the floor over Alistair's body, a Swiss Army knife sticking out of her abductor's neck. "Garneault! I thought you were dead!" She scrambled to his side.

He slumped forward onto Alistair's prone body, their blood mingling in a grisly puddle on the cement floor. "I am sorry, *cherie*," he whispered. "But you are safe now."

"No! Wake up!" Cherise shook Garneault's unresponsive body, and then looked around wildly. "Somebody help!" Then she saw him. Another man down in a pool of his own blood.

"Dirk!" With a strangled cry she stumbled across the floor toward Dirk's fallen form.

Tempest and Stella were already bending over him. "Hang in there partner," Cherise heard Stella say as she applied pressure to his stomach. Blood was seeping through her fingers.

Tempest's hand rested on Dirk's forehead, her other tightly in his grasp. She was saying something soft and gentle - perhaps a prayer - and he was gazing up at her, glazed eyes fixed on her face.

"Oh, God, no! Dirk, you can't die!" Cherise threw herself at his body.

"Give him space," someone said behind her and she felt strong arms pulling her away from her brother. Her mind struggled to decipher the voice.

Roberto.

"Get away from me!" she screamed. She flailed her arms, trying to beat him with her fists. "It's all your fault. You're a monster! A drug dealer and killer!"

Roberto grabbed her wrists and held them in a steely grip, even as she flung her body from side to side to try and get away. "Settle down! I'm a cop. One of the good guys."

Sirens sounded in the distance and every last bit of fight drained from her body. "A cop?" Her chest heaved. "You're a cop?"

Roberto nodded. "Yes."

"Why didn't you tell me?" she whispered. Her whole body slumped and she slid to a sitting position on the cold floor.

"I couldn't." Roberto knelt down by her side. His eyes held apology but not contrition. "I'm sorry."

"But all that time... in Boston... here in Rome -" She choked on the last words. "You used me."

"When you're under cover you're expected to do things that would seem... authentic."

"Authentic? Is that what you call it?"

"I'm sorry," he said again. "Not all of it was an act."

Sirens blazed to a stop as police vehicles and an ambulance screeched into place outside the doors. Roberto stood up and strode to meet them.

With the surreal quality of a dream, stretchers were wheeled into the garage as ambulance attendants and police bustled about. A woman came to her side with a blanket and helped her stand. She glanced at Dirk, covered with blood, an oxygen mask over his mouth and nose. Nearby, Garneault was already on a stretcher, as was Alistair, a sheet pulled over his face.

Tempest and Stella threw their arms around her and although she hugged them in return, her wounded mind could hardly register what was happening. It was too much to take in. So she closed her eyes and let sleep take over.

Cherise

CHAPTER 1

The hem of the bride's gown lifted with the breeze, the only movement beneath the canopy as the couple stood statuesque beneath its white canvas. The bride was petite, even in heels, with black hair piled on top of her head and wearing a simple white halter dress that showed off her deeply tanned shoulders and back. The groom was also tanned, but his skin had an elemental texture bordering on leathery from many hours in the sun. His dark brown hair curled around his ears, and his nose - although slightly sharp and a bit too long - gave him a hawk like quality that suited him.

A sudden snap from one of the overhanging canvas flaps brought the entire crowd to attention, hurrying the proceedings along.

The priest cleared his throat, stood more erect, and announced the familiar declaration with practiced solemnity. "I now pronounce you husband and wife." The rest of his instructions - probably, "You may now kiss the bride," was lost as cheers erupted from the crowd of onlookers.

Poor things. They looked so hot. At least the movement gave them some reprieve from the afternoon heat. Some fanned themselves with paper bulletins that had been passed out by the ushers. A sheen of moisture touched every face - even the well made up ladies.

Cherise turned her attention back to the happy couple, a smile on her lips as the bride and groom remained locked in a passionate kiss that should have brought embarrassment - if they weren't so oblivious to the onlookers.

Stella and Zane were a handsome couple and Cherise Hillyer clapped her encouragement along with the rest. As the maid of honor she stood nearby, and she couldn't be happier that her best friend had found true love. Apparently, such a thing really did exist.

"It's so beautiful," Tempest Ross, the other bridesmaid, whispered close to Cherise's ear. "I'm so happy for them." Tempest dabbed at a tear. She wasn't wearing her usual glasses for the occasion, and Cherise wondered that Tempest could even see. "I promised myself I wouldn't cry. I don't want to ruin my makeup."

Cherise smiled and nodded. "They do look good together. And happy," she added for good measure.

"Stella looks radiant. I suppose it's what love does to a person." Tempest said dreamily.

"Think so? You look pretty radiant yourself." Cherise gave her friend a little nudge with her elbow. Tempest did look beautiful. She had finally blossomed into the knock out Cherise knew existed all along beneath the bad clothing. Her friend had always had good 'bones', but her conservative style and lack of self-esteem had made her fade into the background. Today, the butterfly had finally emerged from its cocoon. A new romance could do that for a woman. Give her a glow that no amount of makeup could match.

Tempest's cheeks suffused with color and her eyelashes fluttered downward. "I have no idea what you mean."

Cherise suppressed a grin and turned her attention back to the bride and groom, finally coming up for air. Stella Crayton -

now Stella Shepherd - made up the third cog in their tightly bound sisterhood. Tempest, Stella and Cherise had been best friends since their days at middle school. Stella looked even more radiant than Tempest - exactly as a bride should look on her wedding day. That's what love could do for you. Stella had found her soul mate in Zane Shepherd and Cherise was happy for them. Really.

Except... everyone had someone but her. She pasted on an even brighter smile. My, how the tables had turned.

Cherise wasn't used to being alone. She had never lacked for male companionship in her life. When they were kids, Stella and Tempest used to tease her that she was 'boy crazy'. Well, it was probably true. Until two months ago, anyway. Since then she had sworn off men - at least for a while. It was safer. Literally. Her last affair had almost cost her life. If it weren't for the relentless-ness of her friends, she might not even be here to enjoy the nuptials.

The priest was saying his final benediction. The breeze ruffled the hair at the nape of her neck and Cherise welcomed the breath of air. Even in September, with a canopy to shade the bridal party, the Texas sun beat strong and hard. At least the sundress was sleeveless - even if mauve wasn't her color. She glanced at the men in the wedding party. Full tuxedos were an instrument of torture in this heat.

The best man caught her eye and winked. He was the groom's brother. A smile turned up the corners of his handsome mouth and she returned it. Blue Shepherd was cute; there was no doubt about that. He wasn't tall - about five foot ten, but he was well built and had a handsome baby face, blue eyes, and shockingly long lashes. His hair was a sandy blonde and curled past his collar in a shaggy style. She'd never actually met either of the Shepherd brothers before the rehearsal dinner last night and wasn't quite sure what to expect. Blue turned out to be friendly and outgoing, just like Stella had always described, but there was an underlying tension that Cherise had picked up on, too.

Cherise snapped back to reality as the music swelled and she watched Stella place her hand in the crook of Zane's arm. Soon her friend was floating down the grassy aisle on the arm of her rugged new cowboy husband. She should get herself one of those... Cherise blinked and then shook her head. She was on a man-diet.

She slid into place beside Blue Shepherd and placed her arm through his as they followed the married couple. "Better duck," Blue advised. Rose petals and rice showered over them the moment they emerged from under the canopy. Cherise lifted her other arm to shield herself and laughed out loud. Blue Shepherd just might be the cowboy to chase these melancholy blues away - if she was looking, that is.

WHITE CANVAS PAVILIONS sheltered the reception area. Cherise glanced around, wine glass in hand, and surveyed the festivities. Stella's father's ranch was a picture perfect location for an outdoor wedding. The extensive grounds had been decorated simply with white gossamer and daisies to reflect Stella's no nonsense nature and country roots. Even the slight whiff of cattle that wafted by every once in awhile added to the charm.

Stella's father, Rod Crayton, sat at a nearby table with his wife Helen. His bald head glistened under the iridescent lights that had come on with the emergence of darkness. Zane's father, Duke Shepherd, sat with them, both men submerged in deep conversation. Duke was the foreman of Rod's ranch and the two families had a long history together. He looked leathery and somewhat wizened, and his leg was pumping up and down in a nervous tattoo.

Cherise's attention shifted as the emcee announced the first dance. She thought she saw a few tears glistening in Rod Crayton's eyes as he watched his daughter and her new husband move toward the open area set up for dancing.

Her own father would never have allowed himself to show such emotion publicly. He would school himself into the strictest decorum if and when she ever walked down the aisle. Not that he'd ever approve of any of her prospects. And not that she had any at the moment, anyway.

The music started and Stella and Zane began to sway in each other's arms, oblivious to the rest of the guests who looked on with sentimental smiles.

Cherise took a small sip of her wine, resisting the urge to down it and get another. She was determined not to over indulge. The last thing she needed was to make a fool of herself in front of the very people who had risked their lives to save hers.

She looked up as Blue Shepherd sauntered into her line of vision. He was holding out his hand in an invitation to join him in a dance. Cherise set down her wine glass and tried to smile. The man was far too sexy for his own good, and with her new found sense of propriety, she wasn't sure close contact was a good idea.

"It's expected," Blue said. "The best man has to dance with the maid of honor."

"Of course." Cherise took his hand and stood in one fluid motion. Blue Shepherd was easy on the eyes and the old Cherise would have jumped at the chance to spend some time with him. But that was the old Cherise. The new Cherise was trying to behave. Move on from her man-crazy ways.

Blue's arms were warm as they encircled her waist, making her whole body tingle at his touch. With her four inch heels, she and Blue were about the same height. It made it easy to look into his blue, blue eyes. She wondered if that's where he got his name.

She had always been a sucker for a good looking man. Roberto with his debonair Italian ways who turned out to be a nark... French secret service agent Jean Yvres Garneault who had rescued her from Alistair's clutches only to be abducted and hurt himself... They were the last two in a long line up of 'Mr. Wrongs'. She just needed to quit falling for the first good looking guy who paid her a little bit of attention. She needed to be on high alert with Blue Shepherd. Though not her usual type, he still posed a threat. She could tell because of the way her body was responding to his touch.

Cherise blinked and glanced away. Tempest was dancing with the other groomsman, one of the ranch hands from the Crayton spread. Like Blue had said, one dance together was expected. She better not start reading anything else into it. Or injecting anything. It would be oh-so-easy to slip back into her flirtatious ways and let Blue Shepherd satisfy her dormant libido. She would have to be careful if she was going to get away from this wedding without breaking her resolve.

"So? You still recovering from your ordeal?" Blue asked.

"My ordeal?"

"Yeah. The whole kidnapping thing."

"Oh right. I suppose everyone here knows about that. Yes, I suppose I am." Truthfully, she still woke in a cold sweat some nights to the sound of her abductor's laugh. Alistair Montgomery had been her brother Dirk's best friend. Of course she had trusted him. When she went running off after her Italian lover several months ago, and subsequently suspected him to be involved in the drug trade, Alistair had offered to help her escape. As it turned out, he was the real criminal.

"I wouldn't say everyone knows, but I was in the know cause I kind of helped them figure out the rescue plan."

"Oh, I didn't know that." Cherise glanced at Blue with new eyes.

He smiled disarmingly. "Sure. Stella and I used to be pretty close."

"Used to be?" Cherise asked. "I thought you still were. Like siblings or some such thing, Stella used to say."

Blue glanced toward his brother Zane as he and his new bride swayed to the music. "Right. Now I guess she's my sister for real."

Although he still smiled, Cherise caught a slight edge to Blue's voice. There was definitely some tension there. She just wasn't sure of the cause. "So me chasing my boyfriend around the globe must have seemed foolish."

"I'm no judge. All I know is that you must be pretty special for them to go to the lengths they did to rescue you."

Blue's words warmed her inside and out. Of course he didn't mean anything by them - he was just being civil; carrying on polite conversation.

The music stopped and Cherise disengaged herself from Blue's arms. "Thanks for the dance." She turned and scurried back to the safety of her table. This wasn't going to be as easy as she'd hoped.

CHAPTER 2

*C*herise sighed and focused on the white table cloth instead of the dancers. Blue was dancing with yet another woman, apparently no worse for wear. A guy like him wouldn't be without a companion for long. She downed the last of her wine and set the stemmed glass on the table with a little more force than necessary.

"That went down fast." Tempest raised an eyebrow. "Maybe you should slow down."

"It's what weddings are for. Having fun." She trained her gaze on Tempest. "You should try it."

Tempest blinked. "I am having fun."

"Oh really? Then why aren't you up there two-stepping or whatever they do down here in Texas."

"Why aren't you?" Tempest countered.

"Because I've sworn off men, remember?"

"Oh right. I forgot you'd said that…"

Cherise surveyed her friend. "Don't believe me?"

Tempest shrugged. "Well… I'm proud of you, and all, but don't you think you're taking it a bit far? Changing your ways doesn't mean you have to swear off men altogether. Just the wrong kind of men."

"Sorry if I haven't found a hunky, altruistic FBI agent like yours. Apparently they're in short supply."

Tempest fingered the stem of her wineglass. "Um… about that. Don't tease me about Ryan. Please?"

Cherise blinked, truly focusing on her friend's distraught features for once. "What do you mean? Did you break up?" As an FBI agent, Ryan O'Toole had been assigned to the drug smuggling case that Cherise had inadvertently found herself involved in. He'd been part of her rescue and afterwards it seemed as if he and Tempest had hit it off.

Tempest gazed over the top of Cherise's head, avoiding eye contact. "Well… I'm not sure, really. I haven't seen him in awhile. He's on assignment."

"Which is why he didn't come to the wedding."

"Yes." Tempest looked away.

"And?"

Tempest closed her eyes briefly and then sighed. "I don't know. Just forget it, okay? I'm sure it's nothing."

Cherise leaned forward, crossing her arms on the tabletop. "Did you sleep with him yet?"

"No!" Tempest exclaimed. "I don't believe in sex before marriage. You know that. And for your information, Ryan is also a Christian, so neither does he."

Cherise held up her hands. "Sorry. I just have a hard time believing that a hot blooded, good looking guy like Ryan is a virgin."

"I didn't say that, exactly."

"So he's not a virgin?"

Tempest fidgeted with the strap on her dress. "I - we haven't discussed it. Our past experiences, I mean."

"Sorry. It's none of my business."

"It's okay."

"Not really, but thanks anyway. I really am trying to change." Cherise smiled and placed a hand on top of Tempest's. "It's just hard to break old habits, I guess. I envy you."

Tempest shook her head. "You shouldn't. I still feel… mixed up. About my relationship with Ryan, I mean."

"Relationships suck. At least that's my general perception. I don't think there's such a thing as a relationship that's true."

"Like true love, you mean?" Tempest asked. "Like in a fairytale?"

"I suppose. It just doesn't exist."

"I don't know about that." Tempest nodded toward Stella and Zane.

Cherise followed Tempest's gaze to where Stella and Zane stood together talking to some guests. "They are cute together, aren't they?"

"More than just cute. They look like they were made for each other."

"So you do believe in fairytales?" Cherise smiled.

"Maybe." Tempest smiled back. "I'm hopeful, anyway." She hesitated for a moment before asking, "How's Dirk?"

Cherise's eyes widened. "I'm surprised you care."

"He is your brother."

"Still suffering, I suppose. I don't really talk to him much. I think he actually cared about you, which is something for Dirk."

"That wasn't my fault. I never meant to lead him on. You know that."

"No worries. We Hillyers are resilient."

"And I'm trying not to harbor any hard feelings, but I admit it's been hard. Who thinks killing someone's pet would make them love you?"

"I'm sorry about that, too. I can't explain it and I have no real excuses for what he did. I suppose I could blame our parents. That's always been my line of defense, but I'm not sure what he did falls under any reasonable category." Cherise looked around, and then lowered her voice when she spoke next. "I'm not trying to make you forgive him, or anything, but he's changed you know, Temp. I think he really did love you, which is something for him."

"I've forgiven him already. It's what a good Christian does."

That trapped feeling began to tighten along Cherise's chest and she sat up straighter. "Wow. I really need another glass of wine."

Tempest leaned forward. "Cherise, why do you get so defensive every time I mention my faith?"

"What are you talking about? I don't get defensive. In fact, you'll be happy to know that Dirk has started going to church, so you've been a good influence on someone."

"Really? Cherise, that's fantastic. Tell him I'm happy for him."

"Not sure he's any happier for it. No surprise there. He's never been satisfied with anything in his whole life."

There was a moment of uncomfortable silence until Tempest filled the void. "Why so afraid?"

"Afraid? Of what?"

"You seem afraid of God. Believing in Him doesn't make you weak."

"I'm not afraid. I just don't think heaven is ready for the likes of me." Cherise stood. "Now, excuse me while I find another glass of wine."

WINE WAS DEFINITELY NOT strong enough. A few mojitos and those pesky companions, guilt and shame, were banished somewhere to the basement of her heart, taking any inhibitions along with them. Somehow Cherise found herself dancing with a cowboy. There was no point in denying herself. She was who she was.

Cherise giggled. "I like your moves, Cowboy." She ground her hips into the unnamed cowboy's for a couple of seconds and he responded in kind.

"You seem to have a few moves yourself."

"You don't know the half of it." She wound her arms around his neck and was about to lean in for a kiss when the music stopped. The cowboy released her and she took a staggering step back. Good thing she'd long since discarded her heels or she might have toppled over.

"Steady." An arm slipped around her waist, keeping her afloat.

Cherise turned to her rescuer with a ready smile. Blue Shepherd. With effort she straightened. "I'm fine."

"Sure you are." He humored her with a smile.

"I am." She swiped at a stray hair that had begun to fall out of her carefully rendered coiffure. "What's going on?"

"Time for tossing the bouquet, I reckon."

Cherise couldn't help the smirk that wanted to become a full blown laugh. "You reckon?"

Blue turned innocent eyes her way. "What? This is Texas." He pointed. "Now hush up."

The emcee tapped on a microphone with his finger, creating a loud 'buff-buff' sound that echoed across the night. "Hey, y'all. It's time to throw the bouquet. But first, the groom's gonna get that garter off his new missus." Whoops followed.

Cherise frowned and steadied herself by leaning a little more into Blue's side. Just what went on at these country weddings?

The band started a seductively jazzy tune as Zane and Stella were ushered up onto the stage. It looked like Stella was protesting, but Zane just shrugged and grinned. Someone brought a chair and Stella proceeded to place one high heeled foot on top of it while she hoisted her skirts to reveal the leg underneath. Wrapped around it was an elasticized garter midway up her thigh.

The emcee continued. "Okay, Zane. You know the rules. You gotta get that garter off. No hands allowed."

Cherise's eyes widened. No wonder Stella had been protesting. Zane, red-eared but determined, proceeded to remove the garter, quite efficiently, with nothing but his teeth. At the end of it all, midst a sea of catcalls and whistles, Zane stood triumphant with his arms raised, garter in mouth. He snatched the talisman from his teeth, and gave Stella a resounding kiss on the lips as she settled her skirt back into place.

"And who will be the lucky gentleman to catch the garter?" called the emcee.

"Why aren't you going forward like all the other guys?" Cherise gave Blue a poke in the arm.

Blue shrugged. "I'm not interested in marriage."

Zane turned around with his back to the audience, lifted the garter over his head, and sprung it like an elastic band into the crowd.

Blue's arm flew up and he caught the garter like an infielder catching a fly ball. The crowd erupted again and Blue held the prize high for everyone to see before pocketing it.

"Thought you said you weren't interested," Cherise said. "I'm not sure I should be standing so close under the circumstances."

"Can I help it if I have cat like reflexes? Don't put any stock in it. Now it's your turn."

"Huh?" She hadn't been paying attention to the emcee and she turned to Blue in confusion.

"Go," Blue instructed. "With the other unmarried ladies."

"But… what if I catch it?"

"Like I said, just a silly tradition." He gave her a little shove and she stumbled forward.

A crowd of tittering women congregated in a cluster near the front of the stage. Most of them were between 16 and 35, but there were a few specimens well beyond that.

These country traditions were getting creepy. What if she caught the bouquet right after Blue caught the garter? What if…?

The bouquet sailed above her head as if in slow motion until the emcee's voice snapped her back to reality. "And it looks like one of the bridesmaids has caught the bouquet!"

Cherise craned her neck to see a pink faced Tempest holding the bridal bouquet like a hot potato. Cherise laughed out loud, relief flooding through her body.

She turned around and bumped straight into Blue's chest. "Oops!"

"Steady on." He clasped her forearms to help balance her wobbly frame.

She giggled. "Looks like you're safe."

"From what?"

"You know. Having to marry me."

"Not sure that's how it works," Blue said with a chuckle and released her.

"How does it work?" Cherise stepped closer and laid her hand on his lapel, right above his heart. "Just cause I'm not interested in marriage doesn't mean I'm not interested in anything else."

Blue tucked a stray hair behind her ear. "I see. I wondered if it was true."

"What... what do you mean?"

"At the rehearsal dinner last night, you seemed pretty... how can I say it? Tame. Normal. Not what I expected."

Cherise pulled back a little to look at Blue's face. "Ah. Meaning my reputation precedes me?"

"Something like that." He blinked away. "Look, sorry. That was rude."

Cherise shook her head. She deserved it. "It's okay. Stella warned you, I take it?"

"Forget I said it. We've probably both just had too much to drink. And for the record, I'm not opposed to... not getting married."

He was standing so close. Close enough that she could smell the mixture of alcohol and spearmint chewing gum on his breath. She leaned a little closer.

And then someone tapped her on the shoulder and the spell was broken. "I've barely had time to talk to you all night."

Cherise whirled around. "Stella!" She threw her arms around Stella's torso as if they hadn't seen one another in months. "This whole thing was so beautiful. You're the most beautiful bride ever! And Zane, well, may I just say that you done good, girl-friend." Cherise stopped as a hiccup enveloped her. She put a hand to her mouth. "Sorry."

"You're having a good time, I see." The tone of Stella's voice didn't quite match her smile.

"Everything is beautiful. The flowers, the decorations, the ceremony..."

"Um, would you excuse us for a second, Blue?" Stella interrupted.

Cherise couldn't help but notice the strained look that passed between Blue and Stella as the latter led her away by the arm. None too daintily either. Cherise finally snatched her arm away from Stella's steely grasp when they stopped at a secluded corner of the yard, away from the general hubbub.

"What's up?" Cherise managed, steadying herself.

Stella released a deep sigh. "I suppose I should just let it go. You've had too much to drink."

Cherise screwed up her forehead. "I wasn't making a specta-cle, was I?"

"Not yet."

"Well, that's good." Cherise snorted and then laughed. "I wouldn't want to embarrass you or anything at your wedding."

"Look. This is a little harder than I thought it would be. Let's sit down." Stella pointed to a nearby swing secured in the branches of a tree. It was large enough for two, with a back.

"Okay." Cherise allowed herself to be led to the swing and settled in next to Stella. Stella gently pushed off with her toe and they began to swing back and forth.

Cherise clutched the rope. "Whoa. Can we stop? Too much movement."

Stella brought the swing to a halt and waited until it stopped moving. "You know I love you, right?" Cherise nodded and Stella continued. "And I know how you are... your tendency to flirt and everything."

"Um, okay."

"And normally I wouldn't care. But Blue... Blue is sensitive. I don't want to see him get hurt."

Cherise's eyes opened wide. Then she laughed out loud. "Oh, so that's it. You *did* warn him off me."

"Blue has been through a lot recently. He's vulnerable."

"Give the man a little credit. I'm not offering him anything he doesn't want."

Stella pushed off again. "I'm not kidding, Cherise. For you, a one night stand is nothing. Blue is more sensitive than that. He's been hurt and I don't want him doing anything that he'll regret later."

"Like sleeping with the likes of me?" Cherise asked, her voice laced with sarcasm.

"I didn't mean it that way..."

"Just say it, Stella. You may be my friend, but you think I'm a slut. You've always thought that. You think I'm not good enough for him."

"Cherise, you're taking this the wrong way. I... I can't tell you everything. Just trust me. Please stop flirting with Blue."

Cherise wiggled off the swing and almost lost her balance. She righted herself with as much dignity as possible. "And all this time you thought I was the snob."

"I never said that and you know it." Stella jumped from the swing. "You are the sister I never had. But I know you, Cherise - and your track record."

Cherise was about to retort but a sudden sense of shame enveloped her. It would take a lot more mojitos than she'd consumed to keep that companion away. She swiped at a tear with the back of her hand.

Stella placed her hands on Cherise's shoulders. "Look, you're my friend, but Blue is my friend, too - like the brother I never had, only now he really is my brother. I don't want to see either one of you get hurt. Especially not with each other."

Cherise shrugged her shoulders free and crossed her arms. She let the pout she had perfected speak for her.

"Please?" Stella looked deep into her eyes until Cherise looked away. "For me? It's my wedding, remember."

Cherise swiped at another errant tear and pushed her bottom lip out just a bit more before giving in with a sigh. "Okay. But it won't be easy."

"Thank you." Stella wrapped her arms around Cherise. "I knew you'd understand."

Cherise didn't, but she let Stella think so. After a moment, she stepped out of Stella's embrace. "You should probably head back to that husband of yours. I might stay here for a bit and cool off. No use jumping right back into temptation's way."

"You're the best." One more quick squeeze and Stella was hitching up her skirt and trotting back to the party.

Cherise watched her go, suddenly feeling drained from the effects of too much alcohol. She plopped back onto the swing, hanging on for dear life until she got her balance. Then she let the momentum of her own body weight move the swing in a rhythmic arch as she leaned back.

Stella was right. She'd come to Texas determined not to fall back into her old habits. She was stronger than that. She needed to prove, especially to herself, that her worth was not dependent on her ability to attract male attention. The problem was, she had been doing it for so long that it was difficult to imagine it otherwise.

CHAPTER 3

"*H*ey, Sleeping Beauty. Time to get you inside."

Cherise's eyes fluttered open. Blue's face filled her vision and she struggled to sit up.

"Relax. I didn't mean to startle you." He was kneeling over her prone body as she lay on the grass a few feet from the swing.

It was pitch black out. With a little help from Blue she slowly sat up. "I must have fallen asleep."

"Passed out, you mean." Blue grinned. He offered her his hand and she took it as he hauled her up to her feet. "Steady," he said, placing his hand on the small of her back.

"I didn't drink *that* much," she protested.

Blue raised a brow. "That's your story and you're sticking to it?"

Cherise let out a small laugh. "Yeah. I guess."

She looked around for her shoes but then remembered she'd been barefoot. They'd turn up somewhere. "We better get back. Stella's probably wondering where I am."

"She and Zane left for their honeymoon already."

Cherise stopped in her tracks. "What? Without me?"

Blue chuckled. "I don't think they were expecting you to come along. Might be awkward."

Cherise frowned, trying to clear her head. "No, I mean, without saying good-bye."

"I thought that's what you two were doing." Blue gave Cherise an inquisitive look. "Earlier."

"Not exactly." Cherise touched her hair and frowned. "I must look a mess."

"Let me help." Blue reached over and took out the remaining hair pins.

It didn't exactly cascade down like in the movies. Cherise could feel her hair trying to become one with gravity, but with all the spray and back combing, it was probably sticking straight out at right angles. "Great. That fixed everything." Cherise grimaced, patting the unruly mass of blonde tresses with her free hand.

"I don't mind messy." Using both hands he gently massaged her hair until it fell more naturally. "There."

His touch on her scalp sent a thrill through Cherise's body. She swallowed hard. Keeping her promise to Stella wasn't going to be easy.

"We should get back." Cherise started walking in what she hoped was the right direction.

"No hurry. Everyone's gone to bed."

"What? I was sleeping that long? And nobody came looking for me?" She crossed her arms over her chest.

"What am I? Chopped liver?" He grinned.

"My knight in shining armour."

"As much as I like the sound of that, I was just trying to clear my head when I found you sleeping."

"So you didn't come looking for me."

Blue shrugged. "I wasn't tired, so I figured a little moonlight stroll might do the trick. Good thing, too. Wouldn't have wanted some night creature to find you."

Cherise's eyes widened. "Could that happen?"

"What do you think? Just listen."

She tuned her hearing toward the sounds of the night. It was eerily still except for a backdrop of cricket song. Then a lone coyote yelped and she jumped. "What was that? A wolf?"

Blue laughed. "A coyote."

"So it could have been dangerous for me to be out here all night."

"Doubtful, but stranger things have happened."

"Well, thanks for finding me. I hope Tempest isn't worried. We're sharing a room."

"I'll escort you back to the house," Blue offered.

"Okay." They started sauntering back toward the scene of the wedding reception. "It sure was a nice wedding," Cherise said.

"I guess it's what girls dream about. Their wedding, I mean."

"Not me. Well, maybe I did at one time, but I'm kind of putting that fantasy on hold for awhile."

"Since your ordeal," Blue said.

Cherise nodded. "Yeah. Since my 'ordeal.'"

"You'll bounce back."

"You think?" Cherise perused him out of the corner of her eye. "What would you know about it? Bouncing back, I mean?"

Blue shrugged his shoulders. "I don't know. Maybe I'm working on it myself, is all."

"Care to share? From one 'bouncie' to another?"

Blue shook his head. "Not right now. It's a little too close to home."

"Fair enough." They had reached the patio that adjoined the house. Underwater lights lent a mystic glow to the turquoise pool. Beyond that the white lights adorning the reception area still twinkled like fairies flitting in the trees. Cherise turned her head to look at Blue's profile. "The wedding happened awfully fast, don't you think?"

Blue seemed to hesitate for a moment before replying. "Both our dad's – Stella's and mine – have cancer. They wanted to have the wedding while they were both around... before either one of them got any worse."

"Oh, of course!" Cherise felt suddenly foolish. Her mind had been so preoccupied with her own troubles that she'd completely forgotten. "Some friend I am. No wonder Stella is mad at me."

"Stella is mad at you?"

"No, not really. Forget it." Cherise picked a few stray blades of grass off the silk material of her bridesmaid dress. "I did know about Stella's dad, but I had no idea that your father was sick as well. He didn't really look too bad at the wedding."

"Trust me, he's sick. He's just too stubborn to show it, that's all." Blue's laugh was anything but humorous.

"That seems kind of crazy, that they'd both be sick with cancer at the same time. Kind of a cruel coincidence, don't you think?"

"They handled some hazardous materials together, back in the day. Stella's dad seems to be in remission at the moment. Maybe all the chemo. But it isn't the kind of thing you wait around for."

"And your dad?"

"He refuses any treatment. Says when it's his time, it's his time." Blue's eyes rested on a spot far away. "Like I said, he's stubborn. Anyway, Stella and Zane wanted them both around to see them tie the knot."

"And they did. Which is what Tempest would call a blessing."

Blue snorted. "Some blessing. To get cancer. Makes me wonder at the guy upstairs."

"You mean God," Cherise stated.

"Sure that's what I mean."

"So you believe in him, then. God?"

Blue raised an eyebrow and glanced at Cherise. "Yeah, I guess so. I mean I always did until recently. Been to Sunday school and all that. My dad goes to church most Sundays and I think Stella's folks have started going again, too. It's amazing how a crisis will force people back into religion."

"You sound skeptical."

"Maybe just disillusioned."

"Tempest believes. She has a strong belief. And I know Stella is Catholic. It's just never been for me." Cherise shrugged one shoulder. "Once a heathen always a heathen." She meant it as a joke, but it didn't sound funny.

"I'm not feeling especially saintly these days, either." He looked at her and smiled.

"Good, then that makes two of us."

They were quiet for a few moments until Blue spoke up. "So what did Stella want to talk to you about? When she took you away? It seemed important."

"Girl stuff. You wouldn't be interested."

"Was it about me?" Blue asked.

Cherise's eyebrows rose slightly. "Maybe. Not telling."

"I know how you women operate. Can't wait to share all the sordid details about us men."

Cherise laughed. "Now you're flattering yourself."

Blue's mouth was somewhere between a grin and a grimace. "You can't tell me she hasn't shared the sorry state of my love life with you."

"She just said you were vulnerable right now. But no details, I promise."

"Vulnerable." He gave a derisive snort. "She's the one who broke my heart."

Cherise's mouth dropped open. "Stella? You mean you and Stella were an item?"

"Not exactly. In my mind we could have been, but she didn't feel the same way."

"Oh, Blue. I'm so sorry." Cherise placed a hand on his arm.

"I'm not putting any blame on her," Blue clarified. "I mean, it was my own silly hopefulness that got me into trouble."

"It explains the tension. And she does love you," Cherise offered.

"Yeah, but not like that." He took a deep breath and let it out slowly. "So there you have it. Pretty pathetic, huh?"

"We can't always choose who our heart loves."

"Which is why I had to get away."

"Oh?" Cherise's brows rose. "I didn't know."

"Yup. I left the ranch shortly after your rescue. Only been back twice to visit my dad."

"I see."

"I love my brother. And I want him to be happy. And Stella, too, of course. But I just couldn't take seeing them together as a couple. Sharing little looks; sneaking little kisses when they thought nobody was watching. Zane thinks I'm over it. That I just wanted a change of scenery. It would kill him to think other-wise. But Stella... well, she's smarter than that."

"I'm really sorry, Blue. I wish there was some way I could help." Cherise meant it. "Now I understand why Stella was so protective. She feels guilty for breaking your heart, and in her own way she loves you enough to not want to see it happen again. It's why she told me not to flirt with you."

"She actually said that to you? Kind of rude, don't you think?"

"My reputation precedes me, remember? You said so yourself."

Blue rubbed the back of his neck. "Sorry about that. Must have been the liquor talking."

"She knows me, Blue." Cherise smiled and reached out to touch his sleeve again. "She knows us both. She knows your heart is still raw, and she knows my... tendencies. Maybe she's looking out for both of us."

"Still... she didn't show much faith in me. I'm a grown man."

Cherise laughed. "Yeah, but I eat men for breakfast."

Blue gave her a sidelong glance. "That seems like a funny thing to say about yourself."

Cherise shrugged. "It's true and Stella knows it. I've had more than my share of relationships. None of which worked out very well. I'm cursed at love."

"Who said anything about love? Sometimes people just need something to sooth the pain."

Cherise raised her brows. "Exactly."

Blue reached for her hand and rubbed his calloused fingers against the soft skin of her palm. Her breath caught in her throat and she waited, teetering on the brink of a precipice.

"So… what you said earlier. About not being interested in marriage not meaning you weren't interested in… other things." He kept rubbing her hand.

Cherise felt her libido sparkle into recognition, like a shimmering body about to appear on the transporter platform in an old Star Trek episode. "Um, what did you have in mind?"

"How about we start with a kiss?"

"Blue, that's probably not a good idea." The vestiges of her atrophied sensible side was making one last attempt to salvage her resolve.

"Says who? Stella? Well, she's not here."

Any further protests were silenced as Blue's lips descended on hers. Cherise's head was swimming with reasons to stop kissing Blue, but her body said otherwise. It had instantly ignited with the pent up heat of two months of celibacy.

Cherise pulled her mouth away, trying to clear the cobwebs of passion. "Um… I promised Stella." Her brain was muddled, still not completely clear of the effects of too many mojitos.

"She'll never know. She's on her honeymoon. With my brother."

"But you're on the rebound," Cherise said between kisses.

"You can help me get over it." His hands were roaming to places that hadn't been touched in months.

"I'm no good for you. Remember, I eat guys like you for breakfast," she whispered.

"Yeah? Then order up."

Cherise sighed and melted into his embrace as all rational thought vanished.

CHAPTER 4

The foreman's house was just a short walk down a gravel path that wound through some bushes. On the veranda leading up to the Shepherd's residence, Blue's caution to be quiet because his dad was a light sleeper took some of the edge off Cherise's heightened passion, but when she suggested that they just call it a night, Blue easily rekindled her desire with a few more kisses and they tiptoed down the hall to his bedroom like kids sneaking in after dark.

The sex was great - no doubt about that. But the afterglow combined with too much alcohol and the lateness of the hour, had Cherise sleeping soundly within minutes. She woke up alone in a strange bed in a strange room, sunlight beaming in through the window. With a groan she hauled herself up to check the time. The clock on the nightstand said nine a.m. Great. Now she'd have to sneak across the yard in her bridesmaid's dress. She just hoped Blue's father was already out the door. The last thing she wanted was to meet him in the hall. And as for Blue? Who knew where he was?

After freshening up in the bathroom, she donned the wrinkled mauve dress. It was going in the trash as soon as she got home to

Boston. She felt miffed that Blue had abandoned her in his bed. The least he could have done was wake her when he got up. Now she was forced to make her way back to the main house as discreetly as possible and hope that no one but Tempest had missed her.

She tiptoed down the hall, checking from side to side until she reached the front door. She opened it a few inches and peered outside. She had a good view of the main driveway from here, a long tree lined alley that ended in a circular affair in front of the rambling ranch house the Crayton's called home. There didn't seem to be anybody about, so she stepped out onto the veranda and shut the door. Everything looked different in the daylight, but she vaguely remembered taking a sheltered path that wound back to the poolside patio. She was pretty sure she'd left her shoes there, and it would afford a lot more cover should anyone be out to see her sneaking from the Shepherd's home.

The path was gravel, a fact that had her stepping gingerly. She certainly didn't remember having any trouble navigating it last night. Her mind had been on other things, apparently.

"Good morning, Miss Cherise."

Cherise stopped in her tracks. She slowly turned in the direction of the voice. Great. Duke Shepherd was standing under a tree on the path behind her. "Um... good morning, Mr. Shepherd."

"Nice time for a stroll. It ain't too hot yet." Duke pushed his dusty cowboy hat back on his head. Was he playing dumb or did he really not know she had spent the night under his roof in his son's bed? The elder Shepherd strongly resembled Zane, or was it the other way around? Of course, his hair had turned to salt and pepper, his face was leathery and crinkled from time in the sun, and his wiry frame was somewhat stooped. Still, she could see the resemblance in the thin face, somewhat sharp nose, and eyes that were alert like a hawk's.

Cherise swallowed hard. "Yeah... well, I better be off."

She turned to scurry away but Duke stopped her with

continued conversation. "I wouldn't advise going barefoot. Them rocks is sharp, and you never know when you might come across a snake."

Cherise's eyebrows rose. "A snake, you say? I'll remember. Thank you." She took another step.

"And by the way, if you're lookin' for Blue, he done left already for Fort Stockton."

Cherise's eyes widened. She stopped again. "Oh?"

"I told him it was yella, sneaking away like that in the wee hours of the mornin'. Ain't no way to treat a lady. Sure as heck he was raised different, but I reckon he's got a mind of his own. Well, good day." Duke Shepherd tipped his hat and turned to leave.

"Thanks..." Cherise trailed off, watching the man's stilted gait. So old Mr. Shepherd wasn't so dumb after all. Now the question was, who else knew?

TEMPEST WAS JUST COMING out of the adjoining bathroom when Cherise walked into their room. She stopped drying her hair in mid motion and glared in Cherise's direction. "It's about time. I was worried sick about you when I woke up this morning and you weren't here. Where were you?"

Cherise raised a brow and flopped down on the still unmade bed. "What are you? My mother?"

"Seriously, Cherise." Tempest perched beside her on the bed, her green eyes penetrating.

Cherise looked away. "I hooked up with a guy."

Tempest's eyes got wider. She set the towel down. "Really? But I thought you said you were taking a break from... well, you know... from that for awhile."

Cherise rolled her eyes. "Sex, Tempest. Just say it. Sex."

"Okay. I thought you were taking a break from casual sex. That's what you said."

Cherise shrugged and rolled onto her stomach. "So I changed my mind. It's what's supposed to happen at weddings."

Tempest shook her head and stood. She grabbed the towel and folded it in half as she walked back to the bathroom. "So who was it?" Her voice echoed from within. There was just a tinge of curiosity mixed with the disapproval.

"Just a guy."

"One of the hired men?"

"Um... yeah. One of the hired men." Technically it was true - kind of. Blue had worked at the ranch for most of his life.

"I can't believe you slept with one of the hired men!" Tempest emerged, brushing her short chestnut hair. "What if Stella gets wind of it? Or Zane?"

"What if?" Cherise pushed herself up into a sitting position and tried slipping her arms out of the bridesmaid's dress. She heard a small tearing sound. "Hey, can you help me with this thing?"

Cherise stood up as Tempest crossed to the bed. She unzipped the back and helped ease it over Cherise's head. "It's got grass stains. And there's a huge tear in it near the zipper." Cherise could hear rather than see the frown on Tempest's face.

"Yeah. I guess I was in a hurry to get it off last night." Cherise laughed. "I'm trashing it anyway."

"You're not going to keep it?" Tempest's eyes were wide with shock.

"Absolutely not. And I would advise you to do the same. Mauve is not your color."

"Well, in any case, back to the hired man. What was his name?"

"Aren't you the curious cat?" Cherise teased.

"Cherise. Seriously," Tempest huffed, crossing her arms.

Cherise shook her head. "Nope. I'd rather just forget about it, to tell the truth. I do have a little bit of shame left in me."

"So he wasn't much good, I take it?" Tempest hauled her suitcase onto the bed and opened it, proceeding to rummage around for something to wear.

"Right," Cherise lied. She reached over and pointed to a flowered blouse. "Wear that one today."

Tempest unfolded the blouse and shook it out. "I just don't get it sometimes. How you can be so... blasé about sex and all."

Cherise shrugged. "Takes practice, I guess." She flipped her stiffened hair off her forehead.

"I think you're selling yourself short."

"There's no point in beating myself up about it. What's done is done. Besides, I won't be seeing him again, anyway." Cherise took a deep breath and let it out on a dramatic sigh. "Now, I really, really need to take a shower. You need anything else in the bathroom?"

"No, go ahead."

Cherise locked herself in the bathroom and readied herself for her shower. If only these melancholy feelings could be so easily washed away. She wasn't prepared for the disappointment she'd felt when she'd found out Blue had left without even saying good-bye. So much for Stella's concerns that he couldn't handle a one night stand. He seemed to be handling it just fine.

She, on the other hand, was a mess. She could almost hear Stella saying, "I told you so," although, hopefully Stella would never find out. It's one reason she hadn't wanted to confide in Tempest. They'd always been so close - told each other everything. But now that the first secrets were beginning, who knew where it would end?

CHAPTER 5

*A*rriving back in Boston would put things into perspective. At least that's what Cherise hoped. She felt a familiar sense of relief as she pulled her Porsche into the driveway of her family's Boston mansion. The two story brick structure with its grand facade of pillars and over-sized windows spoke of wealth, but to Cherise it was just home. Coming from a wealthy family had it perks, but life could be empty, too.

Cherise was greeted at the side door by Crosbie, one of their servants. He was a middle aged man with a ramrod straight back and thinning grey hair. He'd been part of the furniture since Cherise could remember. Sometimes she wondered if he ever smiled or had any fun outside of these walls. Of course she knew he had a life elsewhere, but still, it seemed that so much of his time was spent within the confines of their petty circles that she wondered how he stood it.

"Are Mother and Daddy home?" Cherise asked as she stepped inside the spacious foyer. The ceiling in the entrance rose over-head the full two stories. A large gilded mirror hung over an equally elaborate side table a few feet inside the doors.

"I'm afraid neither one are home at the moment." Crosbie

bowed slightly.

Of course not. "Thank you." Cherise smiled in a way that she hoped was civil. It wasn't Crosbie's fault that her parents had distanced themselves from their children. They were always off doing their own things. Charities, benefit dinners at the country club... it didn't really matter how worthy the activity, the fact remained that they'd spent precious little time with their own offspring. They were snobs, if the truth be told, and although she liked to think differently about herself, she knew in many ways she and her brother Dirk were turning out just the same. Her 'ordeal' in Italy had changed that quite a bit, but now, two months later, it was becoming increasingly easy to step back into the old role of pampered princess.

Dirk had actually changed the most. He had been the quin-tessential rich playboy before she'd run off to Italy with her then boyfriend Roberto. He'd stepped up to the plate when he'd found out she had been kidnapped, and he'd even taken a bullet for her during her rescue. Part of his change was also due to Tempest. Somewhere along the way he'd fallen in love with her shy friend. He'd gone to drastic measures to prove to her that he wasn't the flake she thought he was, but in the end Tempest didn't love him. It had been a hard blow for Dirk. Still, the change in attitude seemed to go deeper than the surface and he had become much more responsible and caring since.

He'd even started going to church, as if that would help any.

Cherise crossed the polished white marble floor and started up the curving grand staircase. She found Dirk in his room on the second floor. His wing was more like it. Each of the siblings had an entire wing of the house to themselves. His bedroom door was ajar but she tapped on it anyway before entering.

Dirk looked the same since their adventure in Italy. Oh, he had lost some weight after getting shot, but he'd gained it back for the most part and had worked hard at getting back into the shape that could have landed him a job as a male model. They shared their mother's blonde good looks, although Dirk didn't bother with any enhancement like Cherise did. And they had the same blue eyes. She wished sometimes that Tempest would have just fallen for Dirk instead of her FBI agent. The haunted expression in her brother's eyes made her sad. But as she'd said to Blue not long ago, you couldn't help who you fell for.

"Hey Sis. How was the wedding?" Dirk looked up momentarily from what he was doing and smiled.

"Beautiful. As weddings go." She took in the open suitcase on his bed, the clothes piled next to it and the open bureau. "What's up? Looks like you're packing."

He nodded. "Very observant."

"You going on a trip?"

"Kind of." He folded another shirt and placed it in the open bag.

"Change will do you good," Cherise said with a nod.

"Exactly what I thought. So, tell me more about the wedding."

Cherise sighed, flopping down in the chair next to the bed. "Oh you know... the usual. Lots of food, wine, speeches... The bride was a vision, yaddy-yadda..."

"In other words, it was a drag."

Cherise shrugged. "It was good to see everyone again, but I feel as if I've lost touch. I know it's only been a couple of months, but still. Sometimes it feels like a lifetime. I don't think anything will ever be the same between us. Me, Stella and Temp, I mean."

"And how is Tempest?" Dirk's voice was purposefully nonchalant, as if he was just making small talk. Cherise knew better.

"Fine. She looks happy." She surveyed her brother out of the corner of her eye.

"Still with what's his name?" Dirk busied himself with the items of clothing on the bed.

"You know very well what his name is. It's Ryan." As far as their status as a couple, Cherise wasn't entirely sure, but she didn't tell Dirk that. No point in getting his hopes up.

"As long as she's happy. That's the main thing." With robotic precision, he placed the rest of the items into the suitcase.

Cherise sat forward. "Dirk. You've got to let go. You know she'll never get over what you did. I still can't believe you went to such drastic measures."

"What? I thought it would drive her to me." He slammed the case's lid.

"Obviously that backfired."

"Obviously."

Cherise's mouth turned up at the corners just a bit. She tried not to let it show. "I can't believe you killed her cat. That was just about the dumbest thing I've ever heard."

Dirk turned toward his sister, his hands on his hips. "I didn't kill the cat, if you remember correctly."

"No, you hired someone else to do it for you." Cherise was full on smirking now.

"I didn't know he would actually kill it. I just said get rid of it. There's a difference." He sat down on the bed with a bounce and clasped his hands between his knees. "Anyway, that's a moot point now, isn't it? She's with what's-his-name and I've moved on."

"Ryan." Cherise sobered. "And have you?"

"Trying."

"Good."

Dirk was quiet for a space. "But it's hard."

"I know."

He looked up and caught Cherise's gaze with his own. "You still hurting, too?"

She shrugged. "No. Maybe."

"Over which one? Roberto or Jean Yvres?"

"You're terrible."

"You didn't answer my question."

"Neither. Both." Cherise sighed and then expelled a small derisive laugh. "I slept with Blue Shepherd at the wedding. You met him, remember?"

Dirk's eyebrows raised a notch. "Yeah, I met him. And?"

"And nothing. I'm a screw up. Maybe I'm just not cut out for settling down. Maybe neither of us are."

"I would have said the same thing once."

"Until Tempest."

"Yeah. Until Tempest." Dirk slapped his knees with his hands and stood up. "Which is why I'm changing my focus."

"Okay... this have anything to do with the packed suitcase?" Cherise gestured to the luggage with her head.

"It does indeed. I'm off on a mission trip to Mexico."

Cherise squinted her eyes in disbelief. "Wait a sec. A mission trip? To Mexico? I thought Mexico is where you go for white sandy beaches and margaritas."

"That too. But this is different. I'm going to help out in an orphanage for a couple of weeks. I'm going with a group from the church."

"Whoa! Hold on there, mister! I can't believe my ears. My brother, Dirk Hillyer, is going to help in an orphanage? You hate kids! They're dirty!"

"Ah, that was the old Dirk." His voice was reasonable. "But the new Dirk loves children and can't wait to do something to help out his fellow man." He grinned.

"Just back up a minute." Cherise held up her hand. "You're not doing this to try and impress Tempest, are you? Cause that bridge has already been burned."

Dirk placed his hands on his hips. "Can't I do something good for a change? I might have a philanthropic bone or two in my body."

"Try one of mother's charities if you want to be a philanthropist," Cherise snorted.

"Seriously. I'm hurt." Dirk stared at her until she wiped the grin off her face.

"Okay, fine. Go off and do some good for a change. But you never answered my question. Is this a ploy to get Tempest's attention?"

Dirk shook his head emphatically. "No."

Cherise's mouth hardened into a line. "You're lying. I can see it. You know you can't lie to me."

"Well, maybe." Dirk shrugged one shoulder.

"Dirk!" Cherise wailed. "Please don't do this."

"I have to at least try, don't I?" he countered. "What kind of man would I be if I didn't at least try to fight for the woman I love?"

"It's crazy. I just came from a weekend with Tempest and she's not interested."

"Be that as it may, I still have to try. Besides that, doing some unselfish work for a good cause seems pretty appealing right now." He sighed heavily. "I'm tired, Cherise. Tired of the meaningless pit my life has become. There has to be more, you know?"

"So you're determined?" Cherise asked.

"If going to Mexico is the only way to get my mind off Tempest, then yes, whether she approves or not. It's a way for me to start fresh."

"Do they even have running water at the orphanage?"

"It's not totally primitive."

"What about a steam bath and saunas?" Cherise's eyes crinkled at the corners.

"Now you're mocking me," Dirk huffed.

"You won't be able to fall back on your spoiled rich boy habits," Cherise warned.

"You calling me a spoiled rich boy?"

"If the shoe fits..." Cherise grinned. She jumped off the chair and gave her brother a hug. He was stiff at first; startled. They weren't normally a family that showed a lot of affection. But life and death situations had changed that for both of them. "I'm proud of you. For taking the plunge. Making a change."

Dirk reciprocated the hug before releasing her. "Thanks, Sis. I needed that."

"So what do Mother and Daddy think?" Cherise fingered the edge of the expensive luggage. She wondered how it would stand up to the trip.

"I haven't told them." Dirk's blue eyes twinkled. "I'm pulling a page right out of my sister's playbook."

Cherise swatted him and smiled. "Just don't keep your whereabouts a secret. We both know how that can turn out."

"Indeed."

Cherise cocked her head to one side. "Maybe I should go with. Do you think they could use another pair of hands?"

Dirk's eyes widened. "You? The conditions aren't exactly five star. And you might have to get your hands dirty, you know."

"If you can do it, I can," Cherise countered.

"I'm not even sure I can. I'm going on a wish and a prayer. Besides that, this is a Christian mission."

"So I'm not good enough for the club? Is that it?"

"I never said that."

"That's the problem with Christians. They think they're better than everyone else." Cherise sauntered back to perch on the chair.

"I think you've got that wrong."

"Anyway, I was just teasing. I have no desire to work in an orphanage with a bunch of snotty nosed little kids." She put up her hands in a defensive gesture. "Not that I don't think it's wonderful for you. I'm proud and I mean that. But me? Not a chance."

The trouble was, she needed a change in focus as badly as Dirk did. Obviously, sleeping with the next available guy just wasn't cutting it anymore, but traipsing off to some third world orphanage wasn't her style either. There had to be something to set her free from this mountain of remorse and vulnerability she'd buried herself under. She just had no idea what it was.

Dirk

*D*irk Hillyer focused on the road ahead as he sped along the six lane freeway in his brand new Escalade. He'd arrived in Los Angeles earlier that day by plane and had headed straight for a car lot. Someplace that specialized in rugged trucks and SUVs. His plan was to drive down the Baja coast to the orphanage and meet the rest of the church group there. No point in renting a vehicle. He'd just sell the thing on the way home. Or donate it to the orphanage. The cost was nothing to him. Maybe it would even help him score a few points with Tempest.

Dirk frowned and gripped the wheel a little tighter. He needed to reconsider that last thought. He would give the vehicle to the orphanage because it was a good and generous thing to do, not because it served his own purposes. They could probably use a reliable vehicle for hauling stuff around. Sometimes he recognized flashes of his former self during his thought process. The old Dirk was a selfish, self centered snob. A man who felt entitled simply because he had money. A man who saw women as accessories, or worse, simply conduits to his own pleasure. Then came Tempest. He genuinely admired her caring and honest ways. It was what drew him to her in the first place.

He'd left Boston several days earlier than the rest of his group, citing business that he needed to take care of in LA first. Business all right. Business of the heart. He'd called Tempest when he arrived, and she'd actually picked up. Probably because he used the car lot's phone so she'd see a local number. In any case, she didn't sound too thrilled about his visit, but she had agreed to meet him at a neutral location. That's where he was heading now. A little seaside restaurant near the place she used to live. She was probably shacked up with Mr. FBI by now, though. He just hoped the other man didn't decide to tag along.

Dirk pulled the shining black vehicle into the parking lot of Shelley's Seafood Delights. It was an unassuming establishment - a takeout joint more than anything - situated on the coastline. A low flat roofed structure with a large billboard on top proclaimed 'The Best Seafood Around' while a smiling yellow fish gave a thumbs up - or rather a fins up - beside the proclamation. A blue and white striped awning along the entire front, which was open for taking orders, flapped in the ocean breeze. Umbrella shaded tables dotted the wooden outdoor deck.

He'd taken Tempest here once when she'd first moved out to LA and she'd needed his help to get settled. It seemed like a long time ago and a lot had happened since. Still, familiar surroundings and memories of a happier time might do the trick.

Dirk stepped down from the high cab and swung the driver's door closed with a bang. The place had one thing going for it - the view. He had an unobstructed line of sight from the parking lot to the board walk and beach. He watched for a moment as people and dogs, skateboarders and joggers, milled about or whizzed past.

With a sigh, he turned from the view and scanned the occupied tables. He spotted Tempest immediately. And Ryan. She was sitting with her back to him so hadn't noticed him yet. He wasn't so sure about O'Toole, on the other hand. The other man was still wearing those interminable dark glasses. Dirk straightened his shoulders, brushed the hair off his forehead that had blown into his eyes, and schooled his features into a pleasant mask.

"Thanks for meeting me," Dirk greeted as soon as he was near. "Nice to see you again."

"Just like old times." Ryan's tone held a sarcastic bite.

Dirk stood for a moment longer. Tempest still hadn't made eye contact. "May I sit?"

"Oh... sure." Tempest colored slightly and Dirk couldn't help but notice Ryan placing a comforting hand over hers. The remains of their lunch, wicker baskets with paper liners and disposable cups, littered the table.

"So..." Dirk cleared his throat as he sat down. "Thanks for meeting me."

"You said that already," Ryan cut in.

"Yes. Well..." Dirk rubbed the back of his neck. "My, this is awkward, isn't it? Listen. I have some things that I need to say to Tempest. I was hoping we could have a couple of minutes alone, if that's possible?"

"I want him here," Tempest replied, gesturing at Ryan.

Dirk could just imagine the glint of triumph in the other man's eyes behind the dark glasses. "Okay, then. I'll just go ahead and spill it, shall I?" When they continued to wait, he cleared his throat again, and angled his body toward Tempest, away from Ryan's gaze. "Tempest. You must know how sorry I am. I'd apologize a hundred times over if that's what it would take for you to forgive me. You have to believe I did not order the... the... well, what happened to your cat. I just thought if she got lost for awhile you'd need me."

Her erect posture didn't change. "Of course I forgive you."

"Forgiving me because you feel you have to and actually doing it, here," Dirk pointed to his chest, "are two different things."

"You heard her, so just leave us alone," Ryan interjected.

"I wasn't talking to you," Dirk directed at Ryan. He shifted slightly, focusing on Tempest once again. "Please? I need to see it in your eyes."

She immediately lowered her gaze. "You lied." Her voice was small. Quiet.

"Yes, I lied," Dirk admitted, "but you have to cut me a bit of slack. I've been lying most of my life." He tried to soften the statement with a self-depreciating laugh. "But I'm trying to change. I started going to church."

Tempest looked up in surprise. So, he'd caught her off guard with that revelation. "Are you really going to church? Cherise told me, but I wasn't sure."

"It's true." Dirk smiled and then got lost in the beauty of her gaze. Her irises were an exotic green like emeralds. He couldn't stop staring. "And... You're not wearing your glasses."

"Lasik surgery," Tempest replied. "And?"

He shook himself back into focus. "And... I've been learning a lot of things. Like about forgiveness, for one."

"Nicely played." It was Ryan and he sounded skeptical.

Tempest sighed. "Of course you're right. I must forgive you. I *have* forgiven you."

"Are you sure about that?" Dirk asked.

She just shrugged.

"I know what I did hurt you deeply. Just give me another chance."

"A chance at what?" Ryan sat up straighter, gripping Tempest's hand more possessively. He was definitely getting territorial.

Dirk ignored him. "Remember when we used to be friends? That's all I want, Temp. For us to be friends again. I swear, I'm not asking for anything else."

Tempest's eyelashes fluttered. "Well, I guess it is the Christian thing to do."

"Thanks, Temp. You won't regret it, I promise." Dirk took her free hand and squeezed. It was a bit awkward, holding one of her hands while his rival held tightly to the other, but still, it was something. "Oh, and by the way, you might be interested to know that I'm actually on my way to Mexico on a mission trip. I'm going with my church to work in an orphanage for two weeks." Dirk smiled broadly. That got her attention.

"Really?" She seemed genuinely pleased.

He nodded. "Mmhm. That's why I'm here. I thought I'd buy a vehicle and drive it down and then donate it to the place when I leave."

"That's very generous." Ryan with his skepticism again.

"It's nothing." Dirk shrugged. "It's the least I can do. After all, I'm trying to do penance for my former sins."

Tempest frowned. "That's not how it goes. God forgives unconditionally if you're really sorry. You don't have to do penance." She stopped and looked up. "Oh dear. Now if that didn't sound like a hypocrite, I don't know what does."

"It's okay," Dirk said. "You have a right to be angry."

Tempest shook her head. "No I don't. I'm sorry for not forgiving you sooner, Dirk. Please forgive me."

"Of course." Dirk smiled and squeezed her hand again. "And I was just joking about the penance thing. I have been learning something listening to all those sermons." He held her gaze for a few more seconds.

Ryan cleared his throat and looked at his watch. "We wouldn't want to keep you."

"It's no trouble."

"What I meant was, Tempest and I should probably be going now."

"Oh. Of course." Dirk released Tempest's hand, albeit reluctantly, and stood to his feet. Ryan stood also, but he certainly didn't let go of Tempest. "I'll keep in touch. Let you know how things are going down at the orphanage."

"I changed my phone number. And cancelled all my profiles on Social Media."

Dirk retrieved his cell phone from his pocket. "No problem. I'll just put in your new number."

"Um… Maybe we'll just stay in touch through Cherise."

Dirk tried to smile, still holding his phone aloft. "Why not eliminate the middle man? Or woman, as the case may be."

"You heard her. It's for the best," Ryan said.

Dirk let his arm drop to his side. Of course Mr. FBI was acting all protective and superior. "Suit yourself. Anyway, I'd better get going."

He walked as casually as he could muster back to the Escalade, aware that all the while they were probably staring at his backside. Things weren't turning out exactly the way he'd envisioned. She was still with Mr. FBI. But he'd made a dent in her armour, of that he was certain. Once Tempest found out he was serious - that he'd really changed - she might come around.

CHAPTER 7

*D*arkness cloaked the small Mexican village when Dirk pulled to a halt in front of the orphanage complex. A large iron gate was securely closed, barring his entrance. He should have known. He squinted at the sign attached to the gate, just to make sure. There was a security light shining down from one of the posts, but it cast a shadow which made it hard to read what the sign said. "Beacon of Hope Mission," he read aloud. "Well, at least I'm in the right place."

With a sigh he considered his next move. He'd left Los Angeles in good time that morning, but heavy traffic from LA to San Diego added an hour to his trip at least. Then, line ups at the border into Tijuana, pit stops, and pot holes the size of his truck once he got off the main highway, turned what he calculated as a six hour trip into ten. Still, he'd arrived in one piece. Now he just had to survive the night in a strange Mexican town.

He peered past the gate, trying to get a glimpse of the buildings beyond. It looked to be a well kept up facility, but it was hard to tell in this light. White stucco and arches, as far as he could see, typical of Mexican architecture. His options were to sleep in the truck or try to find a hotel. The town was rather small, surrounded by farm land, and was a combination of cement structures and ramshackle shacks. Still, there was bound to be somewhere to rent a room for the night.

He was about to back up, opting for the room, when he saw a man approaching on the other side of the gate. The man looked to be wearing some kind of official uniform. Great. The last thing he needed was to be caught trespassing late at night in a strange Mexican village. Dirk rolled down his window, not daring to get out of the truck. His only experience in Mexico had been at five star resorts. He certainly wasn't going to risk being mugged, or worse, arrested.

The guard opened a walk through gate in the side of the high wall that surrounded the complex, closed it again, and approached the truck. "*Buenas noches.*"

"*Buenas noches.*" Dirk nodded at the other man. "I'm supposed to be meeting my group here to work at the orphanage. I got waylaid and I'm afraid I'm later than I anticipated."

The man looked puzzled, so Dirk repeated it in Spanish as best he could, adding some hand signals and a few English words. Unfortunately his Spanish didn't go much beyond ordering drinks or asking a pretty girl to dance.

"Name?" the man asked, raising a dark brow.

"Dirk Hillyer."

The night watchman repeated it twice as if to get it right. Dirk nodded his agreement each time. The guard took out his radio and spoke into it in Spanish, explaining that a 'Dirk Hillyer' was outside the gate. After a moment, he clipped the radio back on his belt and gestured for Dirk to stay put. Once back through the walking gate, he opened the driveway's barricade from the inside, swinging the prison like doors inward one at a time. Finally he waved Dirk through.

Dirk put the truck in gear and rolled forward. Once through, he glanced in his review mirror to see the man closing and locking the gates behind him. He supposed one couldn't be too careful. Not with the evidence of poverty he'd seen on the drive through the countryside.

The wide driveway branched off in several directions, but Dirk followed the signs and turned to the left where it merged into a large cul-de-sac. This was lined with buildings, one of which said '*La Oficina*' on the front. He rolled to a stop beside the main door and another man immediately emerged from within.

The man looked to be in his forties, with neatly trimmed salt and pepper hair and a tanned face. He wasn't tall, but carried himself with confidence and wore a light colored golf shirt and khaki trousers. Dirk figured it was safe to get out of the vehicle, so he cut the engine, unbuckled his seatbelt, and jumped down from the driver's side in time to meet the man in front of the truck.

The other man extended his hand and grasped Dirk's with a steely grip. "Ah. You must be Mr. Hillyer."

"That's right." The handshake lasted longer than normal and Dirk finally retrieved his hand. He flexed his fingers as he surveyed the stranger. The man was shorter than he was, perhaps about five foot eight, and was deeply tanned, his eyes crinkling at the corners in a friendly way. Despite his coloring, he was obviously an American. His accent gave him away. Probably from the deep south.

"James Gallagher, administrator. Welcome to Beacon of Hope Mission."

"Thanks. Pleased to meet you." Dirk stretched his back. He felt stiff from the long hours in the truck, luxury interior package or not.

"We were expecting you. Otherwise Ferdinand might not have been so cordial." James smiled, his teeth gleaming in the darkness against his tanned face. "The rest of your group arrived around five o'clock. They've already eaten, had a quick tour, and are at the evening service."

"Oh. Sorry," Dirk apologized.

"It's alright. As administrator, I expect interruptions."

"It took me longer than expected to make the trip."

James chuckled. "One doesn't judge distance in miles here. It's all about road conditions."

"As I discovered."

"We lock the gate at eight o'clock each night. It gets dark by six these days, but most of the town's folk appreciate what we do here, so we don't have a lot of vandals. Not from the locals, anyway."

"But others?"

"Some of the migrant workers see us as an opportunity."

"So you're pretty much locked in each night."

"We have curfew for the children, of course, but the staff are free to come and go after hours if they choose. You met Ferdinand at the gate already. As long as you show your pass, he or one of the other night watchmen will let you through."

Dirk nodded, wondering when they could quit the chitchat and he could find his room. He felt the need to unwind. The reality of what he had committed to was beginning to sink in.

"I'll hop in your truck and show you where you can park. Then we'll walk back over to the chapel together. You won't have the need for driving much while on the property." James was already hauling himself up into the passenger seat. "Nice wheels."

Dirk felt himself blush and was thankful for the cover of darkness. He hadn't considered that arriving in a brand new expensive vehicle might be in poor taste. "Thanks. I just bought it."

James directed Dirk to a parking lot behind one of the many buildings. There were several other vehicles resting there, including a paneled van, a beat up truck with a flat bed, and two Volkswagen beetles. "You'll be staying in the men's dorm, which is right on our way, so if you want to drop your bags off, I'll show you where it is."

Dirk pulled his small duffel bag out from behind the seat and slung it over his shoulder. His rolling suitcase was in the back of the truck under a custom tarp that rolled back electronically.

"Is that it?" James asked, gesturing at the suitcase.

"I tried to pack light."

"Fine, fine." James nodded. "I'm just used to folks coming down here laden with extra stuff to give away."

Dirk's eyebrows rose slightly. "Oh. I never thought of that."

"That's okay," James assured. "It's on our website. A list of possible things that the locals need. Tarps, jeans, even mittens, if you can believe it. It can get cold here at night during the winter months. We're a beacon of hope to the community at large, not just for the orphans who live here."

Dirk tried not to become defensive, but he was beginning to feel inadequate in front of this man. He hadn't really done much research, if the truth be told. He'd just happened to hear about the trip one Sunday and thought it sounded like a good opportunity - on many levels. Offering to pay his own way upfront without any fundraising, not to mention coughing up a healthy donation to boot, had ensured him a spot. In fact, he didn't really know the other people on the team very well. He'd only been going to the church in Boston for a month, and he'd picked it more by accident than anything. He figured that if he was ever going to make amends with Tempest, he better start somewhere.

James continued to talk as they walked along the cement sidewalk to the dorms, pointing out which buildings housed the school, the clinic, the kitchen and mess hall, and a complex of cottages around a central courtyard that housed the children with their 'house parents'. "We try to create as much of a family atmosphere as possible," James explained. "Of course, we rely heavily on volunteers like yourself, which is why we have dorms for the staff and volunteers when they come. Over there we have a campground for folks who like to bring their own accommodation. We always encourage that. It cuts down on our costs."

Dirk nodded absently, not really trying to remember everything James was telling him. He was too tired and it was too dark. The wheels of his suitcase were creating a lulling thrum that almost had him dropping on his feet.

"Well, here we are." James gestured at a two story square building, rather nondescript with its white stucco front and small windows. "You're on the second floor. Sorry, no elevators, I'm afraid." James produced a key from his pants pocket. It was attached to an elastic wrist band. "You'll want to keep it with you at all times. We assume that everyone who comes here to help is honest, but we can't be responsible for any lost goods."

"Thanks." Dirk took the key and headed up the stairs that were on the outside of the building under a cement canopy. James was close behind. He found his room number, inserted the key, and opened the door. When he flicked on the light switch he blinked. Sparse was the word that came to mind. Cinder brick walls, two single beds with a nightstand, and one lamp. Two benches at the foot of each bed were presumably for luggage, since an open soft sided suitcase spilled its contents on top of one. Dirk turned to James, who was hovering nearby. "I'm sharing a room?"

"It was all in the package sent to your church. I presume you decided on room assignments before you left." James' eyes had narrowed slightly. "Didn't your church do an orientation session before leaving?"

"Oh, of course." He hadn't gone.

"Good." James surveyed him for another moment. "This isn't a hotel, you know, and you're not on a holiday."

Dirk straightened his back and inhaled sharply. "Of course not." He turned and swung his own bag onto the unoccupied bench.

James checked his watch, a large faced affair with an intricately carved crystal face. It looked suspiciously expensive, but Dirk assumed it was a knock off. "We should hurry. The singing was already over and I'd like to get back to the chapel to catch the rest of the message."

"I'll just take a minute in the washroom, first, if that's okay," Dirk said.

"Of course! I didn't show you the men's bath house, yet." James did an about face into the open air corridor.

Dirk's eyes widened as he glanced around the room again. There was only one door, and that led out into the hallway. He pursed his lips, determined not to show any more disgust than necessary. If he'd known he would have to use a communal washroom, he might not have signed up after all.

WHAT JAMES CALLED a chapel could be more correctly termed a gymnasium. The place was large and square with a high ceiling, plain white walls, and a cement floor. It seemed purposefully devoid of decoration. A large stage spanned the far end and housed a piano, various other instruments, and a pulpit. The floor space was lined with cushioned stackable chairs. Gigantic ceiling fans whirred overhead.

The pastor was speaking when Dirk and James entered. James directed Dirk to an empty seat near the back. James slid in next to a thirty something woman with limp brown hair and a plain face. "This is my wife Linda," James whispered. She nodded at Dirk as he sat next to James. "We always sit near the back in case I get called out."

Dirk smiled a greeting and then turned his eyes forward. The pastor was a rotund Mexican man, probably in his fifties with a comb over 'do. He was gesticulating and pacing, mopping his face occasionally at intervals as he preached for all he was worth. It was all in Spanish, and Dirk had a hard time following. He finally gave up altogether and relaxed against the back of his seat.

"I should have given you a headset," James whispered, leaning closer to Dirk.

Dirk's eyes popped open and he sat up a little straighter. He hoped he hadn't just nodded off. He looked questioningly at James.

"A headset." James tapped his ears. "We have someone translating the message for those who don't speak Spanish."

Dirk glanced around the room, noticing for the first time that many of the people were wearing the devices. As he turned his gaze back to the front, he made eye contact with a pretty woman making her way toward the exit. Her chocolate brown hair hung down her back with arrow straightness; her eyes were large and luminous. Their eyes met for a milli-second and she smiled before averting hers and continuing on her way. Dirk glanced over his shoulder to watch her exit.

When he swiveled back in his seat he had a smile on his face. Hopefully she was part of his church group and they could strike up a conversation. He hadn't noticed her at church before, but he hadn't really been that attentive. Tomorrow wasn't looking so bad after all.

CHAPTER 8

$\mathcal{D}$irk was so exhausted after the service that he didn't actually care that a stranger lay in the single bed not far from his. He was still operating on Boston time, so he figured he deserved a break. Of course, his roommate wanted to talk. Harmon was a middle aged tradesman; an electrician who'd made the trip for the past three years in a row. His wife had to stay in the women's dorms. Apparently there were no accommodations for couples at the moment unless you brought your own trailer. When Dirk mentioned the bathroom situation, Harmon just laughed. "Think of it like camping," he advised. Dirk had never been camping.

The morning dawned far too early. Harmon was up with the sun and out the door before Dirk even had time to roll over. He better get a move on. Breakfast was at seven sharp - James had repeated it more than once the night before. With a sigh, Dirk sat up and rubbed his eyes. A hot shower would help him wake up.

Half an hour later, Dirk emerged from the communal bathrooms. The building itself was clean, but primitive. Cement floors, cement walls... everything was constructed out of cement - even the showers. And so much for a hot shower. The hot water tanks were on the roof and were heated by the sun. If a person wanted a hot shower, you had to wait until the afternoon or evening. Morning showers were strictly cold. If this was camping, he didn't see the charm.

Dirk made it to the mess hall right on the dot of seven. The place was huge and once again very Spartan, but clean and serviceable. It was his first glimpse of the children. They ranged in size from about four years of age to young adults. All had dark hair and tanned skin and most striking of all, they all wore identical uniforms. Light blue shirts were combined with shorts or skirts of navy, along with white socks and oxford shoes. He supposed it helped eliminate any stigma. Everyone had the appearance of equality here. There were some signs of individuality, though, especially among the girls. Some sported brightly colored hair bows or barrettes, while others had small earrings in their lobes.

The place seated five hundred at least, and besides the children, there were people of every skin tone, age, and physique, many of whom he assumed were volunteers. At the end of at least twenty tables were babies and toddlers in high chairs, already getting fed by an adult. Some people were eating, while others were still in line getting their food, cafeteria style. Suddenly a horn sounded.

Like magic, the cavernous room became completely quiet. As if by one mind, all of the children and many of the adults began to sing in Spanish - a simple grace. Just as abruptly, the room began to buzz again once they were through as folks continued to eat or get their food. Dirk took his place in line, in awe at the seamless organization that seemed to reign. He supposed it was necessary.

Dirk took his tray and scanned the room for a place to sit. He was one of the last to get his food; a bowl of oatmeal and some fruit. There weren't any options, except for his choice of beverage. You got what they gave you. As James said, this wasn't a hotel. He opted to sit by an older couple who were already finished their breakfast.

"May I sit with you?" Dirk asked politely.

"Certainly." The woman waved him to sit. "We were almost ready to pack up our dishes, weren't we dear?" She looked at her husband, who nodded, still sipping his coffee. "Which group are you with?"

"Um, I'm with the group from Boston," Dirk supplied, taking a bite of his porridge. It wasn't bad. Either that or he was hungry. "We just arrived last night."

"This your first time?" the woman asked.

Dirk nodded. His mouth was full.

"We come here every year, don't we George?" George nodded and she continued. "We're retired. From Texas."

"I have a friend in Texas," Dirk said. He supposed Stella could be called his friend. Sort of.

"I'm Hilda, by the way. It's such a wonderful cause and we love to help out. Of course we bring our own fifth wheel. And we only stay for a week at a time. When you get to be our age, well, there's only so much you can do." She stopped and scrutinized Dirk's bowl. "You better eat up. They don't like you to dawdle. Devotions are right at 7:30."

"Devotions?" Dirk's eyebrows rose.

Hilda nodded. "All the volunteers meet in the prayer room next to the administrative building. After a short devotional and prayer, everyone gets their assignments for the day." Hilda smiled and patted Dirk's hand. "Don't worry. You'll catch on. It can be a bit overwhelming on the first day, but this place works like clockwork. There can be a hundred volunteers or more here at a time." Another horn sounded. "That's our cue. The trays go over there on those carts."

Dirk gulped the last of his coffee and stood up. He scooted to the rolling racks and slid his tray into one of the slots. Hilda was a fount of information. Perhaps he should have been more attentive last night while James explained some of the rules. Either that or he should have attended the orientation meeting back in Boston.

He managed to exit the mess hall and slip in with a group of people walking toward the administrative building. With relief he thought he recognized a couple of familiar faces, so he knew he must be headed in the right direction. They entered en masse through a set of double doors in the side of the structure, and once through a shallow foyer, they were in the 'prayer room'. Dirk was struck again by the inadequacy of the names for these places. He'd envisioned a cozy space with stained glass. This room was large, and the first that he'd seen that had carpet, albeit a faded dark turquoise color. The room was lined with wood paneling and there were rows of stacking chairs in perfect align-ment - enough for about one hundred.

Dirk found an empty place next to his roommate Harmon and a woman whom he presumed was Harmon's wife. The room filled up within three minutes and James took his place in front of the group.

James checked his watch and Dirk couldn't help sneaking a peak at his as well. Seven thirty on the nose. Not bad for effi-ciency. Without preamble, James began reading from the Bible; a passage about the body of Christ working together in harmony. After that he said a prayer asking for God's blessing and protec-tion for the day and thanking Him for the people who had come to work so selflessly here as volunteers. "And now, for those who have already been assigned a team, Jessica has your assignment for the day."

A pretty Mexican woman with a bushy ponytail stood up and waved. She was wearing a flowered dress and had a clipboard in her hands. "Hi. So, all the team leaders need to meet me out in the far corner of the courtyard. From there I'll give you your orders and you can get to work." She smiled widely, her teeth flashing white against her dark skin. At least half of the assembly stood and made their way back outside through the double doors.

James took over the meeting again as Jessica and her group exited. "Now for the rest of you, we've taken the questionnaires you filled out from your orientation packages and tried to put you with a team that best suits your skills. Skilled trade's people, people with carpentry skills, kitchen help, cleaning, mending, grounds keeping.... And of course we also need people to volunteer in the daycare and nursery. For those who didn't fill out a questionnaire or forgot to add certain skills, you will need to go to the administration office and do that now. Everyone else will stay for a short orientation session and then we'll get you grouped with your team leaders."

"Well, I guess that's me," Dirk whispered under his breath to Harmon as he stood up. Harmon smiled and nodded before Dirk stepped his way over several other people's legs in order to get to the aisle. There was only one other person doing the same, a man of about twenty with a beard, glasses, and a bandanna on his head.

"Just through that door and to the left," James directed them. Dirk smiled and nodded, but couldn't help notice the stiffening of James's jaw as they passed.

"Oops. I guess we dropped the ball on that one," Dirk offered quietly to bandanna boy as they passed into the hall.

"What?" The other man looked puzzled.

"The questionnaire," Dirk explained. "I think the director is slightly miffed with us. For not filling it out before we got here."

"Oh, I didn't notice. I'm Dillan, by the way." He stuck his hand out and Dirk shook it. Dillan's protruding beard bobbed when he talked. He was wearing a T shirt that proclaimed, 'Jesus took the nails' and a huge cross pendant made out of spikes.

"You here with a group?" Dirk asked.

"No, I just rolled in yesterday afternoon. I'm touring the coast, just passing through, but my friend told me about this place. Said I should check it out."

Dirk nodded. He should have guessed. The guy looked the part of a vagabond hipster. And a do-gooder one at that.

They arrived at the front counter and Dirk recognized James's wife Linda at the reception desk in the admin office. She was no more attractive than she was last night, poor thing. He smiled. "Hi. Apparently we need to fill in a questionnaire?"

Linda stood up and retrieved some questionnaires from a filing cabinet nearby. "Here you go. Make it as thorough as possible, please." She handed each of them a stapled packet, never making direct eye contact. Dirk nodded his assent, wondering simultaneously how she came to be married to James. She was a lot younger than James, he'd wager; tall and very thin, but not like a model. She stooped slightly, as if to hide her height. Perhaps it was to compensate for the fact that she was taller than her husband. It struck him as strange since the administrator came across as a man in charge; a guy who would want a trophy wife, not a timid mouse. Oh well. The old saying that opposites attract must be true in their case. He wasn't sure what it was about the other man, but there was something about him that rubbed the wrong way. Of course, that was just silly. The guy was a missionary.

Dirk found a seat next to Dillan in the reception area and they both proceeded to fill out the questionnaire. It asked practical questions like, "Do you mind hard work?" and "Are you physically fit?" There were also places to check off various skills like sewing and carpentry. Finally, there was a 'would you be willing to' section. Would you be willing to work in the kitchen, work outdoors, work in the nursery etc. Dirk had never really considered that there would be so many jobs around a place like this, but apparently they kept their volunteers busy. There were also some questions of a spiritual nature. Dirk thought for a minute and then wrote some things that he hoped sounded acceptable.

How was he supposed to know when he first 'accepted Christ'? He'd always believed in some form of supreme being, or at least he thought he had.

With a flourish, Dirk checked off the last of the boxes and handed the package back to Linda.

"Thanks," she said, keeping her eyes focused on the papers. "It might take a while to get this processed and get you on a team. Why don't you go back to the prayer room and see where James would like you to go until them? There's probably something you can do until we get you placed."

Dirk turned to head back to the prayer room. He felt like he'd just been in an unemployment line. Not that he'd ever have to do that in reality, but he imagined it might feel something like that. Humiliating.

James was still in the prayer room, straightening out the chairs into precise rows. "So? What are you interested in doing this morning? We should have you placed on a team by tomorrow, but until then you might as well make yourself useful."

"What is there for me to do?" Dirk asked.

"You could help the construction crew. We're in the process of building more houses."

"Houses? For whom?"

"At present we have twelve houses with a variety of ages in each household and one set of house parents, just like a real family. We'd set a limit of twelve children per unit, but we've had to up that to fifteen. It's not ideal." James looked him over. "Ever done any construction work?" Dirk shook his head and James grunted as if to say he figured as much. "How about kitchen work? They always need help prepping for the next meal. We feed up to five hundred people a day what with children, staff, and volunteers."

"Sure. Lead the way."

James walked as far as the double doors and then just pointed. "You know the way. Kitchen's in back of the mess hall. Just go into the back and ask for Ruby. She's the head of kitchen staff. She'll put you to work, I'm sure."

Dirk nodded and stepped out onto the cement patio. It was a short stroll back to the mess hall and he breathed deeply. The air was warm and fragrant. He liked the way most of the buildings had such clean lines and were constructed around a central courtyard. Planter boxes and benches were built in and there was always at least one tree in the center for shade. It was simple yet beautiful at the same time, and very functional. He'd like to take a walk around the entire grounds sometime, but knew he better be heading over to the kitchen asap.

His footsteps echoed in the large dining hall when he entered. It was strange to be in the room when it was devoid of people. There was no clinking of cutlery on plates; no animated chatter. The only sound was some muffled voices coming from behind the double swinging doors situated beside the serving area. They must lead back into the kitchen.

He swung through the right side, hoping the entrance operated under the same rules as driving. The volume instantly increased; the white noise of chatter mixed with the clack of knives on chopping blocks, the hum of a blender, and the flow of tap water. The room was long and narrow, with gleaming stainless steel everywhere. He only had a moment to survey his surroundings before a short, plump woman in a staff uniform of two tone blue caught his attention with a barked greeting. "Are you looking for something?"

"Oh. James sent me. I'm looking for Ruby."

"That would be me." The aforementioned woman dried her hands on a towel and strode to where Dirk was standing. "Ever done any kitchen work?" she asked, her voice rich with her Mexican accent.

Dirk just shook his head.

With a sigh, Ruby waved for him to follow her to a side cupboard. "First thing you need are some gloves and a hair net."

Dirk's eyebrows rose, but he took the items and donned them anyway. "We got twenty pounds of onions to chop. And that's just for starters."

Dirk nodded and followed her to a work station where she explained how she wanted him to perform his duties. She was a no nonsense kind of woman and ran her kitchen in military style. There was no way he was going to protest, and he certainly wasn't about to show any signs of fear. The fact that he'd hardly even seen an onion in its natural state didn't matter at the moment.

He struggled with the first couple of onions, peeling back each layer in separate, papery strips. Finally, a younger woman also wearing the staff uniform gently took the onion from his hands and demonstrated a more efficient way of extracting the outer layers in one piece. He got the hang of it after a few more tries, until he had a pile of onions on the block just waiting to be chopped. He watched the woman to his left, taking note of the smooth strokes downward with the cleaver type knife. She was hardly even looking as her arm pumped the knife like a person priming a well. He tried to emulate her movements, much more slowly and carefully of course, until he got his own rhythm going. It was actually kind of fun.

It didn't take long before the sting in his eyes was making him literally cry like a baby, however. A few more minutes and he could hardly see.

Suddenly the knife slipped and he felt the sting of onion juice as it penetrated a slice in his finger that went right through the glove's thin plastic barrier. "Ow!" He ripped the glove off and flung it down on top of the already chopped onions and stuck the finger in his mouth. The taste of raw onions made him yank the finger from his mouth and spit to the side.

"What happened?" Ruby demanded. She was beside him in seconds. "Let me see."

He unclenched the finger from his opposite fist and showed

her. It immediately oozed more blood, some of it dripping onto the butcher block.

"Ah! You have ruined the whole batch!" she scolded. She said something else in Spanish and the other girl wearing the official kitchen uniform scurried over and took the contaminated onions away, block and all.

"It's probably nothing," Dirk said, trying to sound nonchalant. It was hard when he was still squinting from the onions.

"No way. Get to the clinic," Ruby said. "We don't want no problems with insurance later on, and you no good for working if you don't get looked after."

"You're the boss."

"You need help finding?" she asked, her hands on her hips as she stared up into his face.

Dirk shook his head, finger back inside his mouth. "No, I got it." It came out garbled.

He was pretty certain he could find his way. He didn't want these people thinking he was totally incompetent. In a way he was glad for the injury. It got him out of chopping any more onions.

CHAPTER 9

irk opened the glass door that led into the clinic and stepped inside. It smelled just like a hospital should smell; antiseptic and something else that bordered on feces. It was also cool, something he noticed instantly. At least they had the decency to keep it air conditioned. The entrance was little more than a vestibule with a row of chairs along one wall. A set of wide doors barred any further entrance. There was a window like in a ticket office at the movies in one wall. He walked up to it and rang the bell on the outside.

A small woman with characteristic dark hair and complexion scurried into the room on the other side and peered through the window. "Yes?" She wore an old fashioned nurse's hat, the kind that looked like an origami boat pinned to her hair.

"I, uh, I hurt my finger..." He held it up for her to see.

She asked him a few questions in stilted English and then had him sign a form. It was difficult with the sliced finger and he winced. He wondered what they would have done had his injuries been worse. They probably had protocol for real emergencies.

The nurse hit a button and a buzzing sound indicated that the main doors were now unlocked. She gestured him through and he found himself in what looked like a real hospital. Linoleum floors, a long corridor with examination rooms leading from it, a cart parked to the side lined with blue and green linens stacked in precise piles, and a circular desk that looked like the nurses' station. The small woman waved a hand for him to follow and he entered an exam room, outfitted like any other he'd seen in the States.

"Sit." She pointed at the bed. He did and she pulled a privacy curtain across to shield him from the open door. Then he waited.

He was preoccupied glancing around the room at the equipment, when he heard footsteps. His eyes widened in surprise when a familiar face pushed past the drapery. She was perusing a piece of paper on a clipboard. "Dirk Hillyer?" She looked up and smiled, no apparent recognition in her gaze. It was the same woman who'd caught his eye on the way out of the church last night. His luck was changing.

He nodded. "That's right."

"It says here you cut yourself?"

Dirk shrugged, trying to appear nonchalant. "Probably no big deal, but they made me come."

"Gotta stick to the rules." Her voice was conversational and pleasant. "Let's take a look."

Dirk held out his finger and allowed her to unwrap the make shift bandage of paper towel. He watched her as she examined the injury more closely. She was as striking in her nurse's scrubs as she had been last night in church. Her long brown hair was now secured into a neat bun on the top of her head, little wisps curling at the nape of her neck. She was of average height and had a well rounded figure that pressed softly against her uniform; not fat by any means, but full and curvaceous. When she looked up he was startled by the brightness of her blue eyes. They were large - almost too big for her face - and thickly lashed. Her mouth was small and pert, her cheeks round and flushed with a rosy complexion, and there was a sprinkling of freckles across her slightly turned up nose. She reminded him of one of those waifs you'd see in a painting. The perfect poster child for an orphanage.

She straightened. "So how did this happen?"

"Chopping onions." Dirk gave a wry smile. Not the most glamorous scenario. He squinted at her name tag. 'Anne-Marie' it said.

"Ah." She nodded and smiled. "I thought I smelled something. It actually looks pretty deep. It might need a stitch or two."

"Oh?" Dirk raised his brows.

"I'll get the doctor and be right back."

"Okay. Thanks Anne-Marie." Dirk smiled when she hesitated just a moment after he'd said her name. Then she touched her name tag as realization dawned and smiled back at him before leaving the exam room.

Dirk watched her exit, enjoying the sway of her backside. He was beginning to understand some men's preference for a healthy booty. Hers was noticeably well proportioned. The old Dirk would act on the attraction. Of course, he was no longer like that. He was turning over a new leaf, he reminded himself. Besides, he had feelings for Tempest.

Anne-Marie returned in a few minutes with the doctor. The newcomer was entirely too handsome and the smile on Dirk's face faded. With his square jaw, tanned face, dark wavy hair, and trim physique, the good doctor could be a model for the latest brand of expensive cologne.

"Hello. I'm Dr. Smythe. I hear we had a mishap in the kitchen." The man had a distinctive Australian accent. Score another point for the doc.

"Um, right." Dirk held up the finger for the doctor's inspection.

"Hm... It needs a suture or two." The doctor straightened and smiled at Anne-Marie. It was apparently his signal for her to get the supplies. She found what was needed on a nearby shelf and began sterilizing the wound. Dirk winced. "Be done straight away and you can get back to your duties," the doctor assured.

Great. Just what he wanted to hear. Dirk braced himself for the first stitch but Anne-Marie had applied a numbing agent and he didn't feel a thing. He avoided watching, though. The last thing he wanted was to faint in front of them.

"So?" the doctor said to Anne-Marie. "What do you think of James' grand vision?"

Anne-Marie shrugged. "I think it's good to think big. The whole orphanage was founded on faith, so why not believe for something even bigger?"

"I suppose. Rather like Nehemiah, though. Rebuilding the walls while our enemies laugh in our faces."

Anne-Marie shrugged. "That's not such a bad analogy. In the end, Nehemiah saw his vision through. With God's blessing."

Dirk didn't understand the reference and listened as their exchange continued. He was decidedly an outsider looking in.

"Well, that should do it." Dr. Smythe swiveled on his stool and then stood up. "Come back in a week and we'll take those out." He didn't bother looking at Dirk again, but turned to Anne-Marie. "Are you on call again tonight?"

She shook her head. "No. It's Franchesca's night."

Dr. Smythe nodded. "Good. We should go out for pizza later."

"Sure. But not until after the service. I'm enjoying Pastor's series."

So that's how things were. Dirk frowned. He watched the doctor stroll from the room. He suddenly had a deep desire to go to church again that evening, too.

THE REST of the day passed quickly. Dirk went back to his kitchen duties, donned a fresh glove and was a lot more careful with sharp objects from then on. He helped serve during lunch, marveling again at how efficiently a large group could be fed when run like a military operation. He got to eat after the line-up was through, so other than a quick nod at Nurse Anne-Marie as she went through the line, he didn't get a chance to talk to her again. Tonight would be a different story, however. He was going to church early.

His feet hurt by the end of the day. The floors were hard tile and he'd been standing in one spot most of the time. He wondered how regular staffers like Ruby could stand it. Hopefully his name would appear on one of those regular rosters tomorrow and he'd be assigned something other than kitchen duty. Not that he wanted to be a complainer, but he'd never actually had to do anything in the kitchen before. That's what servants were for. Then again, he hadn't done much of anything that resembled hard labor. Maybe kitchen duty was the lesser of other, unknown evils.

Dillan, the wandering vagrant and his partner in crime sat beside him at supper time. "So what wonderful tasks did you get to do today?" Dirk asked.

"They actually have a macadamia nut grove here on the property," Dillan responded. "It'll be harvest time fairly soon, so they had me working with the grounds keeper. It was actually really interesting."

Dirk nodded absently. Maybe he could swing a similar gig tomorrow. He looked around for Anne-Marie, but he didn't see her anywhere, so he went back to his meal - nondescript beans, rice, pork, and a flour tortilla on the side. It was plain food, but he was surprisingly hungry and it filled his stomach. There was no dawdling here at meal time. You were expected to shovel it in, clean up your mess, and move on. Lingering over conversation or coffee wasn't part of the program.

After he cleared his dishes, Dirk sauntered back to the dorms to pick up some clean clothes and his toiletries. He was determined to have a second shower that day. He was sweaty and tired and wanted to freshen up before the evening service. Hopefully the water would still be warm.

At exactly ten minutes to seven, Dirk stood just inside the chapel entrance. The shower had been lukewarm, but passable. He smiled and nodded to several people he'd met on kitchen duty, but declined all offers to sit with any of them. He was waiting for someone, he said. It was true. At exactly three minutes to seven, Anne-Marie walked in. He heard her tinkling laughter even before she entered. He had a smile ready, which faded only slightly when he saw the good doctor by her side. He doubted they would have stopped, except that Dirk made the first move by catching her eye and waving.

"Hi. How's the finger?" she asked conversationally. Dr. Smythe didn't say anything, but raised his brows as if he was interested. Unlikely.

Dirk held the finger up. "Still attached."

"Good." She smiled and then looked around. "Waiting for someone?"

"Not really."

"You can sit with us if you like," she offered. The doctor may have frowned. Dirk couldn't tell for sure. Maybe he was reading too much into the other man's reactions, but for some reason, the Aussie doctor made his hackles rise.

The doctor put a hand lightly on Anne-Marie's back as she scooted into an aisle of chairs. Dirk frowned. Did Doc purposely place himself between them? Apparently so. After they were seated, Dr. Smythe dominated the conversation with clever anecdotes about the day's events until the service started.

The singing was lively, and part way through a troupe of dancers - girls between ten and eighteen wearing full swishy skirts and white blouses - did a choreographed routine to the last few songs. It was the first time Dirk had ever seen dancing in church, that was for sure, but he found himself enjoying it. They were in no way provocative, but seemed to be full of joy, using their bodies in a very lively and expressive way.

Then came the sermon. He'd forgotten about the head sets and had to endure another long lecture with little clue as to what was being said. He spent most of the time trying to sneak glimpses of Anne-Marie without her knowing it. He didn't suppose it was the kind of distraction he should be having in church, but give a guy a break. When you can't understand a word and a very attractive woman is sitting just two seats away...

Finally the service was over. Dirk prepared himself for what he would say when given the chance. Unfortunately, it didn't seem he'd get it. For some unfathomable reason, Super-Doc suddenly wanted to converse.

"That was a mighty good message, wouldn't you say, mate?" The doctor looked Dirk straight in the eye, daring him to admit he hadn't understood a word.

Dirk shrugged. There was no use lying about it. "I didn't understand much, to be honest."

"You can ask for a headset at that back counter over there," Anne-Marie said, turning and pointing to the sound booth at the back of the church. "The sermons are always translated."

Dirk nodded his thanks. "I'll do that next time."

Immediately, Dr. Smythe turned his back and started talking about something the pastor had said. Dirk listened for awhile, but gave up and looked around the room instead. He obviously wasn't going to gain Anne-Marie's attention through theological means. Doctor Know-It-All had that all sewed up. He'd just have to think of some other way to get her attention. In the old days, that would have been easy. Drive up in his latest sports car and flash a bit of money around. Somehow he didn't think Anne-Marie would be the kind of girl who'd be impressed by that.

As Dirk was mulling this over, a new thought came to mind and along with it a wash of guilt. He hadn't thought about Tempest all day.

CHAPTER 10

"We're putting you with the crew building the new cottages," James announced the next morning after breakfast.

Dirk's brows rose but he didn't protest. "Okay." He didn't have a clue when it came to construction. He thought he'd made that clear yesterday.

Dirk followed the rest of his work crew to the site of the new cottages. His roomy Harmon was walking among the group, so Dirk picked up his pace and caught up with the older man. "Looks like we'll be work buddies, now, too. I haven't a clue how. I have absolutely no skills when it comes to this kind of work."

Harmon glanced at Dirk as they walked. "I suggested it."

Dirk's eyes widened. "You did? Why?"

Harmon smiled. "You seemed kind of down last night. I figured kitchen duty wasn't up your alley, so I suggested something different."

"You might be sorry." Dirk held up his finger. "I tend to be accident prone."

"Nah. Kitchen duty is just too dangerous. Besides, this way I can keep an eye on you. Keep you from killing yourself."

"Seriously? Now I need a babysitter?" Dirk grinned.

Harmon shrugged. "Not sure. Maybe just a friend." Harmon surveyed Dirk as they walked. "You seem a bit like a fish out of water."

Dirk snorted. "That obvious, huh?"

They'd reached the work site. It was cordoned off by a temporary roll up fence, beyond which was the expected gravel, cement mixers, and piles of building materials. Two cottages were under construction, the first in what would be an outer ring of cottages behind the twelve that already surrounded a central courtyard. The basic structures were already up and the tiled roofs were complete.

Harmon slapped Dirk on the back. "Just stick with me and you should be fine."

Dirk was going to do just that. "So what are we doing?"

"According to the docket, we're going to stucco the outside and start framing the interior walls."

"At the same time?"

"There's enough people."

"We're working on the interior, I hope?" Dirk shaded his eyes with his hand and squinted at the exterior. He didn't know the first thing about applying stucco.

Harmon raised an amused brow. "Ever swung a hammer?" Dirk shook his head in the negative. "Used a drill?" Again a negative response. "That's why we're working on the outside. Maybe tomorrow I'll show you how to do some carpentry work."

Dirk frowned. The sun already felt warm and he suspected it would be sweltering by mid-day. "And how much easier is stuccoing?"

"Who said anything about easier?" Harmon grinned. "It just takes less skill."

The foreman started barking out orders, and the crew split up. The first step in applying the stucco was to wrap the house in a wire mesh that would help hold the stucco in place. The mesh came in huge rolls and it took two men to unroll and tack it flush along the entire surface of the building. With Harmon's help, Dirk started attaching the mesh using a stapler of sorts that he swung like a hammer. Once enough surface was covered, someone else came behind with the thick stucco which was troweled on top. It was hard work and Dirk soon shed the button up shirt he wore. He still had a good tan left over from the summer and of course, there were artificial ways to keep up such a glow. He felt the sweat trickling down his front, back, and into his eyes.

"That's quite a scar." Harmon nodded to the mangled red skin peeking up over the waistband of Dirk's jeans.

Dirk glanced down. "My battle scars." The scar in front was an irregular circular shape and was still an angry red. Another scar in back was larger, like a paint splat. They spoiled the smoothness of the rest of his torso, but he was kind of proud of them, too, and didn't mind showing them off.

"What happened, if you don't mind me asking?"

"I, uh.... I took a bullet." Dirk gauged the other man's reaction. Harmon was suitably impressed. "This is where the bullet went in, and in back," he reached around to point, "is the exit wound."

"Seems there must be a story behind those two. They look fairly fresh." Harmon wasn't about to give up.

"My sister was being held by a psycho. A guy involved in the drug trade. I was trying to rescue her." Dirk shrugged. For some reason he liked the way the story made him sound. Dangerous.

"And it turned out okay, I take it?"

Dirk nodded. "Yeah. She's safe and sound now. The crazy thing is the guy who kidnapped her was my best friend."

Harmon tacked another piece of the mesh in place. "So... before you came to the Lord, I take it you ran with a pretty rough crowd?"

Dirk frowned, unsure for a moment what Harmon meant. Then the light bulb went on. "Oh! You think I was involved in drugs myself." He laughed. "No, I'm just a regular guy." He smiled at Harmon. As regular as a man who was independently wealthy and didn't have to work could be. For some reason the image of a low-life from the wrong side of town who'd scratched his way out of his hole sounded much more intriguing than the truth.

"So how did you come to know Christ?" Harmon asked.

Dirk blinked. He wasn't sure. Did he actually know Christ in the way Harmon implied? He made something up instead. "Um, it was through this girl. My sister's friend." He smiled and hoped that was enough.

It seemed to be. "Nothing like a pretty girl to bring a man to his knees," Harmon chuckled.

The dinner bell rang off in the distance. Time had gone much faster than it had in the kitchen yesterday. They were about one third done the building and would presumably have to finish after lunch. Dirk couldn't believe how hungry he felt.

"Good work." Harmon slapped Dirk across the back. "Now, next time you volunteer for something, you can actually say you have some skills."

Dirk smiled. Harmon was a good guy. The fact that he would volunteer for such a dirty and labor intensive job in the heat, just to take the time to get to know him better, spoke volumes. He wasn't sure anyone had ever done something like that for him before.

CHAPTER 11

*D*uring the next several days, Dirk discovered muscles that he never knew he had. Hard physical labor was a lot different than working out at the gym. It brought a certain sense of satisfaction, too. Perhaps for one of the first times in his twenty-seven years, he felt as if he was doing something that mattered. He was making a difference in the lives of other people in a real, tangible way. Not to mention he'd discovered a whole new skill set. He was actually getting pretty good with a nail gun.

By the end of the workday, the lukewarm shower felt absolutely perfect. He was famished by that time, too, ready to wolf down the plain fare in the allotted time with no qualms whatsoever. Even the narrow bed felt heavenly each night when he fell into it. He and Harmon hardly had time to exchange a few pleasantries about the day before they both drifted off.

Not that they didn't have plenty of time to talk during the day. Harmon had taken Dirk under his wing, so to speak. Not only was the older man teaching him a few practical skills, but they had deep conversations about what it meant to be a follower of Christ. Dirk had never heard things explained in quite that manner before, despite a month of sermons back in Boston. Harmon talked about Jesus as if he were a real person. A friend.

There was only one down side to the last few days. Dirk hadn't had a chance to spend any time with Anne-Marie. He'd made it his mission to get to know her better, if possible. Not that anything would come of it, he reasoned. But he was intrigued by her none the less. He'd attended each and every evening service, hoping to get a chance to speak with her again. Unfortunately, most nights she was already seated with a group - including Dr. Smythe - and afterward it was difficult to get through the crowd without seeming too anxious. Once he'd managed to sit right next to her, but the good doctor was also present, monopolizing the conversation as well as Anne-Marie's attention.

Problem was those two seemed to have this deeper level thing going on... the church club that involved knowing glances and references to Bible verses that Dirk wasn't familiar with. Christian-ese, someone had labeled it. Now he knew what they meant. Well, he would just have to try harder. It was exactly one week since he'd arrived; half way through his allotted stint at the orphanage, and he was running out of time. But Dirk Hillyer wasn't one to give up that easily.

Dirk spotted Anne-Marie as she entered the chapel. She looked pretty in a loose floral sun dress and her hair hung down her back almost to her waist in a shining brown cascade. He'd come early tonight and loitered just inside the doors. He slid into step beside her, trying not to make it too obvious that he'd been waiting for her. "How are you this evening?"

"Just fine. Yourself?" Anne-Marie flashed him a smile.

"Fine." He held up his finger, minus the bandage. "I was going to come in to get the stitches removed, but my roomy shamed me into letting him do it."

"Oh?" Anne-Marie's already large eyes widened even further. "Let me take a look. You don't want to get an infection."

"Let's find a seat first," Dirk suggested. He stepped aside, gesturing for her to go first. Anne-Marie slid into an aisle and sat down, Dirk close at her heels.

"So, let's see it." Anne-Marie's no nonsense tone matched the expectancy in her eyes.

Dirk produced the injured digit. "Harmon said he couldn't afford to let me out of work for something as simple as removing a stitch."

"Two stitches. "Anne-Marie squinted and turned the finger to another angle.

"Right. Two stitches." Dirk inhaled her scent. Her hair smelled fresh like flowers, matching her dress, and it partly curtained her face. "I was planning to come into the clinic tomorrow, though, anyway. Just to make sure." Just to see you, he could have added, but didn't.

"Who's Harmon?" Anne-Marie released his finger and sat back in her seat, her face turned to look directly at Dirk.

"My roommate. So? What's your expert opinion? Am I gonna live?"

She nodded. "Looks like it healed well. Dr. Smythe did a good job. Pretty soon you won't even see that scar."

Dirk's gaze wandered away from Anne-Marie's large eyes toward the front of the church where the worship team was just taking their places. "Doesn't matter. I have worse scars."

"Yeah?" She captured his gaze once again with the simple question.

"Maybe I'll show you sometime." Dirk smiled.

"Hm. Not sure how to take that."

"Don't worry. It's not in a spot that's too private." Dirk stopped talking and looked around. "Speaking of Dr. Smythe, I don't see him around."

"He's on call tonight. Must be with a patient."

Dirk couldn't help the satisfied smile that flickered on his lips.

~

"JUST LOOK at the size of the moon tonight!" Anne-Marie exclaimed.

Dirk raised his eyes to where she pointed. The moon was indeed very large and full. It shone like a silver spotlight on an inky black backdrop. "Very pretty." He turned his gaze back to the woman at his side, watching her rapt expression as she regarded the sky above. They were standing together just outside the chapel doors. A slight breeze lifted Anne-Marie's hair from her back, and her sun dress molded itself against parts of her figure. Even prettier.

His attention was averted as a large group spilled out of the chapel, parting around them like a river splits for an island. Most were chattering in Spanish as they headed for their dorm rooms or to the front gates where the night watchman would let them pass. Many townsfolk came to the services in the evening. As James said, the orphanage served the whole community, not just the orphans in their care.

"When I look up at the moon, I think, 'That's the same moon that my parents are looking at right now.'" Anne-Marie's mouth curled up in a contented smile.

"And where might that be?" Dirk asked. They started walking in the general direction of the dorms, in no real hurry.

"A small farming community outside of Edmonton, Alberta." She looked across at him. "That's in Canada."

He feigned a look of disdain. "I know where Alberta is."

"Not everyone does. At least not around here."

"That's a long way from home. What brought you here?" Dirk asked.

"Adventure, I guess." Anne-Marie shrugged her shoulders, sauntering along beside Dirk as she spoke. "That, and the fact that I like to help people."

"Of course you do. You're a nurse."

"I'd done some nursing up north in the North West Territories." She glanced at Dirk with an impish grin. "That's also in Canada. And then I heard about Beacon of Hope through my church. I signed on for a six month term. I'll be going home at Christmas."

"So you're about half way through," Dirk noted. "Me, too."

Anne-Marie's forehead furrowed. "What do you mean?"

"I'm half way through my two weeks and you're half way through your six months."

"Oh, I see. You'll be leaving next week then?"

Dirk wasn't sure whether he imagined the disappointment in her voice or not. "Unless they let me stay on longer."

"You don't have a job to get back to?" Anne-Marie asked. "Or... someone?"

Dirk shook his head. "No. I'm currently at loose ends on both accounts." The fact that he'd never actually had a job to speak of wasn't important. "Do they let people stay on?"

"I don't see why not. I mean, there's always something to do, and as you know, the mission relies heavily on volunteers. I get paid, of course, but most of my earnings come from outside sponsors."

"A real missionary." Dirk smiled at Anne-Marie's profile in the darkness. He liked the smooth look of her skin and the way her nose turned up just a bit at the end.

"Exactly. It's that way for most foreigners here."

"I might have to look into staying a bit longer, then," Dirk said. "Tell me more."

"Well, Beacon of Hope funds a lot of worthwhile projects besides this orphanage. They do food campaigns once a week throughout the countryside, bringing a hot meal to the migrant workers that work on the farms close by." She looked over at Dirk. "You may have noticed the shanty towns dotted along the highway. Those people have so little and many of them can't make enough to feed their families on the wages they get from the big corporations."

"I saw that, yeah."

"They also run a sister orphanage out of Tijuana. It's not as well established and the conditions are a lot different in a border city like that. I was thinking about working there after my time here is finished."

"After Christmas."

"Yes."

They'd reached the spot where their paths would split. The ladies' dorm was to their right while the men's was off to the left.

"Well... I guess I'll be seeing you." Dirk kicked at a spot on the sidewalk with the toe of his shoe.

"Right. Thanks for walking with me." Despite her words, Anne-Marie didn't make any move to depart.

"It seems like too nice a night to go in yet." Dirk put his hands in his jeans pockets and looked around at the quiet grounds.

"Exactly what I was thinking," Anne-Marie agreed. "How about a little stroll? I love walking at night."

"Sounds good to me." Dirk smiled and they started walking once again. "Where too?"

"Anywhere." Anne-Marie shrugged. "There are plenty of places to sit down if we feel like it."

The night sounds greeted them as they sauntered along the cement sidewalk. They reached the end of the courtyard and started off along a gravel path that led into the macadamia nut grove. They walked for a space, ducking under the trees as they went. "Be careful," Anne-Marie advised. "The leaves are pretty sharp. I wouldn't want to have to treat you for scratches, too."

Dirk reached up to touch one of the leaves. He instantly jerked his hand away again. "Ow!"

"Warned you," Anne-Marie said with a smile. "It's why not too many people stroll in the orchard. You have to be careful about where you walk."

The trees themselves varied in height, some of them little more than six feet high while others seemed to tower over their heads. The leaves were sharp and brittle, similar to holly used at Christmas time, and Dirk could see the clusters of green nut pods hanging thickly from their branches. "How do they manage to harvest these beasties?"

"Protective clothing. Gloves. I'm not an expert, but I know harvest time is coming in about a month and then they hire out a lot of the labor. Sales of nuts help fund the mission. It's kind of a big deal around here."

"I met a guy my first week who was working out here. Dillan. Kind of a drifter. I think he left already."

"Not surprising."

They walked for a space, Dirk ever cognizant of the fact that he had to watch not to brush up against the trees.

Anne-Marie spoke again. "I'm surprised at you, actually."

Dirk turned to look at her as they walked. "Oh? And why is that?"

"About wanting to stay on. I had you pegged differently. Most people come here for their allotted two weeks and then forget all about us once they get home. Sort of a 'feel good' project. It's different when you're here every day and get to know the kids and the regular staff." She stopped walking and glanced up at Dirk. "I'm sorry. That sounded ungrateful and a little bit like a snob. I didn't mean to imply..."

Dirk laughed. "Forget it. You probably had me pegged correctly in the first place. I *am* a bit of a snob. This experience has been good for me."

"You a snob? I can't believe it."

"You don't know the real me," Dirk joked.

"So? What's the real Dirk like?" Anne-Marie smiled, beckoning him with her encouraging eyes.

In truth, he wasn't sure he was ready to reveal the real Dirk to

Anne-Marie. She seemed wholesome and regular. Kind of like Tempest. "You go first," he hedged.

"Oh dear. Really?" She shook her head and looked down, suddenly shy. "There's not much to say."

"I doubt that."

"Seriously. I feel uncomfortable talking about myself."

"Just tell me everything, no matter how silly. I'm listening."

"Let's see." Anne-Marie furrowed her brow. "I'm twenty-six years old. I have a younger brother named Tyler. He's studying engineering at the University of Alberta. That's where I studied nursing. My mom is an office administrator for a small accounting firm. My dad runs his own construction company. I've attended the same church all my life..." She trailed off.

"Good start. But tell me some fun stuff. What kinds of things do you like? Your favorite food, music, things like that?"

"You want the full meal deal, do you?" Anne-Marie laughed. "Okay. I went on a trip to Thailand last year with a friend. Never been to Mexico before..."

"Male or female friend?" Dirk interrupted

Anne-Marie looked quizzically over at Dirk. "Female, of course."

"Go on," he encouraged with a wave of his hand.

"I like musicals, especially the classics like 'The Sound of Music'; eighties rock ballads 'cause I was forced to listen to them when I was a kid; and I am very, very competitive at board games." She grinned and waited for Dirk's nod to continue. "Favorite author is Jane Austen hands down. Favorite color is green. Favorite time of year, fall 'cause I like the rustle of the leaves in the trees."

Dirk nodded, taking it all in. It was a far cry from tennis, the yacht club and womanizing rich girls. She was plain and simple; enjoyed life for what it was. Dirk smiled and shook his head.

"What?" Anne-Marie asked, noting the gesture.

"Nothing. Your list is just somewhat different than mine, that's all."

"Okay, let's have it," she dared.

"Not so fast. You aren't done yet. Food?"

Anne-Marie sighed dramatically. "I like cheese pizza with nothing else on it, chocolate fudge sundaes, and Christmas turkey. My favorite." She patted her stomach. "And I always knew I wanted to be a nurse. There. That about sums it up. Now you know everything there is to know about me. Your turn."

"Not quite," Dirk said. "You didn't mention anything about your love life."

She shrugged. "What's to mention? I've never been in a serious relationship."

Dirk's eyebrows rose. "I find that hard to believe."

"Believe it." Her tone was curt; defensive. "A woman's self worth doesn't need to be attached to a man."

"Of course not. I agree totally, but -"

"Furthermore, I have been very busy with school and then work." By her tone, it was obvious that *that* part of the conversation was finished. "Enough about me. It's your turn."

Dirk inhaled a deep breath and let it out with a huff. "Okay..."

"See? Not as easy when it's your turn, is it?" Anne-Marie's eyes had regained their twinkle.

"Right." Dirk rubbed the back of his neck. "Born and raised in Boston." He turned to her with a grin. "That's in Massachusetts, by the way."

Anne-Marie gave him a playful swat. "I knew that."

He continued, "One sister named Cherise. Favorite color... not sure."

"Come on! Not fair," Anne-Marie called.

"Okay. Blue... maybe. Favorite food... um, it changes. Least favorite drink: beer. I hate the stuff."

"Boring, boring, boring," Anne-Marie teased. "Let's get to the fun stuff."

Dirk frowned. What else could he say? That he enjoyed picking up strange women at night clubs? That he liked fast cars, short skirts, and getting blitzed while cruising on the family yacht? "Um, there's nothing else to say. Just a regular guy, I guess."

"You never said what you did for a living. I know you're between jobs, but what did you do before that?"

"Between jobs?"

"Isn't that what you said? At 'loose ends'?"

Dirk nodded, his mouth suddenly dry. "Oh right. I've been involved in the family business. Investments, mostly."

"So you're a stock broker?" Anne-Marie asked.

"Sort of. My father does the investing and I... worked for him." It was only a small lie. "But I'm ready to try something else."

Suddenly a twig snapped somewhere in the grove. A swishing of grass or leaves had both Dirk and Anne-Marie swiveling in that direction. "Oh my!" Anne-Marie's eyes were even rounder than normal. "That startled me!"

Dirk peered into the darkness. "What do you suppose it was? A wild animal?"

"I doubt it." Anne-Marie let out a long breath and laughed. "Probably just a cat. There are lots of strays that hang around."

Dirk nodded his agreement. "Probably right." Unless they were being followed. The thought sounded paranoid, even to him, so he kept it to himself.

"Now, you were saying?" Anne-Marie had regained her composure and started walking again.

"Um... what was I saying?" Dirk rubbed the back of his neck and followed her lead.

"You were telling me all about yourself," Anne-Marie reminded with a smile as she swung her hair back out of her way.

Dirk watched the thick dark mass swing against her backside. He blinked, resisting the urge to reach out and rub a few strands between his fingers. "That's it. Nothing more to say."

"What about relationships?" she asked with a raised brow. "Since you were so interested in that topic."

"I've been in a few. Nothing that lasted." He looked at her and flashed a sheepish grin. "I'm not exactly proud of my track record."

"A real playboy," she quipped, but there was a smile in her voice.

"All in the past, believe me." Tempest flashed before his mind's eye and he shrugged the thought away. The 'get to know me' game had suddenly lost its appeal.

"What about those scars you mentioned earlier?" Anne-Marie prodded.

Dirk's eyes widened and he smiled. "Oh yes. The scars."

"So?" Anne-Marie's eyes lit up playfully. "Now that we're alone you're too shy to share?"

"It might shock you."

She stopped walking and placed her hands on her hips. "I'm not asking you to strip, although I am a nurse, you know. Just tell me about them."

Dirk glanced at her face to make sure he could see her reaction. "I took a bullet once. I've got two scars. One where it went in and one where it came out." His voice held a hint of pride.

Anne-Marie's eyes widened. "Oh my."

Dirk raised a playful brow. "You wanna see? It's not anywhere too indecent."

"Okay. Sure."

Anne-Marie waited while Dirk held up his shirt with one hand and used his fingers to lower the waist band of his jeans just a tad to give a full view of the marred flesh. "In through the front, out through the back."

"Goodness. Those are impressive." She was bent slightly at the waist to get a better look. When she straightened she smiled impishly. "And you wear them like a badge of honor."

Dirk flushed and let the shirt fall back into place.

"I take it there's a story to go with those?" she asked.

"I was trying to rescue my sister. She'd gotten mixed up with some shady characters. Drug dealers."

"Oh dear. In Boston, I take it?"

Dirk shook his head. "In Italy, actually."

"The plot thickens. So what was the medical care like in Italy, if you don't mind me asking?"

Anne-Marie's interest in medicine had her asking more questions which Dirk didn't mind answering. Her rapt attention to his descriptions of the hospital and their procedures had him wishing he had more to tell. By the time the topic was exhausted, they had walked a full circle through the macadamia grove and were back at its edge.

"I can tell you really love your work," Dirk said, scrutinizing Anne-Marie's face in the semi-darkness.

She nodded. "Someone once said that if you find something you love to do, you'll never have to work a day in your life."

Dirk laughed at that. He hadn't found such a thing, and he still didn't work.

Anne-Marie frowned. "You disagree?"

"No, no. I was just thinking that you're probably one of the lucky few who have found what you love."

"Don't worry. You'll find something fulfilling."

Their attention was drawn several feet to the right as another figure emerged from the macadamia grove. It was Dillan, or 'bandanna boy' as Dirk liked to call him. The younger man seemed startled to see them, but nodded cordially. "Nice night for a stroll," he called before continuing toward the dorms.

"You know him?" Anne-Marie asked.

"Kind of. He's the guy I mentioned earlier that was working in the grove." Dirk frowned. "Except, I thought he'd left already."

Anne-Marie shrugged her shoulders. "Apparently not."

They walked toward the courtyard and their respective dorms. "Well, here we are. I, uh... I had a nice time tonight."

"Me too."

"We should do it again, sometime." Dirk waited for a response.

Anne-Marie's gaze scooted to the side, as if she was embarrassed to look straight at him all of a sudden. "Yes. Yes we should."

"As long as the doctor doesn't mind," Dirk added. He wasn't sure why he said it, but there it was. His jealous nature was out in the open.

Anne-Marie's gaze swung back to his, questioning in her eyes. "The doctor? Do you mean Harry?"

"Harry?" Dirk frowned.

"Dr. Smythe. I don't know what he has to do with anything, or why you'd even ask." Her tone was defensive again.

"Not sure. I just thought maybe the two of you were, you know, more than just friends." Dirk waited, trying to gauge her reaction.

"Harry - I mean, Dr. Smythe - and I are definitely just friends. And colleagues, of course. But nothing more."

"Good to know." If he could actually see her color in the moonlight, he imagined a faint blush on her cheeks. "Anyway, I'll see you tomorrow."

"You will?" She sounded breathless.

He nodded. "At church."

They parted and he watched her retreat to the stairwell on the side of her building, exactly opposite to the one on his own. A full blown smile of satisfaction had blossomed on his face. First thing tomorrow he was giving James notice. He was staying for awhile.

Blue

CHAPTER 12

*B*lue flipped the page attached to the wooden clipboard, and scanned the next items on the list of inventory. The farming supply store stocked everything from small garden supplies, to horse tack, to parts for farm implements. A rancher's 'one stop shop', or so the paid advertising said. It was the first available job Blue had come across when he left the ranch, and the proprietor was more than willing to hire him with his first-hand knowledge and experience. Trouble was, the job was down-right boring at times. Like today. He longed to be outdoors instead of cooped up inside a warehouse checking stock. On days like this, it was hard to keep his mind on work.

If he stopped to admit it, it wasn't just the lack of fresh air that had his mind wandering. It was the picture of a certain blonde beauty that kept popping into his brain. He frowned and tried to snap back to the present. He wanted nothing more to do with Cherise Hillyer and that was final.

It's not that Blue didn't like her. It was the exact opposite. Their one night together had him running scared. He wasn't prepared for the depth of emotion he'd felt while she was in his arms. And there in lay the problem. He had betrayed Stella.

Originally, Blue thought making love to other women would help ease the pain in his heart. It hadn't. The relief was as temporary as the act itself. In fact, it might even have made things worse. He'd caught himself more than once imagining the girl in his arms on any particular night was Stella.

But with Cherise it had been different. He thought it'd be just another temporary balm for his wounded heart. But he'd been fully cognizant of just who he was making love to that night. And his thoughts that morning and afterward had not been of Stella, but of Cherise. Taking hold of his reason, he argued that he really couldn't be blamed. Cherise was the typical bomb-shell; sexy and provocative and very willing. He was human after all. Still, it was more than his physical response to her that had him scared.

For some reason it felt like he was betraying Stella. The fact that she could never be his now that she was married to his brother didn't lessen the feeling any. He'd been convinced - had vowed even - that she was the only woman he would ever truly love. He was an unreliable traitor.

It was why he'd high-tailed it out of there before the feeling could take any deeper hold. First of all, Cherise was Stella's friend. Second, Stella had warned him, via Cherise herself, that the latter was not the kind of woman you could build a lasting relationship with. He didn't need his heart completely trampled to pieces.

It was best to cut and run. The only person who knew they'd slept together, as far as he could tell, was his father. They'd had words. His father wasn't too happy about the whole pre-marital sex thing under his roof, not to mention the fact that Blue had chosen to just leave afterward. But Blue knew there was no other way. Forget decorum. It was a matter of self preservation, plain and simple.

In any case, Cherise had probably moved on to the next guy's bed by now. She was the kind of woman who would think nothing of a one night stand. Just like he didn't care either. Or at least, that's what he pretended...

"How's that list coming?" John Marethorpe's voice echoed in the warehouse chamber from cement floor to twenty foot ceiling.

Blue waved at his boss and lofted the clipboard above his head. "Almost through."

"Good. You can put that on my desk when you're finished. I'll do the purchase orders first thing tomorrow. I wanna get out of here early tonight." John Marethorpe was a giant by normal standards. Six foot six at least and barrel chested with tree trunks for biceps. His thinning hair was the only part of his anatomy that wasn't super sized.

"Oh? Something special going on?" Blue bent to peer at some replacement parts for a grass mower on the bottom shelf. He noted the number of items, and jotted them on the list before standing.

"Yup. My niece is leaving town and we're having a family dinner. She worked all summer in Dallas and didn't get home but once. Now she's moving there permanent. Snagged herself a fancy job with some oil company or something, so we're celebrating and saying farewell all at the same time."

Blue joined his boss near the warehouse doors. "Well, have fun."

"Say, you should come along." Big John, as he was called, narrowed his eyes and scrutinized his employee. "Maybe a good lookin' young buck like you is what Beth needs to convince her to stay put."

Blue laughed self consciously. "I don't think you want your niece taking up with the likes of me."

"Why not? You're a hard worker, conscientious..." The big man grinned. "And maybe you need someone like my niece to convince you it's time to stop sowing those wild oats."

Blue laughed again, but couldn't meet the other man's gaze. "I'd hate to spoil your family time."

"Nonsense. You're practically like family." Big John slapped Blue across the back. "I'll call Millie and tell her to set another place. Dinner's at six-thirty. Don't be late."

The other man was already leaving. Blue'd had a few beers with Big John at a local pub since moving to Fort Stockton, but he would hardly call those grounds for being part of the family. Apparently the matter was settled, however, whether Blue had accepted the invitation or not.

BIG JOHN ROARED WITH LAUGHTER, slapping the table so hard he made the silverware jump. This brought on a burst from the others seated around the table, to which he joined in. He'd just finished one of his 'stories' - something about a hunting adventure he'd been on a few years ago. "Never saw that ole bear again." He stifled a chuckle with a sip from his water glass.

"You and your stories." John's wife Millie shook her head, an amused expression on her face. She was middle aged like John, with short dark hair, snapping brown eyes, and she was tall enough to look her giant of a husband in the neck. "If I've heard them once I've heard them a hundred times."

"Just cause you've heard them all before..." Big John grumbled.

"I've never heard that one, Uncle John." His niece Beth smiled over at her uncle and patted his hand. She sat next to him at the table, across from Blue, while Millie sat at the other end. The Marethorpe dining room was open to the kitchen. It was homey, large, and a little outdated. Kind of like Big John himself.

If Blue had known the family meal was going to be this intimate, he might have reconsidered. He'd expected other members of the family, like Beth's parents and maybe a sibling or two. Big John had never explained before tonight that his niece was more like the daughter he and Millie never had. They'd raised Beth as their own when her parents died ten years ago. No wonder Big John wanted Beth to stay put in Fort Stockton.

Beth was petite and pretty in her own way. She had hazel eyes, small features, and honey colored hair that hung past her shoulders. It was fine and straight, and one of her ears kept peeking out through it on the left side of her head, possibly because it stuck out farther than the other. It wasn't visible unless you looked at her straight on, and as long as she had her hair tucked behind that ear, it wasn't really noticeable. Blue knew he was being too critical. He wasn't perfect by a long shot. Nobody was. Well, he could think of a couple of women. Very different and best friends, in fact...

Blue jerked his attention back to Big John. "What was that?"

"I said, why don't you and Beth go out onto the porch for a bit while I help Millie clean up the plates." Big John winked.

Blue averted his eyes, feeling heat rising around his collar. Surely Beth had seen the gesture and knew her uncle was trying to set her up. He glanced her way and to his surprise she was smiling at him.

"Come on. No use arguing." She flashed him a smile as she rose from the table.

Blue followed suit and trailed after Beth as she led him to the front porch. He thought he heard Big John's baritone chuckle as he exited through the front door.

"Sorry about that," Beth offered. "Uncle John is desperate to keep me here in Fort Stockton. He keeps trying to set me up."

Blue expelled a pent up breath along with a simultaneous chuckle of his own. "So I'm not the first."

Beth shook her head. "Afraid not. It's rather embarrassing."

The porch was a classic wrap around; narrow and made of wooden floor boards that sloped a tad too sharply away from the house. There was a pair of old style folding lawn chairs at one end. Beth headed straight for them and sat, gesturing for Blue to do so as well.

"Can I get you a beer or something?" Beth asked.

"Not unless you're having one."

"Sure. I'll be right back." She hauled herself back out of the chair.

Blue watched as she retraced her steps to the front door and disappeared inside. She was small, but well proportioned. She might be an interesting diversion, but then again, Blue wasn't sure he wanted to tangle with Big John if things didn't work out between them. Somehow he didn't think Big John had casual sex in mind when he wanted him to meet his niece.

Beth came outside a few moments later with two open bottles of beer. "Thanks." Blue smiled and took the beer, noting again the ear thing. He looked back down at his hands.

Beth sat down in the lawn chair and crossed her legs. Blue let his gaze linger for a moment at the smooth skin of her thighs. She was wearing shorts, even though it was a bit chilly outside, but she'd donned a bulky knitted sweater. "Uncle John doesn't seem to realize that the best way to scare a guy off is to push too hard. Besides, I'm moving to Dallas one way or another. I've had it with this town."

"Why's that?" Blue pulled on the beer, and then released the bottle with a satisfied sigh.

"No reason. I'm just ready for a change. I've been away at college for the past couple of years and, well, I just don't want to move back. There's nothing here for me anymore."

"Except your aunt and uncle," Blue reminded.

Beth took a swallow of her own beer and nodded. "Yeah. Of course."

"How long you been living with them, again?"

"Since I was eleven," Beth said. "And I'm almost twenty-one. So that's nine... ten years, give or take the time I spent in Dallas."

"I don't blame them for being attached." Blue gazed at her over the top of his bottle while he took another swig.

"I know, but even if I was their biological child, which I'm not, sometimes kids need to find their own way, you know? Fly the coop and experience life, even if it means making mistakes."

Blue couldn't have said it better himself. "I know exactly what you mean. It's why I left home."

"Tell me about that. Uncle John said you worked at a ranch about an hour from here?" She looked him in the eye as she tipped her bottle back for another drink.

Blue nodded. "I grew up there. My dad is the foreman and he and my brother still live there."

"So why'd you leave?"

Blue shrugged. "Same as you, I guess. I needed to get away. Find my own place out from under my brother's shadow." And the proximity of his wife, he wanted to add, but didn't.

"Running away, in other words." Beth grinned over at him and raised her eyebrows in question as she downed the rest of her beer.

"Maybe."

A loud burp escaped Beth's lips. They both laughed. Blue finished his next and set the bottle down on the floor beside him.

"Want another?" Beth gestured with her head to the empty bottle.

"I don't want your uncle to think I'm trying to get you drunk to take advantage of you."

"I'm a big girl." Beth swung her legs to the floor and padded to the front door with the two empties.

Blue frowned, wondering what John and Millie were doing inside the house and why they weren't outside chaperoning their niece. Beth emerged a few minutes later with two more bottles of beer.

"Where'd your aunt and uncle get to?" Blue asked, taking the bottle Beth offered.

"They'll be out in a few minutes." She swept her hair off her shoulders and tucked a few strays behind her crooked ear.

Blue didn't say anything but took a long drink from the bottle.

Beth snorted derisively. "I think it's my uncle's idea of giving us time to get to know one another."

"Which we are," Blue offered. He smiled in a way that he hoped would put her at ease.

"You know, I don't need my uncle to set me up. I can get a date just fine on my own." She sounded defensive.

"I'm sure you can."

"In fact, it kind of ticks me off," Beth continued. "Under normal circumstances, I'd think you were cute. But I can't possibly go out with you now."

Blue's eyebrows shot up. "Why not?"

"And make Uncle John think he's won? Never." Beth grinned mischievously and took a sip of her beer.

Blue allowed a lazy smile to form slowly on his lips. "Then let's not tell him."

BLUE KNOCKED on the office door, even though it was open, and stuck his head into the tiny, windowless room. "You wanted to see me?"

Big John waved him further into the room. "Yup. Take a seat."

Blue took two steps and was already in front of the only unoccupied seat on the opposite side of Big John's desk. He wondered how Big John managed to run such a successful business. His desk, which dominated the small space, was cluttered with teetering piles of paperwork and dirty coffee mugs. The room itself was lined with oppressive wood paneling, mostly covered with advertising paraphernalia from various suppliers, including several calendars randomly pinned directly on its surface. Most of these were of scenery or animals. Millie wouldn't stand for any of the 'pin-up' variety.

"What's up?" Blue settled himself comfortably in the vinyl covered chair as he hooked his right boot up on his left knee.

"Oh, just wanted to talk, that's all." Big John pushed the reading glasses he only wore while in the office up onto the top of his head. He leaned back in his chair and fixed his eyes squarely on Blue. "We haven't had a chance to talk since we had you over the other night."

A sense of foreboding crept up Blue's spine and he could tell his face was heating up. Just what had Beth told him? "Um, right. Thanks for the invite. I enjoyed it." He focused on the calendar beyond Big John's head. It depicted a lake with trees and a mountain reflected in the pristine water.

"So? What did you think of Beth?"

"Um... She's nice."

"And?" Big John leaned forward.

"And what?"

"You seemed to be getting along okay."

Blue nodded, squinting to bring the deer in the foreground of the picture into clearer focus. "Yes. I think so. She's... nice."

Big John chuckled and relaxed back in his chair. "I'm not gonna give you the third degree. I just wanted to know what you thought of her. I think she likes you, by the way."

Blue expelled a breath. A man who suspected something wouldn't seem so open. "Oh? What makes you say that?"

"I know my niece." Big John smiled and clasped his hands behind his neck. "You're a good lookin' young buck and I almost think she seemed sad to leave the next morning."

"You don't say." Blue shifted in his seat and rubbed his hands up and down his pant legs.

"We're heading to Dallas this weekend with the rest of her stuff. I was thinking maybe you'd like to tag along. When's the last time you been to Dallas?" Big John cocked his head to one side as he surveyed Blue.

"Um... it's been awhile," Blue hedged.

"Wouldn't take much to make her change her mind. A little encouragement of the right kind would go a long way."

Blue dared to look straight into Big John's gaze for the first time since the conversation had begun. "You're not suggesting I... seduce your niece to get her to come home, are you?"

Big John's eyes narrowed and he unclasped his hands, rocking forward in the chair. "Seduce is a bit strong. I'd string you up and quarter you myself if I thought you were dealing dirty with her. I just meant if she had a reason to come home, other than two old relatives who aren't even her own parents."

Blue leaned forward and clasped his hands between his knees. "Don't get me wrong. I like your niece. She seems really nice and she's definitely attractive. I just... I just don't think a relationship would work out between us and I wouldn't want to hurt her by leading her on."

Big John held Blue's gaze for a few more seconds before he relaxed. "You're alright, you know that kid? Honest. I like that." He let out a short chuckle before continuing. "Here if I didn't think there was more goin' on the other night than met the eye."

Blue cleared his throat. "What do you mean?"

"Oh, she went out shortly after you left. Said she had some last minute things to do, but it was kind of late when she came home. Thought she mighta been goin' out to meet you. Guess I was wrong." The smile had disappeared from Big John's face and he pinned Blue with his eyes.

Blue felt the color drain from his face. "Nothing happened, Sir. I mean that."

Big John's eyebrows rose. "So you did meet up?"

Blue nodded. "But nothing happened," he repeated. "I swear."

"You're sure about that?" Big John squinted in Blue's direction.

Blue just nodded again.

Big John let out a harrumph. "If you say so. And I know she won't tell me any different if I ask."

Blue swallowed hard and took a deep breath before speaking. "I won't lie to you, John. You've been good to me. Gave me a job and treated me right. I... we... well... me and Beth went to a pub.

Had a few beers. And, well, we could have done more. Your niece is nice, like I said, and we seem to get along. But I... I didn't want to use her like that. I have too much respect for you and for her to do that to either of you."

"Thank you," Big John stated. He surveyed Blue closely. "So she came on to you and you rejected her? Maybe that's why she seemed so sad in the morning."

"I'm sorry, John. I like her, but I'd just end up hurting her, I think." Blue kept his gaze fixed on his clasped hands between his knees.

"If I didn't know better I'd say you were pining for someone else."

Blue shrugged. "Maybe."

"That why you left your home?" When Blue didn't answer, Big John shook his head and went on. "Funny I never noticed it before."

Blue took a deep breath and sat up straight. "Anyway, I couldn't come to Dallas with you this weekend even if I wanted to. My brother called this morning and said my dad's taken a turn for the worse. I figure I better go pay him a visit while I still can."

"Good idea," Big John said. "There's nothing more important than family."

"Um, right." Blue swallowed and slapped his hands on his thighs before standing up. "Well, I better get back to work now."

With a nod, Big John dismissed him and Blue fled the office. Big John was smart and observant and Blue felt like he'd just dodged a bullet. Trouble was he might be heading for more gunfire once he got home. He hadn't talked to his father since their argument. And he hadn't seen Stella since she and Zane had actually tied the knot. He wasn't sure which he was looking forward to least.

CHAPTER 13

$\mathcal{B}$lue thought about his conversation with Big John as he drove the hour to the Crayton ranch after work. He should have known something was up the moment Big John called him into his office. He'd half expected the big man to fire him on the spot. He wasn't sure exactly what, if anything, Beth had told her aunt and uncle, but it sounded like she hadn't said much. Just as well.

The truth was, they didn't have sex, so Blue's insistence that nothing happened was technically true. But they'd come pretty close. A few more beer had loosened their inhibitions, if there were any there in the first place, and they'd gone back to Blue's apartment. It was more of a one room bachelor pad with a minuscule kitchenette in one corner, a table for two, a double bed and a dresser with a TV on it. That was the extent beyond the bathroom. Still, it had served him well enough. The girls he usually brought home didn't seem to mind the close quarters.

Things had been progressing with Beth as per usual, and they were both half undressed before a sudden sense of claustro-phobia overcame Blue as they wrestled on the bed. He'd pushed himself off of her and went straight for the bathroom, splashing his face with cold water as he leaned over the sink, trying to catch his breath.

He'd been transported back to his own bedroom on the ranch. To the last time he'd slept in his own bed. With Cherise. Which brought back all his feelings of guilt - toward Stella for betraying her, toward Cherise for leaving her without a word of good-bye, and toward his father for not visiting more often. Guilt. Shame. Remorse. It was enough to overwhelm him completely. He sure wasn't about to add to his burden by using Big John's niece to ease his own pain. Big John had been good to him so far and he didn't want to spoil that.

Beth had been confused; miffed, but eventually understanding when he explained it in terms of wanting to respect her as a person. She had dreams to move to Dallas and he didn't want to get in her way. She'd bought it. Now if he could just fool himself as easily, things would be perfect.

It was already dark when Blue pulled up beside his father's house and parked his truck. The familiar sound of cattle lowing in the corrals greeted his ears as he jumped from the vehicle. His childhood home was an older two story, complete with veranda and peeling paint. Sheltered behind some trees, it felt like a private oasis despite the fact that it was situated just steps away from the big ranch house. There was a light on in the house, and he took the porch steps two at a time.

It was quiet inside; eerily so. He set his duffel bag on the floor beside the coat rack just inside the door, and then headed straight for his father's bedroom at the back of the house.

The bedroom door was slightly ajar and he poked his head in before slipping inside the room. The bedside lamp cast a dim glow over the outdated floral wallpaper, a remnant of his mother's influence from so many years ago. His father lay in the bed, propped up with some pillows against the rounded metal posts of the headboard. Stella was sitting in a chair nearby. Blue stopped in his tracks. He hadn't expected to see her first thing.

"Look who's here," Stella said, her voice a quiet sing-song. He couldn't read her expression.

Duke's eyes opened and his gaze flickered to Blue. A smile crept along his lips. "Hello, Son."

Blue crossed to the bed and sat gingerly on the rough patchwork quilt that covered his father's form. "Hi, Dad." He avoided Stella's gaze. "How you feeling?"

"Like heck." Duke tried to laugh but it came out like a cough. "I suspect that's why you're here. I told Zane not to bother makin' you come all this way. I'll be feeling better in a day or two. Just caught a bit of a cold is all."

Blue snorted. "Cold my foot."

"I'll leave you two to visit awhile," Stella offered, rising from the bedside chair.

Blue couldn't help but watch her retreating figure; the way her hips swayed gently. She belonged to his brother now. He best not forget that.

"She's a good girl, that one," Duke said, following Blue's gaze.

Blue snapped his eyes away from the now empty doorway and focused on the montage of jean and flannel that made up the heavy bed cover. "Yup."

"Best daughter-in-law I've got." Duke chuckled at his own joke. "She's good for Zane. She can stand up to his stubborn streak and makes sure he doesn't work himself to the bone."

"He needed a little softening up," Blue agreed with a wry smile.

"They're good together. It's the way the good Lord meant it to be, I think." Duke stopped and surveyed Blue closely.

"Right." Blue sighed and rose from the bed.

"You've got to let her go, Son." Duke's voice was quiet; sympathetic.

"I don't know what you're talking about." Blue rubbed the back of his neck.

"Oh, I think you do, but I won't press you." There was silence between them until Duke grasped Blue's hand. "I'm glad you're here."

Blue gazed at his father. His hand was still rough and calloused, hardened by manual labor. He looked paler than he had at the wedding. His face was thinner, his eyes deeper set than normal, and his nose seemed to hook out at a more prominent angle. "Me too." It was barely above a whisper.

"I didn't like the way we parted after the wedding."

"Nothing I didn't deserve." Blue squeezed his dad's hand before releasing it. He sat down again on the bed.

"That's true, but all the same, it's important not to leave things unsaid. I apologize for interfering."

"Don't worry. We'll have plenty of time for more fights in the future." Blue smiled, meaning it as a joke. Inside he wished it were true.

"You're a grown man now and like it or not, I have to let you live your life the way you see fit. Not that I condone what you done on your last night here. I just hope that someday what I tried to teach you about being a gentleman; about having some moral values, sinks in."

"Dad," Blue began. "This is the twenty-first century. So I slept with Stella's friend. It was just a spur of the moment thing - for both of us. No big deal."

"I'm not just talkin' about that time." Duke's forehead scrunched into a row of lines, made more prominent by the distinct tan line from his hat where part of his forehead was a weathered leather color, while the top part near his bushy hairline was white.

"What are you talking about, then?" Blue asked.

"You runnin' away from the ranch, is what. I know why you done it in the first place, which I understand perfectly. But that don't mean livin' a loose life of women and booze is gonna make things better."

"Yeah? And what is gonna make it better?"

"Time. Prayer."

Blue let out a small, barking laugh. "My way is more fun."

"That don't excuse what you did to that poor young thing you left sleepin' in your bed. You shoulda seen her the next morning. Bewildered, embarrassed."

"I doubt that. You obviously don't know Cherise." Blue stopped and looked directly at his father. "You talked to her?"

Duke nodded. "When she was trying to sneak back to the main house."

Blue's eyes rolled to the ceiling. "Great. What did you say?"

"I told her that scurrying off like a scared pole-cat is not the way you was raised."

Blue groaned. "You actually said that?"

"More or less. Maybe not in those exact words..." Duke trailed off. He let out a heavy yawn.

Blue shook his head. "Whatever. It's over and done with and I probably won't see her again."

"That's no excuse. That young girl has feelings like any other, no matter her reputation. Why, I'd say she's been hurt and that's why she does what she does. It's her way of coping." Duke squinted up at Blue. "Kinda like what you're doin'."

"So now you're a psychologist," Blue said sarcastically, folding his arms over his chest.

Duke ignored the gibe. "You can't go foolin' with people's feelings like that. Treat them like they don't matter. It's not how you was raised and it certainly don't make the good Lord happy."

"We're bringing Him into this again?" Blue expelled a weary sigh.

"He's been in it all along, like it or not," Duke said. "Just cause you turned your back on Him doesn't mean He's turned His back on you."

"Let's just drop it, okay? I don't want to fight with you right now."

"I just want you to think about it, is all. Make peace with God."

Duke hesitated, his voice suddenly cracking. "Tell me you'll at least think about it."

Blue nodded mutely, not looking at his father. He didn't really want to make peace with God, but how could he refuse a dying man? "Okay."

"Good." Duke let out another yawn and settled back into the pillows.

Blue turned his attention back to his father. "So, do you need anything? A drink? Another blanket?"

"No, Stella got me all set up just before you got here." Duke closed his eyes.

"I imagine you're tired."

"Always. That's the worst of it. Got no energy no more."

"I suppose I'll leave you to rest then." Blue patted his father's knee through the thick covers then stood up.

Duke opened one eye and surveyed his son. "That don't mean we won't talk more on this tomorrow."

Blue just shook his head and smiled. "See you in the morning."

"Goodnight." Duke's words were soft, like he was half asleep already.

The last thing Blue wanted was to continue this conversation in the morning. He knew his father was right about some things. He was using sex and booze to cope with his broken heart. The heart he'd lost to Stella. But now things had become a whole lot more complicated. All he'd done was have a little fun with Stella's friend and now he was all mixed up inside. He wasn't sure at times who he was pining over, Stella or Cherise. And he wasn't sure his usual methods were going to work anymore.

BLUE SLIPPED into the hallway and almost ran into a shadowy figure leaning up against the wall. Zane.

"How long you been standing there?" Blue whispered, pulling

his father's bedroom door so that it was barely ajar. Just how much of the conversation had his brother heard?

Zane shrugged in his characteristically nonverbal fashion. His older brother had always been a man of few words. When he had something to say, you knew it was important.

"Dad sure doesn't look too good," Blue continued, moving quietly away from their father's semi-closed door.

"He's taken a turn. That's why I called." They'd reached the living room. "We should talk. Outside." Zane's eyes bored into Blue's.

That familiar yet distinct feeling of apprehension filled Blue's chest. Like they were kids all over again and Zane was about to call him out for doing something behind their father's back. "Okay." Blue tried to sound unconcerned.

They stepped out onto the front porch. The coolness of the night air greeted them and Blue inhaled deeply. He did miss the place, despite everything that had happened. He heard a coyote howl and the answering bark of a dog. This was home. They stood and just listened for a few minutes, enjoying the peacefulness of the ranch. Finally, Zane leaned against the railing, clasping his hands in front of him. Blue followed suit.

"I heard what Dad said in there." Zane's voice was low, not only because of its natural timbre, but flat with no hint of emotion. It was typical. His way of keeping his opponent off balance.

"What part?" Blue tried to keep his voice just as steady.

"You and Cherise."

"Oh." A gust of relief swept over Blue's body. That part of the conversation he could handle. "So?"

"So?" Zane repeated. "She's Stella's best friend."

"And what's your point?"

Zane shifted. "Stella was worried about her. Figured she was vulnerable after what happened to her over in Europe."

Blue shrugged. "She seemed fine. Besides, she's a big girl."

"So you two had a roll and then you just up and left without a word?" Zane didn't look in his direction but Blue could hear the censure in his voice.

"You make it sound like I forced her or something." Blue laughed. "Believe me, she was willing."

"Still, that's no way to treat a lady." Zane eyed his brother with a cocked brow before looking out into the night once again.

"I expected as much from Dad, but not you." Blue let out a derisive snort.

"It's not the way you were taught."

"So I've been told."

Zane was silent for a moment and then shook his head. "Stella won't be happy."

Blue frowned. "You gonna tell her?"

"Shouldn't I?" Zane glanced over at his brother with a steely blue gaze.

"I don't see any point in it, but I suppose you two don't keep secrets." It sounded just slightly sarcastic even to Blue's own ears.

Zane didn't respond.

"Look," Blue tried to explain. "We both had too much to drink and it was just one of those things. There's no going back now, no matter what you, Stella, or Dad think. Besides, what's the big deal, anyway? She's probably moved on by now. I know I have."

Zane pursed his lips and nodded. "I think Dad's right. You're trying to bury your troubles. Just don't start on drugs next."

Blue's eyes widened. "Thanks for the vote of confidence. What makes you think I'm burying my troubles, anyway? Can't a guy want a change of scenery without everyone going crazy?"

"Change of scenery is one thing. Running away is another. What are you running from, Blue?"

Blue let out a gust of air, but just shook his head.

"Is it Stella?"

"No." The one syllable came out too quickly.

Zane released his own heavy sigh. "I'm sorry. There's not much more I can say."

"Don't. I'm over Stella." Blue was almost sure he meant it. "Just confused about some other things, that's all."

"I never meant to hurt you. You know that." Zane glanced over at Blue for a mere second before gazing out over the darkness again.

"I know. And for real, it's not Stella that's keeping me away. Not anymore, anyway."

"Then what?" Zane asked.

Blue shook his head. "Not sure, exactly. It's like I need to find myself, or something. For you, this place... the ranch... it was always your destiny. For me, well, I was just here by default."

"You could move back home. Give it another shot."

Blue laughed derisively. "I don't think that's the answer."

"No? All I know is, we're worried about you, Blue. All of us. Dad, me, Stella."

"Yeah, well, you can tell my sister-in-law to quit worrying about me. I'm happy in Fort Stockton and that's final."

"If you say so." Zane shrugged. "Just remember. You're family, and you'll always be welcome here. No matter what." He pushed off the railing.

Zane descended the steps without a backward glance, his boot heels clacking on the boards. Blue watched his brother's lanky frame disappear in the direction of the barn.

Blue's assurances that he was over Stella suddenly felt quite real. It had been a shock to see her again tonight when he first walked into his father's room, but now he felt strong, like he could see her again in the morning and it wouldn't mean a thing beyond their long time friendship. Maybe time was healing his heart after all. Time, and other things.

CHAPTER 14

*B*lue rotated his left shoulder and winced, leaning on the pitch fork with the other arm. Cleaning the horses' stalls felt surprisingly cathartic. There was comfort in the familiar even if it strained certain muscles. Dolly, one of the older horses, snorted her thanks and he reached to pat her on the side of the head. "Good to see you, too," he said.

"You're up early."

Blue swung his head to see Stella's approaching silhouette. "Might as well make myself useful."

"That's a switch. If I remember correctly, mucking out stalls wasn't one of your favorite activities." Stella teased. The morning sunshine was bright behind her, streaming in the open barn door.

Blue smiled back. "True enough. I've missed spending time with the horses, I guess."

Stella stroked Dolly's nose. "Almost like you knew I'd be coming out here for my morning ride about this time." She glanced over at him and raised a brow.

Blue shrugged. "Guilty."

"Oh? So what is it?"

"Can't a guy want to see his sister-in-law?"

"Sister-in-law, yes, but friend, first." Stella looked him straight in the eye. "What's up?"

Blue glanced down at the cement floor. The truth was, he was testing last night's revelation. Was he really over Stella? Or was his own emotional confusion clouding his judgment? "I just wanted to make sure you're okay."

"Why wouldn't I be?"

Blue shrugged. "Since I haven't seen you since the wedding, I wanted to make sure Zane is treating you good. The way you deserve. Make sure you're happy." He looked up. "Are you happy?"

"Yes. Very happy."

"Good. Then I'm happy, too."

"Are you really? You seem tense."

Blue let out a pent up breath. "Seeing Dad so weak kind of surprised me. I should have come sooner."

"It's taking its toll on everyone." Stella took a visible breath. "Look, Blue. I hope you haven't been staying away on account of... well, you know. On account of me."

"What do you mean? This is your home."

"Don't play coy with me, Blue Shepherd. You know what I mean. On account of the feelings you had for me - and the fact that I chose Zane. I thought we'd gotten past that."

"We have gotten past that," Blue said.

"Good." She squinted at him. "You sure?"

"Of course."

"I hope you're telling the truth, because I love your brother with every fiber of my being and it would break his heart to think you ran away because of us being together."

Blue just smiled and made a face. "What am I? A teenager? It's all good. I just needed a change of scene, that's all. Like you said, farm work isn't my thing, but how do I know what else there is if I don't try something?"

"I guess." Stella stroked Dolly's neck. "But working in a farm supply store?"

"My resume is kinda short, so options were limited. But, my boss is good to me, so I can't complain." Blue gestured to Dolly. "You gonna give her some exercise or what? I think she's getting impatient."

"Right."

"Let me help."

Stella led the way to the tack room and Blue followed. Stella found Dolly's bridle while Blue hoisted her saddle off its resting place. Together they outfitted the horse for her morning ride.

"I feel as if I should apologize to you for the way I acted at the wedding." Stella glanced his way as she fitted the bit between Dolly's teeth. "With you and Cherise."

Blue cinched the saddle in place, keeping his eyes averted. "Oh? Why's that?" Exactly what did Stella know? Had Zane shared last night's conversation with her? She was his wife, after all, and keeping secrets didn't seem their style. Or maybe Cherise had told her something. Who knew what kinds of details girl-friends shared with their BFFs?

"Oh, just the way I warned you off of her. It was stupid. I should have trusted you more than that."

Blue stood up straight and looked at Stella over Dolly's back. "No biggy."

"I mean, she has a history. Baggage, you could say, that makes her do things. I just didn't want to see you get sucked in. It would have made things really awkward later if you two had hooked up."

So she didn't know. Blue smiled. "Crisis averted. Now take this horse for a ride, already!"

MORE CHORES, a quad ride in the hills, and time at his father's bedside filled the rest of the weekend. The fact that his father perked up enough on Sunday to sit on the couch in the living room, a blanket tucked around his knees, made Blue feel less guilty about his prior absence. The old guy looked ten times better than he had on Friday night when Blue had arrived.

"Pass me the remote," Duke said, waving a hand in the direction of the coffee table.

Blue picked up the remote control and clicked on the television. "What do you want to watch?"

"There's a preacher I like on Sundays. Just hand it over."

"Oh. Him." Blue tossed the remote control onto Duke's lap and the older man wasted no time flipping through channels until he found the one he wanted.

Blue kept his mouth closed while his father listened in rapt attention to the evangelist on the TV. The guy was practically yelling at them. It was super irritating, but Blue didn't allow himself to criticize out loud. If a dying man needed to soften the blow of his own mortality a bit, so be it.

A knock sounded at the door. Blue stood up but Rod Crayton had already opened the door without waiting for an answer.

"Come on in," Duke called. He switched off the TV.

"I like that preacher," Rod said as he crossed to an overstuffed chair and sank into it. "Doesn't pull any punches. You can leave it on if you like."

"It's almost over," Duke said.

"Thank God," Blue said under his breath.

"Yes, I do," Duke countered. "Every day."

Rod looked at Blue. "Heading out soon?"

Blue nodded. "Gotta work in the morning."

Rod grunted an acknowledgment then turned his attention back to Duke. "There's a couple of things I wanted to discuss with you before tomorrow." The two went on to talk some ranch business at length. It was surreal seeing them together. Two men afflicted with the same disease, yet still chatting about life as if they had all the time in the world. Work on the ranch would continue, with or without them. It was a sobering thought.

"So, you enjoying life in town?" Rod asked, turning back to Blue.

Blue blinked and sat up straighter. "What's that? Oh, yes. I am."

"Staying out of trouble, I hope?"

"Trying." Blue grinned.

"Not too well," Duke put in, his voice gruff, but with a hint of humor.

"Boys will be boys, I guess," Rod said with a shrug.

"I been telling him he needs to start going to church. Hasn't been to church since he left home."

"How do you know that?" Blue asked. "You got a spy on my tail or something?"

"Well, have you?" Duke asked, his brows raised in question.

"No." Blue shook his head, focusing on a hangnail.

"Never too late to think about the afterlife," Rod agreed. "I was telling Stella that not long ago. Don't wait until you're in dire straits to get right with the Almighty. It took a pretty loud wake up call for me to listen."

Blue frowned. "You make it sound like God made you sick on purpose. That doesn't sound very fair to me."

"Life's not fair," Rod mused. "I wouldn't say God made me sick. But He can use bad situations for His good. 'What Satan means for harm, God can use for good.' That's a good quote to remember."

"Amen to that," Duke joined in. "The old devil thought he had us in his grasp. But we fooled him, didn't we?" He smiled.

"I don't get how you can be so... positive about it. Either one of you. This sucks big time." Blue shook his head. "And that's all there is to it."

"Agreed," Rod said. "But on the other hand, I like to look at it this way. Everyone's in the same boat. We're all dying. Your dad and I just happen to know it'll be sooner than later."

Duke nodded. "Well said."

The conversation was more than Blue could handle. He took a deep breath and slapped his knees before standing up. "Well, I hate to break up this party, but I really should be going. I'd like to get back to town before dark." He looked over at his father. "Do you want me to help you back into bed before I go?"

Duke shook his head. "No, Rod will help me when I'm ready, won't you Rod?"

Rod nodded. "Like the blind leading the blind." They both chuckled.

Blue couldn't help a small smile. "You are a pair."

Rod stood up and reached out his hand to grasp Blue's. He gave it a solid pump. "You take care now. Listen to your old dad and make your peace with God. I got the drift that you've been struggling lately. I don't know what about, but the good Lord does."

'Thanks." Blue felt a lump forming in his throat.

"I'll be praying for you," Rod said. "Me and Helen, both."

Blue crossed to his father, bending to give him a hug to hide the emotion that he knew must be emanating from his eyes. "See you next weekend." His voice sounded gruff.

"Coming back so soon?" Duke asked, his eyes twinkling.

"Lord willing." Blue winked.

Blue found his cowboy hat near the door and put it on his head. He didn't wear it much in Fort Stockton, but it felt disrespectful not to wear it here. He touched the brim before exiting the house. Two dying men had almost brought him to tears. It was time to get back to town where he could pretend everything was normal. At least for another week.

UP AT SIX, work by seven-thirty, home by five-thirty. A shower, a prepackaged frozen meal, and then off to the pub to drink himself into a state of forgetfulness. It was Blue's MO since coming back from the ranch. Every night he ended up leaving his truck in the parking lot of the bar and taking a cab home, only to have to pick it up again before work in the morning. Not the most efficient - or cost effective - way to get around. Still, drinking himself silly meant he didn't bother with women. Women complicated life beyond what they were worth.

Blue's cell phone rang and he pulled it out of his back pocket. He normally wouldn't take calls at work, but it was nearing the end of another work day, and with his father so sick, Big John understood the need to stay in touch just in case.

Blue checked the number. Zane. Butterflies started in his stomach and he pressed the talk button. "Hello."

"I've got some bad news." Zane's voice sounded more stoic than normal.

Blue felt the blood drain from his face. He searched for some place to sit, spotted a stack of palettes and plopped down on them. "Dad?"

Zane cleared his throat. "Um, no."

Blue breathed a sigh of relief and looked up at the ceiling.

Zane continued. "It's Stella's dad. He... he didn't wake up this afternoon when he went for a nap."

Blue blinked, trying to take it in. "Rod? But, he looked so good the last time I saw him."

"I know. We're all in shock."

"When's..." Blue swallowed hard. "When's the funeral?"

"We're still trying to figure that out." Zane cleared his throat again, obviously trying to settle his own emotions. "I... we... you should come home. Stella's taking it hard and Dad..." Zane stopped and caught his breath. "And Dad is, too. They were close."

Blue nodded, not cognizant of the fact that Zane couldn't see his response.

"Blue?"

"I'll leave as soon as I can."

Blue hung up, stunned by the news. The older man had seemed so alive last time they'd talked. Like he was fighting the disease and winning. Everyone was sure Duke would go first. But apparently fate - or was it God - had other plans.

CHAPTER 15

*W*hy did it always seem to rain at funerals? Some people said it was God crying, but it was a sadistic joke, as far as Blue could tell. Why not take the most horrible day of a person's life and make it even worse?

The scene was actually quite picturesque. The grass was a brilliant green, despite the time of year, and the trees overhanging the spot where Rod Crayton would be laid to rest brought some shelter. Still, it seemed cruel, like adding insult to injury. It kept the crowd relatively small. There were only about thirty people brave enough to weather the elements at the graveside service, despite the packed church earlier. The rest of them were all waiting for the family to arrive back at the reception hall. As if anyone was hungry.

Blue stood next to his own father, who was next to Zane. Zane was sheltering Stella with one arm tightly around her waist and the other holding an umbrella overhead. The tears were running freely down her face, but she wasn't sobbing. Gabriella, the Crayton housekeeper and cook, had that well in hand. She stood in the family circle with Rod's widow Helen, sucking in huge breaths and letting them out again on a wobbly note. The minister, several ranch hands, and a few other close friends rounded out the group. They were a cluster of umbrellas around the casket, watching the rain bounce and drip off its polished surface as the minister recited familiar words of commencement into the afterlife. In a place where rain was rare, Rod's funeral was apparently the day for a deluge. Maybe God really was crying. Rod was a good man and he would be missed.

Duke Shepherd dabbed at his eyes with a handkerchief. The fact that he had insisted on coming out to the graveside in his weakened condition spoke volumes about the relationship between the two men. Blue squeezed his father's shoulder with his free hand. Soon they would be repeating the process, minus the man standing next to him. It brought a shudder to Blue's chest and he held his breath for a moment, steeling himself against the emotion that wanted to burst forth like the clouds in the sky.

Finally the ordeal was over. Blue wasn't even sure what the minister had said or when he had finished, but he sensed a general shuffling of bodies and turned away from the casket. The grounds' crew would look after placing it in the ground and covering it up. He heard a cry escape from Rod's widow, Helen - a primal wail that registered in the distance of his mind - and he felt his father leave the shelter of the umbrella and go to her. There was a bobbing of color as the umbrellas shifted and began to move in the general direction of the waiting vehicles.

Blue took one last glance at the lonely casket and then turned to join the others. As the crowd parted he saw two figures he hadn't noticed before, huddled under their own brightly printed umbrella, arm in arm. Cherise and Tempest.

Blue stopped and did a double take. When had they arrived? Of course, he had been preoccupied in the last few days with comforting and supporting his father. Zane had been too busy attending to Stella, not to mention helping Helen with the funeral arrangements. Still, he was surprised he hadn't heard anything. He hadn't even noticed them at the church, but then that wasn't really a shock, either. He and his father had entered the church with the family, walking in a morbid procession down the aisle of mourners as if to flaunt their grief. Whoever invented such a tradition was obviously a sadist. Blue had kept his eyes focused firmly ahead, afraid if he made eye contact with anyone he'd burst into tears like a baby.

Stella broke away from Zane's grasp and hugged each of her friends in turn. When they let go of each other, Zane managed to shuffle her toward the waiting hearse, snuggling her against his side in a protective manner. At that moment, Blue made eye contact with Cherise. She blinked and then looked away. She and Tempest turned as one, holding onto the umbrella between them. He watched them trip toward the lineup of vehicles parked along the perimeter of the cemetery.

Blue took a deep, steadying breath, and then took long strides to the limousine reserved for family. He and his father qualified. He didn't make any move to catch the women. They'd have time to greet one another later. Hopefully by that time he'd have something to say.

THE WARMTH of the reception hall and a cup of coffee helped settle Blue's nerves - some. He kept an eye on Cherise while making the rounds of guests, greeting those he knew and introducing himself to those he didn't. He'd always been the people person in the family, but today he was operating on autopilot.

He had not expected to see Cherise again. At least not like this. His emotions were too raw. He wasn't sure if he could handle it, which gave him all the more reason to mingle with the crowd. Keep busy and she might just go away.

"My poor, poor boy!"

Blue stiffened but then allowed himself to melt into Gabriella's sizeable embrace once he realized who had accosted him. As the longtime cook and housekeeper at the big house, she had become mother to the motherless 'orphans' at the ranch - himself, Zane, and Stella included.

"Such a shock for everyone." Gabriella pulled back, held him at arm's length, and then smoothed some of his hair into place.

Blue touched the spot on his head after her arm dropped. "I know. We all thought Dad would go first."

"At least, Mr. Crayton is free of pain now, in the arm's of Jesus." She glanced heavenward.

Blue shrugged. "If it helps to think so…"

Gabriella's eyes widened and she made the sign of the cross over her ample bosom. "I know so! No more of that from you, young man. It's disrespectful."

"Sorry." Blue smiled sheepishly. One didn't get away with such talk around Gabriella - then or now.

"You should eat something," she stated. "Grief takes a lot of energy and needs to be fed."

"Alright." Blue gave her another hug. For Gabriella, food was the remedy for all life's problems.

He obediently made his way to the buffet table even though he wasn't hungry. Grief and apprehension had masked his need for food, but sudden light headedness confirmed Gabriella's advice and he knew his body needed more than caffeine. The last thing he wanted was to collapse at Rod's funeral. He filled a paper plate with a couple of dainty sandwiches and a few pickles and then popped the first sandwich into his mouth whole. When he turned around, the food caught in his throat and he had to swallow with purpose, washing the food down with some coffee. Cherise was standing just feet away with her back to him. Alone.

He found a resting spot for the coffee cup and set the plate down beside it. He really wasn't hungry after all. With an exaggerated intake of air, he filled his lungs, expelled the breath, and then moved to stand behind Cherise. He leaned in just a bit to whisper over her shoulder into her ear. "I'm surprised to see you here."

Cherise whirled around, her eyes wide. "Oh!" She placed a hand over her heart. "You scared me."

"Sorry." He looked at his feet, wishing he'd brought the plate if only to have something to occupy his hands. He had not forgotten how classically beautiful Cherise Hillyer was, but being up close again set him off balance.

"Temp and I knew we had to come as soon as we heard."

He looked up briefly and then down again, rocking back and forth on his heels. "That's awfully good of you."

"Stella is like a sister. Of course we'd come."

Blue nodded, not sure what else to say.

"We got here late last night," Cherise supplied, answering his next question before he could ask it.

"That's why I didn't see you, I guess."

"Right. Well..." Cherise shifted her gaze, glancing around the room. "I suppose I should find Tempest."

"Wait." Blue rubbed the back of his neck. "Do you think we could... talk somewhere?"

Cherise's eyebrows rose slightly, drawing attention to her blue eyes and thick lashes. "A wedding is one thing, but a funeral? I don't think so." Her tone was haughty.

Color rose to Blue's cheeks as he realized what she was implying. "No, no. Nothing like that."

"Good, because if you think we can just take up where we left off, you're mistaken."

"Actually, about that. I need to apologize." Blue sighed heavily. "I'm sorry for just running off like that."

Cherise surveyed him for a moment before answering. "Then why did you?"

Blue shrugged, a frown marring his features. "I'm not entirely sure. Scared, I guess."

"Of what?"

"You."

Cherise raised her brows. "Me? Why?"

"Why?" he repeated. That was the million dollar question. He glanced around the room, looking for a place they could talk privately. "It's complicated."

"Ah," Cherise said, nodding her head. "Because of your feelings for Stella. We're best friends and you're worried she might find out. Well, don't worry. The only person who knows is my brother, and he's off somewhere in Mexico doing good deeds."

"Dirk?" They had met once before. "He didn't strike me as the type, but…"

"Yes. And your dad, of course. Do you think he'll tell?"

She was partly right about him running away because of Stella. At first, he'd believed that was the real reason for his flight. But then his own feelings had started to change, in more ways than he could have predicted. Now he wondered if fear of falling for Cherise Hillyer wasn't the real root all along. Seeing her again, being near her and talking to her, even for just a few minutes, was enough to make him forget every other woman in the world.

"Hello! Earth to Blue!" Cherise snapped her fingers in his face.

Blue shook his head. "What?"

"Are you worried that your Dad told Stella that we slept together? If that's it, I can talk to her myself and smooth things over."

"Sh!" Blue looked around the room. "Not so loud."

Cherise shrugged her pretty shoulders. "I really don't know why it's such a big deal."

Blue steered her closer to the outer perimeter of the room. "No, I don't think my dad will tell and Stella doesn't know, either. But that's not really the issue. It's a bit more complicated than that."

"Okay. Explain." Cherise folded her arms under her chest.

Blue blinked, his attention suddenly drawn to Cherise's

attributes. He yanked his gaze upward, seeking her eyes instead. What *was* the real issue? That he was lost in some kind of self destructive funk that he couldn't seem to shake? That he had real feelings for her but he couldn't admit it since she so obviously didn't feel the same way? He took a deep breath. "I can't explain. Not here."

"So where?" Cherise asked.

Blue's gaze darted around the room again, trying to gauge whether anyone had paid them any attention. It seemed Stella and Zane were well occupied with Gabriella. His own father was engaged in conversation with Tempest, so that had them out of the way for a few minutes, too. He turned back to Cherise. "It's raining too hard to go outside, but there's a basement in this building. The stairs are over there near the kitchen, just down the hall from the washrooms."

"We're going to go down into some musty basement?" Cherise shuddered.

"It's not musty. Just used for storage. You head that way as if you're going to the washroom and I'll follow in a minute or two. Nobody will even notice we're gone."

Cherise cocked an eyebrow. "And this conversation can't take place right here?"

"No." Blue didn't say any more but just stood waiting. With a flip of her blonde tresses, which were curling around her face more than usual due to the moisture, Cherise turned on her heel and headed for the public washroom sign.

Now he just had to muster enough courage to tell her the truth about how she felt.

THE BASEMENT, a monochromatic grey, was dimly lit. Cherise was waiting for Blue at the bottom of the stairs. "So? What's so important we have to sneak into the dungeon to talk about it?"

"This way." Blue placed his hand under Cherise's elbow to guide her to a more secure location. They walked past several shelves lined with boxes until they reached a large steel door. Despite the sign which read 'Mechanical - Keep Out', Blue twisted the knob and pushed her into the small room before hitting the light switch.

"The sign says 'Keep Out'." Cherise looked over her shoulder as Blue entered behind her. A convolution of metal ducts coming from a large boiler filled most of the space.

"It's just a suggestion," Blue said.

Cherise gazed around the room, eyes wide. "But what if it's dangerous?"

"Nothing dangerous in here."

"How can you be sure?"

"Been down here lots of times as a kid. Weddings, church do's, dances... all kinds of functions where kids are bound to get bored. Me and my buddies explored this entire place from top to bottom."

"Hm. I see." She turned in a circle, as if to case the joint, and then swung back in his direction. "So? What was so important that you had to drag me to the basement to talk about it?"

"I... um..." Blue's mind was suddenly muddled. All he could focus on was Cherise. Her dress, while appropriate for a funeral, made her look ultra feminine. He knew exactly what lay beneath the soft silk, and imagining it was more torturous than seeing the real thing.

"You're staring."

Blue shook his head. "Sorry. It's been a really... emotional day."

Cherise took a step toward him and placed a hand on his forearm. "I know. It's been a rough day all around."

Blue stared down at her hand. The heat pulsing from her palm felt like a branding iron. He raised his gaze and looked into the sympathy he saw emanating from Cherise's eyes. "I, um... I was just going to explain something about that night."

"Yes?"

He stopped. What had he been about to say? That he was over Stella? That he was afraid of the strong feelings he had for her, Cherise, instead? Somewhere the words drifted away, lost forever in the pull he felt from her gaze. Sudden emotion overwhelmed him and he felt tears pooling, but he was helpless to stop them.

"Oh, Blue!" Cherise pulled him toward her. "It's okay to cry. You were close to Stella's dad. Just let it out."

He did, allowing her to cradle him against her like a mother with her child. He let them out, tears that he didn't know he'd been harnessing so ferociously. Mourning for Rod Crayton. Grief for his father. Remorse for his own selfishness in the face of these tragedies. He swallowed and pulled away, embarrassed by the spectacle he was making.

"Here, let me get you a tissue." Cherise dug in her purse and produced a small packet.

He used several, pocketing the evidence in his suit jacket. "Thanks. I didn't expect that. Sorry." He sniffed.

"It's okay. Everyone needs to cry sometimes." Cherise smiled. "Even guys."

Blue rolled his eyes. "I'm so embarrassed. Let's get out of here."

"But what about what you came to say?"

Blue reached for her hand to draw her toward the door. "Forget it. It was dumb and I'm over it now."

Cherise planted her feet. "Absolutely not! You had something to say that was obviously important and I want to hear it."

Blue shook his head. "No, really. Just forget it."

"You were going to explain something about that night." She still held his hand and she stepped closer.

Blue allowed himself to look into her gaze. Big mistake. She was so darn beautiful. And at the moment she seemed open. Receptive.

"So?" she prompted again.

"I... may have forgotten."

"Really? I doubt that." She laughed.

Without warning, he leaned in and placed a kiss right on her mouth. He just couldn't help himself. At first she blinked, startled by the sudden movement. "Sorry," he said, drawing back. "That was uncalled for."

She licked her lips. "No need to apologize." Then she smiled, slowly and provocatively. "Did I mention that men who cry turn me on?"

It was Blue's turn to blink. "Is that so?"

"Oops. I always blurt things without thinking." She was closer now, touching his collar and running her other hand along the side of his cheek.

"My dad says honesty *is* the best policy," Blue said.

"Smart man."

Was she a sorceress? The hold she had on him was beyond his control. "Despite my better judgment, I'm thinking how much I'd like to kiss you again," he heard himself say. "For real, this time."

"Despite *my* better judgement, I'd like that."

All the sorrow and uncertainty came rushing out as their lips came together, transformed into pure passion as one emotion morphed into another.

Cherise pulled away first. "Wait." She put some distance between them by laying her palms on Blue's chest. "Wouldn't it be disrespectful to - you know. Go any further at a funeral?"

Blue dropped his arms and took a deep breath. "Right. Of course."

"People might be wondering where we are, so if you have something to say, you should say it." Cherise smoothed her dress over her hips.

"I think maybe you already know."

"Try me."

Blue took a deep breath. "Okay. After that night... well, at first I felt like I'd betrayed Stella. But the whole time since..." Blue stopped and captured Cherise's gaze. "I wasn't thinking about Stella. I was thinking about you." There. He'd admitted it. And it felt good. Liberating.

He was sure he saw her features soften, like she was about to lean in for another kiss. Then she straightened her spine. "Thinking of me how?"

"You know. Just how good we are together." It sounded lame but it was the best he had at the moment. He wasn't even sure himself what he felt; what he expected from a relationship. All he knew was she'd gotten under his skin and he needed more.

"Oh, right. Of course. It was fun."

"Fun?" Blue repeated.

"It was a one time thing and it was fun, but seriously?" Cherise flipped her hair and laughed. "We're both grown ups. No need to get hung up over a one night stand, right?"

It wasn't the response he'd expected. He'd just bared his soul and she seemed as cool as a cucumber, despite their passionate encounter just moments ago. Or maybe he was reading more into it than was actually there.

"If that's it, we should head upstairs. I don't want Stella to worry."

"Good idea." Blue tugged at his suit jacket, determined to maintain a calm aloofness. He'd just released his feelings only to have them sputtering and spurting around the confines of the tiny space like a deflated balloon. He was a fool.

He opened the mechanical room door and held it aloft like a gentleman holding a carriage door for a lady until Cherise passed through. She ascended the stairs first, with Blue one step behind, careful not to focus on her derriere.

She pushed the door open and light from the upper hall flooded the dimly lit stairwell. There, standing at the top were Stella and Zane. They didn't look happy.

CHAPTER 16

"*H*ow could you? At my father's funeral?" Stella stopped pacing for a moment, sending daggers with her eyes directly at Blue.

He shifted in the leather chair, not daring to maintain eye contact. The small group of five had gathered in Rod Crayton's study, hushed and huddled while Stella wore out the carpet. Blue let out a frustrated sigh. "Nothing happened. I already told you that."

"Then what were you doing in the basement, Blue? *The basement*." Stella enunciated the words slowly for emphasis.

"We needed somewhere private to talk. That's it." Blue looked over at Cherise for support. She sat beside Tempest on a cushioned loveseat and was looking down at her hands.

"Talk? I bet!" Stella let out an unflattering laugh. "At my father's funeral." Her glare bore into Blue until she melted before their eyes and burst into tears. She turned away, covering her face with her hands.

Zane was by her side in a second, placing an arm around her slumped shoulders. "It's okay. You're just wound up."

"Wound up? You bet I'm wound up. My father is hardly in the

ground and I catch my friend screwing *your* brother in the basement - at my father's funeral!" She flung the last part over her
shoulder at full volume.

"We didn't 'screw'!" Blue slapped the armrests of the chair.
"How many times do I have to tell you?"

"I trusted you. Both. How could you?" Stella's voice was
muffled through her hands.

Zane rubbed Stella's back, his chin resting on her head. He
gazed over her head at Blue, his eyes not revealing anything as he
spoke. "We'll talk about it tomorrow. You're tired -"

Stella cut him off, pushing him away. She spun around, her
attention now focused on Cherise. "And what have you got to
say? I know you're horny all the time, Cherise, but really?"

Blue jumped up. "Hey, that was uncalled for. I realize your
nerves are shot after such an emotional day, but that doesn't give
you the right -"

"That doesn't give *you* the right!" Stella shouted and pointed at
Blue. "Or you!" she added, pointing at Cherise.

Blue gazed around the room at the sorry state of his friends
and family. Rod's study was large and masculine, like the man
who had occupied it, with lots of leather and a hardwood desk.
The seat behind it was ominously vacant. There was no one there
to bring some sanity to the situation. Zane was shushing a now
sobbing Stella. Tempest was holding Cherise's hand. Cherise
seemed unusually quiet and stoic. Blue let out a deep sigh. "Look,"
he said, trying his best for a reasonable tone. "Yes, we did sleep
together, but -"

"Aha!" from Stella.

"But not today," Blue finished quickly.

"I just knew it!" Stella glared at them both. "When?"

"Who I sleep with is none of your business," Blue said.

"I want to know when," Stella repeated.

Blue hesitated before finally giving in on a sigh. "After your
wedding."

146

Stella's eyes narrowed and she turned her gaze toward Cherise. "I thought I warned you."

Cherise kept her gaze averted. "You did. But I've never been good at celibacy. You know that."

"I wasn't asking for celibacy, Cherise! I asked you for one thing. Specifically. Stay away from Blue. That's it! And you couldn't even do that one thing?" Stella shook her head. "I thought you had more respect for me than that."

"It's not like you have any right to decide, by the way," Blue spoke up. "You married my brother, not me."

"Oh…" It was the first time Tempest had spoken. She looked over at Cherise. "You said it was one of the hired men…"

"Technically…" Cherise began.

"You knew?" Stella interrupted, her ire now turning on Tempest.

"Settle down," Zane said, his voice gentle but commanding. "They're consenting adults."

Stella turned to her husband. "I suppose you knew, too?"

His silence was answer enough.

Stella threw her hands up. "So everyone here knew that Cherise and Blue were having an affair except me? Was I ever going to be let in on this little secret? Hm?" She looked around the room from one person to another.

"It's hardly an affair…" Blue said.

"Maybe people were afraid of your reaction," Tempest offered tentatively. "Not that I knew for sure..." She trailed off, focusing on her clasped hands.

"Thanks, Tempest," Stella bit out. "Of all people, I thought I could trust you."

"Why are you so upset anyway?" Blue asked. "Cherise is one of your best friends. You went around the world, putting yourself in danger to save her. Am I not good enough for her?"

"Maybe it's the other way around," Cherise said quietly.

"Of course that's not it!" Stella clipped.

147

"Then what?" Blue asked.

Stella pursed her lips for a moment. "I just trusted you. And you let me down."

"But why should it matter?" Blue asked. "We'll always be friends. You know that."

Stella shook her head. "I can't explain. I care about you both and I don't want to see either of you get hurt." She put her hand to her temple. "I think I just need to lie down."

Zane encircled her shoulder with his arm. "That's it. Everything will seem different in the morning." He steered her toward the study door and opened it for her.

At the thresh hold, Stella turned around. "And you're right, of course. I can't control your choices, but I did try to warn you."

"She's just acting out of grief," Tempest said once Stella and Zane had gone.

"It's what I love about you, Temp," Cherise said. "Always the optimist."

"It's true. Her dad just died. Sometimes people say things - do things - they don't really mean when they're grieving."

"This started before her dad died," Cherise said. "She's always looked down on me."

"Hey, that's not true." Tempest put her arm around Cherise. "She loves you, the same way I do. It's why she put her life on the line for you."

Cherise sighed. "I know. But will I ever be able to repay you?" She smiled in a resigned sort of way. "I don't think so."

"Enough of this. I think we should take Stella's lead and all get some rest. Okay?" Tempest stood, waiting for Cherise's response.

"How anyone will possibly sleep after all the drama, I have no idea," Cherise said.

Blue had been watching the exchange. Theirs was a complicated relationship, these three friends. He might never understand it, which is probably why he couldn't quite comprehend Stella's current issue with him and Cherise. He offered a smile.

"How about a drink?" He pointed to the the liquor cabinet beside some bookshelves. "I'm sure Rod wouldn't mind."

"I don't think so," Tempest replied. "I'm beat and bed really does seem like the best option right now. You coming, Cherise?" She gestured toward the open door.

Cherise hesitated.

"A walk then?" Blue suggested. "The rain stopped earlier and it might help clear the cobwebs."

He noted the exchange of glances between Tempest and Cherise.

Tempest sighed. "I won't wait up," she said over her shoulder and left.

"Ah. She's smart." Blue smiled.

"I'm not so sure. Every time we take a walk together we end up in compromising situations."

"Is that what you call it?" Blue smirked.

"Well, that's one way to put it," Cherise said. "But seriously, perhaps it's not such a good idea. I was surprised by how strongly Stella reacted when she found out about our... rendezvous."

"Me too."

"Although, she did apologize afterward. Sort of."

"Not much of an apology. Those were some hurtful things she said to you," Blue offered.

Cherise shrugged. "Whatever. If the shoe fits, I guess. It just seems weird that she'd be so dead set against... well, you know."

"Yeah, weird."

Cherise furrowed her brow. "Why do you suppose that is? That she's so against us getting together?"

"I don't know."

"Do you think she still has feelings for you?" Cherise asked. "Maybe she's sorry and thinks she chose the wrong brother."

Blue sucked in a breath and shook his head. "Don't even go there. She is head over heels for my brother, just like he is for her."

"Still, it's a possibility. If it was true, how would that make you feel?"

"I want you to put that thought right out of your head. If it was true, which it isn't, I've moved on. Stella is off limits and frankly, my attention has turned elsewhere."

"Oh." She was quiet for a moment. "But, still, you're probably feeling guilty -"

Blue took the two steps needed and stopped her with a kiss. He pulled her against him, his mouth silencing any further protest as passion ignited. "Make love with me again, Cherise. You're all I've thought about since the last time."

"But, Stella..."

"I don't want Stella. I want you." He took her mouth again, with more urgency.

Cherise pulled her head to the side. "But what if she's mad? She's my best friend! I owe her my life."

"A debt that should never be mentioned again, if she's really your friend. You can't let her dictate you life."

"But..."

"She'll be fine. She's just emotional." Blue kissed her again.

"It's still her father's funeral day..."

Blue pulled back just enough to consult his watch. "Not for much longer."

"No, this is wrong." Cherise disentangled herself.

"Why is it wrong?" Blue took her hands in his. "Give me one good reason."

"Well..."

"Exactly," Blue said before she could think of anything. "We'll go to my house. My dad's meds make him sleep sound as a baby and Tempest isn't expecting you anyway." He grinned and placed a quick peck on her lips. "And for the record, I won't run out on you this time." To seal the promise he lowered his head and kissed her again, gently this time.

"You're making this really hard," Cherise whispered against his lips.

"Just come with me," Blue begged. His voice had gone gruff, full of emotion.

"I told her I wasn't that strong!" Cherise wailed.

Perfect. He was banking on it.

BLUE STRETCHED and then inhaled deeply, letting his senses bask in the aura that was *her*. The second time around was even better than the first, if that were possible. He was sure he'd never experienced anything like making love to Cherise Hillyer.

He rolled over and opened his eyes, ready to greet her with a gentle kiss. Her side of the bed was empty.

Blue sat up, looking for evidence of her presence. Nothing. He flipped off the blankets and pulled on some jeans and a T-shirt. When he padded out to the living room, he found his Dad watching TV in his usual spot on the sofa.

"Morning," Duke said. "Lawyer's coming over around ten for the reading of Rod's will. Apparently, he wants us there."

"Really? Okay. Say, you haven't seen…"

"That gal who slept over again last night?" Duke shook his head. "Young people. Probably back at the big house."

"Thanks."

As quickly as he could, Blue got cleaned up for the day and headed to the main ranch house. He entered through the kitchen at the back without knocking, an arrangement both Shepherd boys had kept with Gabriella since childhood. The large Mexican matron was preparing breakfast, while Tempest sat at the kitchen island nursing a ceramic mug of coffee. Relief flooded through Blue's body. Cherise and Tempest had come together, so she was probably in the shower or something.

"Morning," Blue said. "Coffee smells good."

"You know where the cups are," Gabriella responded. Her ample frame blocked the view of the stove where she worked. "Just another minute and the toast will be ready to go with these eggs."

"I can butter it," Tempest offered, sliding off the high stool.

"Absolutely not." Gabriella pointed her spatula in Tempest's direction. "You're a guest in this house and guests don't butter their own toast." The toast popped and she turned to Blue. "Get that for me, will you?"

Blue just smiled and did as he was told.

Helen, Rod's widow, clacked into the kitchen, her low pumps resounding on the tiled floor. She was fully dressed already in dark pants and a fitted white blouse. She gave a quick nod in the direction of her house guests and then turned her attention to Gabriella. "Have you seen Stella or Zane yet today?"

"Zane's already had his breakfast and gone outside," Gabriella answered. "Probably making sure the chores are getting done properly."

"I hope he won't be too long." Helen wrung her hands, her lips in a tight downward bow. Her eyes were puffy and red. "The lawyer is coming out this morning for the reading of the will and he needs to be there. All of them do. Zane, Duke and you, too, Blue."

"So my dad said," Blue offered. "Although, I can't imagine why."

Helen's gaze flickered to Gabriella. "You as well, Gabriella."

"Me?" Gabriella frowned. "Now what's that husband of yours gone and done?" She shook her head, her tightly pinned black hair never moving. "Duke and the boys I understand, but me?"

Blue felt an uneasy stirring in his gut, but finished buttering the toast and joined Tempest at the island with his coffee. Whatever it was, they'd all be finding out soon enough. Gabriella set two plates down with a clatter as they connected with the island's polished granite top. "This one for me?" Blue asked.

"No, it's for Stella, but I'll fix you some, too, if you like," Gabriella said.

"I'm fine." Blue wasn't sure he could eat even if he tried.

Stella walked into the room, dressed for the day in jeans and a button up shirt. "Morning."

"You're wearing that to the reading of the will?" Helen's brows rose.

Stella looked down at her attire and back up at Helen. "Oh. I didn't think it mattered since it was just us."

Helen pursed her lips. It looked like she might cry.

"I'll go change," Stella offered.

"Never mind. Mr. Morrison will be here at ten, so make sure everyone is ready. I'm going into the study if you need me. I want to make sure everything is in order."

Gabriella clucked her tongue once Helen was out of earshot. "Poor thing. What's she gonna do now without your dad around, hm?"

"Hopefully lighten up." Stella said. "We've been getting along pretty well recently. I hope she's not going back to her military ways."

Gabriella frowned, making no attempt at hiding her disapproval. "You're not the only one hurting around here, Miss Stella." She used her spatula as a pointer again. "The poor woman just lost her husband. I think she deserves a bit of grace. Now eat your breakfast."

Stella blinked, her face turning a shade of red as tears rushed to her eyes. "I know. Sorry." She swallowed and made a production of mashing her fried eggs and then piling them on her toast.

Blue cleared his throat. "Um, so has anyone seen Cherise this morning?"

"Cherise?" Tempest asked. "Uh…"

Just then Zane strode into the room. His long strides took him directly to Stella. He placed a resounding kiss on her cheek, and then took a sip of her coffee with a grin.

"Hey, get your own cup," Stella protested, but she was smiling.

"He knows where the mugs are," Gabriella threw over her shoulder as she washed up the frying pan at the kitchen sink.

While this was playing out, Tempest leaned toward Blue and whispered, "I thought Cherise was with you."

"She was, but…"

"Well, she wasn't in our room this morning, so I just assumed -"

"What are you two whispering about?" Stella asked.

Tempest cleared her throat. "We were just wondering if anyone has seen Cherise this morning."

"She's not in your room?" Stella asked.

Tempest shook her head.

"That's strange." Zane looked directly at Blue and raised his brows questioningly.

Blue held up his hands in surrender. "Okay, before anyone says anything else, I'll come clean. Just don't freak out."

"You hooked up again," Stella stated. She shook her head but kept her mouth in a tightly drawn line.

"Yes, we did spend the night together last night, but after our… talk last night we thought you'd understand. You said yourself we're free to make our own choices."

"But you knew I would still be upset," Stella said.

"Let's not start this now," Zane interrupted. He squeezed Stella's shoulder.

"Wait! I never checked my phone yet this morning," Tempest said. She tapped her cellphone and read briefly. "She left me a message saying she took our rental and left early. She says she hopes someone can give me a ride to the airport…" She looked up. "Can someone give me a ride to the airport?"

"She just left?" Stella asked. She looked directly at Blue. "What did you do?"

"That's a bit personal…"

Stella shook her head. "This is exactly why I warned you both."

"I'm sure there's a good explanation," Zane offered.

Blue agreed with his brother. Cherise was giving him a taste of his own medicine. He'd been played.

Trio

CHAPTER 17

*D*irk checked his watch one more time. Two minutes to chapel and Anne-Marie still hadn't shown up. It wasn't like her to be late for the evening service, but maybe she was on call at the clinic and there was an emergency.

A twinge of jealousy washed over him. If Anne-Marie was still at work, the good doctor was probably with her. Dirk tamped the feeling down, giving his head a shake. She worked with Dr. Smythe - a fact of life that he just had to get used to.

Actually, he'd done a good job of horning in on the doctor's territory now that he was a regular staffer. Dirk made sure to come up with a question of a spiritual nature by the end of each service, which often led to long walks. Of course, he was more interested in the one on one time than in the answer to his questions, but he was learning a lot, too. Dirk fully admitted to himself that he was attracted to Anne-Marie in a man to woman kind of way, but so far she had been very careful about her responses to his attempts at flirting. She just laughed them off as jokes. What was it with the good ones and their insistence on being 'just friends'?

Anne-Marie came into his line of vision, walking briskly along the cement path leading to the building. Dirk pushed off the stuccoed wall with his shoulder and got in step with her as they entered the sanctuary.

"You shouldn't have waited," Anne-Marie whispered.

"I wasn't waiting long," Dirk said. "Something come up at the clinic?"

"Something like that," she barely mouthed.

The service had begun and someone was praying up at the front. They found two empty seats near the back and slipped into the row of chairs. Dirk smiled inwardly since there was no third seat available, thus cutting the doctor out of their circle should he also arrive late.

Next, the singing began. Dirk clapped along, not really trying too hard to follow the Spanish words projected on the screen, and let his mind wander. The place was packed as usual - community members, children, staffers… it was a mixing pot of people of all ages and economic background, coming together with one purpose - to praise God and learn about the Bible. If someone had told him a few months ago that he'd be here, he would have laughed in their face.

His entire perspective on life had changed. Sure, sometimes he wished he could soak in a Jacuzzi tub, drive fast in one of his cars, or just sit and do nothing. But for the most part, the shift in outlook felt good. Cleansing. Life had meaning beyond himself - a rare sensation for a socialite playboy.

James, the administrator, had been reluctant when Dirk first asked if he could stay on, making it very plain that there would be no wages involved. The budget had already been set for the year, so he would have to raise his support like the rest of the missionaries on staff. Dirk smiled. Him - a missionary? If they only knew!

Naturally, raising the money wasn't a problem. Anne-Marie had commented about how quickly he'd come up with sponsors, but Dirk had just shrugged it off. He'd been put on construction duty and was proud of the calluses developing on his hands and even the dirt that got under his nails. This was true, honest work.

His misconception that everyone else who worked there was perfect had been shattered, too - another truth that surprised him. The rest of the regular 'staffers' were actually real people with flaws. Tempers flared on occasion, there were insider cliques, and even some thinly veiled gossip about the administration - things that the short term volunteer never saw or heard. It was hard to keep up the facade of Christian patience at all times, and it was good to know he wasn't alone.

Another thing that surprised him was his love for the kids. He was getting to know many of them as individuals, and they were as varied in temperament and personality as the rest of the population. He'd taken up playing basketball with the older boys when he had time. If he could just scoop each and every kid out of this poverty stricken environment and take them back home to Boston, he'd be a happy man.

But that was unrealistic. These kids needed more than money to help them get on their feet. What they got here was unconditional love and a sense of self worth - something that seemed to come through their reliance on their Creator. In many ways, Dirk felt like he was getting as much from them as he was giving. Maybe more.

Dirk blinked back to reality. The evening service was ending with the usual prayer and he hadn't a clue what the sermon had been about. How was he going to ask Anne-Marie a theological question based on what they'd heard when he hadn't actually listened?

"Um... how'd you like the sermon?" Dirk asked as they made their way with the rest of the throng to the exit.

Anne-Marie smiled. "I often feel like he's talking directly to me. Don't you?"

"Yes, yes. So true." It was dark as they emerged into the night, and Dirk took advantage of the dim lighting to glance over at Anne-Marie's profile. "What was it that caught your attention this time?"

He listened, more to the cadence of her voice than the actual words as she explained how the love of Christ overwhelmed her at times. She was so beautiful and it took his breath away. Her hair was free, as it so often was after hours, and occasionally a strand would find its way across her face and she would have to flick it out of her way. She was wearing another loose fitting dress, this one with a blue, orange and white geometric pattern. It fluttered against her legs when she walked and he caught the outline of her shapely limbs.

"I guess the fact that He brought me here for such a time as this makes me feel small - insignificant - but in awe at the same time. To think that the Creator of the universe would orchestrate every detail like that. I'm just so grateful that I can help out in some small way, knowing that it's all part of a grand design and I'm just playing my part."

Dirk nodded. "I know what you mean. It's mind blowing." He stopped walking and looked up at the night sky. "What else do you dream about? Beyond your work here?"

"I don't think about it much. There is just so much to do. 'Take no thought for tomorrow for every day will take care of itself. Sufficient unto the day is the evil thereof.'"

Dirk grinned. "You always put me in my place by quoting the Bible. I don't know how you do it."

"I think that was a bit of a mash up, to be honest."

"A Bible mash-up. I like it."

They both laughed and took up strolling again.

"Seriously, though," Dirk persisted. "If you could see yourself in say, ten years from now, what would it look like?"

"Hm. By that time I might like to settle down. Have a few kids of my own."

Dirk nodded. "The family aspiration. I should have pegged you for that one."

"Why? What's wrong with family?" She smiled across at him, swinging her arms at her sides as they walked.

"Nothing. As long as you come from a good one."

"Good people have troubles, too. Just because a person comes from a loving family, doesn't mean they don't have problems."

"But your chances are better, I think. Of being normal, I mean."

"Define normal," Anne-Marie said.

"Loving parents that care about their kids. Spend time with them, not just ship them off to wherever. You know, parents who watch them play little league and all that." Dirk laughed. "Okay, maybe it doesn't exist after all."

"I get the feeling you're talking from personal experience."

"I guess. My parents were always too busy doing their own things to spend much time with my sister or me."

"That's too bad."

"Don't get me wrong. Many of their 'things' were - are - good things, but... it might have been nice to just spend some time together."

"It's never too late," Anne-Marie suggested lightly.

Dirk snorted. "You don't know my family."

"And your sister? What's she like?"

"Spoiled."

"You mentioned that you saved her from a drug ring. Is she... involved in things like that?"

"You're asking if she's a crack head or a prostitute." Dirk raised an eyebrow in Anne-Marie's direction.

"Sorry. I wasn't trying to pry."

"The answer is no. Unfortunately, she has a knack for picking the worst guys to date." He shook his head. "You've heard the term 'dumb blonde'? Well, Cherise isn't exactly dumb, except when it comes to men. Then she's hopeless."

"She must be pretty." Anne-Marie's voice sounded wistful.

"She's my sister, but, yeah. She is. They say the good looks run in the family." He meant it as a joke, but when he looked over at Anne-Marie she wasn't smiling. "Um, that was a joke."

"Why? You're a very good looking man. I imagine you get all kinds of attention from women."

"Well... that's a bit of an exaggeration." The old Dirk had cultivated that sort of attention. Lately he hadn't tried that hard.

Anne-Marie laughed. "Of course it isn't. I've seen the way some of the other women look at you when your back is turned. Even some of the girls. You'll have to be careful. You wouldn't want any scandal."

Dirk's eyebrows rose clear to his hairline. "You're joking, right? I mean, I would never, never do anything to compromise one of the girls in care. Never."

"Relax. You'd think you were guilty the way you're carrying on."

"I swear -"

Anne-Marie gave him a playful shove. "I was just kidding, okay? Nobody has said anything. I just notice these kinds of things. The way people react and such."

"Oh." He knew he was good looking. He'd always known it and used it to his advantage. But lately, he hadn't bothered looking in the mirror except to quickly shave each morning. He hadn't had a haircut in weeks and his usually styled tresses were now more in line with a shaggy surfer's do.

"Sometimes I think people wonder how you and I got to be such good friends. They're probably thinking you could have done better. Not that we're dating or anything, but -"

Dirk stopped in his tracks. "Wait a second. What do you mean by that?"

Anne-Marie frowned and shrugged. "Nothing. Just that people probably think a handsome guy like you shouldn't be hanging out with a girl like me."

"You're a very attractive woman, Anne-Marie. You must know that."

Anne-Marie let out an unladylike snort. "Attractive? That's a nice way to put it, I suppose. Most guys want the skinny little model. They don't take the time to get to know girls like me."

"What do you mean, 'girls like you'?"

She shrugged. "Big boned."

"Big boned!" Dirk's eyes widened.

"You know. Large." She made little quotation mark signs with her hands.

Dirk shook his head in disbelief. "Your bones seem pretty well proportioned to me."

"Typical male response. The only thing I've got going for me is my big chest. But then there's the rest of me that goes with it." She gestured to her lower body with a sweep of her arms. "I've always struggled with my weight."

Dirk slapped his forehead with his palm. "I can't believe my ears. You do not have a weight problem."

"Stop it. You're just being nice because we're friends. I know who I am, Dirk. I'm the fat girl and I'll always be the fat girl. But I'm okay with that. I've come to like myself just the way I am." It sounded like she was giving herself a pep talk.

"Listen to me." He gripped her forearms and gave her a little shake. "You are not fat - by any means. You look perfect, and that's no lie."

"Stop." She tried to pull out of his grasp. "You're just saying that."

Instead of allowing her to go, Dirk pulled her toward him. He stared for one moment into her eyes. "If that's so, why do I have the urge to kiss you right now?" Anne-Marie's eyes opened wider, but before she could say anything Dirk bent his head and captured her lips with his own.

Anne-Marie was obviously taken by surprise, but about one second in, Dirk could have sworn she was kissing him back.

Then suddenly she jerked out of his grasp and backed away. "That wasn't funny," she whispered, her voice shaking with emotion.

Dirk shook his head to try and clear the fog. "I'm sorry." He stopped and scrutinized her face, which was pinched as if she was trying to hold back tears. "And it wasn't supposed to be funny."

"Whatever. Just don't ever do it again." Anne-Marie angled her body away from him and hugged herself tightly around the middle.

"I, um... I'm not sure I can promise that."

Anne-Marie's nostrils flared. "Stop it. Just stop."

"Hm." He rubbed the back of his neck. "I guess I hoped you wouldn't find it as unpleasant as all that..."

"That's not what I mean and you know it."

Dirk frowned. "I'm not following."

"You're teasing me. Playing the sympathy card. Or worse, making fun of me."

Dirk shook his head. "I have no idea what you're saying. But if I'm reading it right, it makes no sense." He took a step toward her and planted himself right in front where she would have to look at him. When she didn't back up immediately, he reached out and ran a finger over her forearm. She tensed and he dropped his hand to his side. "You really have no clue, do you?"

"No clue about what?" She raised her chin in defiance.

"How gorgeous you are."

"There! You're doing it again."

Dirk shook his head. "No, I'm not. I'm just telling the simple truth from the way I see it."

Anne-Marie spun on her heel and started walking briskly in the opposite direction.

"Wait." Dirk rushed to catch up and grabbed her arm to stop her.

She resisted slightly, but stopped, shaking his hand off her arm in the process. "I thought you were better than this." She let out a huge sigh and rolled her eyes heavenward. "This is ridiculous. I feel like a teenager again."

"Hey." His voice was gentle as he reached for her and slowly spun her to face him. "I'm not teasing or making fun of you. And I'm certainly not playing the sympathy card." He searched her eyes before she dropped her gaze. "I genuinely find you very attractive. I thought you'd have caught on to that by now. And I'm sorry about kissing you like that without warning. I won't do it again… unless you want me to."

Anne-Marie's eyelashes fluttered upward and then down again. She shook her head. "I'm not sure I'm comfortable with this kind of change in our relationship. I thought we were friends."

"We are. And I won't kiss you again if it makes you uncomfortable. Unless you want me to, that is…" He smiled slowly, trying to encourage her to trust him.

A tentative smile crept along Anne-Marie's lips as well. "That's the second time you've said that."

"So it is." He bent his head, his lips hovering near her mouth. He kept his gaze fixed on hers. "So? May I?" Her answer was an imperceptible nod as her lips rose to meet his.

"Oh, sorry, man."

Dirk and Anne-Marie jumped apart at the sound of the male voice. Bandanna Dillan and his ridiculous beard. He'd emerged from the grove just feet away. He gave a small salute and scurried away.

"Him again," Dirk said on a sigh.

"Working late?" Anne-Marie suggested. She was looking down at the ground, seemingly too shy to look Dirk in the eye now that they had actually kissed.

Dirk's eyebrows furrowed even deeper. "I haven't seen him

around lately. Strange." He purposely relaxed his features and turned back to Anne-Marie. "One thing for sure. He has terrible timing." He reached for her hand and drew her gently toward him, preparing to take up where they left off. Another rustling sound stopped them again. This time it was James Gallagher, the administrator.

Rather than appear startled, James looked at ease, striding with purpose from the grove as if he did it every evening. Maybe he did and they just hadn't noticed him before. A slight frown of disapproval flashed across his face when he noticed their clasped hands. "Evening," he offered and kept going.

"Oh dear." Anne-Marie let out a little wail and snatched her hand away. "That was awkward."

"Are there rules about workers having relationships?" Dirk asked.

"I'm not sure," Anne-Marie replied. "This is a Christian mission."

"Got it. No hanky-panky." Dirk grinned. "But a little kiss is pretty harmless."

Anne-Marie didn't smile, but just looked away, stress furrowing her brow. "We should go."

"Hang on." Dirk grabbed her arm and stopped her before she could barrel ahead into the brighter lights of the courtyard. "I hate to start something and not finish it." He surveyed her nervous expression; her fluttering eyelashes and pert little mouth that was pinched into a rosebud, just begging him to kiss it. "Please?"

He took her silence as a yes. Without further hesitation, Dirk placed his lips on hers and allowed the sweetness of them to envelop his senses. She kissed him back, just as he'd hoped, but he lingered only a moment before pulling away. He didn't want to overwhelm her too soon. "Come on. We better get back before James thinks we're doing something scandalous."

With a nervous giggle she trotted hand in hand with him back to their dorms. For a woman who had traveled the world she was awfully wary when it came to matters of the heart. Someone's insensitivity had hurt her deeply and it was his new mission to heal those wounds.

CHAPTER 18

*C*herise lifted the lacy curtain and stared out at the grey mist. From this vantage point, sitting on the window seat in her little girl bedroom, the scenery was that of an old black and white horror flick. Blurry, dull, and monochrome. The kind of cold, inhospitable weather that was the precursor to winter. Inside, she felt just as chilled.

Cherise sighed and let the curtain drop. Running away seemed like the best idea at the time. She knew that to her friends she must appear unfeeling and selfish. Maybe she was. That's what everyone thought, so why not play the part?

Her phone buzzed and she glanced at the screen. Tempest. Again. She'd received at least ten messages that first day, wanting to make sure she was okay. At first she hadn't even answered, but guilt - and Tempest's persistence - had gotten the better of her and she'd answered with something short and upbeat, promising to call when she had time. Looks like Tempest had run out of patience.

"Hey, I was just going to call you," Cherise lied, putting on the most cheerful tone she could muster.

"Oh? I'm not interrupting anything, am I?" Tempest asked.

"No. Just contemplating the weather." At least that was true. "It's raining again."

"I see. So what's going on?"

"What do you mean?"

"You know exactly what I mean, Cherise. Why did you take off so suddenly after the funeral? Everyone was worried."

"No beating around the bush, I see."

"Well… It was rather sudden. I figured there must be a reason and I just wanted to make sure you were okay."

"I told you I'm fine. I just needed to get out of there. I don't do well at funerals. Too morbid."

"That sounds rather selfish under the circumstances."

"Thanks." There was a sarcastic edge to Cherise's voice.

"Which is not like the Cherise I know," Tempest added.

"Maybe I've been fooling you all these years," Cherise said quietly. Self loathing, conceived in Italy and incubated these past months, had become an unshakable companion. "What if I'm actually just selfish? If the shoe fits, as they say…"

"Stop it, Cherise. Deep down you're a kind and compassionate person and I know something happened that made you run."

"Very deep, apparently."

"Stop feeling sorry for yourself and talk to me."

"Did Stella put you up to this?"

"Of course not. Stella is still grieving. I've just been worried - about both of you. Now that I'm back home I thought we could talk about it. Freely."

"Without Stella asking questions, you mean."

"She has a lot on her plate right now."

"True, but there's nothing to explain. I told you already."

Tempest sighed on the other end. "Look. I wanted to hear you admit it, but I might as well tell you that everyone knows you and Blue slept together again."

Cherise stopped and took this information in. "Who told you?"

"Blue. Is that why you took off when you did?"

"I told you, I didn't just take off, I -"

"Stop!"

Cherise blinked. Tempest had never been the forceful one, but obviously she was changing. They all were. They weren't the little girls they had been in boarding school all those years ago. Life and circumstances had forced them to mature, but she wasn't sure it was for the better, at least in her own case.

"Please tell me you're okay," Tempest said, her tone back to its normal soft cadence. "I know there is more to this than you're letting on. Otherwise, you would have waited and left for home with me the next day, as planned."

Suddenly, unbidden, a tear rolled down Cherise's cheek. "Oh Temp! I'm dying inside! What if I made a mistake?"

"It's okay. I'm here," Tempest soothed.

"I know you are, but I don't deserve you."

"That's silly and you know it. You, me, Stella... friends forever, remember?"

Cherise nodded, even though she was aware Tempest couldn't see the response. "Yes. That's what I keep telling myself. You've both done so much for me already - risked life and limb. All over a silly infatuation I had only a few months ago. It's why I had to leave - why I couldn't face any of you again. I'm just such a flake!"

"It's going to be alright. Just let it all out."

"Well... Oh never mind! It's nothing."

"You can't do that. Just start and then not finish."

"It's crazy," Cherise said.

"I'm used to your 'crazy'."

"Okay." She took a deep breath. "But you can't tell Stella."

There was a moment of silence on the other end. "Um... okay, I guess. May I ask why not?"

"It would hurt her and she might not understand."

"Cherise, I'm not sure I can keep it from her if she asks."

"Fine. I just don't want to hear her say 'I told you so.'"

"She wouldn't do that."

Cherise let out a derogatory snort. "You sure about that? You saw her the other night. Heard what she said…"

"She was grieving. You know that. People don't always say what they mean when they're in pain."

"In any case, can you at least keep it secret for a little while? She already feels like I've betrayed her, and maybe I did. Just don't say anything until, well, until it blows over."

"Until it blows over…?" Tempest repeated.

"Yes." Cherise took a deep breath. "I think I'm in love. For real this time."

There was silence on the other end of the line.

"See? I knew you wouldn't take me seriously. And you're right to be skeptical. I know my track record isn't the best."

"No, no. I'm listening. With Blue, I take it?"

"Yes. It's why I had to leave. I'm just no good for him. He deserves better."

"Well, I don't know about that -"

Cherise cut Tempest off. "Of course it is! We both know it! What happens when I suddenly lose interest? It would break his heart and I can't risk that. That, and the fact that it would hurt Stella. She's my friend and I care about her feelings, too."

"I thought you said it was different this time," Tempest said. "How do you know you'll lose interest?"

Cherise shrugged. "It's just the way I am, I guess. It's why I had to leave before he got hurt."

"Hm. Just think about that for a second," Tempest said. "Blue is the first guy you've been willing to sacrifice for."

Cherise furrowed her brow. "What do you mean?"

"It's the first time you've broken it off because you didn't want to hurt the other person. You care more about his feelings than your own."

A pinprick of hope shone at the end of the tunnel. "Wow. You know, I think you're right?" A smile spread across Cherise's face at the revelation. "With every other guy it's been all about me. How he makes me feel, how much I want to be with him…"

"So maybe this is the real thing after all," Tempest said. "Now the question is, what are you going to do about it?"

CHERISE SCANNED the message one more time to make sure it said exactly what she wanted it to. Sending a text was a bit of a cop out, but at least she was taking action. It was the least she could do. Try to explain herself and make Blue see why she had to break it off before they got any more involved. Try to do some kind of penance so that maybe, just maybe, God, fate, the universe - whoever was in charge - could overlook her idiosyncrasies.

I FEEL good about the fact that I helped you get over Stella - if that's true. It wasn't a healthy situation, so I'm glad I could help. But Stella was right when she warned you about me. Everything she said is true. I'm fickle. When it comes to love there is no other way to put it. I might think I feel something right now - and for the record, I do feel something for you - but that could change overnight. It's happened before. I think that's why Stella was so against it. She doesn't want to see you get hurt and with me, you will get hurt. I've lost track of how many times I've been in love, pathetic as that sounds, and I'm not even counting the times I've had casual sex. I'm not even sure I know the difference between love and lust. Maybe there isn't one. I haven't figured that out yet. When we made love the first time I wasn't too worried. I thought your heart was already taken. But now? I can't guarantee I'd be faithful and that's not fair to you. I didn't want to hurt you, but chances are pretty good that I have already. That's why I left. It's what's best. I know you will find someone someday that will love you the way you deserve and I wish you all the happiness in the world. Sincerely, Cherise.

CHERISE TOOK a deep breath and hit send.

CHAPTER 19

*B*lue leaned against the wall where the headboard should be. He didn't own a couch and the bed was the only place to sit if you wanted to watch TV. Not that he was watching. It was on, providing some background noise, but he really couldn't say what show it was. He drained the last of his beer, crushed the aluminum can with one hand, and tossed it across the room, missing the garbage by a few inches. The crumpled can lay with its compatriots, a testament to the day's inactivity. Blue let out a loud burp, and considered whether he had the will to roll off the bed and get another beer from the fridge. His next trip he'd just bring the whole case, even if they did get warm.

He felt things too deeply. It was a weakness he could fully admit - after a few drinks. He'd shed the last bit of romantic longing he'd felt for Stella, but in its place was a love so melancholy, so overpowering, he wasn't sure he'd ever recover. Cherise had crumpled him up like a piece of paper and thrown him in the stove, letting him burn up to nothing. That's what his life felt like at the moment. A pile of ash ready to blow away in the wind. To think he'd let himself be played so skillfully. It was pathetic, really, and he needed to buck up and get on with life.

Or...

Maybe he should just curl up in the fetal position and let the world go by. He wouldn't bathe or shave and in a few weeks someone would complain about the smell and the paramedics would find him in his little bachelor pad, emaciated.

The thought made him smile and he let out a half chuckle, half snort.

Blue shook his head. Of course he wouldn't do that. He would carry on like the good cowboy his father had raised; smiling at the world while inside he was dying a slow death. He needed to be strong for awhile yet, if not for himself, then for his father and the rest of the family. He'd made a promise to visit the ranch every weekend, and he intended to keep that promise, even if it killed him. It might give him some focus and it was important to all of them, especially since Rod's will had been read.

Rod Crayton had divided the ranch three ways between his wife Helen, daughter Stella, and friend Duke. Of course, that meant that when his own father died, his part would be divided between his sons, Zane and Blue. Blue wasn't sure what fraction that would be, but his intention was to give his share to Zane, anyway. That way, Zane and Stella would have controlling interests. Not that Helen didn't deserve her share, but in his opinion, she should move on. Buy herself a condo in the city and let Zane and Stella have full run of the place. Rod had also provided for Gabriella's retirement with a sizeable pension that would provide for her and her family until she died. Rod was a good man, putting others first even to the end.

In any case, Blue had no desire to ever move back there himself. That chapter of his life was firmly over, and once his father was gone, he doubted he'd even visit much except maybe at Christmas.

Blue sat up a bit straighter and flipped through several channels, but finally threw the remote across the room with the beer cans. It landed with precision right in the garbage. He let out an oath. He'd have to remember to fish it out before garbage day.

His cell phone lay beside him and he grabbed it, scrolling through his messages with the kind of purposeful concentration that only drunks displayed. He stopped when he found the last message from Cherise. He knew it by heart, but read it over anyway. The torture helped him focus. Maybe he should call her right now and beg her to reconsider. Beg her to come to Fort Stockton and live with him. He smirked at the thought. She could cook and clean his dinky apartment while he worked at the warehouse. Just what a high class broad like Cherise Hillyer would want to do. Stranger things had happened. People did a lot of things for love.

Except she didn't love him. She'd made that clear. Maybe he'd call her and give her a piece of his mind instead. Use every foul word he knew and make a few up besides.

That thought also made him smile, but soon enough it turned to a frown and he felt on the verge of tears. He was pathetic.

The impulse to throw the phone was strong, but he kept himself in check, scrolling back several messages instead. Beth. Big John's niece. Now there was a girl who'd welcomed his advances. And Big John was anxious to find a way to get her to move back home.

Blue pressed the message button and started texting. "How you been? I might come to Dallas sometime. We should get together."

He let out a drunken snort. Take that, Miss Cherise Hillyer. He'd just found a replacement.

BLUE SHIFTED from one foot to the other, keeping his eyes fixed on the calendar behind Big John's head. He'd come for a favor, but was beginning to have doubts about the wisdom of the errand.

"So? Spit it out," Big John said, finally looking up from his paperwork.

"I was wondering if I could leave a bit early today."

"Something wrong at home? Your dad take a turn?"

"No. It's not to go to the ranch. It's to... well, you see, Sir..."

Big John frowned and sat back in his chair, surveying Blue with intensity. "You seem awfully nervous, boy. Take a seat and get whatever it is off your chest."

"I'd rather stand, Sir." Blue straightened his shoulders. "See, I'm off to Dallas for the weekend."

"Dallas?" Big John blurted.

Blue nodded. "To see Beth, if that's alright with you."

Big John sat there for a minute, rubbing the stubble on his chin.

"We've been communicating quite a bit these last few days. She invited me up."

"Communicating? What in tarnation does that mean?"

"Texting mostly," Blue replied.

"Texting!" Big John shook his head. "Young people. Can't even carry on a real life conversation."

"She invited me to come for a visit," Blue repeated. "I thought you'd like to know. And of course, I can just leave after work, but I thought this way I'd get to the city at a decent hour."

Big John's desk chair squeaked as he leaned forward. "Where are you staying?"

Blue could feel the heat creeping up around his collar and he gripped his cowboy hat in his hands, not daring to meet Big John's penetrating gaze. "A hotel, of course."

"Good." Big John relaxed again. "I said before I thought you two would make a good pair, but I expect you to treat her like a lady." He waved his hand. "Oh, I know I can't expect her to save herself for marriage or anything like that, but I do expect a little decorum - at least on the first date."

"Of course, Sir."

Big John tapped a finger on the desktop, all the while staring at Blue. Finally he spoke. "Alright then. You can take off right after lunch." He consulted his watch. "Which is now."

"Two o'clock would be fine."

"Who's the boss around here?" Big John pushed away from the desk and stood with slow motion precision. "Now, you better get a move on. It's a long drive to Dallas and my niece deserves a nice dinner out."

Blue nodded. "Thank you, Sir." He made a bee-line out of the cramped office and Big John's intensity.

Misgivings danced a gig inside Blue's stomach as he trotted toward his pick-up. He was actually going to do it this time. Take the steps necessary to move on with his life. One night stands and drowning his sorrows in booze hadn't helped one bit. He needed to find a stable relationship with a nice girl. Someone he could depend on. Someone he could build a future with. Someone like Beth.

The thought of her didn't fill him with the same sense of urgency he felt when he thought about Cherise, or even the warm longing he'd felt for Stella. Two perfect examples of why a relationship should not be built on emotion. He was choosing to pursue Beth, not getting forced into it by some unseen force. Following your heart did nothing but get it broken and he was done with that. A new strategy was in order, starting this weekend.

Of course he'd have to convince Beth that his motivation went deeper than trying to cauterize the wound that had him bleeding to death inside. He would be the perfect gentleman; wining, dining, even bedding her if necessary - with or without Big John's permission.

Blue didn't stop to analyze why the thought of the latter didn't bring more excitement as he revved his engine to life. He was sure his libido would kick in at the appropriate time, whenever that time came. It was a brilliant plan and one that Blue was determined to carry out. Otherwise, he just might die in his misery.

CHAPTER 20

*D*irk plunked down on one of the cement benches in the courtyard. "What do you mean you want to come down here and volunteer for awhile?" He held his cell phone to his ear with one hand and ran a hand through his hair with the other.

"It means I need a change of scenery," Cherise responded on the other end of the line.

A stray basketball bounced toward him and he caught it in one fluid motion. "I get that, but running away isn't the answer." Dirk sent the basketball back to the open air court where 'his' group of teens were playing.

"Says the guy who just ran away."

Dirk expelled an impatient puff of air. "Touché." He bent forward, one elbow slung across his knees. They were a deep brown, darker than any salon tan he'd ever had. "This isn't a holiday destination, Cherise. You actually have to work. Hard."

"You don't think I can do a little work?"

"And there are no amenities. Not like you're used to anyway." He'd taken his T shirt off during the game and began using it to wipe the sweat off his brow and shoulders.

"Be specific."

Dirk looked out over the basketball court. Only three boys remained. If he didn't shower soon there might not be any hot water left. "Okay. How about no private bathrooms and no guarantee of hot water?"

"Oh dear."

Dirk smiled. He could hear the hesitancy in Cherise's voice and imagined her look of disgust at sharing a bathroom. "Plus, you have to go to church every night."

"They make you do that?"

"They don't make you, but it is kind of expected."

"Well, I suppose it couldn't hurt," Cherise said.

"I can't believe my ears." Dirk laughed. "My sister actually agreeing to go to church?"

"Maybe I've changed. People do, you know. You're not the only one with dibs in that department."

"What are you not telling me?" Dirk asked. "Something's up. I can tell."

"Can't I just want to do some good in the world?"

"I suppose. Plus there's not much else to do here in the evenings. It's no holiday."

"You said that already."

Dirk looked up when he saw someone's shadow approaching. He smiled when he recognized Anne-Marie. "Hi," he mouthed.

Anne-Marie sat down on the bench beside him. She was still wearing her scrubs.

"I'm kind of sweaty," Dirk said to her.

"That's okay," Anne-Marie responded.

"Sweaty?" Cherise asked.

"What? Oh, yeah. I was just playing basketball with some boys." Dirk leaned over and gave Anne-Marie a quick kiss on the cheek.

"Is someone with you?" Cherise asked.

Dirk sighed and readjusted the phone to his ear. "Um, what's that?"

"You seem distracted. Who are you talking to?"

"Nobody."

Anne-Marie gave him a little shove and he laughed, nearly falling off the bench.

"Is that so?" Cherise asked.

"Just a co-worker," Dirk said.

"A Mexican beauty, knowing you."

"A beauty, anyway." Dirk winked at Anne-Marie and she swatted him, smiling shyly.

"Hm. Are there lots of eligible singles there? I could use a distraction."

"It's not like that here," Dirk said, all humor dissipating.

"Apparently it's enough for you to get over Tempest. Pretty quickly, I might add."

Dirk cleared his throat and switched the phone to his other ear, away from Anne-Marie. "That was actually rather unkind and certainly uncalled for."

"It's the truth, isn't it? You ran away to get over Tempest and it seems to have worked. Maybe I need a dose of that same medicine."

"Listen, Cherise. I don't want to talk about it right now."

"I think it's a good thing. You and Temp just weren't meant to be. I'm glad you're getting over her."

"Cherise..." Dirk ground into the phone.

"What? It's true. And maybe coming down there will do the same for me."

"It's not the same," Dirk said.

"Why? Cause you're a guy and I'm a girl? You're every bit the slut I am, brother, only it's okay for guys, apparently." Her tone was haughty.

"Can we *not* have this conversation right now?" Dirk bolted

185

from the bench and spun away from Anne-Marie's penetrating gaze.

"We're more alike than you think. Which is why I was thinking that if this 'boy scout thing' - or whatever you want to call it - can work for you, maybe it can work for me, too."

"It's not a 'boy scout thing'," Dirk protested. "It's a Christian mission for orphans. And they do real work here. Good work."

"Okay. So maybe I need a bit of religion then, too. Tempest would certainly be happy."

"You can't just show up here, Cherise. There are protocols. Background checks. You're working with kids."

"And you think I'd be a bad influence?"

"I didn't say that." The last thing he wanted was his sister hanging around spoiling his chances with Anne-Marie.

"Then tell me why. And not just because there's work involved."

"It's just… you couldn't handle it."

"Wanna bet?"

"Cherise, please…"

"I've made up my mind. I need this Dirk. Probably even more than you." There was a wobble in her voice.

Dirk looked skyward and sighed. "Don't cry, okay? I'll talk to someone. See what I can do."

"Thank you. You're the best."

Dirk glanced over to the bench where Anne-Marie still sat, waiting. "But under one condition."

"What?"

"Tell me the truth. What happened this time? And no crap about just needing a change. I know you better than that."

There was silence for a moment until Cherise spoke, quietly this time. "I finally met Mr. Right."

"Um, okay…" He rubbed the back of his neck.

"I know you think it's just another one of my infatuations, but this one is for real. I'm sure of it."

"And that makes you want to run away because…?" He knew his tone didn't sound all that sympathetic.

"It's because I love him that I had to end it. I'd ruin his life. The way I ruin everything." A small sob escaped.

Dirk closed his eyes. "Hold on, now. That's not true -"

"Isn't it? I almost got you killed, Dirk. You, Temp, Stella, not to mention Roberto, and Jean Yvres - you all risked your lives for me, and for what? I honestly can't tell the difference between a real relationship and a shallow one and I couldn't do that to him. I couldn't hurt him like that. So I jumped ship. And now I need a way to pay for it - all of it."

"What do you mean, 'pay for it'?"

"You know!" She let out an exasperated sigh. "You're the one in Mexico doing good deeds. I need to make up for my wandering eye. For all the affairs gone wrong. All the guys I've tossed overboard without a thought or a care."

"And you think that coming down here and volunteering at an orphanage will help square you away with God? I didn't think you even believed in a higher power."

"I don't. Or at least I didn't think I did. But Tempest has been preaching at me for years, so maybe some of it has rubbed off. In any case, it couldn't hurt. I'm dying inside, Dirk. I need this."

"From what little I know, forgiveness isn't quite that simple. It's not about doing good deeds to balance out the bad."

"No? Then what is it about?"

"I…" Dirk looked over at Anne-Marie. How could he explain when he wasn't even sure himself? "Listen. I'll talk to the administrator. But you have to be willing to stay for a full two weeks. That's their rule."

"I can do that." Her voice held hope.

"No going home when the going gets tough. Got it?"

"I won't let you down. I promise."

"I'll call you by tomorrow afternoon. Then all you have to do is book a flight from Boston to Ensenada, about a half hour drive from here. I'll pick you up."

"Thanks Dirk. You may have just saved my life."

"Don't thank me just yet," Dirk chuckled. "You might be cursing me after the first day. Love you, Sis." He hung up.

"Your sister?" Anne-Marie asked.

He nodded as he scooped his T shirt from where he had tossed it on the bench and pulled it over his head.

"Who's Tempest?" Anne-Marie asked, one eyebrow raised expectantly.

"Ah. You heard that." Dirk screwed his face into a grimace. Anne-Marie just nodded, but she was still smiling so he figured he wasn't in too much trouble. "You jealous?" he asked.

"Of course not!" Her answer seemed a little too quick.

"No need, for the record. She's just an old crush. I kind of came down here to forget her."

"I see."

"It worked." He grabbed her hand, intending to pull her closer. She resisted. "So, I'm the rebound?"

Dirk released her hand. "It's not like that."

Anne-Marie blinked but then visibly relaxed. "Sorry. I don't like it when girls get catty like that. It doesn't matter one way or another."

Dirk surveyed her features. "You sure?"

"Of course."

He wasn't sure he could believe her, but to push the topic seemed pointless and things might get awkward. "Good." He reached for her again but she continued to resist. "What now?"

"You're all sweaty," Anne-Marie protested.

Dirk laughed. "So I am. Sorry." Instead of letting go, he yanked her forward like a dancer doing the jive and encircled her in his arms. "But not that sorry."

"Brute," she teased and wiggled out of his embrace. "You never told me what your sister wanted."

"I'll tell you about it later," Dirk promised. "I need to shower before suppertime."

That way he would have time to decide which parts he wanted to tell and which parts he needed to keep secret.

DIRK AND ANNE-MARIE walked hand in hand in the darkness, their arms swinging gently back and forth between them. They were quiet. Contemplative.

The pastor's sermon that night had struck a chord with Dirk, and apparently it had with Anne-Marie as well. It was a straight up salvation message, something Dirk had heard a lot of since coming to Mexico, but for some reason this one really hit home. What was he doing here? Really? Playing at philanthropy? Stroking his own ego? Or had God directed his steps to this place for a deeper purpose?

"What you thinking about?" Anne-Marie broke the silence with her question.

"Just wondering what on earth my sister is going to do if she actually comes here," he responded, going for the next thing that was on his mind rather than the first.

"Nursery duty, kitchen duty, teaching..." Anne-Marie listed. "I'm sure she'll find something she's interested in, and as you know, they're never short of jobs."

Dirk laughed out loud. "You don't know my sister."

"Tell me about her." Anne-Marie smiled encouragingly.

"For starters, she's stubborn. Once she gets something into her head, she won't let it go."

"A family trait, perhaps?" Anne-Marie asked mischievously.

"Maybe. She's determined to come down here and it looks like she will, whether I like it or not."

"I'm looking forward to meeting a member of your family. It

might shed some light on the real you." She gave him an impish grin.

Dirk grunted. "Exactly why I'm not happy about it."

"Why?" Anne-Marie's face suddenly fell. "Are you embarrassed for her to meet me?"

Dirk jerked his head sharply in Anne-Marie's direction. "Of course that's not it. Why would you say that?"

"She's probably really beautiful. You did say you looked alike."

Dirk stopped in his tracks and turned Anne-Marie to look at him. She was still so sensitive and very insecure, especially about her appearance, despite his assurances to the contrary. "To me she's just my sister. And you are positively gorgeous." He kissed her long and hard and when he released her mouth he hoped she would understand that he had eyes only for her.

"So what is it then?" Anne-Marie asked.

Dirk retrieved her hand and they kept walking. "There are just some things about my family that you don't know. That I haven't told you yet."

"Bad things?"

"Not exactly..."

"My goodness! Then what is it? You mentioned taking a bullet for her. Does it have something to do with that? Or some other deep, dark secret?"

Dirk rubbed the back of his neck, expelling a pent up breath. "I'm not quite sure how to say it."

"You might as well spit it out," Anne-Marie said on a laugh. "It's easier in the long run."

Dirk glanced sidelong at Anne-Marie's expectant expression. "You promise you won't think less of me?"

"I'm pretty much expecting the worst, so you might as well just come right out and say it." Her expression had sobered. "Besides, as a Christian, your past is no longer relevant. You're a new person."

Dirk felt a twinge of guilt at her comment, but pressed on.

"Okay. Here goes." He took a deep cleansing breath and then let it out again. "My family is rich, which means I'm rich." He waited for her response, watching her features as she digested his revelation.

Confusion was the only thing that registered on her face. "And...?"

"That's it."

"You're rich," she repeated.

He nodded. "I don't mean sort of rich. I mean very rich, as in wealthy. And once Cherise gets here, there will be no hiding it. You'll know what I mean when you meet her. She... I don't know exactly how to explain it."

Anne-Marie's eyes widened. "You're not part of the mafia, are you? A mob family?"

Dirk laughed. "No! Nothing like that."

"Then what's the big deal?"

Dirk shrugged. "I don't know. People try to take advantage when they know you have money. Or they don't take you seriously."

Anne-Marie cocked an eyebrow. "So you thought I might try to take advantage of you for your money?"

Dirk laughed. "Not you. But maybe you wouldn't have given me the time of day if you'd known. You know. Been intimidated or something."

"My, we are full of ourselves, aren't we?"

"See?" Dirk grinned. "Now that you know, you're treating me differently already."

"So how much money are we talking about?"

"Would you believe it if I told you I've never actually had a job?" He tried to gauge her reaction.

"What about working with your father?"

"Doesn't really count. He wants me to step into his shoes when he decides to retire, but he's too much of a control freak to ever let that happen. Besides that, he just keeps an office in downtown Boston for looks. He doesn't really do much. His investments are solid, as are mine, so I don't have to work."

"Ever?" Anne-Marie's eyes had widened even further.

"Ever."

"No wonder you had no trouble getting sponsorship. Not to mention talking on a cell phone all the time - in a foreign country." She looked at him and grinned. "I should have guessed right off that first day when you came into the clinic. All perfectly tanned and every hair in place."

"I hope it's not that obvious anymore."

She reached over and gently touched his hair with her finger tips. "Kind of scruffy these days, but you'll do."

Her touch sent a shock wave through Dirk's body and he grabbed her hand and kissed the palm. "Please don't think any less of me now that you know. I don't want anything to change between us."

"Don't worry. I feel obligated to keep you. I just don't get why you didn't tell me sooner."

She was teasing him, Dirk knew, but he felt desperate to ensure that things didn't go downhill from here. "Seriously, I've felt freer here than I've ever felt. Free to be myself. To accomplish something on my own merits, not just because I have money and a family name. All the money in the world can't compare to doing something good with your hands. Or making a difference in people's lives. That's priceless."

Anne-Marie kissed Dirk gently on the lips. "So are you."

Before Dirk could seal the moment with another kiss, they heard voices nearby. They were whispering but definitely angry if the sharp hiss of their tone was any indication. Dirk put his finger to his lips and he and Anne-Marie moved silently into the shadows. Dirk winced when the sharp leaves of one of the macadamia trees pricked him through his shirt. He sheltered Anne-Marie as best he could with his own body and they waited as footsteps crossed dangerously near their hideaway. In a moment, James Gallagher, the orphanage administrator, emerged from the trees. He looked both ways and then continued on his way in the direction of the central courtyard.

Dirk realized he'd been holding his breath and let it out slowly. "Now for sure I'm suspicious," he said in a whisper.

"Why? He probably just likes taking walks - the same as us."

"No, there's something different. You heard it. He was arguing with someone. And the way he stopped and looked from side to side. Someone is hiding back there in the trees."

Anne-Marie furrowed her brow and shook her head. "I'm sure it's nothing. You're just being paranoid."

"Call it what you want. I plan to find out."

"My hero," Anne-Marie teased. "Taking bullets has gone to your head. Come on. We better head back."

Dirk checked over his shoulder once more before following Anne-Marie's lead. He tried to shake off the feeling of foreboding that had suddenly enveloped him. Maybe this was why God had brought him down to a Mexican orphanage. To uncover some sinister evil that lurked in a macadamia nut grove.

CHAPTER 21

"Get out and don't ever come near me again!"

Blue ducked as his duffel bag rocketed toward him, spewing a T shirt and a pair of socks on the way like a space craft shedding its thrusters. "Hey! I'm sorry, okay?" He rolled off the rumpled bed and stood.

"You're sorry? Is that all you can say?" Beth's nostrils flared.

"What more do you want?" Blue bent to pick up the bag and the stray items, and stuffed them inside. "It was nothing."

"Nothing? Calling me by another woman's name while we're making out is nothing?" Beth stood across the room, hands on hips.

Blue advanced cautiously. "I thought you just wanted to have some fun. Isn't that what we were doing?"

"I'm not interested in being runner up. Now, get out of my apartment before I call the cops."

By the look on Beth's face there would be no arguing. With a sigh, Blue turned away from her seething countenance and found his shirt lying at the foot of the bed where he'd shed it only moments before. He thrust his arms in the sleeves, not bothering to button it, and then zipped the duffel bag's closure with a jerk.

He gave it one last shot. "You're sure about this? It really was just a slip of the tongue."

"Get out!" she yelled.

Blue put his hands up in surrender before slinging the duffel bag over one shoulder. He found his shoes near the bedroom door, and strode from her tiny apartment without another backward glance. If she wanted to be stubborn about it, then he could be, too.

So much for a weekend getaway. So much for exorcising his demons. Blue walked to his truck and tossed the limp bag onto the passenger seat. He started the truck with a roar and jerked it into gear. He just hoped Beth wouldn't spew to her uncle.

He'd arrived in Dallas yesterday with every intention of courting Beth. Their first evening together had been nice and they'd even ended with more than a little heated kissing. Beth had wanted him to stay the night with her but Big John's remark about getting his own room was still ringing in Blue's ears. Either that or he was making an excuse.

Their second evening together promised to be different, however. Blue was determined to put all thoughts of Cherise Hillyer out of his mind and if that meant getting down and dirty, then so be it. Somewhere between dinner and a night cap at Beth's apartment, things had gotten hot and heavy. And then it happened. He'd said Cherise's name and all hell broke loose.

Served him right. He would have done the same had their roles been reversed.

With a sigh, Blue pulled out of Beth's parking lot and merged into the traffic on the street. There had to be more to life than chasing his own tail. Despite the late hour, he'd head straight to the ranch since he wouldn't be able to sleep anyway. Perhaps there he'd find some peace.

~

BLUE STOOD beside the grey mare, combing her coat with methodical movements. It was dim and cool in the stables - almost too cool now that fall had settled in. He wished he'd thought to wear his buckskin coat, but he'd left it hanging on the hook beside the front door. He'd just have to let the exercise of grooming the animal warm him. Besides keeping his blood pumping, it was cathartic. Calming. Not that there was anything to be anxious about.

Yeah, right.

He'd arrived at the ranch in the early hours of the morning, so managed to avoid his brother and sister-in-law. He just didn't have the energy. After a couple hours sleep, he spent the rest of the forenoon in the company of his ailing father, which was exhausting in its own way. The elder Shepherd insisted on talking about spiritual things, understandable in his present state. Anything for a dying man.

After that Blue had gone for a short ride, and planned to head back to Fort Stockton as soon as he finished looking after the horse. It would be dark again by the time he got back home to his own place, but that was a good thing. Less time to think about life. His only obligation would be to fall into bed and start the circus all over again in the morning. Except this time he might have some explaining to do to Big John.

Blue tensed when he heard footsteps entering the stables. Zane. He'd recognize his brother's gait anywhere. He glanced in the direction of the open doors just to make sure. He really wasn't interested in a conversation right now. It was one thing to endure his father's recriminations, but quite another to explain his failures to someone like Zane.

"I was hoping I'd find you here." Zane stopped a few feet away and crossed his arms.

"Just came in from a ride." Blue kept his arms moving, even though the horse was thoroughly groomed already.

"Haven't seen much of you lately," Zane stated.

"I'm busy."

"Must be."

"I mean to get out to see Dad every weekend, but I had to go to Dallas on Friday. That's why I got here so late."

Zane just nodded.

"And while I am here, I just want to spend as much time with the old man as possible, you know?" Blue continued. "Sorry for not coming to see you and Stella."

Zane nodded again. "I get it."

Blue didn't know what else to say, so busied himself with hanging up the grooming tools on the wall behind him.

"What's in Dallas?"

Blue blinked, and glanced over his shoulder at his older brother. "Just a friend."

"Anyone I know?"

"Aren't you the nosy one. Your wife put you up to this?"

"Just asking."

Blue patted the horse on the neck and then swung the gate to her stall closed. It latched with a click. "If you must know, I went to see a girl." He looked pointedly at Zane and then headed in the direction of the exit. "Anything else you'd like to know?"

Zane followed him out into the yard. "It's your business, I guess. Just seems sudden."

"Sudden why? You were expecting me to be a blubbering mess? You don't expect me to become a priest, do you?" Blue took his cowboy hat off and brushed at the dust on the rim before placing it on his head again. Then he looked directly at Zane. "Besides that, I thought you'd be pleased. Stella did her best to keep me and Cherise apart and now that she's succeeded, everyone should be happy."

"That's not very fair," Zane said, his voice low.

"Don't talk to me about fair, Zane. You of all people have no right."

"Because of Stella?"

"Yes, among other things." Blue shoved his hands in his pockets and avoided Zane's gaze.

"I'm sorry if you're still hurting over… you know." Zane kicked at a pebble. "The heart has a mind of its own."

Blue laughed and looked skyward. "Don't I know it. But no need to keep apologizing. I'm over Stella. I told you that already."

"I believe you."

"Good. And Stella was worried about Cherise being unstable. Maybe I'm just as fickle, which in this case is a very good thing for you."

"I suppose. But I hate to see you hurting," Zane said.

"Who says I'm hurting?"

"It's as plain as the nose on your face."

"Well, you'll be happy to know I'm taking steps to fix that."

"The girl in Dallas?" Zane asked.

Blue shrugged. "Or so I thought."

"It didn't go so well?"

Blue rubbed the back of his neck and allowed a sheepish grin to form. "I said Cherise's name while we were making out."

"Ouch."

"You said it! She tossed me out of her apartment so fast it made my head spin."

"Nothing you didn't deserve," Zane said.

"Thanks, brother."

"Doesn't sound like a man who's moved on."

"Yeah, well, I might have been lying earlier about not being a blubbering mess. I am a mess - minus the blubbering, but a mess none the less." Blue sighed. "You know, at first I might have been using Cherise to get over Stella. But that changed. Now I can't stop thinking about her."

"Maybe you should call her," Zane suggested.

Blue's eyebrows shot up. "And risk the wrath of my sister-in-law?"

"Stella was just worried for you both, but she'll come around if it's meant to be."

"I don't know. You're a brave man for even suggesting it," Blue said, shaking his head.

"It's not like that. From what Stella says, Cherise comes across as really confident, but deep down she's scared."

"Of what?"

"Commitment. Getting hurt."

Blue nodded. "I gathered as much. Still, you didn't read the text she sent me. She made it pretty clear she was moving on."

The soft shuffle of boots on gravel alerted both men to an approaching figure. Stella's silhouette glided toward them, obscured from detail due to the late afternoon sun behind her. She stopped beside Zane and went up on tiptoe for a kiss before addressing Blue. "Nice job of letting us know you were here."

"You ganging up on me, too?" Blue said with a grin. The display of affection did not affect him as it used to. They deserved happiness and he was thankful that he hadn't stood in their way.

"Hardly. Just coming out to see what's taking my husband so long. It's supper time. You'll stay, of course."

"No, I gotta head back before it gets too late. Gotta work in the morning."

"You're sure?" Stella asked.

"We were just talking about Cherise," Zane said.

Blue raised his brows. His brother was full of surprises.

"Oh?" Stella said, looking from one to the other.

"What he means to say is, he was trying to give me advice on my love life," Blue said.

"Was he, now?"

"Of a sort," Zane admitted.

"And?" Stella prodded.

"I was telling him about this girl I've been seeing in Dallas," Blue said.

Zane grunted.

"I take it something went wrong?" Stellas asked.

"You could say that," Zane offered.

"I told him in my attempts to get over a certain friend of yours, I may have gone and upset my boss's niece."

"You never said anything about her being your boss's niece," Zane said.

"Must have skipped that part."

Stella placed a hand on Blue's forearm. "Can I be blunt?"

"Seems to me you always are, with or without anyone's permission."

"Have you tried calling Cherise?"

"I didn't think you approved."

"I didn't. But I've had some time to think about it and, well, I feel as if I had no business sticking my nose between you two. If you want to see each other then you should. And if it works out, what could be better than two of my best friends together?"

Zane caught Blue's eye and imperceptibly raised an eyebrow as if to say 'I told you so'.

"She made it pretty clear that she was moving on and I should, too," Blue said.

"Just call her," Stella advised.

"Why? You know something I don't?" Blue asked.

"Call." Stella gave Blue one last stare and then grabbed her husband's arm. "Gabriella won't be happy if we're late."

"Wait!" Blue reached for Stella to stop her. "I will. Thanks, Sis."

"Sis, now is it?" Stella teased.

Blue released her with a grin. Suddenly the future didn't seem as bleak.

CHAPTER 22

*C*herise cradled the mug of hot tea in her hands, watching the steam rise and dissipate into thin air. If only her own feelings could disappear so easily. She looked up and smiled as Tempest joined her on the futon. Tempest's 'new' apartment was small and boxy; one room to be exact, above her employer's garage. One window framed by limp, filmy drapes afforded a view of the cement driveway and a couple of distant trees. It was a definite step down, but Tempest wasn't one to complain. It was the first time Cherise had been to visit her since she'd moved out of the place Dirk had secured near the beach when she had first moved to L.A. It had only been a few months, but it seemed like a lifetime.

"You're sure you want to go through with this?" Tempest asked. "Going to Mexico?"

"I've made up my mind," Cherise said. "Besides, the weather will be so much nicer than in Boston this time of year. I hate the cold."

"Working in an orphanage might not be what you think."

"Dirk has already given me plenty of warning. He tried to talk me out of it, in fact, but I managed to twist his arm."

"It'll be totally different than going to a Mexican resort. You know that, don't you?"

"Why does everyone assume I can't handle a bit of work?" Cherise asked with a sigh. She took a sip of tea.

"Well…"

"All right, I admit, I haven't had the opportunity to prove myself, but I know I can do this, Tempest. I *need* to do this. For once in my life, would you let me be the 'good' person for a change and not the one who needs rescuing?"

"You are good, Cherise. I just worry that you might be biting off more than you can chew."

"It's only for two weeks, remember? Then, if I want to stay longer, I will."

"It does seem a bit extreme."

"Why? I flew all the way to Italy for a man, why not go to Mexico to get over one?"

"True. At least Dirk will be there."

Cherise smiled. "I'm happy to hear you say that. It makes me believe you really have forgiven him."

"I'm trying to give him the benefit of the doubt." Tempest gave a half hearted smile. "After all, nothing is impossible with God. In any case, I'm glad it brought you here first."

"Of course I wanted to stop and see you on the way. You always help ground me and I need that right now before I go off into the wilderness." She gestured dramatically with a sweep of her hands.

"I'm glad. I don't know when we'll get together again next. Stella's Dad's funeral was unexpected, but there's nothing else coming up."

"We don't need a reason to get together, do we?" Cherise asked.

"Not all of us have unlimited funds for flying around the country," Tempest reminded. "Plus, I have a job."

"Oh right. You're a reporter now. How is that going?"

"I was a reporter back east, too. Did you forget?"

Cherise shrugged and flipped her hair out of her way. "Of course not. I just meant… oh, never mind. I'm a terrible friend."

"No, you're just preoccupied with other things."

"Which is about to change," Cherise declared and sat up straighter. "Good works here I come! Maybe there'll even be a cute *chicano* to distract me. Take that, Blue Shepherd!"

"Cherise! I thought you said you were going off men - at least for the time being."

Cherise sighed. "I am. I think…"

"And by the way, I don't think you used 'chicano' in context…"

"Whatever. You know what I meant." In her heart, Cherise knew it would take more than a well tanned male distraction to make her forget about Blue, but it was easier to keep up the old front than admit the depth of her despair. She sat up and smiled. "And what about you? You haven't mentioned anything about good looking Ryan O'Toole since I got here."

Tempest shrugged. "He's away on assignment again."

"Oh. I'm sorry. I just thought…"

"Don't worry about it. We're just taking it slow."

"If you say so."

There was silence for a moment. Tempest blinked and let her lashes flutter downward. "Cherise, I have something I need to admit."

Cherise looked up. "Okay…"

"I told Stella. About what you said… that you were in love with Blue." She took a deep breath and the rest came rushing out. "I know I told you I'd try not to tell her, but then we talked and she mentioned something about it herself and it seemed wrong to keep it from her." Tempest searched her friend's face. "I'm really sorry."

"I see."

"I think she feels badly for the things she said to you after her father's funeral. She was under a lot of stress and wasn't herself."

Cherise waved a dismissive hand. "Forget it. I took action, like you said, and now I'm moving on."

"What kind of action?"

"I wrote him a text explaining it was over for good."

"Was that wise? What if there was still a chance?"

"What's done is done." Cherise set her empty mug on the floor beside her feet. "And now I say we take those poor mongrels of yours out for a walk."

There was no point in re-hashing what had already been finalized. Was there?

CHERISE LAY with her eyes wide open listening to Tempest's soft breathing on the futon beside her. Thankfully Tempest's dogs had been relegated to their kennels for the night or it would have been a foursome. As it was, the bed was rather narrow.

With slow motion precision, Cherise sat up, flipped the covers off her legs, and swung them over the edge of the futon. She waited a beat before standing, and then tiptoed to the kitchen table where she'd left her phone.

She clicked on the screen, shielding the light with her free hand as she scrolled through her most recent messages. She stopped when she got to Blue's name, and re-read the message she had sent to him. She rested her head against the wall, letting her mind wander to all the 'what ifs'. What if they could make a go of it? What if he was Mr. Right? Was there even such a thing? She shook her head and began scrolling again. She had done the right thing.

She hadn't spoken to Stella since the day she'd left the ranch and her finger hovered over the keys, but it was too late to do anything about it now. If what Tempest said was true, Stella might not be as opposed to her dating Blue as she had once been. Still, it hurt, knowing that someone she loved and trusted didn't think she was good enough. Scratch that, *she herself* didn't think she was good enough. It was different with Blue somehow, and she'd made the right decision.

Cherise sighed. Maybe tomorrow she'd call or text Stella and they could put any hard feelings behind them.

"Can't sleep?" Tempest's voice sounded groggy and far away.

"No. I didn't mean to wake you," Cherise whispered.

A low rumbling whine came from the large kennel where Jupiter, Tempest's Great Dane, was supposed to be sleeping.

"Sh, Jupiter," Tempest said in a hoarse whisper. "Don't wake Paddy."

As if on cue, the terrier let out a frenzied yelp.

"I'm so sorry," Cherise said, moving toward the kennels. "I've gone and woken everyone."

Tempest joined her and opened the kennel doors. "There'll be no peace unless I let them out," she said.

They spent a couple of minutes petting the dogs until they both settled.

"Well, want to make it a foursome?" Cherise asked.

Tempest smiled. "You don't mind?"

"Why not? It'll make my last night in the States one to remember."

Hopefully, it would also help her forget.

CHAPTER 23

*D*irk leaned one elbow on the counter at the reception desk in the administration office, simultaneously glancing over its edge at the neat and tidy desk on the other side. James Gallagher's wife Linda usually manned the station, but no one was there at the moment.

"Can I help you with something?"

Dirk glanced up at the pretty Mexican woman who was searching through a filing cabinet further away. Jessica, if he remembered correctly. She'd helped with orientation that first day. "Not sure. It's about another volunteer who wants to come down and help for a bit."

Jessica nodded her head, her bushy ponytail bobbing in time. "Good, good. We're always happy to welcome more volunteers. I'll just be a minute." She rolled the open filing cabinet drawer back into place.

Just then Linda slid into the room and went straight for her desk. "No need. I'm back."

Dirk supposed the poor woman could have been attractive if she held herself differently. As it was, her stooped posture made her look like a praying mantis that was trying to fold into itself.

"What is it you want?" Linda's gaze was focused on repositioning an already aligned container of pens. She tucked a stray strand of limp brown hair behind one ear.

"Right." Dirk stood up straight. "My sister wants to come volunteer for a couple of weeks. I thought I should mention it to someone rather than just have her show up."

Linda's gaze met his for a millisecond over the tops of her glasses, though she never moved her downturned head. "Correct. And that someone would be me."

"Okay. So… this is me letting you know my sister is coming. Her name is Cherise Hillyer."

Linda gave him a withering look. "You can fill out the form as best you can and then I'll get her to sign it when she arrives." She swivelled in her chair, about to get up, but Jessica was already by her side with a blank form.

"Here you go," Jessica said cheerily and set the papers on the high reception counter.

"Thanks." Dirk took the paperwork and used it to salute the women. "I'll have these back by this afternoon."

James Gallagher strode through the door of his private office into the main reception area. "Ah! Mr Hillyer. Just the man I was hoping to see. Can you join me for a moment?" He gestured at his inner sanctum.

"Sure." Dirk looked at Linda. "May I?" he asked, pointing to the path around her desk which led to the inner office.

She just nodded.

"Enjoying your late night strolls?" Dirk asked conversationally as he sauntered around Linda's seated form.

James blinked rapidly. "Pardon me?"

"Your late night strolls," Dirk repeated. "I've seen you a few times, now, coming out of the nut grove. Late at night," he added for emphasis.

Linda had swung around to stare at her husband but she didn't utter any words.

"There are plenty of reasons why I need to walk the property." James puffed himself up and gestured once again at his open office door. "Now, if you please?"

Dirk put on his most charming smile and entered ahead of James, who immediately shut the door behind them. He would just bet that he'd rattled James Gallagher just a tiny bit. For some reason it gave him a small sense of satisfaction. The guy was definitely hiding something.

As Dirk lowered himself into a chair, James spoke. "No need to sit. This won't take long."

Dirk's brows rose slightly, but he straightened and waited. "Okay… What's this about?"

"I might as well get straight to the point."

"I'm listening."

"This is a Christian organization, Mr. Hillyer."

"Yes…" Dirk nodded slowly.

"And as such we do not condone… we do not approve of…" James frowned, searching for words. "We discourage couples pairing off, as it were, during their time here. It can get messy and quite frankly, it sets a bad example for the children in our care."

"Oh! You think Anne-Marie and I are… you know. Doing something immoral. I can assure you, nothing like that has happened. We're just getting to know one another and -"

"But something *could* happen," James stated. "It's why we discourage such behavior."

"I see."

"So? Do you agree to stop this relationship before it goes any further?" James asked.

Dirk furrowed his brow and thought for a moment. "Well… would you let *me* have this conversation with Anne-Marie, first? I promise I'll make her understand."

"Well, I suppose that would be acceptable. I often let my wife handle the women in these types of affairs. Saves on awkwardness. But that should do nicely."

"Perfect. Consider the conversation handled." Dirk pivoted and then stopped. "Is that all?"

James rubbed the back of his neck. "I must admit, I was expecting more of a fight."

"Don't worry about a thing," Dirk reassured. "I will definitely take care of everything."

And he would. He'd handle it, alright, and hopefully make Anne-Marie understand the depth of his feelings for her. There was no way he was telling her anything about this conversation, though. With her conscientious leanings, she just might agree to ending their relationship and that was not happening - not when things were going so well.

But that wasn't all. Dirk was determined to find out what James Gallagher was up to on those late night strolls. He wasn't exactly sure what he was looking for, but he'd know it when he saw it.

DIRK'S first step was to follow James the next time he headed into the macadamia grove. Doing that and staying undetected might prove to be tricky. Tonight was his best bet, since Anne-Marie was on call at the clinic and had left the evening service after only one song. It was his perfect opportunity to slip out himself and hide somewhere in the grove - and hopefully catch James at his game, whatever it was. He'd been watching the administrator these past couple of nights during the services and without fail, James always seemed to be called out. This time, Dirk would be waiting.

Dirk slipped out of the auditorium and walked as quickly as he dared to the beckoning trees. The last thing he wanted was to raise suspicion, so he'd worn a hooded jacket to the service that night, just in case, and he was glad for the relative protection it afforded against the prickly leaves.

Once inside the shelter of the trees, he found a spot near the outer fence that had some shrubbery growing around it. The grounds crew kept the grove in such pristine condition it was hard to find a secure hiding spot. Still, if he crouched down and kept really still, he figured nobody would notice.

His legs were just beginning to cramp up when he saw a lone figure approaching. James. He felt his heartbeat speed up and purposely tried to slow his breathing. He just had to watch and wait. James would either lead him to whatever it was or he would prove himself innocent.

James strode into the grove, not bothering to look to the right or to the left as someone with something to hide might. Dirk was beginning to have his doubts. There was no one else around, however, so maybe James was feeling confident enough not to worry. Dirk watched until he could no longer see James but could still hear his footfalls on the grass. He better move soon, or he might lose him altogether.

Dirk slowly straightened, much to his joints' protest. He couldn't wait for the tingling sensation to dissipate. He had to get moving. With the thrill of participating in some kind of spy movie, Dirk ducked from one tree to the next, staying far enough back and out of James' line of sight. Once James stopped in his tracks and stood silent, listening. Dirk held his breath. Then he continued on, straight to the far reaches of the grove and the high fence that marked the edge of the property.

Dirk positioned himself beneath a fairly small tree, perfect because if its low branches for camouflaging his presence. He could see another entrance, similar to the main gates, with a small booth for a watchman. He had never considered before that there was another entrance onto the property. A packed dirt road followed the fence line to a large storage building. It looked to be a maintenance shed or garage of some sort, which made sense since they did need equipment for mowing and yard maintenance as well as harvesting and transporting the nut crop.

He watched as James waited while the night watchman opened the gate and a paneled fifteen passenger van drove through. It was white and very similar to the one owned by the mission. They used it to transport food and other supplies to the community at large during their weekly 'outreach' trips. As well, it was used to transport groups of children when they were going on an outing. The van drove up to the shed and the driver got out. Dirk squinted to try and get a better look at the man. It was hard to tell in this light, but he certainly resembled his old friend Dillan, the hipster with the beard.

James and Dillan talked and then they both went into the shed. A few minutes later they came out. Dillan waved at James and proceeded to exit the premises on foot. Once the gate was securely closed, James turned and headed back the way he had come.

Dirk held his breath as James passed within a few feet of where he was standing. He made sure the older man was well out of the grove before he finally emerged from his hiding spot and walked back through the trees himself.

Dirk had a sneaking suspicion that whatever had just taken place was not above board. Regular business took place in the daylight, not under the cover of darkness. And Dillan had long since gone on his way to explore more of the Baja peninsula, or so he had said. The younger man showing up, driving one of the mission's vans, and then leaving on foot, just didn't add up.

Or maybe it did. It added up to no good.

"I JUST CAN'T BELIEVE there is anything to this, Dirk." Anne-Marie's eyebrows formed a delicate line. "James is a long time missionary. He loves God - and he loves this place. I'm sure whatever you saw has a perfectly logical explanation."

Anne-Marie sat next to Dirk on one of the benches in the courtyard. They had just finished lunch and soon they would both need to head back to work.

"Do you want to go ask him?" Dirk raised a brow.

"Of course not." She looked down at her lap, worry written all over her face.

"Exactly. Cause there might be something to it."

Anne-Marie glanced up. "So what are you going to do?"

"Keep an eye on James. Watch for any more strange comings and goings."

"I still think you're being paranoid."

"Maybe, but it's better to know for sure, don't you think?"

"And just how are you going to accomplish all this surveillance, hm?" Anne-Marie cocked her head to one side.

"Well, I actually have a plan if you'd like to hear it."

"Go ahead."

"A new batch of volunteers arrive tomorrow and I thought I might volunteer to show them around; help with their orientation."

"And?" Anne-Marie prompted.

"And maybe I can get a closer look at that shed. See what's inside."

"I can tell you exactly what's inside that shed, if you'd only asked. Drying racks for the fresh harvest and processed nuts waiting for shipment, that's what."

"I figured as much, but my guess is there's more to it than that. There must be some other secret activity going on."

"Like what?" Anne-Marie's tone was skeptical.

"Who knows? Drug smuggling, people smuggling... it's what I hope to find out."

"Now you're being ridiculous."

"Time will tell."

"What about your sister?" Anne-Marie asked. "When is she due to arrive?"

"Same afternoon. I'm going to pick her up - another opportunity to do a little watching while no one is expecting me to work."

Anne-Marie laughed. "You sound as nutty as this whole thing."

"I'm only nuts about you," Dirk said and grinned.

"Enough!" She gave him a playful swat and stood up. "Tomorrow we'll be laughing about this whole thing when you don't find anything."

"I don't know." Dirk shook his head. "I've been right to listen to my gut before and my gut says there's something fishy going on around here."

"Maybe your sister can talk some sense into you."

"My sister believes in my gut. It saved her life."

Anne-Marie gave him a withering look. "I better get back to work. And you should do the same."

Dirk wanted Anne-Marie to be right. But his gut, a pretty reliable barometer, was telling him otherwise.

CHAPTER 24

*J*ust call. The advice echoed in Blue's mind.

He stared at his cell phone for a moment and then with a deep intake of resolve, he brought up Cherise's number and hit dial. He waited until an automated voice came on, informing him that Cherise was either busy or out of range. Yeah, right. How about choosing not to answer? With a sigh, he set the phone down.

He stood up and sauntered to the TV set sitting atop his dresser. He flipped it on but almost as quickly shut it off again. Who was he kidding? He was driving himself crazy.

The last couple of days had been a roller coaster ride of ups and downs. He'd come back to Fort Stockton full of hope, but now? He was worse off than ever. So far, Big John hadn't said anything to him about Beth, but he knew an interrogation was coming. It was just a matter of time.

Maybe he'd bring it up himself at work today. Take the bull by the horns. What's the worst that could happen? Death by strangulation at the hands of Big John?

Blue smiled. Better that than the slow death he was now experiencing.

∽

BLUE LOITERED outside Big John's office, hat in hands. He took another steadying breath and then cleared his throat upon entering the overcrowded space.

"Come in, come in!" Big John bellowed, gesturing with his paw for Blue to enter. "I've hardly had a chance to talk to you these last few days. Never heard about your weekend getaway yet."

"Um, right." Blue stood in the doorway fingering the rim of his hat.

"Well, sit already!" Big John gestured at the vacant chair on the other side of his desk.

"Okay." Blue sank onto the cracked vinyl seat.

"So?" Big John propped his reading glasses on the top of his head and then gave Blue his full attention, clasping his large hands on top of the desk. "How's Beth?"

"She's good," Blue said, barely above a whisper.

Big John stared at Blue for a moment and then started to laugh, a hearty, right-from-the-gut sound. "Don't look so scared! I don't expect you to tell me all the details. I know my niece isn't a little girl any more, so if that's what you're worried about, don't be. I just wanted to know if you had a nice time together, that's all."

Exactly what did the other man know about that weekend? Had Beth already called and confided in her uncle, telling him all the sorry details about his slip of the tongue and how she threw him out on his ear? Blue swallowed the lump in his throat. "Have you talked to Beth recently?"

"No. That's why I'm asking you." Big John narrowed his eyes.

Was Big John baiting him? Blue cleared his throat. "Well, about that…"

The telephone rang. "Just a minute." Big John held up one finger as he picked up the receiver and put it to his ear. "Hello?"

Blue let out a pent up breath. He considered making a beeline for the door, but Big John would finish the conversation one way or another so he might as well wait and face the firing squad.

Big John hung up. "That was the wife. She says to expect a surprise, but darned if she wouldn't tell me what it was." He shook his head and then looked square at Blue again. "So, you were saying?"

"Yes, well -"

"Surprise!"

Both men snapped their attention to the open doorway. Beth was standing there with a tentative smile on her face.

"Beth!" Big John was up and at the door, enveloping the girl in a bear hug before Blue could even register what had happened. "We were just talking about you!"

Beth made eye contact with Blue. "You were, were you?"

Blue stood up and gave a slight nod in her direction, but didn't say anything.

"Blue was just going to tell me about your weekend. Minus the private parts, of course," Big John said with a chuckle.

"Oh. Well, I wouldn't want to miss that," Beth said, raising a brow in Blue's direction.

"But first, what in tarnation are you doing here?" Big John asked. "When Millie phoned and said to expect a surprise I didn't know what to think. But this is the best surprise ever." He held her at arms length.

"You might not think so when I tell you," Beth said.

Blue's stomach clenched.

"Why? Did something happen?" Big John frowned and looked her up and down.

"Nothing too bad," Beth said and wiggled out of her uncle's grasp. "At least I hope it's not."

Blue gestured at the chair. "Take the chair, Beth. I should get back to work." *Or pack my things and leave since I'll probably be getting fired.*

"Now, wait just a minute," Big John said to Blue. "I still want to hear about your weekend after Beth says her piece."

Blue leaned one shoulder against the door jam and waited for Beth's revelation, keeping his eyes solidly fixed on a spot on the worn linoleum.

"So?" Big John asked as he returned to his throne behind the desk.

Beth took a deep breath. "I quit my job."

Blue blinked and stole a glance at Beth. It wasn't what he had expected.

"You what?" Big John's volume rose.

"I know you just helped me move, but the big city isn't what I thought it would be. I'd... I'd like to move home. Back to Fort Stockton."

Big John's expression was unreadable. Blue felt sorry for Beth. Her uncle was an intimidating figure and it couldn't be easy facing him under these circumstances. "So, I'm just supposed to make another trip all the way to Dallas and pack all your belongings back here when I just got you settled?"

"I know it's a lot to ask, but -"

Big John's face split with a smile as wide as the Rio Grande. "Of course I'd be happy to do it. There's nothing I'd love better than to have you back where you belong."

"Good. Except..." Beth hesitated. "There's one condition."

"You have conditions, now, do you?" Big John harrumphed.

"I'd like to get my own place," Beth said.

"And how are you supposed to afford that when you don't even have a job?"

"Well, I was thinking that maybe I could apply at this really great hardware store I know," Beth said. "Rumor has it they're in need of some tech upgrades."

Big John's brows rose. "You want to work here?"

"Aunt Millie says you're always moaning about how you're

reaching retirement age but can't retire because no one knows how to run the business. You can teach me and then, when the time comes, you can take more time off. Ease into retirement gradually. Besides, it's time to move into the twenty-first century. It's what I'm trained for."

Big John perused his niece with narrowed eyes. "Sounds like you and Millie have it all worked out."

"You deserve a vacation." Beth smiled hopefully.

Big John rocked back in his chair. "So, you want to learn the family business, do you?"

Beth nodded.

Big John smiled again. "Well, I think this calls for a celebration! I'm calling Millie and we're all going out for lunch!" He turned to Blue. "What do you say?"

Blue blinked. "Um, I think this sounds like a family deal. I wouldn't want to intrude."

"Nonsense!" Big John bellowed. "It'll give me time to interrogate you, and with Beth there you won't be able to pull the wool over my eyes." He winked.

"Right…" Blue looked at his toes.

"I'll fill him in," Beth said with a slight smirk.

Blue jerked his head up. "But -"

"Sounds like a plan. Now back to work and we'll meet at lunch time," Big John said in no uncertain terms.

Blue gave Beth one last questioning stare and then left the office. Once she told Big John the truth, he'd be the one looking for a new job.

"WE NEED TO TALK." Beth's voice came from the other side of the shelving unit in the storage compound.

Blue closed his eyes momentarily and then opened them

again, steeling himself for the onslaught of verbal abuse he knew was coming. Served him right for thinking he could work for Big John and not run into Beth. Now, if she started working for her uncle as well, it would be impossible. He should just hand in his resignation and find another job.

Beth appeared around the end of the unit and stood waiting, arms crossed.

Blue stood his ground. "If you want me to quit, I will," he said. "Just don't spoil my chances of getting a good reference."

"Is that what you think I'm doing? Moving back here just to make your life miserable?"

"Well, aren't you?"

Beth shook her head and let out a small laugh. "You give yourself way too much credit. I couldn't care less if you stay or go."

"Is that so?"

"Yes, it is. Although…" She took a step closer. "I was thinking that I could use you to my advantage."

"Why does the sound of that scare me?" Blue asked.

"If Uncle John thinks we're a couple, then he'll quit trying to set me up with every random man under thirty-five that he knows. It'll keep him and Aunt Millie out of my hair and give me an excuse when I don't feel like visiting. You know, because I'm out with my boyfriend."

"What if I don't play along?" Blue asked. "Your uncle has been good to me and I won't lie to him."

"No? Then the alternative is I tell him what really happened."

"So be it. If he fires me then he fires me. At least I'll have a clear conscience."

Beth laughed. "Oh, you might get more than that, especially when I tell him how you forced yourself on me. Practically raped me and then left me crying with no one and nobody to turn to."

"What? That never happened!"

Her mouth turned down and her lip began to quiver. "It's why

I had to come home. I couldn't face being in Dallas after what you did to me there."

Blue closed the distance between them in a few strides. "That's a lie."

"Is it?" she asked. "It's your word against mine, and if there's one thing I know, it's that my dear Uncle John has a soft spot for his little Beth." All sadness had been replaced with a malicious grin.

Blue turned away and ran a hand through his hair. "That's just crazy and you know it. Why go to all that trouble just so you can have a little more freedom? I mean, you could always just explain to them that you need some space without getting me involved."

"What fun would that be? This way, I get to see you squirm."

"So you did move back just to make my life miserable," Blue stated.

"No, not really. I honestly didn't like Dallas all that much, but once I saw my opportunity to get you back for what you did, it seemed too good to waste."

Blue shook his head. "I won't do it. It's not right and you don't have any proof."

"It's too late. I already told him about us, so you'll have to go along with it or else."

"Or else what?"

"Oh, I don't know. Now that I'll be working for him, I'll think of something." She narrowed her eyes. "Maybe get in touch with that Cherise person and tell *her* that you're a rapist."

Blue shook his head. "You sound like a crazy person, do you know that?"

Beth shrugged. "Maybe I am."

Blue pointed his finger at her. "Listen, I'm just gonna do my job and mind my own business. You tell your uncle whatever you want if it makes you feel better, but I won't be your puppet." He started for the exit.

"Does that mean you're not coming to lunch?" Beth called.

"Exactly what it means."

Blue strode from the warehouse without looking back. Somehow he had to figure out how to tell Big John the truth without implicating himself or hurting Cherise in the process, but for now, the best course of action was to keep his head down and not cause any waves.

CHAPTER 25

*D*irk loitered just outside the main doors to the prayer room where the new recruits had gathered for their assignments. James had just finished praying and had turned the meeting over to Jessica, the cute administrative assistant. Dirk noticed a couple of stragglers that needed to head to the main office to fill out their task forms and smiled. Seems he wasn't the only one.

He hadn't bothered asking James to be assigned to the orientation group. It was easier to ask for forgiveness than permission. Besides, this way he could come and go as he pleased. As far as his crew boss knew, he was off for the entire day picking his sister up at the airport. It was all working out perfectly.

He tagged along with the group for the first half hour. When they got to the macadamia nut grove, they stood just a few feet within its borders. Jessica was talking about the viable business that had been carved out here and how many of the former orphans now had jobs at the orphanage, including tending, harvesting and processing the nuts.

"How often do you ship and who are your primary clients?" Dirk asked.

Jessica focused her dark gaze on Dirk, as if seeing him in the crowd for the first time. "Hello, Mr. Hillyer. I didn't know you were joining the orientation group this morning."

Dirk smiled congenially and nodded. "I'm off to pick my sister up, but thought I'd tag along for a few minutes until then."

The explanation seemed to satisfy her and she went on to answer his question, turning to the group at large. "The Mission sells a lot of its product right here, to tourists and volunteers like yourselves. Know that every tasty treat you take home is also benefiting a poor child. We also send several shipments per year to our sister orphanage in Tijuana. We have a warehouse there and it makes it easier to send to our markets in America."

Dirk's mind clicked with this new information. Of course. He should have made the connection before. 'Beacon of Hope' had a fledgling orphanage in the Mexican border city. Maybe they were smuggling something into the states via the Tijuana home.

When Jessica was finished her spiel, Dirk slipped further into the grove and waited for the group to follow her to the next location on their tour. Then he turned and strode with purposeful steps in the direction of the storage shed. He met up with two workers on the way but simply waved at them in a friendly manner as if he knew exactly where he was headed and why.

The shed itself was cool inside and there was no one else around. As predicted, long mesh drying racks stacked up like shelves took up quite a bit of space. Along one wall, cardboard cartons of nuts were stacked in neat rows about ten feet deep and six feet high. He opened one with the box cutter he had slipped into his jean's pocket that morning. Inside were vacuum packed packages of macadamia nuts. The wrapping was opaque and each one was labeled with a generic stick on label that declared the contents along with its weight and 'Product of Mexico'. He lifted several out and dug to the bottom. Everything seemed to be in order.

He closed the carton's lid, wishing he'd thought to bring some replacement tape to reseal the carton. There wasn't much he could do about that now, so he set the open carton underneath another to keep it closed and hoped when it came time to ship it they'd blame one of the workers.

Once that was done, he scanned the rows of boxes for anything out of the ordinary. Then he noticed something. One of the boxes had a small 'x' on it, slashed quickly in the upper right corner with a grease pencil. It could mean anything. There was only one way to find out.

Dirk hoisted several boxes to the side until he could get to the one with the mark. Next, he carefully slit the packing tape and opened it. He dug around in the box as before and was about to give up when he touched a package that felt slightly different. He pulled it out and turned it over in his hands. On the outside it looked the same as the others. Brick hard and lumpy where the vacuum seal had molded the plastic to the nuts. But these didn't look like nuts. The contents were smaller - cylindrical, perfectly symmetric and somewhat rectangular. Like a pill.

He poked the bag with his cutter and immediately the package became pliable in his hands. They were indeed pills. He could only guess where they had come from or where they were going.

Now that he had evidence, the urge to get out of there was strong. There may be other packages in other boxes, but for now his only concern was stacking things up as best he could and getting as far away from the shed as possible before someone found out he'd been there.

He had just finished squaring up the stacks of boxes when he heard a vehicle approach and come to a stop outside the building. It sputtered to a halt and went silent. Probably one of the small tractors used to maintain the extensive grounds. Dirk crouched behind the stacks and waited, taking shallow breaths.

A man entered the building - one of the farm workers Dirk had passed earlier. The man had apparently come in to get some kind of tool - a long pole with a basket on one end that resembled a clawed hand. He left the shed, pole in hand, and Dirk heard the engine start up. It made a putting sound like a lawn mower which faded as he drove away.

Dirk slipped out of the shed and kept as close to the cover of the trees as he could until he was back in the courtyard. He had one more errand to run before going to the city to pick up Cherise. That was to warn Anne-Marie.

DIRK BUZZED the bell at the wicket inside the clinic's waiting room and looked around as he waited for someone to answer. The clinic was more like an all inclusive health care facility. It housed everything necessary to take care of minor health issues and was utilized by more than just the orphanage. The community at large relied on it for routine care. Overnight care was a rare occurrence, however, since anyone needing serious medical attention was sent to Ensenada. It also housed a small pharmacy which was attached to the reception room. Patients could wait outside the wicket, and one of the nurses on staff would dispense the drugs, with the doctor's signature of course, if he was unable to do so himself. Dirk had learned all of this from Anne-Marie. Now he could see that the system had definite flaws. Someone was using the clinic to smuggle drugs.

Francesca, one of the other nurses, came to the window. "Yes?" she asked in accented English.

"I'm looking for Anne-Marie," Dirk said.

Francesca gave Dirk an icy glare, but left the window. In a moment Anne-Marie was on the other side. "What are you doing here?" She looked nervously over her shoulder and then back at Dirk.

"I don't need to come inside," Dirk said through the window. "I just need to talk to you for a sec. Can you come around?"

She nodded, and within seconds she emerged through the double doors. "What's up?" Her perfect brow was wrinkled in worry as she surveyed Dirk's nervous stance. He had his hands in his pockets and he was tapping one foot subconsciously.

Dirk glanced at the other occupants of the waiting area. There was one woman, probably in her twenties, with a small child sitting listlessly on her lap. "Can we step outside for a moment? It won't take long because I have to get to the city."

Anne-Marie led the way through the glass doors onto the cement step. "You found something?" she asked.

Dirk nodded his assent and watched as her face changed to a mask of preparedness. She was good at that. Schooling her features in preparation for the worst. Probably something she had to do when dealing with patients.

"I just don't want to alarm you too much, but..."

"What did you find?" she asked point blank.

He placed one of the pills in her palm. "A whole bag full."

"Where?" she demanded, looking up from her palm to search his eyes.

"In the shed. Vacuum packed with the nuts. There may be more but I had to get out of there. One of the workers came and almost found me."

"And where are the rest?" she asked.

"Somewhere safe."

"Dirk!" she protested in exasperation. "You need to go to someone. James. The police. Someone."

"James hardly seems like the best person to approach at the moment," Dirk said dryly.

"The police, then! Someone!"

"Sh!" Dirk looked around, hoping Anne-Marie wasn't drawing too much attention. He turned back to her and placed his hands on her shoulders, looking deep into her eyes. "Trust me, okay? Until we know more, this is our little secret. In the meantime, would you do me a favor?" He took one of her hands in his and rubbed the backs of her knuckles with his thumb.

She nodded mutely.

"I want you to keep your eyes and ears open for anything suspicious. If someone is involved in smuggling prescription drugs, the likeliest source is the clinic. An unusually large prescription, certain drugs missing off the shelves, things like that. Oh, and see if you can identify that pill."

"That could be hard to do." She looked down at the pill resting in her palm. "I'll have to use the lab when no one is around."

"Just do your best."

"This means someone inside the clinic is in on it." Anne-Marie's lips had a pinched quality, like she was trying really hard not to cry.

Dirk rubbed his chin. "I never did trust that Dr. Smythe. Too smooth."

A tiny smile replaced the apprehension on Anne-Marie's face. "You're just jealous cause you think he likes me."

"I know I'm jealous," Dirk grinned. "And now I better let you get back to work and I better go before my sister thinks I abandoned her."

"Be careful," Anne-Marie whispered as she let go of his hand.

Dirk smiled and nodded. The care in her eyes was enough to make him think all of this was worth it, no matter the outcome.

CHAPTER 26

*C*herise rushed through the glass entrance to the baggage area as quickly as her slip on heels would allow - and straight into Dirk's arms. She couldn't believe how good it was to see him again. He looked pleased to see her, too, if the grin on his face was any indication.

"Just look at you!" Cherise held Dirk at arm's length after a prolonged hug. "You look like a surfer, all tanned with your hair long and streaked!"

"And I didn't have to go to a salon for either." Dirk looked her up and down. "You look good yourself. Not the haggard wreck I was expecting."

She glanced down at her attire - fashionable capris and a T shirt in the season's latest color - and then punched him in the arm. "You're horrible."

"Well, the way you sounded on the phone I thought you'd let yourself go completely."

"I'm determined to make a change in my life once and for all. That's what this is all about. A journey of discovery." She smiled, trying to convince herself of the declaration.

"Are you going to tell me about it or do I have to wait for your first melt down?" Dirk asked with an amused smirk.

"You are terrible! I'm suffering from a broken heart - for real this time," she added emphatically before continuing, "and all you can do is make fun of me."

"Anybody I know?"

"You've met him," Cherise hedged, "but that's all you'll get. Suffice to say that I have officially sworn off men indefinitely." She adjusted the large tote bag that was slung over one shoulder, clutching it with two hands to distribute the weight.

"Famous last words," Dirk said with a laugh.

"I mean it." Did she, she wondered? She could already feel a sense of panic rising at the thought of being alone forever. Maybe finding another male distraction would ease the pain... She shook her head to banish the thought.

"Here, let me take that for you."

Dirk reached for the tote bag, but she grasped it tighter. "You can carry my other stuff." As if on cue, one designer suitcase rounded the corner on the baggage carousel. "Oh! There's my bag." She scurried to the moving belt and pointed to the approaching large suitcase. "That one."

Dirk hoisted the bag from the track and was about to leave when Cherise exclaimed again. "Oh, and that one, too."

"How much stuff did you bring?" Dirk grunted as he pulled the second bag from the carousel.

"I tried to pack light, like you said." Cherise blinked, her blue eyes wide and innocent.

Dirk just laughed. "I'd hate to see you pack heavy."

"Anyway, I hope it's not too far to the orphanage. I can't wait to freshen up. And my tummy feels a bit upset. I didn't eat much on the way, but I feel as if I have a cramp or something."

"Hope you didn't drink anything but bottled water."

"Of course not." Cherise flipped her hair.

"And as far as freshening up, I hate to say I warned you. The utilities aren't five star, you know."

"I know." Cherise sighed. "I just want to get settled. Start focusing on something besides myself for a change."

"Now, that is a switch."

Cherise gave him another punch in the arm which he absorbed with an 'Oomph.'

They emerged from the airport building into the blazing sunlight, and Cherise shaded her eyes with her hand. "It wasn't this hot in LA when I left, yet here the sun is blazing. I didn't expect such a difference. Now Boston, on the other hand…"

Dirk stopped and let the unwieldy suitcases rest. "Los Angeles? I didn't know you were taking a connecting flight through L.A."

"Oh, I didn't. I stopped to visit Tempest. She says, 'Hello,' by the way."

"Oh. Well, hello back. Does that mean she's forgiven me?"

Cherise cocked her head to one side. "Mostly, I think."

"Hm." Dirk nodded before proceeding forward to his vehicle with the suitcases.

"But I take it that doesn't matter as much anymore," Cherise said, raising a brow.

"Of course it matters. Tempest is a friend."

"I thought you were over her. That you've found a new love interest."

"I have," Dirk replied. "But that doesn't mean I don't care what Tempest thinks of me."

"She's trying, I'll give you that," Cherise said. They'd reached his vehicle. "Now, tell me all about your new lady love!"

"We've only got an hour," Dirk said with a grin. He hoisted the suitcases into the back and slammed the endgate shut.

"That special?" Cherise asked.

"I think so."

"Oh good! Just the distraction I need!"

"She's more than a distraction, Cherise. If I have my way, she'll be part of the family and I won't let you spoil that."

Cherise raised her brows coyly. "Afraid I'll tell her about the real you?"

"She's a genuinely caring person and I don't want you scaring her with your stories."

"Don't worry, brother. Your secrets are safe with me."

"That's just it. I don't want any secrets, but your spin might not be as... flattering as mine."

"Promise." Cherise made a zipping gesture over her lips before climbing into the passenger's side.

Keeping Dirk's secrets would be easy enough. Keeping her own errant emotions in check would be a different matter all together.

DIRK WASN'T AS forthcoming about the mysterious Anne-Marie as Cherise would have liked, but she was good at reading between the lines. She had never witnessed her brother in such a state of agitation. At least not over a woman. It had to be love.

In fact, she'd hardly recognized him when he came to pick her up at the airport. It was much more than the long hair, deep tan, and Bermuda shorts. She'd never seen him without his suave persona firmly in place before. But apparently, in a little foreign orphanage, he seemed to have let his guard down. He wasn't the confident playboy she remembered - the one always ready to gain attention by showing off. When he mentioned Anne-Marie he acted downright giddy. She just hoped he wouldn't get hurt.

They managed to pass the drive with small talk about home. The scenery on the way consisted of sand, sagebrush, and cactus interrupted by fields of vegetables - obviously irrigated in the dry climate - and glimpses of the Pacific Ocean out the passenger window. They passed through a gate at the entrance to the orphanage and Dirk parked his vehicle in a parking lot near some buildings.

"We'll leave your suitcases in here for the time being," Dirk said. "I have someone I want you to meet first."

"Okay." Cherise linked her arm through Dirk's as they rounded the vehicle. "Bet I can guess who that might be. Imagine! My big brother has finally fallen in love. For realsies!" She squeezed his arm. "I can hardly wait to meet her." She looked around. "Where are we going?"

"The clinic. She's still at work, but this way you two can meet before church tonight."

They walked arm in arm across the courtyard and past the administrative building.

"About that," Cherise said hesitantly. "Does everyone have to go to church every evening?"

"No. But it's part of what people do here. It is a Christian mission, after all." He looked at her pointedly. "Don't say I didn't warn you."

Cherise shook her head. "I still can't quite wrap my head around it. You getting so into religion."

Dirk rubbed the back of his neck. "It's not like that exactly."

"Whatever." Cherise shrugged. "I respect other people's beliefs."

"You sure?" Dirk asked with a grin.

"Of course. Just ask Tempest. But let's talk about something else. Do you think Anne-Marie will like me?"

"She likes most people," Dirk said. "She's very warm and kind. I told you that already."

Misgivings fluttered in Cherise's stomach. What if the saintly Anne-Marie found her shallow and lacking?

Once inside the clinic, Dirk went straight to a little wicket and rang the buzzer. A small, dark skinned nurse came to the window.

"Hi, Franchesca. Is Anne-Marie handy?" Dirk asked.

TRACY KRAUSS

"She might be busy," the Mexican woman said in stilted English. "Wait here and I'll call her." They watched her disappear from the window.

"We should have asked if you could see a doctor, too," Dirk said, sliding his hands into his pockets. "How's your stomach?"

Cherise waved a dismissive hand. "It's nothing to bother a doctor with."

Franchesca came back. "Wait at the nurses' station," she said and buzzed them into the hospital proper.

Once through the large double doors, Dirk headed for the nearby nurses' station with Cherise trailing behind. It was unoccupied.

"Hello."

Cherise swung around to see a good looking man - presumably a doctor, judging by the lab coat - standing behind them.

"May I help you?" he asked.

Cherise took in his Australian accent and tanned features.

"Doctor Smythe," Dirk greeted formally. "We're just here to see Anne-Marie." His tone wasn't the most friendly, Cherise noticed, and she glanced at her brother's sour expression. If she wasn't mistaken, he had his hackles up.

"Is this visit of a medical nature?" Dr. Smythe asked, his tone just as cool.

"Actually, I was feeling some stomach discomfort," Cherise piped up. She gave the good doctor her most winning smile. "I just arrived. Cherise Hillyer, Dirk's sister." She offered her hand and batted her lashes for good measure.

"Your sister?" Dr. Smythe's eyebrows rose as he turned to Dirk. He shifted his attention back to Cherise. "Something you ate, perhaps?"

"I really have no idea, doctor."

"Come into one of the exam rooms and you can tell me all about it." He glanced at Dirk. "Why don't you go fill out the necessary paperwork, hm? I'm sure Nurse Fletcher will be back soon."

Cherise let Dirk's arm go and followed Dr. Smythe. She looked back and waved over her shoulder at Dirk before disappearing into the exam room.

She told herself she was rescuing Dirk from a rival, and it was mostly true. Even though she'd sworn off men, could she help it if men had not sworn off her?

"TAKE A DEEP BREATH."

Cherise obeyed, inhaling slowly as the doctor moved the stethoscope to another location on her chest. His hand had disappeared beneath her T shirt. The instrument was cold to the touch and certain parts of her anatomy had responded reflexively. She surveyed the handsome doctor to see if he had noticed, but his face was a blank. Totally professional.

"In... then out..."

Cherise closed her eyes and tried to relax. Dr. Smythe was handsome, no doubt about that. As if his dark hair and tanned features weren't enough, his Australian accent lent him that extra charm that would have any woman falling over herself to gain his attention. She was in the perfect position to flirt. Too bad she couldn't think of anything provocative to say. She must be losing her touch.

"Your vitals seem fine." Dr. Smythe slung the stethoscope around his neck and sat back on the rolling stool. "It's not uncommon for visitors to feel some stomach sickness. Did you drink anything other than bottled water? Eat any fresh vegetables?"

Cherise shook her head. "I know not to do that. It's probably just nerves."

Dr. Smythe nodded. "Okay. I can give you something to settle things down, like an antacid."

"Thanks doctor. I appreciate it."

"You can call me Harry." He flashed his perfectly straight white teeth. "I imagine we'll run into one another again, so we might as well cut the formality."

Cherise raised a delicate brow. "Okay, Harry. And you can call me Cherise."

"Alright. So what brings you here - Cherise?" He stood up and crossed to a desk to find a small pad of paper on which he scribbled a prescription.

She sighed dramatically. "Trying to find myself? Do something worthwhile for a change? It seems to be working for my brother, so why not me, too?"

Dr. Smythe gave a small laugh. "Ah yes. Your brother." Cherise's eyebrows rose, but the doctor continued smoothly. "Whatever it is you're looking for, I hope you find it." He made full eye contact. "Maybe I can help."

Maybe he wasn't oblivious to her charms after all. Not that she'd been trying. "Thanks. I'd like that." Maybe a fling in a foreign country with a sexy foreign doctor would help her get out of the emotional funk she currently found herself in.

Stop it! She blinked and schooled her mouth into a pleasant smile for the doctor.

"So? Anything else I can get for you?"

"I love your accent. Say 'so' again. It's very cute!"

Dr. Smythe smiled. "No, I don't want to."

"There! You said 'no'! Just as good." Cherise giggled.

Someone cleared his throat. Cherise jerked her head around to see Dirk standing in the doorway. A sudden flush of shame suffused her cheeks but she warded it off with practiced bravado by tilting her chin. "Don't you just love Harry's accent, Dirk?"

"Yeah. Great." He didn't sound enthused. "You about done here?"

"I think so." Dr. Smythe handed Cherise the slip of paper and then took her other hand and helped her down from the exam table. "Nurse Franchesca can get it for you at the front counter. It's not really a prescription, just an over the counter remedy."

"Thank you so much. Hopefully we'll run into one another again."

"I'm sure we will."

Cherise threw the doctor one last winning smile and sauntered to where Dirk loitered by the door. "No sign of Anne-Marie yet?"

"She's with a patient." Dirk frowned as he placed his hand against the small of her back and maneuvered her out into the hall. "What do you think you're doing?" he whispered.

"What do you mean?" Cherise blinked, her eyes wide with faux innocence.

"You know. Flirting with him."

"Why shouldn't I?" Cherise asked. "He's cute. Besides, I like his accent."

Dirk rolled his eyes. "I thought you were coming here to get away from all that. I thought you wanted to turn over a new leaf."

"I have. I'm here, aren't I?"

"Doing exactly what you always do. Throwing yourself at the next available man."

"Is that what I'm doing?" Cherise tilted her chin. Was it? It's why she had warned Blue off. Tears sprang to her eyes and she blinked. "Maybe I can't change who I am, so I might as well just go with it."

"Hey." Dirk put his arm around her shoulders. "You're really hurting this time, aren't you?"

For some reason his sympathy rankled, and she shrugged off his embrace. "Since when did you become such a good judge of human character? Or is this part of the conversion experience? You can read minds now, too?"

"What -"

"Maybe God whispered in your ear," she threw at him.

"Now you're mocking me," Dirk said.

"No, I'm not. Just quit trying to help me." She hugged herself and turned away from his penetrating gaze. Dirk of all people knew her best. Knew she was hopeless.

"I thought you wanted help."

"There's no point."

"That's not true."

He touched her shoulder but she shrugged him off again. "I don't want to talk about it."

"Cherise…"

"Maybe I'm just destined for shallow relationships, okay?" She glanced at Dirk and found more understanding than she could handle, so looked down again. "That's all I'm good for."

"That's not true."

"No? Then why was I flirting with another man when all I really want is -" Her voice hitched.

"Blue Shepherd?"

Cherise turned wide eyes to her brother. "How did you know?"

"It's not rocket science," Dirk said. "What happened? Did he dump you?"

Cherise frowned and then punched Dirk in the arm.

"Ow!" Dirk held his arm with the other hand. "Well?"

"No, I dumped him, but it's for the best. He's history like all the rest. Like Roberto and Jean Yvres and every other man I've ever loved. I'm a screw up, okay? Incapable of fidelity, so just leave me alone." She pressed her palms into her eye sockets to stop the flow of tears.

"Stop fighting me," Dirk said and enfolded her in his arms. This time she let him. "You're being too hard on yourself."

Cherise took a deep breath, willing the offending tears away, and rested her head on Dirk's shoulder.

"There's someone out there for you," Dirk soothed. "You just have to be patient. Maybe don't try so hard."

"I don't think I want just someone."

"Um... hi."

Dirk released Cherise and they both swung around to meet the newcomer.

"Anne-Marie," Dirk said.

Whatever Cherise was expecting, it wasn't the pretty woman in nurse's scrubs that stood just feet away. She was about five foot three and quite curvaceous; not plump but certainly not a willowy model. Her face could best be described as cute, with big eyes, a pixy mouth and dark hair which was neatly secured in a bun at the back of her head. She was everything that Dirk's usual type was not, which is probably why he was so attracted to her. But there was a look of uncertainty in her eyes, too, like she wasn't quite sure what to make of the situation before her.

"I'm Dirk's sister, Cherise." She reached forward with an outstretched hand.

Instantly, Anne-Marie's countenance changed and she rushed to grasp Cherise's offer of friendship. "It's so wonderful to actually meet you. You're just as gorgeous as Dirk said."

Cherise raised a skeptical brow. "He said that?" She snorted in his general direction.

"I know you're still working, but I couldn't wait until church tonight to introduce you."

"I'm glad you did."

"And," Dirk went on, "Cherise has a prescription from the doctor. Maybe you could fill it for her." A look passed between them - an unspoken message reserved for that special someone.

If only she could guarantee her commitment to Blue, like Dirk apparently had done to Anne-Marie. Maybe things could be different then.

Cherise blinked back to reality. Who was she trying to kid? She was Cherise Hillyer - privileged, rich, attractive - and fatally flawed.

CHAPTER 27

*B*lue scowled at the cellphone screen, his thumb hovering over 'send'. With an oath, he hit delete instead and pocketed the device. He'd been trying to reach Cherise for days now. The string of unanswered texts made him look pathetic. Maybe he was, but that was about to change. He'd made his last attempt at contacting her. It was time to move on.

Looking down, he rounded a set of warehouse shelves and skidded to a stop.

"Heads up!" Big John hollered. "You almost knocked me over."

"Oops. Sorry, Boss."

Big John chuckled. "Never mind. You're the one who would have been on his arse, I suspect. Anyway, I was looking for you. Millie wants you and Beth to come over for dinner tonight. Says she's hardly seen Beth since she came back to town, thanks to you."

"You see her at work every day," Blue said.

"Sure, but Millie doesn't. Be there by six-thirty."

Apparently the conversation was finished since Big John strode away without waiting for an answer. Blue sighed and kept walking in the other direction. He'd been lucky enough to avoid

Beth the entire week since she'd been back in Fort Stockton, but he knew it was only a matter of time. That time was now, it seemed.

Blue rapped on the casement leading into Beth's office. Office was stretching it, since it was little more than a closet converted into a work space with a small desk.

"I see you got the invitation," Beth said without looking up.

"About that." Blue leaned against the door casing, staying just outside the room. "I'm gonna tell your Uncle the truth this afternoon. I won't lie to him."

"I told you that wasn't a good idea."

"You can't threaten me," Blue countered. "For one thing, you can't prove anything. For another, I don't care, so it would be pointless. I'd rather lose my job than lie."

"Exactly what I thought you might say." Beth finally looked up, her mouth tilted in a malicious smile. "Maybe you don't care about your own reputation, but what about…" She scanned her phone. "Cherise Hillyer, is it? Pretty posh, by the looks of it."

"How…? Just what are you planning?" Blue stepped into the room proper.

"It was easy to find her. People are so careless about what they post on social media."

"You leave Cherise alone."

The smile had disappeared from Beth's lips. "Cherise is just the start. If you don't play along, I'll involve your whole family. Your brother, your sister-in-law. Everyone you're connected to."

"What makes you think you can fabricate something so terrible that it will affect my whole family? People don't believe half of what they see on social media."

Beth laughed. "You forget who you're talking to. It's not just about social media. I can hack into just about anything."

Blue narrowed his eyes. "You'd risk committing a felony - just to get back at me for dumping you?"

"It was the other way around. I dumped you."

"A technicality."

Beth's eyes flashed daggers. "Watch it, cowboy. You messed with the wrong girl."

"Either way, revenge is juvenile. Let's be adults and move on." A notification dinged on Blue's phone and he glanced down but didn't bother opening it.

"Aren't you going to check that?" Beth asked.

"Just a message from my sister-in-law. I'll check later."

"I'd open it now if I were you."

Blue shrugged, but touched the screen to open the message. "WHAT'S WRONG WITH YOU?" it said in all caps. Blue frowned.

"Maybe you should check to see what you just sent her," Beth suggested.

Blue glanced up at Beth, noting the smug expression on her face. Then he scrolled backward in the conversation that he had supposedly had with Stella. When he clicked on his own outgoing message, seductive music blared to the flash of a couple in the act of having sex, followed by the words, "Wanna?"

"What? I never sent that!" Blue bellowed.

"Of course you did," Beth said.

"You hacked my account?"

Beth just shrugged. "These things happen all the time. Pretty annoying, I'd say."

"You… I'll report you!"

Beth rolled her eyes. "To who? The police don't have time for such petty crimes. Besides, you and your sister-in-law had a thing at one time, didn't you?"

"How did you…?" Blue stopped before he admitted anything he couldn't take back. "You don't know anything. And you won't get away with this." Blue scrolled through his security settings. "As soon as I delete that image I'm calling Stella to explain."

"It's already gone," Beth said. "So, good luck in finding any evidence if you do decide to squeal."

"What are you going to gain from all this?"

"I haven't actually decided yet, but the opportunities could be endless."

"You're demented."

"Watch it. You wouldn't want that nasty message going to your brother by mistake."

Blue clamped his mouth into a straight line, refusing to respond to Beth's bait. Instead he sent a quick reply to Stella telling her he'd been hacked and then finished deleting his account all together. When he was done he looked up. "Gone. I'll go offline altogether if I have to."

"As if that'll do any good. Fake accounts are super easy to create."

"And you know enough about me to make sure it looks legit."

"You might as well just give in. I have you over a barrel." Beth smiled in an unpleasant way. "Well, not in the way that couple were demonstrating, but you know what I mean."

Blue sighed. "So what do you want from me, exactly?"

"Just be a good boyfriend whenever I need you. Like a buffer between my aunt and uncle and me. Otherwise, stay clear."

"That's it?"

"Maybe a nice gift now and again would be good."

"I should have known!" Blue threw up his hands.

"Nothing too expensive, since my uncle doesn't pay you very well, but enough to make it look convincing."

"Anything else?"

"Dinner tonight."

Blue sighed again and ran a hand through his hair. "And if I agree, you promise not to hack any of my accounts again? You won't bother any of my family - or friends?"

"You hold up your end and I'll hold up mine."

"How do I know I can trust you?" Blue asked.

"I guess that's part of the fun."

Blue shook his head. "I can't believe I'm agreeing to this."

"Agreeing to what?"

Blue swivelled to see Big John standing on the other side of the small doorway.

"Blue just doesn't want you and Aunt Millie to put too much pressure on us," Beth said. "He's got commitment issues, I think." She giggled.

Big John clapped one of his huge paws on Blue's shoulder. "Never fear, young man. Commitment is just a scary word folks use to ward off true love."

Blue swallowed. "Beth and I, we... we want to take things slow."

"I know that's the fashion these days, but when you find the right one, why wait?" Big John asked. "That's my opinion, anyway. Tying the knot with Millie was the best decision I ever made."

Blue's eyes widened. "We're a long way from that, Sir. I can assure you."

"Now you're scaring him," Beth said as she rounded her desk and stood by Blue's side. She took his hand. "But who knows? Surprises can take place at any moment. Isn't that right?"

Blue just nodded. It was the first true statement she'd uttered.

 irk stood and stretched his back. It had been difficult to concentrate on the evening service, not just because Anne-Marie was sitting beside him - she was always a distraction - but because of the other suspicions that weighed heavily on his mind. He glanced over at his sister and wondered how she had faired during her first taste of church. He'd like to talk to her about it but then wasn't quite sure what he would say, exactly. She didn't look as frightened or confused as he might have expected, but then she was flirting with Dr. Smythe again. Maybe she was beyond help when it came to men.

He frowned and banished that thought. If he believed he could change, then he had to believe anyone could - even Cherise.

"Let's go," Dirk whispered in Anne-Marie's ear. "It's stuffy in here."

"But what about Cherise?" Anne-Marie asked. "Don't you think we should wait for her? It is her first night."

Dirk held in an impatient sigh that wanted to escape. "Of course." He cleared his throat and spoke a bit louder. "You coming Cherise? You must be tired."

Cherise looked over with a ready smile. "Harry was just telling me how he came to the orphanage."

"I won't keep you," Dr. Smythe said. "I imagine you two will be going for your nightly stroll?" he directed at Dirk and Anne-Marie. His voice held just a hint of condescension.

"You're welcome to join us," Anne-Marie offered.

Dirk scowled but kept his mouth shut.

The group made their way to the great outdoors and he was glad for the intake of fresh air once he'd made it past the exit. As usual, the night sky twinkled with stars and the freshness of the air held a belying crispness despite its tropical location. He squeezed Anne-Marie's hand until he noticed her wince and immediately let it drop.

"Count me out," Cherise said. The smile she flashed Dirk told him plainly she understood his need for some alone time with Anne-Marie. "It's been a long day and I'm told that hard work is coming my way tomorrow." She turned to Dr. Smythe. "Perhaps the good doctor can walk me to my dorm?"

"My pleasure." Dr. Smythe extended his elbow and Cherise slipped her arm through.

Dirk's scowl deepened as he watched the two of them saunter away.

"If you frown any deeper it'll freeze your face."

"Hm?" Dirk jerked his gaze away from his retreating sister and her companion and looked at Anne-Marie.

"At least that's what my mom used to say." She smiled and used her finger to smooth out the furrow in his brow.

He relaxed, letting out a pent up breath. "I don't trust either one of them."

Anne-Marie arched a brow. "That seems like a funny thing to say about your sister."

"I told you, Cherise has... men issues."

"How about trusting God for a change?" Anne-Marie linked

her arm through Dirk's and they started to walk slowly along the perimeter of the courtyard.

"Easier said than done," Dirk admitted with a slight laugh.

"So I noticed." Anne-Marie glanced at Dirk before her eyes darted down to the ground. "Actually, I've been meaning to ask you something and maybe now is as good a time as any."

Dirk felt Anne-Marie's hand slipping from the crook of his arm so he placed his other hand over it, keeping her attached to him. "Okay, but I've already told you my deepest secret, so I can't imagine what else you think you need to know."

"It's just that, the whole topic of trusting God makes me wonder." She gazed into his eyes, blinking only once. "Maybe we should sit down."

"Okay." Bewildered, Dirk followed her lead to the nearest bench and they sat.

"Did you like the sermon tonight?" Anne-Marie asked.

"Um, yeah. It was good." Dirk tried to remember what it was about. He'd been so preoccupied that he hadn't really paid attention.

Anne-Marie took a deep breath and removed her hand from its position inside the crook of his arm. Immediately Dirk felt the coldness of it.

She linked her hands together in her lap. "Sometimes I wonder. Have you really accepted Jesus as your Savior? Because the Bible warns about being 'unequally yoked', and -"

Sudden panic gripped Dirk's chest. "Of course! Don't be silly. I'm just a bit off with this whole smuggling pills thing and then my sister showing up out of the blue. I know I need to trust God more, but you know what they say. God helps those that help themselves."

Anne-Marie's troubled expression melted a bit and she giggled. "That's not actually in the Bible. You know that, right?"

"Of course." He smiled back. "Now, speaking of pills, I got the feeling you wanted to talk to me about that earlier. Is that why you were late for the service? Did you find something?"

Anne-Marie nodded her head. "Nothing conclusive. I went through some of the medical requisitions to see if the amount ordered matched the amount dispensed or still in stock."

"And?"

"Like I said, it's not conclusive. I'd need to spend more time and check all the records first."

"But?"

"There definitely seems to be a lot more medicine going through the clinic than I would have expected."

Dirk slammed his fist into his thigh. "I knew it. And I let that slime ball flirt with my sister."

"You don't know for sure who's doing it. Harry could be innocent."

"Who else, then?" Dirk asked.

"Other doctors from Ensenada rotate in and out, especially on weekends."

"And there are the other nurses," Dirk offered.

Anne-Marie blinked, her eyes wide. "I just can't believe that about any of my colleagues."

"Of course, you can't. Always the trusting optimist."

"I know these people. I work with them every day!"

"Stick to the list," Dirk advised. "Everyone is a suspect until we prove otherwise."

"Whatever happened to innocent until proven guilty?" Anne-Marie asked.

"We don't have that luxury."

Anne-Marie sighed. "Well, then, there's the lab techs and the cleaning staff. Or it could be a patient."

"How would that work?" Dirk asked. "No, I think it's an inside job. Who does the ordering?"

"It goes through the main office," Anne-Marie supplied.

"So, someone in admin is probably in on the scam, too." Dirk let his jaw work while he digested this information. "James *has* been acting suspiciously."

"You don't know that!" Anne-Marie defended once again.

"Is there any way we could get in there tonight without anyone knowing? It would be the perfect time to do a thorough search."

"I suppose. We'd have to be careful. We could be in a lot of trouble if we get caught."

"We could already be in a lot of trouble. There's no point waiting for whoever is doing the smuggling to catch on that we know."

And Dirk knew exactly who his main suspect was.

THE EMERGENCY LIGHTS were the only ones on as Anne-Marie and Dirk entered the building. She'd had to punch in her security code so that the alarm wouldn't go off, a fact that meant their visit could be traced. Still, it was the only viable option.

The large inner doors whooshed as Anne-Marie opened them once they'd made it inside. There were no overnight patients at present, and the echoing of their footsteps was an eerie sound that sent shivers down his spine.

"This way," Anne-Marie whispered as she led Dirk around the first corner to their left. She unlocked a door and they stepped into the small room with the wicket that opened into the waiting area. It was closed now, and locked from the inside. The room was little more than a closet, with a narrow counter and a filing cabinet. Along the wall, opposite to the window, was a shelf lined with over the counter medications. It had glass doors, also locked for the night.

Anne-Marie unlocked another door in the back corner and swung the door wide. There was no emergency lighting in this room, so she flipped the light switch. Fluorescent brilliance flooded the space.

"Do you think that's smart?" Dirk asked, his voice barely above a whisper.

"There are no windows," Anne-Marie said. "This is the pharmacy and they didn't want easy access for a break in."

Dirk nodded his understanding. "Maybe we should at least close the door."

Anne-Marie grasped the doorknob and shut the door noiselessly, applying gentle pressure with her other hand.

"Now what?" Dirk asked.

"We keep records of all medicines dispensed over here on this clipboard."

"That seems a bit archaic."

"They also get entered on the computer. It's a backup, just in case, and also saves time if we can't get to entering it right away or if the server is down." Anne-Marie smiled impishly. "That happens out here in the boondocks on occasion."

Dirk glanced around the room, noting the rows of shelves like in a library. There was a fridge in one corner and a counter for dispensing as well as a computer station. He turned back to Anne-Marie. "It's cozy in here. Private, too." He leaned in for a kiss but Anne-Marie batted him away.

"Focus! We're here for a reason, remember?"

Dirk gave his head a shake. "Of course. So? What are we looking for?"

Anne-Marie picked up a clipboard and seated herself at the computer station. "I only had time to look over a few files. But there are definitely a lot more drugs coming into this place than are accounted for. The written records do not match the files on the computer."

"Maybe someone just forgot to enter the information on the clipboard," Dirk suggested.

"Human error is possible, but even then, there are more drugs coming in than is normal for a clinic of this size."

"Okay, so let's focus on gathering some evidence."

Anne-Marie held up a USB memory stick. "Exactly why I brought this along." She inserted the device into the side of the computer and started searching for any orders that looked particularly incriminating. "Once I download a few of these, we'll have to check the shelves and make a comparison. We should probably scan some of these written records as well."

"You say the main admin office does the ordering?" Dirk asked.

"All the staff take note of supplies as they are used, but yes. Doctors also have the authority to do so."

"So it could be Dr. Smythe," Dirk noted.

"Innocent until proven guilty," Anne-Marie reminded.

"I'd say it's probably more than one person. James and Harry could be working together." Dirk rubbed his chin. A sandpaper of stubble had formed since he'd shaved that morning.

Anne-Marie squinted at the monitor. "This is worse than I thought."

Dirk peered over her shoulder. "It's funny nobody noticed it sooner."

"Why would anyone notice?" Anne-Marie turned to look at him. "No one goes back to check the files once an item has been listed. You'd have to be looking for it in the first place." She slumped in her chair. "I just can't believe James would be in on something like this. I trusted him. We all did. He's supposed to be a Christian!"

Dirk shrugged his shoulders. "Don't take it too hard. Some people are good at acting."

"Like you?" she asked.

Dirk frowned. "Where did that come from?"

Anne-Marie shook her head. "Never mind."

"If James is the culprit, how are we going to prove it?"

"We've got all the evidence we need right here." Anne-Marie gestured to the computer.

"If he gets wind that we're investigating, he'll change things. We need to figure out a way to catch him in the act."

"That's a job for the police," Anne-Marie said.

"Ever heard of police corruption? They might be in on it."

"Really? But -"

"Think about it. James obviously isn't doing this alone. There could be all kinds of players here, and I'm not trusting anyone until I know for sure."

"Like your friend Dillan," Anne-Marie suggested.

Dirk snorted. "Hardly my friend, but yes. Dillan is definitely a suspect after what I saw the other night. But there has to be more than just him. Security guards, laborers... Someone is helping him not only get the drugs, but package, transport, and probably smuggle them across the border as well."

"But why? Why would he do this?" Anne-Marie cried.

"Money, obviously."

Anne-Marie put her hand to her forehead. "This is so horrible. I think I might be sick." She squeezed her eyes shut.

Dirk rubbed her back with the flat of his palm. "Don't worry. We'll figure something out."

"I'm worried about what it might mean for the kids." Anne-Marie turned soulful eyes on him. "This place does so much good. If and when this scandal comes out, it could shut the place down."

Dirk blinked. He hadn't really thought about that. He let out a sigh and dropped his hand to his side. "Then we have to make sure we do things right. Only those involved get punished, not the kids, too."

"I just wish I could go to bed and forget any of this ever happened." She expelled a heavy breath.

"What about all your talk about trusting God?"

"You're right of course. We should get going, though. It's getting late."

"One more thing to do, remember? You said you wanted to photocopy some of the written records."

Anne-Marie sighed again, a weary sound.

"Or we could wait and you could try to do it tomorrow," he suggested.

"No, we're better off doing it now." She brushed past him toward the door, clipboard in hand.

As soon as she opened the door they heard a noise. It sounded like footsteps followed by the whoosh of the double doors. Anne-Marie switched off the light and put her index finger to her lips. They waited in silence as the footsteps sounded in the outer waiting area followed by the clack of the outside doors.

"Who do you suppose it was?" Dirk whispered.

"I don't know, but I've got thirty seconds to make sure they didn't set the alarm on us." Anne-Marie dashed through the wicket room, past the double doors and to the outside entrance, Dirk close on her heels.

He waited as she punched in her code before expelling a pent up gust of air.

"That was close," she said.

"Who was it?" Dirk asked.

"Harry. I saw him walking away as soon as I reached the panel."

"Did he see you?"

"I don't think so." Anne-Marie glanced once more out the glass door, and then took Dirk's hand and led him into the shadows.

"So... the good doctor is probably hiding something after all."

"You don't know that for sure."

"Still defending him?" Dirk raised a brow.

"I don't know who to trust any more. For all I know you could be in on it, leading me along to throw me off the trail."

Dirk frowned and surveyed her features. "You don't really think that."

She shook her head. "No."

"Good. Put that thought right out of your head. I would never do that to you." He sealed the promise with a kiss. "Now, let's go scan the rest before we have any more surprises."

CHAPTER 29

*T*oilet brush in one hand, cleaning solution in the other, Cherise stood in front of the toilet, staring down at its white porcelain bowl. "You can do this," she said out loud.

"Well, hello there. I didn't know work detail had placed you here in the clinic."

Cherise glanced through the open stall door. Anne-Marie was smiling at her from the bank of sinks on the other side of the clinic's public washroom.

"It was either janitorial or child care. I don't know the first thing about kids, so I thought it would be safer to take janitorial - for both me and the kids."

Anne-Marie laughed at Cherise's attempt at humor. "I think you're supposed to set out the sign that says the washroom is being cleaned so that people don't come in and try to use it while you're working."

"Oh right!" Cherise gestured with the brush and felt a droplet hit her in the face. "Ah!" She simultaneously dropped the brush and cleaner as if both were hot to the touch.

Immediately, Anne-Marie was by her side. "What happened? Are you hurt?"

Cherise sighed and let out a nervous laugh. "No, I'm fine. It's just… oh never mind."

"What is it? You can tell me."

"It's just… well, I've never actually cleaned a toilet before."

"Oh. Right. Dirk told me…"

Cherise glanced at the other woman. "What? That I'm a spoiled diva?"

"No, that you and your family are well off so haven't had to do those kinds of chores. I'll show you how it's done, if you like."

"That's okay. I already had a demonstration from the supervisor. It's just, I didn't think it would be this… disgusting."

Anne-Marie chuckled again. "I won't disagree. Once you get on to it, though, it won't be so bad. Pretend you're a fictional character - a secret agent on special assignment or something."

Cherise relaxed and smiled also. "Some special assignment."

"I do it all the time when I have to do a job I don't particularly enjoy. Would you believe that I used to hate giving needles? Not a good phobia for a nurse, let me tell you! But I got over it by pretending I was injecting people with a secret super-power or maybe tiny robots that would rebuild them from the inside out. In a way, medicines are like that, so it wasn't that far fetched. You should try it. Don't let the fact that you've never done it before stop you from being the best toilet cleaner on the property."

"Okay. I'll save the planet one toilet at a time."

"There you go! And now, I'll let you get back to work." Anne-Marie began to leave but then stopped and turned back to Cherise. "Make sure you set the sign out. Especially when you go to do the Men's. It could be awkward otherwise."

"Thanks." Cherise stooped to pick up the brush and cleaner.

She could see why her brother liked the other woman. Anne-Marie seemed down to earth and was easy to talk to, like she had genuine interest and respect for whoever she was talking to, not based on stereotypes or worse, rumors.

Forty minutes later, Cherise finished cleaning both public

restrooms in the clinic. With a sense of accomplishment she hadn't expected from completing such a demeaning task, she rolled the cleaning cart down the wide hallway to where she was to meet her supervisor for the next assignment.

"I see you've found gainful employment."

It was Dr. Smythe.

Cherise looked down at the plain blue uniform she wore, her first reaction to run and hide. Then she straightened her spine and smiled back at the doctor. "Yes. That's what I'm here for, although the uniforms aren't the most flattering."

"I can't agree. You look positively charming."

"Thanks," Cherise said. "You know what they say. If you don't work, you don't eat."

"I've heard that, although, I doubt that would really happen. Speaking of which, would you consider dining with me tonight in the village?"

Cherise blinked several times. Should she? "Is it allowed?"

"Of course! We aren't slaves here! There is a little pizza place very near the orphanage. I'll pick you up outside your dorm at six. We should be back in time for the service if that's a concern."

"That sounds fine."

"See you then." Dr. Smythe flashed a salute like wave and continued on his way.

Cherise watched his retreating form. What was she doing? The mixed bag of emotions she'd been feeling of late weren't settling down into anything sensible. One minute she felt like she deserved a bit of fun in the company of an interesting male. The next, she felt like the worst person on planet earth, full of self loathing for betraying the memory of Blue Shepherd, no matter how pointless that relationship had been. Maybe she should have let her fling with Blue continue on to its ultimate conclusion, even if that meant hurting him in the process. The current situation held little to no satisfaction - or promise. If she allowed a relationship to develop between her and Dr. Smythe it could only end in ruin. Just like all the rest.

It wasn't that Dr. Smythe wasn't attractive. And it wasn't that she should have expected anything different. She had been flirting with him after all, and he obviously wasn't a moron. But despite her efforts to gain his attention - misguided as that was - now that she had it, it felt empty. She'd be better off refusing his offer rather than accepting it and having to make an excuse later.

Why did she always get herself into trouble when it came to men?

"Are you lost?"

Cherise turned startled eyes toward an approaching nurse. The woman's accent along with her dark complexion and hair, indicated she was a local member of staff.

"It's alright, Franchesca," Anne-Marie said, coming up behind the other nurse. "She was just waiting for me. We're about to take our break together." Anne-Marie smiled encouragingly at Cherise.

Nurse Franchesca shrugged and continued on her way.

"Park your cart and we'll take ten," Anne-Marie said.

"We can do that? Take breaks whenever we want?"

"Well, no. But I can see you need one and I'm about to take my break, so I figured we could do it together."

"No argument from me," Cherise said and followed Anne-Marie after pushing her cart into the broom closet where it was stored.

They headed outside to some benches situated just beyond the clinic entrance.

"Franchesca is a very good nurse but sometimes she can come off as a bit short with newcomers. I thought I'd better rescue you before she started interrogating you in Spanish."

"Thanks."

"Did you manage to get the washrooms cleaned?"

"Sparkling and germ free. I saved the planet from the next plague," Cherise said.

"Good! You *did* look a bit lost, so I thought I'd better check."

"The work wasn't so bad," Cherise admitted. "But I guess I *was* a bit lost - in my own head, that is."

"Oh? Anything I can help with?"

Cherise shrugged. "I don't know. I'm not sure how much Dirk's told you about me."

"He mentioned a run-in you had with some drug dealers. That you had been kidnapped and he took a bullet for you..."

Cherise nodded. "I owe him a lot. Did he say anything else? About my... penchant for getting into questionable relationships?"

Anne-Marie focused on her lap. "He may have mentioned something like that. No details, or anything. Just that you've had some bad luck when it comes to relationships."

"That's an understatement. I'm cursed at love."

Anne-Marie looked up. "You don't mean that. We don't always make the best choices, but I don't believe anyone is actually cursed."

"No? I think I am. But what about you?"

"What do you mean?"

"How serious are you about my brother?"

Anne-Marie's eyebrows lifted. "Um... well... There's more going on than you know. Between us, I mean. But I can't go into it right now."

"But you'd like to get to know each other better?" Cherise asked.

"I suppose. But, we aren't really that serious, so there's no need to worry," Anne-Marie said in a rush.

"Why would I be worried? You've been really good for him, as far as I can tell. Just don't let anyone - including him - tell you he's not a good guy, cause no matter what he's done, he is. He's the better of the two of us, for sure."

"Oh."

"You seem nervous," Cherise said. "You like him, don't you?"

"Oh, yes! But when he leaves, when he finds something else to occupy his time…"

"Someone else, you mean," Cherise finished candidly.

Anne-Marie blinked. "I suppose that is what I mean."

Cherise shook her head. "I don't think that's likely. I think this is the real thing for him this time."

"You mean other than Tempest."

Cherise's eyebrows shot up. "He told you about Tempest?"

"Not really, but I gathered he was just getting over someone when he came down here. At least, I overheard a conversation…"

"There was never really anything between Tempest and my brother. At least not on her part, and I should know since she's one of my best friends. Besides, she has someone else in her life now, and," Cherise gave Anne-Marie a side long glance, "so does Dirk, apparently."

Anne-Marie looked flustered, her eyelashes batting furiously against her smooth cheeks. "I'm trying not to get too attached. It's not wise under the circumstances."

"But you see each other every day. Go for walks, sit together in church, talk all the time. Have you slept together?"

Anne-Marie's eyes widened. "No! We certainly have not."

Cherise frowned. "Oh right. You religious types don't believe in sex before marriage." When Anne-Marie was silent, Cherise looked at her flushed face and tried to backtrack. "Sorry if that sounded rude. It's just that I've never been good in that department. Staying celibate, I mean."

"It's okay. I like your candor. It's refreshing."

"Good. So, here's another question. What if you really felt like you loved a guy but you knew you would just end up hurting him, so you just ended it. Would you start dating other men?"

"Well, since I have no frame of reference, I can't really say for sure."

"Okay. Say it was Dirk and you knew you loved him but you also knew that it would never work between you so you ended it. Would you date other guys just to help you move on?"

"I... um. I don't know. Are you trying to tell me something?"

Cherise sighed. "Forget it. I just need to let things happen as they happen, I guess. Quit trying to orchestrate life and just let come what may." She slapped her thighs. "Anyway, I should probably check with my supervisor now. I probably have more toilets to clean or something else just as exciting. Thanks for listening."

Cherise noted the worried expression on Anne-Marie's face but waved it off as sympathy. She was such a nice person. Dirk was one lucky guy.

They walked back to the clinic, each in their own thoughts. There was no point trying to figure out too many moves in advance. Life was a chess game and she was just a pawn. She might as well have some fun while she could, since she was probably going to get removed from play soon anyway.

THE PIZZA ESTABLISHMENT was outdated and dark with wooden beams in the ceiling, a bare cement floor, and furnishings that Cherise was sure came straight from a Hollywood movie about bandits who were hiding out in an obscure Mexican village. The set included a couple of local men who sat at one table nursing mismatched coffee mugs. They watched every move as a middle aged woman with a missing front tooth led Cherise and Dr. Smythe to an empty table.

"Don't be alarmed by the decor," Harry said as soon as they were seated. "The food is top notch. I like to eat here every week or so as a change from the plain fare we get at the orphanage. Not that I'm complaining."

"Of course not."

"So? How have your first few days been? Is it everything you expected?"

Cherise lifted a shoulder. "My brother warned me that it was no five star hotel and that it would be no picnic, either. So far, I'd say he was right."

"Ah, yes. Your brother." Harry's lips pursed.

"I take it you two don't get along?"

"I wouldn't say that exactly. As a doctor, I don't expect to make friends with every volunteer who sets foot on the place. I was just surprised that he stuck around after his two weeks were up. He didn't strike me as the type who relished hard work and substandard living conditions."

"Perhaps you don't like the fact that he and a certain nurse seem to be hitting it off," Cherise suggested. She flipped her hair off her shoulders.

Harry shook his head. "I worry about Anne-Marie. She's naive, if I am allowed to say that, and your brother is... well, I don't want to offend you, but perhaps 'worldly' is the word I'm looking for."

Cherise raised a brow. It was very close to her own opinion, but hearing if from the doctor made her hackles rise. "Dirk is a good man. You obviously don't know him if that's what you think."

Harry put up his hands in surrender. "I'm sure he is! There just seems to be something about him that doesn't mesh with the unskilled laborer persona."

"You know what they say. It's best not to judge a book by its cover." She smiled sweetly. Obviously, Dr. Smythe didn't know that she and her brother came from old money. Just as well. She certainly wasn't going to tell him.

"Of course, of course! I am concerned, none the less. They've been engaged in quite a bit of sneaking about lately."

"Sneaking about?"

Harry leaned closer. "Not to shock you, but if I didn't know better, I'd think your brother was involved in something not quite above board."

Cherise narrowed her eyes. "Enough about my brother and Anne-Marie. What kinds of things do you like to do, when you're not doctoring - or analyzing others, of course."

"I see I have offended you after all and for that I apologize."

Cherise took a deep breath. "Apology accepted. I guess blood is thicker than water as they say, and I get a bit testy when it comes to my big brother. He's been there for me in more ways that I can count. In ways you wouldn't even begin to imagine. So, I don't take well to people talking badly about him."

"I shall gladly endeavour to avoid the topic from now on," Harry said. "To answer your previous question, I enjoy playing polo, actually."

"So, you like horses, then?" Cherise sat up straighter. An image of Blue swinging into the saddle came to mind and she smiled.

"Most certainly. And you do, too, I take it?" Harry asked.

Cherise blinked. "Oh. Well, to be honest, I've never really ridden. But I like the idea of horses." And the idea of a certain cowboy who rode them.

"If we ever get the opportunity, I'd love to take you riding sometime."

"So, why polo?" Cherise asked. "I didn't know people actually did that any more. At least not in America."

"In case you've forgotten, I'm not American," Harry said with a grin.

"Of course. How small minded of me," Cherise apologized.

"But you're not far off. Polo isn't the most popular sport in terms of the masses, but it's quite exhilarating and takes a lot of skill and practice. I've been to several tournaments in South America."

"Interesting. I've never seen anyone play polo, but I have a friend who owns a ranch and they have horses. Well, her father owned it, and when he died he left part of it to her." Cherise smiled. "She also married the foreman. He's a real cowboy."

Harry laughed. "A cowboy! How quaint!"

"What's wrong with being a cowboy?"

"Nothing if one likes dusty clothes and the lonely strains of the harmonica while eating endless portions of beans served on a tin plate around a campfire."

Cherise laughed out loud. "That's quite a picture! Too many western movies, I'd say. Very stereotypical."

"Granted. I loved western movies as a kid. John Wayne was my favourite. I wanted to be a cowboy when I grew up, but that wasn't very practical for a city boy, so I became a doctor instead."

"Too bad. That you never got to follow your dream, I mean."

"Not really. I would have made a terrible cowboy. I'm too much of a clean freak for that."

"What's that supposed to mean?"

"I've only met one cowboy. He and his wife came here to volunteer and I swear the odor of manure emanated from the man even though he'd left home weeks before. It led me to believe showers aren't a thing in the cowboy circuit."

"You've never met the right cowboys." A wistful smile played on Cherise's lips.

There was a lull in the conversation as Cherise twisted her fork between her fingers. Blue's image filled her mind. Every moment together, both of ecstasy and frustration, was imprinted in her memory.

"Someone special?"

Cherise blinked back to the present. "Hm?"

"You looked like you were thinking of someone special. A cowboy who got lost on the range?"

"Something like that."

"Is that why you came here? To get away from his memory?"

"Are you sure you're not a psychiatrist?"

"It's a common scenario. More common than you might imagine," Harry said. "I'd know, since I did it myself."

Cherise's eyes widened. "You came here to get over a broken heart?"

He nodded. "So far, it's been working. Maybe even better now that you're here."

"Thank you. I'm flattered." Cherise lowered her gaze. Dr. Smythe seemed like a nice man. He was smart, good looking, successful and he obviously was a good person, too, seeing as he worked in an orphanage. Maybe they could help one another.

Except the image of a certain blonde cowboy, dusty hat and all, just wouldn't be kept down.

irk sat on his narrow bed, rubbing the bridge of his nose between his thumb and forefinger. In his hands he held the evidence he and Anne-Marie had collected. It was clear they had stumbled on something big, but he was stumped at what to do next. His hesitation to alert the police stemmed partly from fear that the orphanage would be shut down and partly from his own gut. He'd snuck out to the storage shed again and all the cartons were still sitting right where he'd seen them the last time. But he couldn't be sure how long that would last. There was only one thing to do. Call for outside help. But who?

A knock sounded at the door and he scrambled to hide the papers under his mattress. "Just a minute," he called. Once they were stashed, he straightened his shoulders, ran his fingers through his mass of hair, and then opened the door.

"Cherise. I wasn't expecting you." He opened the door fully and let her step past him before shutting it again. "What are you doing here? Aren't you supposed to be working?"

"I could say the same to you." Cherise flopped down on his mattress, making it bounce.

Dirk cringed when he heard the sound of crackling paper, but

Cherise didn't seem to notice. The situation would be downright comical if the danger wasn't so real.

"The toilets are endless! Why, oh why didn't I take nursery duty?"

"That was my question when Anne-Marie told me you were cleaning bathrooms." Dirk lowered himself carefully onto the end of the bed.

"I've never been one for kids. You know that." She flipped her head, even though her blonde tresses were firmly held back in a ponytail. "But, if I never see another bathroom, I'll be happy. I need a break!"

"I warned you."

"Whatever. Looks like you're taking a break yourself." She arched an eyebrow.

"I just stopped off here to get something."

"That's what they said when I stopped by the construction site."

"You went by the construction site?"

Cherise nodded. "Sure. I noticed a couple of good looking guys working out in the sun when I passed by the other day. No shirts." She raised her brows several times, Groucho Marx style.

"I thought you went on a date with Harry Smythe."

"I did. Doesn't mean I can't notice some good looking specimens when I see them."

Dirk just rolled his eyes. "Whatever. Sometimes I think you're trying to put on this act, to throw me off the scent."

"The scent of what?" Cherise asked.

"What's really bothering you."

"And that would be?"

"Don't be coy. You're still broken up about Blue Shepherd and you're trying not to show it."

"That obvious?" she asked.

Dirk nodded. "Now, to get to the point. What did you need? I've got to get back to work."

"Just needed a breather. But since you're here… what's going on with you and Anne-Marie?"

"What do you mean?" Dirk schooled his features into a nonchalant mask.

"When she and I talked the other day it was like there's a big secret or something. You're not planning to elope, are you?"

Dirk laughed. "No. Nothing like that. Although, come to think of it, that's not a bad idea."

"You're that serious about her?" Cherise asked.

"Maybe. Not so sure about her, though."

"Hm." Cherise was silent for a moment, then she looked up. "So?"

"So what?"

"What's going on? I know there's something going on around here and I want to know what it is."

"It's complicated."

"I'm good at complicated."

"And maybe even dangerous."

"Good at that, too, in case you've forgotten."

Dirk sat for a moment before answering. Then he sighed. "If I tell you, you have to promise not to tell anyone. I mean it."

"I promise."

"Stand up for a minute."

Cherise did as she was told and Dirk retrieved the paperwork from beneath the mattress.

"We stumbled across some kind of drug smuggling operation." Dirk handed her the papers. "It looks like prescription drugs are being smuggled out with the macadamia nuts. James is the main culprit, but we know there are others, too. Maybe even that Aussie doctor who seems to have taken a liking to you."

Cherise's gaze swung from the papers to meet Dirk's. "Wow. Drug smuggling, huh? I'm feeling a bit of deja vu."

Dirk nodded. "I know what you mean."

She flipped one of the pieces of paper and scanned the next as she spoke. "How do we manage to get stuck in the middle of such things?"

"Luck, I guess," Dirk said with a shrug. "Anyway, I'm not sure what to do next. Anne-Marie thinks we should go to the police, but I have a bad feeling about that. We have to do something soon, though, or the next shipment is going to be gone and we won't have it for evidence."

"Do you really think Harry is in on it?" Cherise asked.

"We don't know anything for sure."

"Since he likes me, as you said, maybe I could be your inside person," Cherise offered.

"I won't put you through that again. It's too dangerous. There has to be another way."

"This whole thing is dangerous! Do you think I'm going to sit back and let you put your life at risk again? No way!"

Dirk took the papers out of her hands and re-stashed them in their hiding spot. "I won't allow you to get involved. That's final."

"I'm already involved, like it or not."

Dirk looked ceiling-ward. "I knew telling you was a bad idea. We just have to think of another way to alert the authorities without compromising the situation. I just don't know who to trust."

"I might have an idea."

"I said no!"

"Will you let me finish?" Cherise asked.

Dirk sighed. "Okay. But if it involves you selling yourself to Dr. Smythe, the answer is no."

"Thanks, brother. Not what I was going to suggest."

"Sorry. Go ahead, then." He folded his arms.

"Ryan," Cherise said.

Dirk's brow furrowed. "Ryan?"

Cherise rolled her eyes. "You know, Ryan O'Toole? Tempest's boyfriend?"

"Oh. That Ryan." Dirk's voice was flat.

"Tempest's FBI boyfriend," Cherise added, stressing the 'FBI' part.

"I don't know if I want her involved in this, either."

"Tempest doesn't have to be involved. Just Ryan." Cherise squinted at Dirk. "I thought you said you were over her."

"I am."

"So why are you acting jealous about Ryan?"

"I'm not acting jealous." His voice came off just a bit too loud.

Cherise shrugged. "If you say so."

"Why would he do that, anyway?" Dirk asked. "Come down here on a whim just because we asked?"

"Because it's his job. It's what he does," Cherise replied.

"Officially. But this isn't official. It's certainly not FBI business - not yet anyway. And it wouldn't be unless we can connect it to drugs crossing the border. For now it's just me with a load of suspicions and a few bits of evidence - all against a very reputable and worthwhile institution."

"So, play dumb then, if that's what you want." Cherise shrugged one of her shoulders. "Forget about it. It's not your problem, anyway."

"You know I can't do that. Not now." Dirk's gaze bore into hers.

"Then call. It can't hurt."

Dirk sighed and ran his hands through his hair. "What if he says no?"

"At least you tried."

"What should I say, exactly?"

"Goodness!" Cherise exclaimed. "Just tell him what you've found. At least that way you've taken it to some kind of authority. Even if he can't get involved himself, he should know what to do. Who to call."

"I don't know. It could be... awkward. "

Cherise put her arm around Dirk's shoulder and squeezed.

"Come on, big brother. Why such a chicken? You know you can trust Ryan."

Dirk nodded. "I know you're right. I'm just not looking forward to it." He sighed. "And now I better get back to work or someone might come looking."

"Ditto. Remind me to thank the housekeeping staff when I get home, okay?"

They both exited and Dirk shut the door with a decisive click.

He had wondered who to call and despite his misgivings - or was it humiliation - he knew Cherise's idea had merit. It wasn't that he still felt anything for Tempest or that he was jealous of Ryan. It was more that he felt shame for so much of who he was during that part of his life and he'd rather put it all behind him, for good. He had changed so much in the past few months and he was afraid that revisiting those past relics might jinx the whole process. Or might jinx what he'd established with Anne-Marie. Once she saw the real man, she might run for her life. He wouldn't blame her. He wanted to run away from that part of his life, too. But instead of leaving it in the past, he was hurtling headlong into the fray.

DIRK DIALED TEMPEST'S NUMBER, tapping his foot nervously as he waited to see if she would pick up or if her answering machine would answer instead. It was almost time for the evening service, but it was the only opportunity he'd had since his conversation with Cherise.

He lowered himself onto his bed. His room was the only place he could think to find any privacy, although he would still need to keep his voice low. At least his present roomy wasn't around. Few people hung around in their rooms, preferring the outdoor living spaces to four cement walls.

Part of him wished for the answering machine instead of

Tempest. He hadn't spoken with her since their meeting in LA before he moved to Mexico and he felt nervous to talk to her, even though he no longer had designs on her affections. He wasn't sure if he should tell her about the latest personal developments or just stick to business.

On the third ring, Tempest picked up. "Hello?"

Butterflies launched in Dirk's stomach. "Hi Tempest. It's me. Dirk."

"Oh!" Alarm rang in the one syllable. "Is something wrong? Is Cherise okay?"

"She's fine. Everything is fine," he assured quickly. "I just needed to talk to you about something."

"Oh." Same syllable but with a whole different tone. Suspicion.

"Yeah, um..." There was an awkward moment of silence. He almost didn't know where to begin. "How are you?"

"Fine. You?"

"Great. The place kind of grows on you. It's good to feel useful."

"Good." Silence. "Is that all you wanted?"

"No. There's actually this crazy favor I need to ask you. It's more of a favor from your... from Ryan."

"Ryan?" Dirk could hear the alarm in Tempest's voice. "What kind of favor?"

"There is some suspicious activity going on here at the orphanage. I thought maybe he could look into it. You know, with his connections and all he might be able to do a little background check on a couple of things."

"I can't speak for Ryan. It's something you'd have to ask him."

"Is he around?"

"Um... yes, he is in fact."

"Can I talk to him?"

Dirk waited as Tempest muffled the phone for a moment. Then she was back. "Sure. Although, I'm not too sure how excited he is about talking to you."

"You can tell him I'm seeing someone, if that helps." There was silence on Tempest's end. "I think she might be the one," he added.

"Oh. Well, that's good. A Mexican girl?"

"She's Canadian, actually. A nurse here at the orphanage."

"I see." Tempest hesitated. "Here's Ryan. You can tell him that yourself."

There was a second of silence as Tempest transferred the phone. Then Ryan's clipped voice came on the other end. "Tell me what?" he asked without preamble.

"That I've met someone here, so you don't need to worry about anything on that front. My favor has nothing to do with Tempest."

"What favor?" Ryan asked.

"Let me explain." Dirk transferred the phone to his other ear. "I, I mean we - my girlfriend and I - stumbled onto what looks like a drug smuggling operation."

"Oh?" Ryan's voice held definite interest.

"It started out with just some crazy suspicions, but then Anne-Marie - she's a nurse - found evidence of large amounts of prescription drugs running through the clinic. I did my own little stake out and noticed some suspicious late night deliveries and even found pills stashed with a shipment of macadamia nuts." There was silence on the other end. "Hello?"

Ryan cleared his throat. "Just taking it all in."

"And?"

"You know you could get hurt, sticking your nose into places it doesn't belong."

Dirk grinned. "You're concerned for my welfare?"

"Funny. As a member of law enforcement, it's my job to keep people like you safe. Selling illegally obtained prescription drugs is big business. There's a huge demand on the black market. The people doing the trafficking aren't always nice. You get in their way and you could end up in Mexico permanently, if you understand me."

"Loud and clear. Which is why I called. I was afraid to go to the police and I couldn't think of anyone else I could trust."

"So you called me." Dirk could hear the disbelief in Ryan's voice.

"Cherise's idea, actually."

"I see."

"But I thought it was a good one," Dirk continued. "For the record, I'm really sorry for any awkwardness I caused when I came to see you last time. And like I said, I'm seeing someone else now, so I'm not trying to win Tempest back or anything."

"As if you ever had a chance."

Dirk smiled, enjoying the sparring match. "Probably true. Anyway, what do you think I should do?"

"First of all, what kind of evidence are we talking about?" Ryan asked.

"Drug orders and dispensing records. We've got a copy on a USB. I've also got a bunch of pills still in the packaging, marked 'Nuts'. I've got them hidden. Other than that, it's just what I saw."

"Which is what again, exactly?"

"A late night delivery one night through the back gate. Plus, the administrator coming and going from the orchard at odd hours."

"Did this administrator see you?" Ryan asked.

"A couple of times."

"Do you have access to a computer? A way to send me those files?"

"I think so. I didn't bring a computer myself, but Anne-Marie should know a way."

"Are you sure you can trust her?"

Dirk frowned. "What a silly question. She's the one who found the discrepancies in the drugs."

"Just checking."

"What else should I do?"

"Nothing. Not another thing until I see what you've got. We've been on a similar case for awhile now. Prescription drugs coming across the border through Tijuana. This just might be the break we've been looking for."

When Dirk hung up he felt a mixture of relief and apprehension. He was glad to have someone as competent at Ryan O'Toole on his side. Again. But this was obviously big. What if he'd just put those he loved in danger?

CHAPTER 31

*B*lue handed Big John the clipboard and waited for him to scrawl his signature across the bottom.

"That should do it." Big John passed the clipboard back to Blue. "Beth says we gotta quit doing things the old fashioned way, but I'm not ready to let a robot start signing my signature. No sir. Not yet."

"She'll have you in shape soon enough," Blue said with a grin. He turned to leave the confines of the office.

"Me?" Big John laughed. "You're the one two steppin' to her tune, if I'm right."

Blue blinked. "Pardon me?" Just what did Big John know?

"Don't look so worried! I just can't help but notice you have the air of the whipped about you. You almost seem scared of her, which is ridiculous since she's the sweetest girl in Texas."

Blue tried to smile in a way that looked natural. "Right." He'd best get out of there. Quick.

"Everything alright between you and Beth?" Big John stopped him with his words.

"Um, sure. Why wouldn't it be?"

"You tell me." Big John folded his arms and waited.

Facing Beth's guardian bear wasn't on Blue's list of things to do that morning. "Everything's fine."

"Having second thoughts?" Big John asked.

"Well, we're really not that serious. Not yet."

"In other words, back off," Big John said.

"I didn't say that," Blue said quickly. "But, you know. Maybe we aren't cut out for each other after all. These things take time."

"Young people!" Big John waved a dismissive hand. "Quit gabbing and get back to work."

Blue scurried from Big John's presence. He didn't need to be told twice. It was becoming more and more awkward and the thought crossed his mind more than once that he should find another job and be done with it.

Except, Beth could follow him anywhere. Somehow, he needed to get that she-monkey off his back. At this point in time, however, the old adage, "Keep your friends close and your enemies closer," reminded him he had little choice.

BLUE KICKED OFF HIS BOOTS, grabbed the remote control off the dresser, and flopped down on his bed. Vegging in front of the TV with a beer seemed like the best antidote for fatigue. The stress of living on pins and needles, waiting for Beth to make good on her threats, was enough to bring on more exhaustion than he'd ever felt after a long day of physical labor on the ranch.

His cell phone beeped and he glanced at the caller. Beth.

He sighed deeply. He probably shouldn't answer it, but he knew she would just keep calling or texting until he did. There would be no peace unless he flushed the thing altogether - which wasn't a bad idea, except for the future consequences.

He answered and put it on speaker, tossing the device on the bed beside him.

"I thought I told you to play nice," Beth said.

"Hello to you, too." He took a swig of beer.

"Uncle John was asking me all kinds of questions at the end of the day. He seems to think you and I are close to breaking up."

"No clue where he got that idea." Blue switched to a sports channel on the TV.

"Don't play dumb. You obviously said something."

"Not that I recall."

"Are you even listening? What's all that racket?"

"I'm watching football."

"Well, quit watching football and pay attention! I'll make your life so miserable that -"

Blue hung up. He knew it was probably a mistake, but he just couldn't listen to any more of her ranting. She was already making his life miserable, so come what may, he would just have to face the consequences.

His phone beeped again. It was a text this time. Curiosity got the better of him and he opened it to read, "You'll be sorry."

He already was sorry. In so many ways, he couldn't even count them.

"Hey, brother. We missed you this weekend," Zane said on the other end of the telephone.

"Sorry. I was busy," Blue said. "Listen, I just need to warn you that if anything weird appears online about me... or you... or Stella... Well, just ignore it, okay?"

"What do you mean 'anything weird'?"

Blue looked up at the ceiling. "Oh, defamatory. Sexual. Inappropriate. Pretty much anything."

"Hm. A little more explanation might be nice."

Blue sighed. "Remember that girl I told you about a while back? The one in Dallas? Well, she's kind of blackmailing me."

"Your boss's niece."

"That's the one."

"Blackmailing you how?"

"She's one of those computer wizards. The kind who can hack people's accounts and stuff. She says if I don't pretend to be her boyfriend, she'll hack me and spread all kinds of rumors."

"It's why I hate social media."

"Exactly what I'm beginning to think. I wouldn't care if it was just me, but she says she'll bring my family and friends into it, too. Which is why I'm calling. I really ticked her off earlier and she's threatening to get back at me. I already deleted all of my accounts, but knowing her, she'll figure out a way."

"Thanks for the warning."

"I mean, she did it once already when she sent Stella that video, but -"

"Wait. She sent Stella a video?" Zane asked.

"Oh. I guess she didn't tell you," Blue said.

"What video?" Zane repeated.

"It was nothing, really. Just some sexual innuendo sent from my account to Stella. Stella already tuned me in about it, and I told her I'd been hacked and it wasn't me. But it just goes to show that Beth knows her stuff and that she can't be trusted. She's a psycho chick."

"If she hates you that much why would she want you to be her boyfriend?"

"She doesn't want me to be her boyfriend, she wants me to *pretend* to be her boyfriend so that her uncle won't keep trying to set her up. He wants her to settle down."

"Seems kind of drastic."

"Like I said. Psycho chick."

"I'll tell Stella."

"Actually, I was wondering… I might need to warn a few other people. Maybe I should talk to Stella myself."

"You want to warn Cherise," Zane guessed.

"Beth specifically mentioned her when she first threatened me, so I wouldn't put it past her."

"Why don't you just call her?"

"I tried, believe me. But she won't answer. I thought maybe Stella could try warning her for me."

"Just a minute," Zane said. "I'll find her and get her to call you back."

They hung up and Blue waited. He had no idea what Beth would try, but he knew it wouldn't be good. Somehow he had to warn Cherise before she got caught in the crossfire.

His phone rang and he quickly answered. "Stella?"

"I am so mad right now! How dare that Beth person! There must be something you can do to bring her to justice. She's messing with the wrong people, that's for sure!"

Blue smiled. Stella, his ever feisty friend turned sister-in-law, would not stand for such an infringement on those she cared about.

She continued, "I can't believe you've gotten yourself into such a mess!"

"What?" Blue's eyebrows rose. "You make it sound like it's my fault."

"In a way it is, but be that as it may, we're not going to let some two-bit hack threaten us. No way. Have you called the police?"

"Not yet."

"What? Why not?"

"It's complicated. She said they'd never be able to prove anything and it seemed easier to just go along with it for the time being."

"No more of that, mister," Stella said. "And no more doing it on your own, either. We stick together and we'll be fighting tooth and nail should she even dare to slander you or any one of us."

"About that. She might be out to target Cherise. Is there any way you can warn her?"

"Why don't you call her yourself?" Stella asked.

"I've tried. Well, not recently, but since she didn't answer when I did, I figured she just didn't want to talk to me, so I haven't tried in awhile. A guy can only be so pathetic, after all." He tried to make it sound like a joke.

"Oh…" Stella let out the syllable slowly. "So, you didn't know she went down to Mexico. That's probably why she wasn't answering."

"Mexico? She went on vacation?" Visions of Cherise on the beach ordering cocktails from a muscular cabana boy came to mind and he had to shake his head to tamp the jealousy down.

"She went to work in an orphanage, of all things," Stella said. "Her brother Dirk is there, too. Something about trying to find herself."

"I remember Dirk." Blue nodded to himself. "Okay. So maybe if I contact him, he'll pass on the message."

"It's worth a try."

Butterflies fluttered in his stomach as Blue said his good-byes. The thought of getting in touch with Cherise again was enough to make his worries about Beth seem insignificant. If it meant a second - or was it third - chance, then it was worth it.

CHAPTER 32

*C*herise noticed Anne-Marie checking her watch - again. She placed her hand on the other woman's arm and smiled reassuringly. The sermon was almost over, and Dirk still hadn't shown up at that evening's church service. "I'm sure he's got a good reason."

Anne-Marie nodded and turned her eyes toward the platform. "Of course."

Cherise focused her attention on the words coming through the headset perched on her head. She hadn't wanted to use them at first, fearing a ruined hairdo, but she'd resigned herself to the reality of an imperfect coiffure after the second day.

The sermon was unlike anything she'd ever heard before. Simple and easy to understand, the pastor claimed giving your life to Jesus was the answer to all life's troubles. At least that's what it sounded like. Lord knows she had plenty of those!

Cherise turned to glance at Anne-Marie once again. The other woman had her eyes closed and was praying along with the pastor. Cherise closed her own eyes and let his words sink in. She felt a warmth creeping over her and she had the strangest urge to go forward at the pastor's invitation. Her eyes snapped open. She removed the headset and flipped her hair back.

"Everything alright?" Anne-Marie asked.

"I... I don't know exactly," Cherise admitted. "I just feel... I don't know how I feel."

Anne-Marie smiled. "Was it something the pastor said?"

Cherise nodded. "Yes. But I don't really understand. I feel confused. I feel..." She threw up her hands. "I don't know! I just feel all muddled up inside. I know it must look like I have everything, and I shouldn't complain, but I just feel so empty inside and nothing seems to make it go away."

"Maybe the Holy Spirit is calling you," Anne-Marie said.

Cherise blinked wide eyes. "What do you mean?"

"God. He's three in one - Father, Son, and Holy Spirit. He's convicting you. Pulling you toward Him."

Cherise nodded. "Yes... I think that's it. Is that selfish of me? To not be satisfied and want more to life?"

"No, it's the way it's supposed to be. God made you and wants a relationship with you. Nothing else will fill that void."

"Oh. I never thought of it like that."

"Do you want to accept Jesus as your Savior?" Anne-Marie asked.

"I don't really know what that means," Cherise said.

"Well, the Bible says that all have sinned and fall short of the glory of God, but God has provided a way, through His Son Jesus, for us to be reconciled - that's re-connected - with Him. You see, on our own we can never be good enough to come into His holy presence, but Jesus made a way, through His shed blood. 'For God so loved the world that He gave His one and only Son, that whoever believes in Him should not perish but have everlasting life.' That's John 3:16."

"You're so smart!"

Anne-Marie laughed. "Not really. It's one of those verses that every kid learns in Sunday School."

"I never went to Sunday School," Cherise admitted with a sigh. "I wish I had, then maybe I wouldn't feel so confused. I've been listening these past few days, and my friend Tempest has tried to tell me about God before, but it never really made much sense. It felt like a fantasy story and I just didn't see the point. But now I'm beginning to think there is something to it. The way people seem so genuinely happy and all." Cherise let her gaze sweep the room, from the front where several people were praying with the pastor, to the crowd still mingling in the aisles. "It makes me feel envious. Life looks so uncomplicated. I wish my life was like that."

"It can be."

Cherise let out a little self depreciating laugh. "I doubt it. You don't know my life."

"True. But Jesus does. He made you, after all."

"Huh. I never really thought of it that way." Cherise looked at Anne-Marie. "So, you're telling me that if I pray that sinner's prayer, all my problems will disappear. Poof! Just like that."

"I never said that. Accepting Jesus doesn't mean all your problems will go away."

"It doesn't? I thought that's what the pastor just said."

"No, he said that with Jesus, we can face whatever comes our way. And we can have joy even in the midst of trials."

"Hm. So not the total fix-all I'd hoped."

Anne-Marie laughed again. "You're funny. Nothing is a total 'fix-all'. We still have to work at life, but Jesus can take away the sense of hopelessness. He gives life meaning and purpose."

"Now, *that* I could use!"

"It's a lot to take in and the biggest decision of your life - which you won't regret, by the way. Do you have a Bible you can read? Maybe if you started there, God will reveal Himself through His word."

"He can do that?"

"Of course! His word - the Bible - is alive and active, like a two edged sword, Paul says. Come on." Anne-Marie stood. "They have some New Testaments at the back. You can take one and start reading."

Cherise followed Anne-Marie to the back of the room. The other woman handed her a pocket sized book bound in faux leather. She turned it over in her hands. "Thank you," she whispered. For some reason the little book felt sacred. Precious. She felt tears pricking the back of her eyelids.

"*John* or *Mark* are good places to start," Anne-Marie said.

Cherise looked up, blinking. "Even if I read it, I double it will make much difference. I'm not a good person, really. I mean, I'm not terrible, but I'm not good either. I've done a lot of stuff. Been selfish and spoiled most of my life."

"That's the point. No one is good enough, remember? It's why Jesus paid the price so that you wouldn't have to. It's His free gift to you."

"But... I don't understand why. Why not fix everything some other way? Or why make people in the first place if He knew we were just going to mess up? And why all the suffering?" Cherise sighed. "See? I'm a bad person! I can't even accept God's free gift without asking too many questions!"

"Asking questions is good," Anne-Marie said. "But allow God to give you the answers." She tapped the cover of the Bible still in Cherise's hands. "Through His Word."

Cherise was fighting with her old nature - the one that didn't like being told what to do. But this new longing was even stronger. She wanted to find the answers to life's questions. She wanted peace.

"You're making it more complicated than it needs to be," Anne-Marie offered. "Jesus doesn't expect you to know all the answers or to even have your life all straightened out before you accept Him. Just give Him your heart and let Him take care of the rest."

Cherise looked down at the Bible and then up again at Anne-

Marie. "Then why do I have to wait until I read this? Can't I accept Him right now?"

Anne-Marie's eyes widened. "Sure. If you want to."

"I don't really want to go up there, though." Cherise pointed to the altar. "Can you pray for me instead?"

"Yes. Definitely," Anne-Marie responded. "But if you want to accept Jesus as your Savior, you'll have to pray, too."

Cherise sighed. "Oh. I thought you said it was easy."

"It is." Anne-Marie took Cherise's hands in her own. "But accepting Jesus is very, very personal. It's not something I can do for you. There's no right way or wrong way to do it and no right prayer or wrong prayer, either. All you need to do is confess that you've sinned and ask Him to forgive you of those sins. The Bible says, 'If we confess our sins He is faithful and just to forgive us our sins and cleanse us from all unrighteousness.' Then, surrender your life completely to Him. Ask Him to help you learn what it means to live like a Christian - how to live a life that is pleasing in His sight. He'll do it! He'll cleanse you and make you a brand new person."

"Okay…" Cherise smiled sheepishly. "Can you get me started at least?"

"No problem. Repeat after me and go ahead and add anything else if you feel like it."

Cherise just nodded.

Anne-Marie took Cherise's hands in hers again and bowed her head. "Dear Jesus, I know that I'm a sinner… I've done a lot of things I'm not proud of… I confess all of my sins to you, both past and present, and ask for Your forgiveness… Please come into my life as my Lord and Savior… I surrender every part of my life to you… I pray that You would fill me now with Your Holy Spirit… Help me live a life that is pleasing in Your sight… in Jesus name…"

Cherise repeated each line as Anne-Marie paused to give her time to do so, but before saying the closing she added, "And Jesus,

I pray that you would help me be a good person like Tempest and Anne-Marie. Thank you for such good friends and for saving my life. Forgive me for being spoiled and focusing on pretty things, even though it really isn't my fault since I was born rich. Forgive me for all the men I've had sex with because I know that sex is bad..."

"Sex isn't bad," Anne-Marie whispered.

Cherise looked up. "It's not?"

"Not in marriage."

"Oh." Cherise closed her eyes again. "Forgive me for all the men I've had sex with when I wasn't married and help me not to want sex anymore unless I get married - which I doubt will ever happen because I have commitment issues. But help me not to have commitment issues anymore - if you can possibly make that happen. And be with the kids here at the orphanage and give them enough food and clothing and everything else they need. And... just take away this sadness and emptiness that I've been feeling ever since I left Blue. In Jesus name..."

"Amen!" they both said together and immediately laughed and hugged.

"I think I do feel lighter," Cherise exclaimed. "Can that really be true?"

"Of course," Anne-Marie said. "It's called being born again."

"I can hardly wait to tell Tempest!" Cherise spun in a circle, giddy with freedom she didn't even know she'd been missing. "I feel like Mary Poppins! Ready to float up in the air!"

"I'm so happy for you," Anne-Marie said. "But now we should go find Dirk."

Cherise trailed behind her friend into the night air. Born again! What might it mean for her relationship with Blue? She smiled. It didn't matter. She had just done something unprecedented. She had just given her heart to a man, but she never had to worry about getting it broken.

CHAPTER 33

*D*irk sat on one of the benches outside the main courtyard and waited. He hadn't bothered going to the evening service once he'd finished his call to Ryan. The possibilities of what would happen next loomed large and sitting in a church service pretending to listen was the last thing he felt like doing.

People started trickling through the auditorium doors, the usual cacophony of Spanish and English mingling in the night air. Dirk kept his eyes peeled for Anne-Marie and Cherise, hopefully minus the doctor, and he stood when he saw them emerge.

"Hey, what happened to you?" Anne-Marie asked as soon as she was near.

"I had a call to make," Dirk replied. "An important call, which I think might help our cause."

"Oh?" Anne-Marie's eyes darted toward Cherise and back again.

"It's okay. She knows what's going on," Dirk said. "She wrangled it out of me this afternoon."

Cherise nodded and smiled. "We're old hands at this drug smuggling thing."

TRACY KRAUSS

"Sh," Dirk warned, looking around at the passersby.

"Why didn't you tell me you knew?" Anne-Marie asked Cherise.

"Sorry." Cherise looked down at her feet. "I wasn't sure how Dirk would feel about it."

"My feelings are the least of our worries," Dirk said. "We need to talk. Somewhere private. Oh, and we need a computer."

"My laptop?" Anne-Marie asked.

"Perfect." Dirk scanned their surroundings. "But we need somewhere private."

"Wait a minute." Anne-Marie looked at Cherise. "Aren't you going to tell him your good news?"

Dirk's gaze swung from Anne-Marie to his sister. "What good news?"

Cherise blushed and her eyelashes fluttered down.

Anne-Marie put an arm around Cherise's shoulders. "You don't need to be shy. You're in good company."

Cherise looked up and her eyes were shining. "I did it. I accepted Jesus as my Savior."

Dirk took a step backwards. Whatever he had been expecting, it wasn't this. "Um, great. When?" He shook his bangs as if trying to clear his head.

"Just now. Anne-Marie prayed with me. I can't believe how free I feel!" Cherise stretched her arms out. "It's amazing!"

"That's... that's great," Dirk hoped his smile was genuine. He was trying to get his own life in order, but he hadn't expected Cherise to beat him to it. It seemed... unfair, somehow.

Cherise giggled. "I know I mocked you in the past, Dirk. For getting religious, I mean. But now I get it - sort of. I mean, I don't really understand what just took place, but I do feel different inside. Like there's hope for me after all."

"Come here," Dirk said as he reached for Cherise. He enfolded her in his arms and gave her a hug. "Of course there's hope for you. I'm proud of you. And happy, too."

Cherise stepped back and wiped a tear from the corner of her eye. "Thanks. I needed that."

"And now we need to go somewhere private so I can tell you about my call. We need to send those files to Ryan asap." He took Anne-Marie's hand and started toward the dorms.

"So, you liked my idea to contact Ryan," Cherise said. "Should I be saying, 'I told you so?'"

"Who's Ryan?" Anne-Marie asked.

"Just a friend," Dirk said. "He's with the FBI."

"More like a rival." Cherise gave Dirk a nudge.

"Oh?" Anne-Marie asked.

Cherise stopped smiling and her eyes got wide. "Oh. But that was before he met you."

Dirk sighed. "Thanks, Sis."

"No big deal," Anne-Marie said. They stopped on the sidewalk between the two dorm buildings. "My room-mate might already be in bed. She's an early riser. I'll head up and grab my laptop, but then we'll have to find somewhere else to talk."

"My room-mate of two days left already," Cherise said. "We can meet in my room."

"Men aren't allowed in the women's dorms," Anne-Marie reminded.

"He's my brother. Besides, there are people breaking bigger rules around this place than that. I'll meet you there."

Cherise started toward the women's building. Dirk grabbed Anne-Marie's hand before she could follow suit. "Cherise talks too much."

"Is this about Tempest?" Anne-Marie asked.

"I thought you said you weren't the jealous type."

"I'm not."

"Then there's nothing to worry about. Whatever I felt for Tempest is totally gone. Vanished."

"Then why do you seem so… touchy about it?" she asked.

"I'm not touchy!" Dirk scowled.

"Okay." Anne-Marie held up her hands.

Dirk sighed and ran a hand through his already dishevelled hair. "Look. Tempest is a thing of the past. For real. But right now we have another matter to think about. Getting that information to Ryan."

Anne-Marie nodded. "Of course. I'll go get my laptop."

Dirk watched Anne-Marie jog up the flight of steps on the outside of her building. He wasn't sure if he had convinced her or not, but he wasn't about to open the subject again. The last thing he wanted was to admit the depths of his desperation when it had come to Tempest. Anne-Marie was still skittish, and if she found out the truth, she might avoid him like a steaming turd.

But he couldn't dwell on that right now. He had bigger worries, and time was of the essence.

Dirk's cell phone buzzed in his pocket. Ryan calling back so soon?

He checked the number and frowned. A strange number had called more than once. With everything that was going down, he was definitely not going to answer it.

CHAPTER 34

*B*lue tried calling Dirk several times, but Cherise's brother seemed to be on the same wave length as his sister. He just wasn't answering. Blue wasn't one to give up, though. He knew he had only one course of action left. Call the orphanage.

"Beacon of Hope," a female voice greeted on the other end of the line.

"Hi." A huge smile broke out on Blue's face. Finally, he'd gotten through to someone. "Is this the Beacon of Hope orphanage? In Mexico, right?"

"Yes, that is correct." There was a pause. "How may I help you?"

"A couple of friends of mine are down there working. Is there a way I can get a message to one of them?"

"Is this a family emergency?"

Blue's grin started to relax. "No. Not exactly."

"We usually just put messages up on the bulletin board and people can check there."

"Oh. Well, it's not an emergency exactly, but it is important."

"I'm sorry. We don't have time to chase people down with personal messages unless it's an emergency."

"Okay..." Blue's smile had totally faded.

"Your name?" the clinical voice on the other end asked.

"Blue. Blue Shepherd."

"And your message?"

Blue rubbed his chin. 'Don't believe anything you see on Social Media,' sounded alarmist. 'I love you, Cherise,' was also out of the question and probably a bit strong to be pinned up on a bulletin board.

The voice cut into his thoughts. "Sir? Hello?"

"Oh, sorry. How about just, 'Call Blue. It's important.'"

"Alright. And who is this message for?"

"Cherise Hillyer."

"Oh. I see." The woman's voice definitely held a hint of conde-scension.

"Do you know her? She's there with her brother, Dirk Hillyer," Blue said.

"Oh, I know them, alright."

Blue frowned. What was that supposed to mean? "Is every-thing alright? They're okay, aren't they?"

The woman's pseudo laugh was more like a snort of disdain. "Just fine. Will that be all?"

What else could he say? "Actually, it is a family emergency of sorts, but I didn't want to alarm either one of them. It's just really, really important that I hear from one of them."

"So now you're saying it is an emergency?" Her tone held cynicism. Blue couldn't blame her.

"Yes, if it means I can be sure she'll get the message."

"If I may, both Hillyers are... how can I put this? Flirts? I'm not sure either of them take our work here seriously."

Blue frowned. "Flirts? What does that mean?"

"If you know them at all, I'm sure you know exactly what I

mean," the woman said. "And now, if you don't mind, I have other important work to attend to."

"Wait a minute! I thought Christians were supposed to be nice. Helpful."

"I am being helpful. I will put your message on the board with the others, but I can't guarantee either one of them will read it. If I were you I'd forget about Miss Hillyer and move on."

"What makes you assume I'm involved with Cherise Hillyer? You don't know me from Adam."

"Are you?"

Blue blinked. "Well, in a way, but -"

"There you have it. I don't think she misses you as much as you miss her. And now I really must be going."

"But -" Blue was greeted by a click on the other end of the line. He frowned down at the cell phone in his hand and then tossed it on his bed. How dare she!

Then again, maybe he needed to hear that. Cherise had moved on, just like she had predicted. And in record time, too, it would seem.

BLUE SLAMMED the driver's door of his pickup and loped across the parking lot to the square industrial building. Running late wasn't usually his style, but he'd stayed up far too late last night trolling social media for any signs that Beth had made good on her threats. So far, so good. There was nothing.

He skirted the storefront door and went around back, hoping to duck into the warehouse without being seen by Big John or one of the other staff who manned the retail side of things.

He was just about to start up the fork lift when Big John entered and whistled for him to stop. "Hold up!" Big John bellowed.

Blue jumped down from the machine and waited the ten

seconds it took for Big John to reach him. His boss looked upset. "If this is about my being a couple of minutes late, I'll stay after hours," Blue began.

Big John's brow furrowed even deeper than it had already been. "Late? That's the least of your worries."

"Oh? Why's that?" Blue scoured his brain for what else might have put his boss into such a foul mood. Had Beth said or done something? Rather than speculate, he waited.

"I think we both know what I'm talking about," Big John said and folded his arms.

Blue shook his head. "Honestly, I wish I did."

Big John narrowed his eyes. "I thought you'd have the decency to come straight with me. After all I've done for you. Then again, there ain't no honor among thieves, so they say."

"Thieves? Are you accusing me of stealing?" Blue asked, his eyes widening.

"Not just accusing! Beth told me about it this morning. Seems one of my employees has been adding items to the orders. Items that aren't accounted for. Probably selling them under the table or online. A tidy little business, I'd say." Big John eyeballed Blue with an intensity that dared him to deny it.

Blue let out a snort. "Of course it was Beth who told you."

"What's that supposed to mean?"

"Well, what makes you think it's me?" Blue asked. "Did she tell you that, too?"

"She didn't want to," Big John said. "She wanted to give you the benefit of the doubt, seeing as you're her man and all, but I wrangled it out of her. Her records point to the orders that you had a direct hand in placing. I'm sorry, Blue, but you might as well fess up."

"You want me to confess?" Blue spun sideways and threw up his hands. "Okay, I will! I confess to being a wimp and a fool by letting your niece blackmail me."

"Blackmail you?"

"Yes, blackmail! Beth isn't the nice girl you think she is. In my opinion, she's a psycho chick and -"

Big John rose up on his toes, like he might explode. "Hold on, now! I won't stand for you bad-mouthing my Beth! If you're having a lover's spat, that's one thing, but no need to get personal."

"We aren't even a couple! That's what I was going to say. She's been threatening to harass my family and friends on social media if I don't pretend to be her boyfriend. All because I hurt her feelings once while we were in Dallas."

"She does have a vengeful streak…"

"Vengeful? She's downright crazy!"

"Hey now!" Big John warned.

Blue held up his palms in surrender. "Sorry, but it's true. She hacked into my account to prove she could do it and sent my sister-in-law some pornography. I had to delete everything. My entire life online! Then she threatened that if I didn't pretend to be her boyfriend, she'd target more people."

"Why would she do that?" Big John asked. "It doesn't make any sense."

"I hate to say it, Sir, but perhaps you're holding on too tightly. She said if you thought she had a stable boyfriend, you wouldn't keep trying to set her up or bother her about her social life. She doesn't want you looking over her shoulder."

"All Millie and I have ever done is try to protect her," Big John protested.

"Maybe you're the ones who need protection." Blue took a step toward his boss. "I didn't steal from you, I swear. But you and I both know that Beth is a whiz when it comes to computers. She could have easily tampered with those accounts, especially now that she's upgrading your systems. You've got to believe me."

"Why should I?"

"Because I have no reason to lie. Not any more. Now that you know the truth, Beth won't have any leverage."

Big John rubbed his chin. He was still frowning but his face was less angry and more sad. "You want me to believe that Beth has been lying to me, but you could be lying to me just as easily."

"Have I ever lied to you before?" Blue asked.

"Not that I know of."

"Has Beth?"

"A time or two, over the years." Big John's body suddenly deflated, like a leaky balloon. "More than a time or two, if I'm honest." He sighed heavily. "We did our best, Millie and me, but Beth was a strong willed child. Angry at the world - with good reason, I suppose. Still, I can't believe she'd do something like this to the business. To me."

"Deep down I think she loves you and Millie, but she's confused. Life's been rough," Blue said. He was trying to soften the truth about what he really thought of Big John's niece, but there was no point in being harsh. "It might be wise not to let her access your accounts any more, though."

"Maybe you're right." Big John surveyed Blue's face. "Sorry for accusing you without hearing your side. I didn't want to believe you'd do a thing like that."

"Beth is family. Of course you'd believe her."

"That she is. Which is why I don't know how I'm going to let her go…" Big John looked up at the warehouse lights.

"I'll leave that up to you," Blue said, "but I would suggest bringing in an outside accountant. Someone who knows the old system and who can check the facts."

Big John clamped a hand on Blue's shoulder. "Maybe I should make you the new manager."

Blue laughed. "I'm just a lost cowboy, not managerial material."

"Don't know about that. Seems to me you've done a good job since coming on board. I need a reliable person I can trust to run things so Millie will stop hounding me about taking more time off, and you seem like the best candidate."

"From thief to manager in less than a minute?" Blue asked, cocking a brow.

Big John cracked a smile. "I knew you were innocent."

"Could have fooled me. You looked about fit to kill me there for a second."

"Good thing I didn't. Would have been awful messy to clean up and with you being the best clean-up boy, I'd a had my hands full."

Blue sobered. "I appreciate the offer. Really I do, but I'm going to have to think about it. I'm feeling a bit unsettled these days and I wouldn't want to leave you in the lurch."

It was the truth. Unsettled was putting it mildly. Not only had he discovered that the person he thought was the love of his life had moved on while in Mexico, he didn't relish the idea of working for Beth's uncle, even if she had no more hold on him. It might make life a bit too complicated and right now he was longing for simplicity.

Like the simplicity of home? He wasn't sure. All he knew was that change was in the air and he needed it if he was every going to breath normally again.

CHAPTER 35

*D*irk opened the door to the administration building and was immediately enveloped in what felt like a cool breeze. Thank goodness for air conditioning. It was a sweltering day outside, but the interior of the office was tolerable. One last errand and he would leave the rest to the experts.

Ryan had been in touch, explaining that the evidence he and Anne-Marie had sent was just what the FBI needed and everything was in place for a bust. Since the FBI had no jurisdiction in Mexico, they had to wait and catch the smugglers once they crossed the border at Tijuana. But they'd be there - in force. Soon it would all be over.

Dirk walked up to the counter and greeted Linda, James' wife, with a nod. "Hi, Linda. I just came over to check on some building materials that should have arrived yesterday."

Linda's eyebrows shot up above the rim of her glasses. "Building materials? I don't recall any building materials being scheduled to arrive yesterday."

"You know how it is." Dirk leaned on the counter with one elbow. "Sometimes things get lost from the paper copy to the office." He smiled his most charming smile.

Linda let out a little huff. "Well, I suppose I could check."

"Actually, I think it was supposed to arrive on one of our own delivery trucks. You know, on its way back from Tijuana?"

"I highly doubt it. That's not how we usually do things." She clicked a few keys and opened a new window on her computer screen. "There. No deliveries scheduled. Just as I thought."

"Wow. That's really weird. The guys said it was supposed to be here yesterday. A shipment of nuts went out, didn't it?"

"Not yet."

"Really?" Dirk shook his head. "I guess somebody somewhere is mixed up. When is that next shipment supposed to go out?"

Linda clicked a few more keys and took a moment to read the screen before answering. "Tonight." She shifted in her seat, a puzzled look on her face.

Dirk leaned over the counter enough to catch a glimpse of the screen. "Everything okay?"

She sat up straighter and minimized the window. Her face was now a nondescript mask. "Fine. But I didn't see anything about a return delivery."

"I'll tell the guys. Maybe they'll have to put in a new requisition. Thanks anyway."

"You're welcome," she said stiffly.

Dirk stood up straight and stretched. "Oh, by the way, you look nice today. Must be the dress. The color suits you."

Linda blinked rapidly. A rosy hue crept into her cheeks and she seemed momentarily speechless.

"See you around." Dirk waved and turned to saunter away. He'd gotten the information he needed. The shipment was scheduled to leave tonight. Now he just needed to alert Ryan and his team.

The heat hit him like a brick when he opened the door and stepped outside. He wasn't sure if Linda was in on the scam or not. Probably not from her reaction when she saw that a shipment was going out tonight. Then again, it was hard to tell with her. She only had two sides. Agitated mouse or condescending librarian. Poor James. Poor Linda.

He had to contact Ryan with this last piece of 'intel' and then get back to work. *"Make sure you carry on as usual. I don't want anything to look out of the ordinary."* Ryan's words echoed in Dirk's head. Life was about as ordinary as a three ring circus.

DIRK CROUCHED BEHIND THE FOLIAGE, careful not to get too close to the sharp macadamia leaves. The darkness cast long shadows across the gravel parking area outside the storage building, the only light coming from the harsh floodlight at the gate. A transport truck was backed up to the loading dock.

Ryan had warned him to carry on as usual, so by rights he really shouldn't be here at all. There was really no purpose in watching things play out. But he needed the assurance that the shipment was actually going out, as scheduled.

From this distance he couldn't tell who was loading the truck, but he kept watching as one of the workers swung the back doors of the vehicle shut and latched it securely. The man banged on the door with the palm of his hand and yelled something in Spanish. The other man emerged from the shadows, swung himself into the driver's seat, and moments later the vehicle rolled away, leaving the other worker to close up the shed.

The night watchman shut the gate and all was quiet, just as if nothing unusual had happened. Of course, to the casual observer, nothing unusual *had* happened. Even though late night deliveries were not the norm, it wasn't like they never occurred. Dirk wondered how many people were actually privy to the truth. Did the night watchman at the gate know what was in that truck? Did the man who had helped load it?

Dirk unfolded his frame and stood, stretching the kinks out of his legs and back. It was all up to Ryan and his team now.

He turned and ran smack into a wall of human flesh.

"James!" The name exploded from Dirk's lips and he jumped back, laughing nervously as he did so. "You scared me."

"What are you doing out here?" James stood military style with his legs apart, arms crossed.

Dirk shrugged. "I like taking evening walks. You know that."

James narrowed his eyes. "I think there's more to it than that."

Dirk tried to laugh. "Like what?"

"Why don't you tell me? Or better yet, how about explaining it to the police?" James stepped to the side and gestured behind him. Two uniformed officers stood in the shadows.

Dirk's eyebrows shot up. "The police? No, no! You've got this all wrong."

"You thought I didn't know, didn't you?" James said. "But I've been watching you. You and Anne-Marie, although she surprises me. I never would have pegged her for a drug smuggler."

"What? No, no!" Dirk repeated. "You've got it wrong –"

James cut him off. "Once your sister arrived, I knew for sure that something was up and I did a little checking. Seems you made the papers. 'Rich socialite gets shot over drugs,' or some such thing."

"If you read those papers you'd know we were the victims."

James shrugged. "Maybe. Or, it could be part of your front. The fact that you lied about your family background is incriminating enough."

"James, this is crazy."

James raised a hand. "You can explain everything once we get to my office." He gestured to the officers and they stepped forward, taking hold of one arm each.

"You don't need to manhandle me," Dirk said. "I can explain."

One of the officers said something sharp in Spanish.

"If I were you, I'd be quiet and come peacefully," James said. "I convinced them not to cuff you. I don't want to upset any of the other staff or worse, the children. But if you keep making a fuss, it could go badly."

Dirk clamped his mouth shut and matched his pace to that of the uniforms. This was definitely not how things were supposed to go down.

DIRK CLASPED his hands together between his knees as he sat on the hardbacked chair in James' office. James stood nearby, as did the two police officers. One of them was writing something on a small pad while the other stood guard, his eyes trained on Dirk. They said they were just here for questioning, but it sure felt like a whole lot more. The bigger bald one kept slapping his billy club into his palm.

"I keep telling you, you've got things all wrong." Dirk leaned forward in an appeal to James. "I thought *you* were the one smuggling the drugs."

"Don't be ridiculous. This orphanage is my home. My passion. And these kids are like my own. I would never do anything to jeopardize that."

"What about the evidence?" Dirk turned his gaze to the police.

"Ah yes. It was convenient for your girlfriend to have a copy." The cop with the pad stopped writing momentarily and surveyed Dirk closely. His accent was thick; his dark hair slicked back.

"Your 'evidence' shows exactly what I thought it would," James put in. "Someone from the clinic - likely your girlfriend - was doctoring the books." He smiled. "No pun intended."

"Now *you're* being ridiculous!" Dirk sputtered.

"Are we?" the officer with the pad asked. "You did have drugs in your possession."

"I kept them as evidence!"

"Very incriminating." James shook his head.

Dirk sighed and sat up straighter. "Look. I've tried to cooperate in every way. It wasn't until after I saw James in the woods talking to that... that hipster Dillan, that I even started snooping around. How do you explain that?"

"Dillan is an undercover police officer," James said.

"Of course." Dirk rolled his eyes. Things couldn't get much worse.

"I'm afraid we're going to have to take you in for further questioning," police officer number one said. Number two continued to slap the baton into his palm.

Dirk swallowed the lump in his throat. "If you must." He stood up slowly.

"Good. I am glad you are cooperating. Much better than your sister did," the interrogating officer said.

"What do you mean?" Dirk's eyes shot from one man to the other.

"She and your girlfriend were already taken in," James explained.

"Shall we go?" the officer in charge asked pleasantly. The other one took a step closer and batted the baton into his palm one more time.

CHAPTER 36

A female officer held the door open for Cherise and Anne-Marie as they entered the small police station. "This way," she said in accented English. She was a tall woman, pretty enough, with streaked hair pulled into a severe ponytail. She escorted them through the outer office which housed a couple of wooden desks and a few filing cabinets toward an interrogation room near the back.

Cherise slowed her steps. "I'm an American citizen. You have no right -"

"You are not in America," the police officer said, not unkindly. She gestured for them to enter the room. Anne-Marie straightened her spine and stepped over the threshold.

Cherise stalled inside the doorway as a wash of anxiety swept over her. "I don't feel well. I think I might be sick."

"There is a garbage over there." The woman pointed to a metal trash can.

With a sigh, Cherise followed Anne-Marie.

"Wait here," the woman said and shut the door. As if they had any choice.

The room was sparsely furnished with one table and a couple

of chairs. There was no two-way mirror like in the movies, just plain panelled walls. Cherise sank into one of the chairs.

"Are you really feeling sick?" Anne-Marie squatted beside Cherise and took one of her hands. "You do look flushed."

"Probably just a flashback."

"A flashback..." Anne-Marie repeated before her eyes lit with understanding. "Of course. You were kidnapped and held against your will. This must be absolutely terrible for you." Anne-Marie stood. "I'll try to get you a drink of water."

"Never mind," Cherise said, not letting go of Anne-Marie's hand. "I just need a minute. I'm mostly over feeling claustrophobic and I haven't had a bad dream in weeks. As soon as they talk to us, they'll see we're innocent and everything will be fine." At least, that's what she needed to tell herself right now. Otherwise she might go into full panic mode.

"We should pray," Anne-Marie suggested firmly. She held out her other hand and Cherise took it, and they both closed their eyes. "God, you see us right now and you see the trouble we're in. Be with Dirk, wherever he is, and keep him safe. You know the truth about what's going on. Help the police find the right culprits so that nothing will happen to the orphanage or the children and staff, and keep us safe until we get released. Amen."

Cherise opened her eyes. Although she still felt uncertain, somehow the simple prayer had calmed her nerves. "What do you think is going on?"

"I'm not sure," Anne-Marie admitted. "If James is responsible - and Dirk seems to think he is - he might be behind our arrest. I just can't believe he would do something like this, though. I trusted him. He's a good man... or at least, I thought he was."

"You know what they say. Don't judge a book by its cover." Cherise lowered her gaze to the cement floor. "I should know. I've been doing it for too long."

Anne-Marie was about to say something but the door opened and she clamped her mouth shut.

"Come," the female officer gestured to Cherise.

Cherise's eyes twitched from the waiting officer to Anne-Marie, every uncertainty rushing back with vengeance.

"Go. He's got this." Anne-Marie pointed toward the ceiling.

Cherise stood and nodded. She wished her faith was as strong as Anne-Marie's. She followed the officer to a bank of cells along one wall and stopped. "A jail cell? I haven't done anything!" The officer gave her a gentle shove and shut the barred door with a clang.

She surveyed the space and then plunked down on the hard bench along the wall. There was no mattress or cushioning of any kind. She leaned her head against the cement and closed her eyes. *Oh God, oh God, oh God!* The phrase rolled around in her head, a silent plea that went beyond words. *I don't know if I'm strong enough. Help!*

Round and round like a carousel, her prayer came full circle until the rattle of keys in the lock startled her eyes open and she shot up from the hard bench. The officer was ushering Anne-Marie into the cell next to hers.

Cherise rushed to grasp the metal bars that separated them. "What happened?"

"I told them everything I know. Apparently, it isn't enough." Anne-Marie slumped into the bars, resting her forehead against the steel. "Beacon of Hope is such a godsend to this community, they don't take it lightly when a foreigner accuses someone associated with it of illegal activity."

"Wouldn't they want to know the truth?"

"I would hope so, but right now they seem more upset about its reputation. I gave them the evidence, but they didn't seem to believe me. They made me feel as if the real crime is me bringing it forward. As if I'm to blame if Beacon of Hope crashes."

"No talking, please," the female officer barked. Her demeanour was becoming less friendly by the minute.

"It almost sounds like they're in on it," Cherise whispered.

"It does, doesn't it?" Anne-Marie glanced at the officer, now sitting at one of the desks. "I don't mind admitting I'm scared."

"This is like a bad nightmare all over again."

A shaft of light arched into the dim interior as the exterior door swung open. A man was shoved, none too gently, into the building.

"Dirk!" Cherise cried out.

"Quiet!" the officer said sternly and rose to meet two of her compatriots, Dirk firmly in the middle between them.

Cherise watched as a burly, bald officer led Dirk to the bank of cells. The other officer had dark, slicked back hair. One of them said something in Spanish to the female, gesturing with his head at Cherise's cell. The woman nodded and proceeded to unlock Cherise's door. Before she knew what was happening, she was being dragged from her cell by the arm. "Dirk!" she called over her shoulder.

With practiced efficiency, the officer unlocked Anne-Marie's door and shoved Cherise in with her friend. With a small cry, they bolted into each other's arms and clung.

Dirk was pushed into Cherise's former cell and all barricades were shut with a clang. "Looks like they're out of real estate," he said.

Anne-Marie let go of Cherise and approached Dirk's cell, pressing herself into the bars that separated them. "What's going to happen?" she whispered.

Dirk grasped her hands through the bars. "It doesn't look good. I'm just hoping that Ryan pulls through."

"Do you think he will?" Cherise asked on a whisper, joining them.

"I hope so. One thing I do know. We can't trust these cops. Or James."

The officer with the bald head sauntered toward the cells. "You've been told. No more talking." He thumped his billy club into his palm. He wasn't even pretending to be sympathetic.

~

SOMEWHERE IN THE NIGHT, Cherise's weariness gave way to sleep. She woke with a horrible backache and gritted her teeth as she straightened into a sitting position. She looked over to see that her cell mate hadn't fared any better.

"That was probably the worst sleep I've had in a long time." Anne-Marie stretched her arms over her head.

"Certainly brings back memories I'd hoped to forget." Cherise winced and rumpled her hair with one hand. "I must look a mess."

"Even in these conditions, still thinking about how you look." Dirk clucked his tongue.

Cherise surveyed her brother through the bars. He didn't look much better than she felt. She stuck out her tongue and he laughed. The sound was out of place in the stark surroundings, but added just the sliver of normalcy she needed right now.

"Good morning. Sleep well?"

Cherise directed her attention at the new voice. It was the female guard who had stayed the night. Unlike the other female officer, she was not just tall but also overweight, her uniform stretched tightly over her curves. She had a gun strapped to her side and her face had a no nonsense look to it.

"You might want to use the *banos*." She picked up a piece of paper from the desk and scanned its contents. "You will be transported to a new facility very soon."

Dirk shot to his feet and clutched the bars. "That's crazy. We're innocent. And we're American citizens."

The woman looked up from the desk. "Not all of you." She flashed an icy stare at Anne-Marie as if to prove she couldn't be hoodwinked. "It doesn't matter if you are American or Canadian. This is Mexico and you must abide by our laws when you are in our country."

Dirk ran a hand through his already mussed hair and turned

to Cherise and Anne-Marie. "This is bad," he whispered. "You know what they say about Mexican prisons."

"Thanks, brother. I feel so much better now." Cherise looked at Anne-Marie. "We prayed! I thought you said God had it handled."

"He does," Anne-Marie stated. "Prayer isn't magic and God isn't a genie. We can't just demand that God do things our way. We just need to trust Him that He will work it out in His time, His way."

Cherise sighed. "This being a Christian is harder than I expected."

Perhaps God was testing her commitment. The euphoria she'd felt after saying the sinner's prayer hadn't abated exactly, but having to trust Him completely was a hurdle she hadn't expected.

CHAPTER 37

*B*lue pointed the scanning gun at the barcode on the box and then checked the numbers against those on the clipboard he carried in the other hand. He nodded to himself. Big John's system may be outdated, but rarely were there any mistakes. Beth must have fabricated her accusations, since so far he could find nothing. Either that or she set things right again before Big John could investigate further. She was smart that way.

He made a check mark in the appropriate column and moved farther down the row of steel shelving.

The clack of cowboy boots on cement brought him to a halt. Beth. He waited until she rounded the corner.

"Just what do you think you're doing?" Beth asked, her tone scathing.

"Checking stock," Blue replied. "Which is part of my job."

"I meant you turning my uncle against me." She crossed her arms.

"I doubt he's turned against you, Beth. Just what are you accusing me of doing?" He scanned the next item, refusing to look her way again.

"He's brought in some old friend of his to go over all the accounts. Says I can go ahead and upgrade the system, but that he'd prefer some things left as is until he can make sure I know the business well enough." She let out a growl of frustration. "As if a bunch of machinery parts is rocket science."

"And you think I put him up to it?" Blue asked. He scanned the next box.

"Of course you did! He cares more about your opinion than mine."

Blue could hear the pout in her voice, but chose to keep scanning.

"Because of you, he doesn't trust me anymore!" she added.

"That's rich," Blue said with a snort. "I'd say you did that all by yourself."

"What? How dare you!"

Blue lowered the clipboard and turned to Beth. "Stop the dramatics. I know about your little attempt to set me up. Figuring that out wasn't rocket science either. Fortunately, your uncle was smart enough to figure it out, too."

"I don't know what you're talking about. There was a glitch in the numbers and it genuinely looked bad, but I was able to find the mistake and everything is fixed now."

"Of course it is," Blue said sarcastically.

Beth's chin lifted. "Yes, it is. I told him it was just a mistake, but now he's gone and hired someone else to do half my job because you turned him against me."

Blue scanned another item and checked it off his list. He took a deep breath before speaking again. "I told him the truth about us. That we're not a couple and that you were blackmailing me. Did he mention that to you?"

Beth blinked, obviously surprised by the revelation. "He won't believe you. No one would be that pathetic."

"Oh, he already does believe me," Blue said. "So you might as well give it up. You have no leverage left."

"I don't need leverage to make your life a living hell." Beth turned on her heel and stomped away, her heels clacking all the way to the warehouse doors.

Blue closed his eyes for a moment, waiting for the heavy clunk of the door as it shut behind her. Now what was he supposed to do? He couldn't continue in this toxic environment for much longer, but the only solution seemed to be finding a hole somewhere and crawling into it. He needed an escape plan.

The peace of his home on the ranch came to mind, but he shook his head. He'd already decided that the life of a cowboy wasn't for him and he'd told his father and Zane as much. Going back on his word seemed like a cop-out.

Or maybe that was just pride talking. He was a failure at love and a failure at finding a meaningful vocation. He might as well become a failure at keeping his word, too.

BLUE RAPPED on the casement with his knuckles and stepped over the threshold into Big John's office. As had happened so many times before, the older man looked up over the rim of his reading glasses and gestured for him to sit. He was fielding a call which Big John had placed on speaker so that he could also peruse a quote that was in front of him on his desk.

Blue lowered himself onto the available cracked vinyl seat and waited, half listening, half trying not to.

A few seconds later, Big John ended the call and tossed his reading glasses on the desk beside him. "Before you say anything, I want you to know I went easy on Beth, even though I know she done you wrong. She's still finding her way and there was really no harm done."

"I know. She told me," Blue said.

"She did, did she?" Big John nodded his approval. "Well, that's good news."

"It wasn't exactly an apology, if that's what you're thinking," Blue clarified. "And she didn't seem to know that I had told you we aren't really a couple, either."

"I didn't want to embarrass her," Big John said. "I figured it would come out eventually in its own way. Oh well, it's all out in the open now, so I suppose there's nothing left to do but move on."

Blue hesitated, not sure if he should mention the new threats. He decided against it. Why ruin their relationship even more? He sat up straighter. "Speaking of moving on, that's what I'm here to talk to you about. I've decided to give you my resignation."

Big John's eyes widened. "Now, wait just a minute! If you think I should have been harder on her, I can have a talk with her this afternoon."

"It's not that. I just think it's time for me to move home for a bit. My father hasn't been well, as you know, and I think I should be with him as much as I can before... well, you know."

"Of course, of course! But a resignation isn't necessary. Just take some time off. As much time as you need. Your job will be waiting for you when you're ready."

"Thanks. I appreciate that, but I wouldn't want to hold you to that in case I find something else."

Big John nodded. "I get it. You're young. Still finding yourself. I was your age once."

Blue fingered his hat brim. "I know I should give you two weeks, but under the circumstances, I was wondering..."

"Absolutely. We'll manage somehow. Your family is more important." Big John stood and came around the desk to pump Blue's hand. "You'll always have a place here if you should change your mind."

Blue stood also and they embraced for a second, Big John thumping Blue's back a bit too heartily. He felt tears trying to prick the corners of his eyes and blinked several times to clear them from his eyes.

He doubted he would be back, but stranger things had happened. He hadn't exactly fit in here, just like he didn't quite fit in at the ranch. Starting over again at square one might be the only way to figure out where he actually did fit - or resign himself to a life of mediocrity.

CHAPTER 38

*T*he rumbling of the transport vehicle should have lulled Dirk to sleep, but his nerves were too shot to find rest. They'd been handcuffed, hands in front, and put into the back of a police van. There was no air conditioning and the air was oppressively close.

He glanced at the women, sitting across from him, and felt another wave of guilt. Cherise's head lolled to the side, her eyes shut. She'd been through too much in the past few months. New found faith or not, she was headed for a breakdown. Maybe they all were. He turned his gaze to Anne-Marie, the knowledge that he was responsible for putting her in danger cutting deep into his gut.

"I wonder where they're taking us?" Anne-Marie squinted out the tiny mesh covered window in the side of the cargo bay.

"Who knows?" Dirk shifted so he could crane his neck and see out the small window. Dry Mexican landscape whizzed past. He recognized the outskirts of Ensenada, the mix of looming cement high-rises and shanty town shacks. It made sense. They'd been driving for about an hour.

The van turned off the main highway and continued on a

street that soon narrowed into little more than a gravel path. Dirk's heart sank even lower. They passed shacks made of metal, tarps, and unpainted plywood, some of them fenced with rows of spiky cacti. This gave way to some larger industrial buildings. Finally the van came to a stop in a parking lot sealed off with chain link fence.

Someone unlocked the back door with a heavy clank and air rushed inside the confines of the van. An officer in uniform waved his arm for them to disembark and Dirk obeyed, squinting as he jumped down onto the hard pavement. His body felt crippled, not only from the long night on the hard bench in the police station, but from the awkwardness of riding with his hands cuffed. By the look of Cherise and Anne-Marie as they spilled from the vehicle, they hadn't fared any better.

"I'll take over from here."

Dirk swung around to see the owner of the voice. Ryan O'Toole. A smile started on his lips and he was about to give the other man a hearty greeting when he noticed the tight lips and steely stare emanating from the other's eyes. Ryan had purposely lifted his dark glasses. He was holding up his identification and he was wearing a flak jacket with FBI emblazoned across the back.

"Prisoners, you will be transported back to the United States as per orders outlined in our governments' joint agreement. There you will be held and tried. You have the right to remain silent..." Ryan proceeded to recite the rest of their rights.

Dirk clamped his mouth shut, grateful that Cherise had the good sense to do the same. Whatever game Ryan was playing, he was definitely going to play along.

They were loaded into a black Suburban by another FBI officer with shortly cropped red hair. He wore the standard issue dark glasses and the same jacket as Ryan. The bench seat was a lot more comfortable than the back of the police van, with or without hand cuffs. A glass panel separated the seat from the front of the vehicle.

"What's going on?" Anne-Marie whispered when the doors had been securely shut.

"I think God just answered our prayers," Cherise said with a smile.

"You know him?" Anne-Marie asked.

"That's Ryan," Dirk said.

The unidentified agent took the wheel and as soon as they started driving away Ryan turned in his seat, hit a button and the glass barrier lowered. "This is Agent Coates." Ryan gestured to the driver who waved a greeting. "Oh. And here. You might find a use for this." He tossed a key onto Dirk's lap.

With a little maneuvering, they managed to get the cuffs off their wrists. "Thanks, man. I was worried we were heading for a maximum security prison where they throw away the key." Dirk rubbed his wrists.

"You might have. Took a little maneuvering on my part to make a deal." Ryan looked squarely at Anne-Marie. "You might want to reconsider hanging around with these two. I'm getting tired of rescuing them."

"Noted," Anne-Marie said with a smile.

"So what just happened back there?" Dirk asked.

"We stopped the shipment at the border and it was clean," Ryan began.

"What?" Dirk interrupted. "But I saw those boxes with the drugs in them myself."

Ryan shrugged. "Someone must have tipped them off. Then we got word that you had been taken in for questioning. We knew we had to make it look like you were arrested and taken out of the way for good. Whoever is behind this operation got scared and we need some time to let things settle so that they can re-emerge from their rabbit hole."

"James?" Dirk asked.

"Not sure, but it could go pretty deep. We've got the full cooperation of the Mexican authorities, but there's always the possibility of a mole. In any case, it looks like your time in Mexico has come to an end."

"I can't say I'm sorry," Cherise said.

"I did warn you," Dirk replied.

"What about me?" Anne-Marie asked. "That's my job. My livelihood. And I left all my stuff back there."

"Sorry. It can't be helped. Once it's all settled and we've caught the real bad guys, you can probably go back. But for now, you're not allowed in the country." Ryan faced the front and secured his dark glasses in place on his nose. "For now just enjoy the ride. As soon as we get you over the border, we'll find a nice place for a bath and a change of clothes."

"We smell that bad?" Dirk asked with a smirk.

Ryan nodded. "Mmhm."

Anne-Marie pursed her lips but didn't say any more. Dirk slipped his hand over hers but she withdrew it. She turned her head and looked out Cherise's window instead.

Dirk let it go. Anne-Marie had a strong faith, but even people like her needed some slack once in awhile.

DIRK WATCHED the lights of Los Angeles out his window until Agent Coates pulled up to the luxury hotel he had suggested. Well, not suggested, exactly. Insisted on. It had been a grueling day. Lots of questions at the border and then the drive to Los Angeles had all three passengers dreaming of a hot bath and a comfortable bed. It was the least he could do.

While the vehicle idled, Ryan turned around to speak. "I need to meet with you tomorrow to go over a few details about the case. Then you're free to go home."

"Will we see Tempest?" Cherise leaned forward in her seat.

"I can probably arrange that." He looked pointedly at Dirk. "Tomorrow is her day off."

"Oh good!" Cherise clapped her hands.

Dirk nodded his approval and then glanced at Anne-Marie. She didn't seem opposed to the idea, so he let any apprehension about meeting Tempest go.

The three scrambled out of the vehicle and waved as Ryan and Coates drove away.

"This looks awfully expensive." Anne-Marie gazed at the canopy of palm trees overhead, her eyes darting to the marble columns that flanked the front entrance.

"After what we've been through we deserve it," Dirk said.

"I don't have my credit card." Anne-Marie frowned. "I don't have anything."

"My treat," Dirk said with a wave.

"But... look at me! I'm a mess!" She gestured down at her rumpled nurse's uniform - the same clothing she'd been wearing when she got arrested.

"Just hold your head up like you own the place." Dirk took her arm and pulled her forward into the spacious foyer. "We'll buy some clothes at the shop on the main floor and have them sent up." At Anne-Marie's uncertain expression he added. "I'll start you a tab. Then after we're cleaned up, we'll go out for dinner."

"Not me. I'm not coming out of the bath until I look like a prune, so I'm getting room service," Cherise said cheerfully as they approached the front desk.

"Well, I'm not comfortable with you paying for everything," Anne-Marie said. "I'll pay you back."

Cherise laughed. "Don't be silly. Didn't Dirk tell you he has loads of money?"

"Yes, but..." Anne-Marie hesitated. "You don't have your credit card, either, do you? They took everything, including our cell phones."

"Don't worry about it," Dirk said. "It'll be fine."

"This isn't the first time Dirk's unloaded his bank account here. They don't forget customers like that," Cherise explained.

Anne-Marie blinked, worrying her hands together in front of her. This was not the confident woman Dirk had met down in Mexico. "Just ignore her," Dirk said in a low voice near her ear. "After what you've been through - what we've all been through - we deserve a bit of pampering." Anne-Marie didn't seem convinced, so he took her hand and gave it a little squeeze. Then he smiled at the waiting receptionist, a bleached blonde with red lips and long nails. "Please make sure Miss Fletcher has everything she needs."

"Of course, Mr. Hillyer." The woman smiled back, her long nails clicking on the keyboard as she entered the information. When she looked up she batted her lashes. "If there's anything else you need - *anything* - don't hesitate to let me know."

"Thank you." Dirk nodded and then turned to the women, handing them each the security code for their rooms. "All set."

Cherise leaned toward Anne-Marie. "Can you believe this guy? Even looking like a lost surfer he attracts the females!"

Dirk made a dismissive sound. "She was just being friendly." He surveyed Anne-Marie's melancholy countenance. She obviously wasn't enjoying the situation. "My sister is *loca*. Ignore everything she says." She didn't look convinced, so he stepped closer and rubbed his hand along her back. "Seriously. It's no big deal. Go buy something nice to wear at the shop, freshen up, and we'll meet in the restaurant in say... ninety minutes?"

Anne-Marie bobbed her head mutely and left without any words.

Dirk watched her for a moment. He hoped a hot shower would also wash away the black cloud that seemed to have descended.

～

DIRK CHECKED HIS WATCH. He let a smile form on his lips and fingered the crystal on the timepiece. It was newly purchased at the hotel jewellers. Luxury did have its appeal. He hadn't missed his old way of life while down in Mexico, but now that he was here, it was rushing back to greet him.

The restaurant was large but still had an intimate quality with candlelit tables and fresh linens. He hoped Anne-Marie liked it. It would be their first real date.

He looked up when he saw Anne-Marie winding her way in his direction behind the maitre'd. His pulse quickened. She looked beautiful, as always, but hardly dressed for a fancy restaurant in slacks and a rather plain blouse.

"Hi." Dirk stood and held out her chair until she was seated.

"Thanks," she said, settling herself. She glanced around the room. "This is fancier than I thought."

"You should have spent more on an outfit," Dirk said. "My treat, remember?"

Anne-Marie looked at him pointedly. "You don't like what I'm wearing?"

"No, no! You look beautiful, as always!" he fumbled. "I just meant, you could have spent more... if you wanted to, that is."

"I don't feel right about taking your money."

"You're forgetting I'm rich, remember?" he teased.

Anne-Marie's lashes fluttered downward but she didn't say anything.

Tension grew as they busied themselves with their order. When the waiter left, Dirk put his hand on top of Anne-Marie's. "What's wrong?"

She shrugged. "Long day."

"I hear you. Is that all?"

Anne-Marie screwed up her forehead for a moment. "Just worried, I guess."

"Ryan will handle it. He's a pro and completely trustworthy. He's a good guy to have on our team."

"I'm sure that's true, but there's more to it than that."

"Like?" Dirk prompted.

"My career, for one."

"You're a great nurse! You'll find another job."

"Easy for you to say. This could ruin my reputation. What if things aren't resolved right away and I can't find another job?"

"Trust. You always say it yourself." Dirk smiled.

Anne-Marie withdrew her hand. "See? You don't know what it's like to be an ordinary person like me. Working at the orphanage was more than just a whim. I don't have family money to fall back on."

Her words stung. Dirk knew it was a jab at his affluence, but he put on a smile anyway. "You could always come to Boston."

Anne-Marie frowned. "And do what?"

Dirk shrugged. "Hang out with me."

She shook her head. "That's another part of the problem. You did a pretty good job of fitting into my world, but I'm not sure I fit in with yours." She gestured to the watch on his wrist. "Take that watch, for instance. How much did that cost?"

Dirk looked down at the watch and then back up at Anne-Marie. "I didn't look at the price."

"See what I mean? I don't even know the real you. I only know what you want me to."

"I let you know I care about you," Dirk said. "That hasn't changed."

Anne-Marie sighed. "Maybe for now."

He didn't know what was going on with Anne-Marie. The ordeal with the police had changed her. He was ninety-nine percent sure he loved her, yet she was distancing herself by the minute. And he wasn't quite sure what to do about it.

~

DIRK LAY on the king-size bed in his hotel room and stared up at the ceiling. The evening had been strained to say the least. Still, he knew it was partly due to the stress of the day and the ordeal they had been through. At least he hoped that was all it was.

When he stopped to think about it, he was attracted to so much more than Anne-Marie's physical attributes. What he really loved was her strength of character; her unwavering faith; her kind and compassionate nature. These were truly beautiful things - things that stemmed directly from her love of God.

And then it dawned on him. He wasn't worthy of a woman like her.

If he really loved Anne-Marie he needed to share her faith - not just fake a walk with God that was dependent on his own needs.

But was he really ready for that? A total surrender to God?

He took a long, deep intake of air and let it out again just as slowly. He'd heard the 'sinner's prayer' enough times at the church services down in Mexico, albeit through a translator, to know it off by heart. Still, the gist was the same, no matter which language was used. It might be worth a try. He had nothing to lose and everything - including the woman he loved - to gain.

Dirk closed his eyes. "Okay God. I think I'm finally ready, so if you're really real, let's do this thing." He took another deep breath. "Dear Jesus. I confess that I'm a sinner. You know it! Please forgive me of my sins and become Lord of my life. I want to live for you from now on. For real, so help me do that. Oh, and please, can I have Anne-Marie, too?"

Almost immediately, Dirk drifted off to sleep, a smile softening his features.

CHAPTER 39

*R*yan's office was not large, but the glass walls that separated it from the rest of the bureau made it feel quite open. Cherise sat across from him along with Dirk and Anne-Marie while he shuffled through a few papers on his desk. She wasn't sure what was going on between her brother and his girlfriend, but there was definitely more tension in the air than even such a visit at the FBI would warrant.

"I've gotten everyone's statements and now it's just a matter of letting our guys do their thing. It could be a matter of days or months before we can wrap this one up. Hopefully it won't come to it, but be prepared to testify if need be." Ryan tapped the stack of papers on the desk to straighten them.

"Is it safe?" Cherise asked. "I mean, for us to just be going about our business while the bad guys are still out there?"

"Since this is a joint investigation, there is only so much I can do to guarantee your protection. Having said that, I doubt that you'll be in any danger. We made sure to protect your identities and to make it look like you were suspects, so the likelihood of anyone risking themselves to cross the border to find you is very slim."

TRACY KRAUSS

"But still a possibility," Cherise said.

"Anything is a possibility." Ryan's no nonsense stare cut through to her core and Cherise lowered her gaze.

"I don't like the sound of that," Dirk said. "Not one bit."

Ryan shrugged. "It's the best I can offer."

"Then I'll be hiring private security for all three of us," Dirk declared.

"Do what you have to do," Ryan said with a shrug. He directed his gaze at Anne-Marie. "What about you? You've been quiet through all of this."

"I was just thinking about home. I'll be glad to get back, even if winter has already set in."

"You're going back to Canada?" Dirk's eyebrows rose.

"Of course. What did you think I'd do? I can't stay in the US indefinitely without a visa and without a job... At least I can stay with my parents until I get myself back on my feet."

Dirk sat forward. "But... how will I know you'll be safe?"

She shrugged. "Trust."

"She's probably right," Ryan said. "There is really no point in any of you hanging around. Carry on with life and let us do our jobs."

Dirk sat back and folded his arms. "We will definitely be talking about this later."

"What about James?" Cherise asked. "Is he the one behind it?"

"I really can't comment, seeing as it is an ongoing investigation. Let's just say he is cooperating fully with the authorities."

"He's guilty," Dirk muttered.

"You might be surprised," Ryan offered. "But that's all I'm at liberty to say." He glanced at his watch. "And now, I've got some work to do before we meet Tempest for lunch. She's very excited to see you." He looked pointedly at Dirk. "All of you."

The thought of seeing her friend again helped dissipate some of the unease that Cherise still felt. She thought giving her life to Christ was going to make her existence less complicated, not

334

more so. Trust was the operative word of the day, it seemed, and so she pasted on a smile and followed the rest to the waiting rental car.

~

ON THE DRIVE to the restaurant in the four seater Ferrari that Dirk had rented, Cherise chattered about things that would have normally consumed her interests - the latest fashion, reality TV stars, and the upcoming seasonal parties they would be expected to attend. It sounded shallow, even to her own ears, but filling the awkward silence in the vehicle seemed like a necessity. Her companions were being morbidly quiet. Anne-Marie's was a melancholy silence, while Dirk's seemed to stem from his anger at the unsatisfactory twist in their situation.

They pulled into the parking lot of the seafood restaurant that Tempest had chosen and Dirk cut the engine. "Hmph. Funny she chose this place," he said to no one in particular.

"What's that?" Anne-Marie asked.

"Oh, nothing. I've been here before is all." He went around to Anne-Marie's side of the vehicle but she had already opened her own door.

Seagulls squawked overhead and the salt sea air filled Cherise's nostrils as soon as she exited the car. "Ah! This is beautiful!"

The seafood restaurant had an open deck that stretched along the harbor and the hostess led them to a table near the outer railing.

"Thanks," Cherise said as Dirk held out her chair once he had done the same for Anne-Marie. "This is simply picturesque! I think I'd love living in California. No wonder Tempest loves it." The breeze whipped a few tendrils of hair across her face and Cherise had to swipe them away with her forefinger. "Did Dirk ever tell you that he helped Tempest move out here?"

"Do you ever stop talking?" Dirk asked.

Cherise blinked. "Oh. Sorry. I was just making conversation."

"No, he never told me that," Anne-Marie responded. "I suppose there are a lot of things he hasn't told me."

"All in good time," Dirk quipped.

"I don't expect you to tell me everything," Anne-Marie countered reasonably. "We've only known each other a short time and we're just friends."

Dirk's frown couldn't get any deeper, Cherise noted. There was definitely something amiss between her brother and his new lady love. She sat up and smiled, pointing at the menu. "Oh look! Calamari! My favourite!" If either of them got any grumpier, she'd have to resort to an all out song and dance routine to keep them distracted.

Much to Cherise's relief, Ryan and Tempest arrived within minutes. "Oh my goodness! Let me give you a hug!" Cherise squealed and jumped from her seat. She threw her arms around Tempest and they hugged tightly before Cherise finally let her friend go.

"I'm so happy about your news!" Tempest said. "After you called me, I couldn't sleep for the rest of the night!"

"News?" Ryan asked, looking from Cherise to Tempest.

"That I accepted Jesus," Cherise said. "Tempest didn't tell you?"

"Oh. I must have forgotten," Ryan said.

"With everything else that's happened, I don't blame you."

Dirk had stood when Tempest and Ryan arrived. "Hello, Tempest. Good to see you again." He gave a slight bow.

"You too," Tempest responded, giving him what looked like a genuine smile.

"May I introduce Anne-Marie Fletcher? We met down in Mexico."

The women acknowledged each other with a nod. "Ryan told

me," Tempest said. They all reseated themselves, Ryan helping Tempest before Dirk could offer to do so.

"I've got new information since our meeting this morning." Ryan unfolded his napkin and gave it a quick snap.

"Oh?" Cherise asked.

"Our contact in Mexico thinks he knows who the mole is. We might be able to wrap this case up sooner than expected. You might want to stick around for a few days, if possible."

"No problem," Dirk said, then quickly turned to Anne-Marie. "At least, I think it's a good idea." She just nodded her ascent.

"Well, I sure don't mind a few extra days in sunny California," Cherise said.

"We can do some touristy stuff," Tempest put in. "Museums, galleries…"

"Shopping," Cherise added and they both laughed. Cherise turned to Anne-Marie. "What do you say? A little shopping on Rodeo Drive?"

"Oh goodness! I can't afford that!" Tempest said immediately.

"Neither can I," Anne-Marie echoed.

"But I can," Cherise countered. "Come on! It'll be fun!"

"Actually, I was hoping that Anne-Marie and I could take a walk this afternoon," Dirk interjected.

"A walk? How boring!" Cherise exclaimed. "What if she wants to come with us?"

Dirk ignored his sister, focusing on Anne-Marie. "Please? I miss our walks. Plus, I have something important I need to talk to you about."

Cherise leaned forward. "He won't stop until you agree," she directed at Anne-Marie. She knew if they were going to mend their relationship, this is exactly what they both needed.

Anne-Marie took a sip from her water. "I suppose."

Cherise sat back with a satisfied smile. Her heart still ached for Blue, but if she could do something to help her brother and the woman he loved, it would all be worth it.

∼

CHERISE AND TEMPEST walked arm in arm along the palm lined street, vermillion hibiscus spilling from planters as each shop window tried to outdo the next with expensive wares tucked behind their arched and gilded facades, an architectural mixture of grandeur and charm.

Cherise stopped to peer at a display of purses in a high-end boutique. "I could get used to this! Maybe I should move here."

"Real life isn't this glamorous," Tempest said, pulling her friend along. "LA is bigger than I remembered as a child and it's a very expensive city to live in." She smiled. "Not that that's a worry for you, but you know what I mean."

"Now that I'm a Christian too, we could hang out together all the time! Go to the same parties and not drink together. How fun would that be?"

Tempest laughed and shook her head. "As a baby Christian, you do need some mentoring, I can see that!"

"I know," Cherise squeezed her friend's arm. "I was just teasing about the parties... maybe. Anne-Marie has been very good about helping me learn things. She got me reading the Bible and I went to church - a lot - while I was at the orphanage."

"She seems like a very nice person," Tempest said. "Do you think it's serious between her and Dirk?"

"I don't know. I would have said definitely, when I first arrived in Mexico, but things have been a bit tense lately."

"You've all been through a lot," Tempest reminded. "Intrigue seems to follow you."

"Tell me about it. I could do with a slice of normal right now, believe me." Cherise sighed. "I just wish normal wasn't so lonely."

"You still have feelings for Blue Shepherd?"

"Yes, I think so. Although, so much has happened that I'm not sure what I feel anymore. I just want to feel secure. Happy."

"That's where Jesus comes in," Tempest said. "No matter what or who lets you down, He'll never let you down."

"So I've been told." Cherise glanced at her friend. "I get the feeling that someone has let you down recently. Can I hazard a guess at Ryan?"

"What makes you say that?" Tempest asked.

Cherise shrugged. "I just have a sixth sense about these things. I haven't been in so many relationships for nothing!"

Tempest shook her head. "I'm not sure what to think about our relationship. Right after we got back from Italy, it seemed perfect. We were both here in LA and I could hardly believe such an interesting and good looking man would want to be with me."

"But...?" Cherise prompted.

"Things have changed recently. I can't quite put my finger on it, but they have definitely changed."

"How, exactly?"

"For one thing, he's keeping secrets from me. I know it."

"That's part of his job. You know that."

Tempest nodded. "I know, but it's more than that. Maybe I'm the one who's changed." She took a deep breath. "Anyway, I don't want to talk about it. I want to know about you and what you're going to do now. Did you know that Blue has been looking for you? At least that's what Stella says."

"Stella? Why didn't she tell me herself?"

"You weren't exactly making yourself available," Tempest said. "None of us could reach you while you were in Mexico."

"Oh, right. Sorry. I was trying to distance myself, I guess. Dive right in and not get distracted by thoughts of home."

"Or thoughts of Blue," Tempest added.

"Exactly."

"I take it it hasn't been working."

"Yes and no."

"Why don't you call him?" Tempest suggested. They stopped in front of an exclusive dress boutique. "Now that you're back in the States and you've made a commitment to Christ, who knows what could happen?"

Cherise shook her head. "I doubt it's a good idea. I'm still no good for him. He's a cowboy and I'm…"

"What? A lonely woman who happens to be in love with a cowboy?" Tempest gazed into Cherise's eyes. "You keep belittling yourself, saying you're no good. But you are good, Cherise. Jesus made you a new creation and who are you to say that the work He's done in you is rubbish?"

"When you put it that way…" Cherise smiled.

"You know I'm right. Maybe the old Cherise had commitment issues. A wondering eye, even. But who knows what the new Cherise is capable of?"

"Do you really think I could give it another shot with Blue?" Cherise asked.

"I do. Stella says he's been miserable without you and as far as I can see you feel the same. Maybe God meant for you to be together."

Cherise straightened her spine and took a springy step forward. "Come on. This calls for some retail therapy. Or is it a retail celebration? Either way, I'm buying you a new dress!"

"I don't need anything new," Tempest protested, following Cherise into the shop.

"I won't take no for an answer!"

And she wouldn't. This time she was going to fly straight to Fort Stockton just as soon as she could leave LA. If Jesus said she was a new creation, then who was she to argue?

irk left the Ferrari parked where it was since Cherise and Tempest had taken a cab for their shopping excursion. It was just a few steps from the restaurant terrace to the boardwalk and the beach proper. He reached for Anne-Marie's hand on their way down the wooden staircase, but even though she accepted, her grasp was limp and unresponsive. She was putting up a wall and he didn't understand why. All he knew was, it needed to come down before it was impenetrable.

"So? What do you think about what Ryan said earlier? Catching the bad guys sooner than later is a win in my books."

"Yes, good news," Anne-Marie responded.

"I don't suppose it changes much, though. About you going back home, I mean." He glanced at her profile on the way down the steps.

"It doesn't. I have to go home either way. Besides, where else would I go?"

"You could come to Boston," he suggested hopefully.

"I can't afford that."

"Then I'll come to Edmonton."

"Things aren't that simple. You're free to fly around the world and do whatever you want. I, on the other hand, have to work for a living."

"So? I'll pay."

"You know how I feel about taking handouts."

"Oh, it's a pride thing," Dirk said with a nod of his head. "I thought pride was one of the original sins or something."

"Now you're making fun of me."

"Well, you're making things more complicated than they need to be."

They stopped, having reached the boardwalk, and Anne-Marie sighed heavily. "Dirk, I don't think you're being realistic about our relationship."

"I'm being very realistic." Dirk turned her to look at him. "I know that I care about you. Deeply. And all this 'We're just friends' in front of Cherise and the others just doesn't cut it. You know I want more than that. Feel more than that."

"Dirk, stop," she protested and withdrew her hand from his.

"No! I won't stop! I don't know what's going on, but somewhere between here and the orphanage you've changed. Where's the confident woman I met in Mexico? The one who trusts God?"

"Maybe she was a figment of your imagination."

"I doubt that."

"When I was at the orphanage, I felt good about myself. I knew I had a purpose and I guess that helped to boost my self confidence. But here, surrounded by all... this," she gestured to the beach thronging with people, "I feel like an outsider."

"You're talking crazy."

"No, I'm not. I'm telling you how I feel." She patted her heart. "So don't dismiss me."

"Sorry."

"See, that's part of the problem," she continued. "You're one of 'them' - the beautiful people - so you see things differently. But being here, among all these perfectly tanned and toned specimens... It makes me feel inadequate."

"Anne-Marie -"

She cut him off with a raised hand. "I'm not finished. I'm not comfortable here and I suspect this is very much who you are. I just want to go back to my work, where I can feel good about myself."

Dirk ran a hand through his hair. "I see this is going to be a tough sell. You've convinced yourself you don't fit in. That you don't like 'my world'. But you haven't given it a chance."

"I'd feel like a fake."

"I have no idea why. You *are* beautiful - inside and out."

"You're one smooth talker, I'll give you that, but I'm not convinced. I don't know what it is about you, Dirk Hillyer, but ever since I met you, I got my priorities all mixed up."

"Oh? Is that a good thing or a bad thing?"

"You had me convinced I was something special -"

"You are!"

"Sh! You're interrupting again. I used to care more about following Jesus and helping others. I didn't put too much stock in outward appearances. I'd learned to love and accept myself - or so I thought. And then you came along and I started feeling inadequate again. About my weight and my clothes..."

"I think your weight is perfect and clothes can be changed," Dirk reasoned.

"On the inside I'd still feel like a phoney. If we started seeing each other, I'd be afraid the whole time that one day you'd suddenly see me for who I am and dump me."

"I would never do that!" he exclaimed.

"How do I know that?" she asked. "I hardly even know you. You're just someone I talked to on moonlight strolls down in Mexico. How do I know the real Dirk Hillyer is who he claims to be?"

"You want a confession?" he asked. "Okay. I have a huge confession to make. I've been waiting to tell you all day, but just couldn't find the right moment."

"Okay…" Anne-Marie said slowly.

He grinned nervously. "Talk about being a phoney. I'm the biggest one yet."

"You mean you're not rich after all?" she asked with a tentative smile.

"No, that part is true." They stopped walking and Dirk looked down, expelling a deep breath. "Okay. Here goes." He looked up. "I lied."

"About what?" Anne-Marie's voice was small and hesitant.

"Actually, you called me out on it awhile back, but I was too embarrassed to admit it to you."

Anne-Marie was blinking rapidly, her eyes filling up with tears. "I knew it was too good to be true. I never should have trusted you." She turned away and swiped at a tear.

"Hey, don't cry!" Dirk put his hand on her shoulder but she shrugged it away.

"I'm fine." She turned around to face him and tilted the corners of her mouth up in a fake smile. "This is about you and Tempest, isn't it?"

"Huh?"

"You lied to me when you said you didn't care about her anymore. Seeing her again made you realize that. I get it."

Dirk shook his head. "You are so silly!"

"Silly? Yeah, maybe I am, to think a guy like you would ever fall for a girl like me."

"Don't tell me you're jealous of Tempest."

"Yes, if you must know. She's very pretty. Sorry, but it's how I feel."

"For the record, you have it all wrong. Our relationship was never more than wishful thinking on my part." Dirk gave a self depreciating laugh. "Thankfully, I came to my senses when I met you."

"But… Cherise makes it sound like there was something deeper. Some terrible dark secret between you two. Even Ryan seemed a bit edgy today when her name came up, and even more so at lunch."

Dirk shook his head. "Oh boy. Talk about confession time!"

"So, there is something." Anne-Marie looked down at her toes. "I'm sorry for prying. You don't have to tell me if you don't want to."

"I don't want to, believe me, but it's not what you think, so I better just get it over with and then if you want to run, you can."

"Oh dear. That bad?"

"Depends on your point of view, I guess." He took another fortifying breath. "Okay, here goes. I wanted to fabricate a way for her to need me. To turn to me in a time of crisis. So, I asked someone to take care of her cat, as in make it go away. I thought it would drive her to me, but instead the idiot killed the cat and left it hanging right in front of the window where Tempest would see it."

Anne-Marie gasped and put her hand over her mouth.

"Terrible, I know. I'm a cat killer - sort of. I kept the truth a secret for as long as I could, but eventually I told her everything. When I did, she almost didn't forgive me."

"And that's what broke you up," Anne-Marie said.

"No! We were never together. I've been trying to tell you that! The interest was all one sided, believe me." He glanced at her profile to gauge her reaction. "That's the real me. Just a depraved and desperate man looking for love and making a disaster it. It's not one of my proudest moments, but I'm grateful that Tempest - and God - have seen fit to forgive me. I hope you won't think any worse of me for it."

"We all make mistakes," she said.

"Yes, which brings me to the real thing I wanted to confess to you."

She turned soulful eyes toward him. "There's more?"

"I'm not lying about my feelings for you, but I have been lying about something else..."

She waited expectantly.

"What I lied about was knowing Jesus."

She closed her eyes. "I knew it! You're not even a Christian!" She turned away, a small sob escaping her lips.

"Now, wait a minute!" He grasped her shoulder and turned her back around to face him. "It wasn't a total lie because I didn't exactly know what that meant. In any case, now I do. I prayed last night and I actually gave my heart to Jesus."

Anne-Marie's eyes widened. "You what?"

"I prayed and asked Jesus to be Lord of my life." He grinned.

Anne-Marie threw her arms around Dirk's neck and started crying in earnest, the tears soaking into his shirt.

Whatever reaction he had expected, it wasn't this. Still, he wasn't about to look a gift horse in the mouth. He clung to Anne-Marie like he would never let go. Maybe God had answered his prayers after all.

hat kind of grown man quit his job and moved home? Blue shook his head. One tired of running, he supposed. Zane and Stella had been understanding and of course, there was always work ready and waiting on the ranch, so it wouldn't be like he wasn't pulling his weight. Still, it felt anti-climactic and definitely knocked his ego down a notch. It was only a temporary arrangement, he kept telling himself. When their father passed on, Blue planned to move on as well. If he settled on the ranch he'd become an old bachelor. Maybe he'd become one anyway, but at least if he left, he could see the world.

Blue entered the big kitchen of the main house through the back entrance, in search of Zane and a good cup of coffee. One of Gabriella's baked goods would do the trick, too. Even though he was the foreman's son, Gabriella had always made him feel like he was part of the family, and now that Zane had married Stella, he supposed he really was.

"Good morning, Blue." Helen Crayton, Stella's stepmother, was pouring herself a cup of coffee from the carafe.

"Oh, hello, Ma'am." Blue nodded and removed his cowboy hat. He hadn't been expecting Rod's widow to be in the kitchen, but then again, it was still her home. "Have you seen Zane this morning?" he asked as a way to explain his appearance.

"I'm afraid not." She took a tentative sip from her travel mug and then secured the lid in place. "I was wondering when I'd see you, since I heard you moved back."

Blue fingered the rim of his hat. "It's only temporary. Till Dad... well, you know."

"Of course. Family should be together at times like these."

Blue nodded.

"Well, I'm off to the city for a few days. I'm sure he's around somewhere." She gave a slight nod and turned to leave just as Gabriella entered. "Oh, Gabriella. Can you make sure the donations for the charity raffle get delivered? Someone is supposed to be picking them up, but I'd feel more secure knowing you were delivering them instead on your way into town tonight."

"Of course, Mrs. Crayton," Gabriella said with a nod.

"Alright. See you in a few days. And make sure someone looks after the pets."

The clack-clacking of Helen's heels diminished.

"Since when *hasn't* someone looked after the pets?" Blue rolled his eyes. "It certainly has never been her."

"Shush!" Gabriella scolded, raising her index finger. They waited until they heard the front door open and close.

"And if someone is picking the donations up, why ask you to deliver them?" Blue shook his head. "I thought that woman had changed since Rod died, but I see she's back to being the control freak she always was."

"That's enough from you, young man," Gabriella said. "Mrs. Crayton has had a hard time of it since the boss passed. Not to mention Stella back and married and living in the house with her. I'd say she's done very well."

"If you say so."

Gabriella placed a steaming mug of coffee in front of Blue, complete with cream and sugar already added. The force with which she set the mug down caused it to spill. The motherly housekeeper seemed to be in a contrary mood this morning, but Blue tried to ignore it. She'd been under a lot of strain, too, since Rod Crayton had passed away.

"Thanks." Blue took a sip of the hot brew and sighed. "Ah! Just the way I like it."

Gabriella stood with hands on hips. "Under the circumstances, I should make you get your own coffee, but I just can't believe it's true, that's all."

Blue frowned. "What? All I said was Helen shouldn't expect you to be a delivery person, too. You have enough to do around here."

Gabriella grunted her disapproval. "You're one to talk about people. The shenanigans I see you getting up to! I just pray you're involved by mistake, or it would break my heart." She got out a mixing bowl and some baking ingredients.

"Shenanigans?" Blue frowned.

Just then Zane and Stella entered the kitchen. Zane went straight for the coffee while Stella plunked down at the granite covered island. "What's this about shenanigans?" Stella asked.

Zane set two mugs of coffee on the counter and joined his wife.

Blue laughed. "Not sure, exactly. Gabriella seems to think I've been getting up to something, but I'm not sure what."

"Now what have you done?" Stella teased.

"Me? Nothing."

"Mr. Innocent," Zane commented and took a sip of coffee.

"Well, I talked to Tempest recently," Stella said. "She says Cherise and Dirk are sticking around LA for a bit since the police are making headway with the drug smuggling case they got mixed up in."

"Tut, tut! Those two are always getting into trouble." Gabriella shook her head, mixing vigorously. "It's a good thing the good Lord is looking out for them. For all of you young people."

"At least He's watching over somebody," Blue said sarcastically. "And how do you seem to know so much?" he added.

"I go on social media," Gabriella informed defensively. She pointed her wooden spoon at Blue. "And He's watching over you, too, and don't you mistake it - no matter what you're involved in."

"Blue keeps his guardian angel well employed," Zane said with a grin.

"Very funny, big brother," Blue shot back. "I'll have you know I agree with Gabriella. That psycho chick I was telling you about could have caused me a world of grief."

Stella was scrolling on her cell phone. "I'm not so sure she hasn't…"

Gabriella popped the muffins into the oven. "You better hope you've been hacked."

"What do you mean?" Blue looked from Stella to Gabriella.

"Have you checked your social media lately?" Stella looked up at Blue.

"I deleted them all after, well, you know," Blue replied sheepishly.

Stella shuddered. "Don't remind me!"

"I don't even bother with it any more," Blue continued. "It's kind of freeing, to be honest."

"Well, that's not what it looks like." Stella held up her phone.

Blue frowned and leaned closer to Stella to take a look. His eyes widened. "What the…? Give me that!" He grabbed Stella's phone and continued scrolling through her feed. Apparently, he had joined a white supremacist group and was spouting about the necessity for purity among the races. "I never joined any such group!" He sat back, stunned and then turned to Gabriella. "You must know I would never, ever promote anything like that! I swear!"

"It's a good thing I gave you the benefit of the doubt, or you would have been wearing that coffee," Gabriella declared.

"Beth?" Zane asked.

"Who else?" Blue slumped forward and cradled his head in his hands. "She warned me."

"You need to report this right away," Stella advised.

Gabriella put her hand on Blue's back. "When the muffins come out of the oven, you get two."

LATER THAT DAY, Blue sat by his father's bedside and stroked the elder's hand. Duke looked so sallow. So weak and small. Not the stalwart cowboy that Blue still saw in his mind's eye. It was frightening how quickly things could change. One day his father was a robust wrangler, still able to carry his share of the work-load. The next, he was a frail shadow of a man, lying in bed just waiting to die.

Blue's own life had changed just as quickly. He went from being a carefree ranchhand at loose ends and back again with little to show for it but a hole in his heart the size of Texas itself. Where he went from here was a mystery, but he knew he couldn't stay at the ranch. This was Zane's destiny, not his. Maybe he would become a drifter. Travel the world bringing home exotic gifts for his yet to be born nieces and nephews. The notion was appealing, if somewhat lonely.

Fortunately, once he'd reported the hack-job, every trace of the supremacist group and his so called involvement in it was deleted. Hopefully, not too many people had seen it, but he supposed there might be some fall out. He knew Beth had a vendetta against him, but the depths of her vengeance seemed extreme next to the misdemeanours that had caused it.

Duke's eyes fluttered open. His breathing had been labored this evening; more so than usual. Blue leaned forward. "Do you need something? A drink? Another blanket?"

Duke shook his head, a very slight movement. He gestured

weakly with his free hand for Blue to move closer. Blue bent even further and Duke's hand flopped to the sheets. Blue turned his ear toward his father's mouth so that he could hear better. "I want to see you in heaven."

Blue furrowed his brow. "What was that?"

Duke took another labored breath. "I said, I want to see you again. In heaven."

"Oh. Of course." Blue patted his father's hand and started to sit up but Duke's frail one grasped Blue's with surprising strength.

"Pray. Now," Duke demanded.

Blue squeezed his father's hand, partly because he wanted to reassure him and partly because the old coot wouldn't let go. Blue took a breath and then closed his eyes. He knew how it was supposed to go, so he started praying, hoping he remembered the proper format for the old man's sake.

"Heavenly Father. I confess that I am a sinner and in need of a Savior. I accept the free gift you gave on the cross when you died for my sins..." Blue's voice hitched.

His chest felt constricted and he wasn't sure he could go on. A gentle reminder in the form of a squeeze to his hand opened his mouth again. "I ask you to come into my life as Lord and..." Blue's voice caught again and this time he gasped as he filled his lungs with air. A sob escaped and tears began to flow.

Blue bent his head and rested it on top of his father's chest. Duke laid his free hand on his son's shoulder as Blue cried into the sheets.

"Oh God! I have really messed up. Big time. I don't deserve your love or your forgiveness. And I sure don't deserve such a wonderful dad as you gave me. Thank you for this godly man. Thank you that he drilled the right way into my thick skull even when I didn't want to hear it. Please God. Forgive me. Forgive me for all the things I've done against you and against myself. Make me a new man. I want that. And I want to see my pa again someday. Please God. That's all I have to say." He raised his head and sniffed. "Amen."

"Amen," Duke said, quite clearly.

Blue sat up fully. "Thank you for being too stubborn to give up on me," he whispered and grasped his father's hand more tightly.

Duke looked into Blue's eyes and smiled - a full sunbeam of love and pride. Then he closed his eyes, a contented look about his face. His breathing steadied and he relaxed into sleep.

Blue sat for a few minutes longer, filled with the wonder that now enveloped his being. A sense of joy and peace like he had never known was hovering over his shoulders and filling his heart, that empty cavern that now felt full to the brim. He listened to the rhythmic breathing of his father and rejoiced in this feeling of happiness. "You always were a stubborn old goat," Blue said with a smile.

Duke took a deep breath, followed by a very slow release that seemed to go on unnaturally long.

"Dad?" Blue leaned forward onto his father's chest. The motion caused air to press out of Duke's lungs like squeezing on an inflatable tube. "Dad?" he repeated and then felt for a pulse. Nothing.

Blue sat for a moment, not quite sure what to do next, but still basking in the peace that had flooded the entire room. A smile spread slowly across Blue's lips. "Stubborn old coot," he said. "You just couldn't leave without me, could you?"

CHAPTER 42

"Anne-Marie and Cherise are here, too. Just a minute and I'll put you on speaker." Dirk hit the speaker option on his cell phone and held it aloft as he, Cherise, and Anne-Marie gathered on the sitting room couch in Cherise's hotel suite. "Okay, go ahead, Ryan."

Cherise took a hold of Anne-Marie's hand and squeezed. They'd assembled in her hotel suite to wait for Ryan's call, but now that it had come, she felt nervous.

"Hi, everyone." Ryan O'Toole's voice came tunnel like through Dirk's cell. "I have an update. I thought you'd like to know that arrests have been made in the Beacon of Hope drug smuggling case."

Relief pulsed through Cherise's chest as the tiny group gave a smattering of applause.

"James, I take it?" Dirk asked.

"No, it looks like James is innocent," Ryan said. "His wife Linda, however, not so much."

Cherise raised her brows at Dirk and Anne-Marie, the latter of whom seemed especially taken aback by the news.

"Huh! Who would have guessed!" Dirk exclaimed.

"She claims it was for, and I quote, 'altruistic reasons,'" Ryan added, "citing the need for more funding to allow for the expansion plans that James was apparently working on."

"That still doesn't make it right," Anne-Marie said. "What about the people she was hurting on the other end?"

"I feel kind of sorry for her," Dirk offered. "She always seemed like such a misfit."

"In any case, it will be up to the court to decide her punishment," Ryan continued. "She's lucky to be coming back to the States for her trial."

"What about poor James?" Anne-Marie asked.

"Apparently, he didn't know anything about it, although he was beginning to suspect something was amiss right around the same time that you did."

Dirk nodded his understanding. "That's probably why he was out walking in the grove late at night."

"Linda claims she did it out of love for James - that the mission's funding had gone down recently and she was just trying to keep things afloat. Again, we'll see if the jury buys it," Ryan said.

"I never liked her," Dirk claimed.

"Dirk!" Cherise punched him in the arm. Dirk winced but didn't say anything.

"Surely there are others?" Anne-Marie asked. "She couldn't have set this up on her own."

"Another local, a nurse named Franchesca Valdez, was also involved."

Anne-Marie gasped and put her hand over her mouth.

Dirk placed a hand on her shoulder. "What about the Aussie doctor? Harry Smythe?"

"Clean."

Dirk snapped his fingers. "Too bad."

"Dirk!" both Cherise and Anne-Marie scolded. He got another punch, this time from Anne-Marie.

Ryan continued. "The two ladies are small fry compared to the outfit behind it all. Probably a drug cartel or other criminal organization. Unfortunately, they aren't as easy to pin down. That part of the investigation is still ongoing, and quite frankly, we might never be able to catch them."

"So, poor Linda and Franchesca are the scapegoats." Anne-Marie shook her head.

"Local police did arrest a driver from Tijuana," Ryan supplied. "He's probably the best informant we've got, but… he'll be prosecuted in Mexico."

"And James' cousin or nephew or whatever he is… Dillan? He really is a cop?" Dirk asked.

"Yes. Very helpful in solving the mystery, although I'm sure James wasn't expecting it to turn out this way."

Anne-Marie frowned. "What is this going to mean for the mission? Will they be able to continue?"

"The mission should be business as usual, and as far as I know, James is free to stay, although I'm not sure he'll want to. I would expect the board of directors is looking for a replacement as we speak. The last thing they need is scandal attached to their good name. It could jeopardize donations," Ryan said.

Anne-Marie sighed. "Why is everything about money?"

Dirk rubbed his chin. "I think I might have a solution for that."

Cherise frowned at her brother. "You're not thinking of applying?"

Dirk laughed. "No. Running an orphanage is definitely not my area of expertise. I was thinking of funding the place, though."

"Really? You'd do that?" Anne-Marie asked.

"Of course. I know how much it means to you, and if the truth be told, it means a lot to me, too."

"Well, that's about it from me," Ryan interrupted. "Thank you all for your cooperation. Hopefully the next time we meet it won't have anything to do with drugs or any other criminal activity."

"Amen to that!" Cherise flopped back against the plush cushions after Ryan had hung up. "I've had enough drama for one year."

"That makes two of us," Dirk echoed.

"What are your plans, Anne-Marie?" Cherise asked. "Now that we can all go home."

Anne-Marie shrugged. "Look for a job."

"I was thinking I might like to try a white Christmas in Edmonton, this year," Dirk said. "Then after that, you could come to Boston for Valentine's day. And then who knows? We might have to settle on someplace in between."

Anne-Marie gave Dirk a wry smile. "You're getting ahead of yourself. I said we'd 'try' a relationship'. And you haven't met my father yet."

"I can be very charming when needed. Just ask Cherise. And I can be patient, too. You'll see."

"What about you?" Anne-Marie asked Cherise.

"Home for Christmas, of course, since it sounds like Dirk might not be there and we couldn't leave our poor parents totally alone for the holidays."

"They wouldn't even notice," Dirk said dismissively.

"They're still family," Cherise said. "But first I'm going down to Texas."

"You are? Since when?" Dirk asked.

"Since I talked to Tempest about it. There's some unfinished business I need to clear up."

"Mysterious," Dirk said, slapping his knees as he stood. "Well, we have flights to book."

Anne-Marie stood also and gave Cherise a hug. "It has been wonderful to get to know you."

"Don't worry. We'll be seeing a lot more of one another if my brother has his way."

Anne-Marie laughed and headed toward the door.

"Good luck." Dirk kissed Cherise on the cheek and then whispered in her ear. "I hope you find as much happiness as I have."

"If we both keep on praying, we should be alright."

Dirk and Anne-Marie left her suite hand in hand and the sight of them did Cherise's heart good. She was truly happy for her brother - that he had found Jesus as well as such a treasure in Anne-Marie.

If only she could say the same. Even though she, too, had found God's saving grace, she still ached at the thought of Blue. Maybe it would always be that way. Maybe God was teaching her to rely on Him and not on a man.

She inhaled deeply and smiled. She didn't need a man to make her feel whole. The creator of the universe had done that all by Himself.

CHERISE SIGHED as she stared out the window of the Uber, watching the scenery surrounding Fort Stockton's airport gradually give way to evidence of industrialization. Large metal buildings surrounded by chain link fences replaced the dusty hills and dark greenery.

The driver pulled into the parking lot beside a square industrial building. After paying the driver, Cherise got out of the vehicle and shut the door with a thud. She smoothed her skirt, a rather tight affair that showed off her attributes. One couldn't blame a girl for pulling out all the stops. With fluid steps she clicked her way across the pavement to the glass door that proclaimed 'open'.

The store was not that big for the size of the building. Metal shelves were lined with gadgets and mechanical parts; leather belts and large gears that she'd never seen before. She supposed it was more of a showroom than anything else, with the majority of the stock in the large warehouse that loomed beyond a cavernous door behind a single counter.

"May I help you?" The young woman behind the counter tucked a straggling piece of hair behind one ear, her eyes narrowing in silent appraisal.

"Yes. I'm looking for Blue Shepherd. I believe he works here?" Cherise put on her best smile and flipped her hair off one shoulder. If the other girl was trying to be disconcerting, she couldn't have done a better job.

"You're Cherise, aren't you?" the girl asked.

Cherise blinked. "Do I know you?"

"Not yet, but you will." The young woman leaned against the counter, her eyes never leaving Cherise's.

Cherise tilted her chin with practiced superiority to look down her nose at her counterpart, a move perfected after years of maneuvering through the boarding school pecking order. "And you are?"

"Oh, just the person your boyfriend was banging on the side."

Cherise's eyes widened. "Excuse me?"

"You heard me." The other girl laughed unpleasantly. "I suppose you thought he was faithful to you all this time, but I think we both know he's not the type."

Cherise inhaled sharply. Her first instinct was to scratch the other woman's eyes out, but now that she was a Christian, she had to rethink that option. She straightened her spine. "You have me at a disadvantage. What's your name?"

"I'm Beth, his boss's niece, but don't worry. I dumped him. Right after my uncle kicked his arse down the road for being the lying, cheat he is."

"I... I don't know quite what to say..."

"Can you believe he was embezzling money right under my uncle's nose?" Beth glanced sideways and then leaned closer in a conspiratorial fashion. "Not to mention he's part of a white supremacist group!"

"A white supremacist group?" Cherise repeated. Her knees suddenly felt weak and she slumped against the counter.

"We've got all kinds of whack-jobs here in Texas," Beth said with a wave of her hand. "I'm just glad I found out before he proposed to me."

"Oh my! You were that serious?" Cherise's head was swimming and she thought she might faint.

"Beth!"

The bellowed syllable jolted Cherise upright and she turned to watch a giant emerge from a doorway tucked out of sight in the far left corner of the show room. "That is quite enough!" The man was middle aged but built like a linebacker. "My niece is full of hot air, Miss," he directed at Cherise, before turning back to Beth. "I have no idea what you're doing, but whatever it is, it stops now!"

"It was nothing." Beth rolled her shoulder. "Just a joke."

"Well, it's not funny." The man pointed a finger in her face. "I don't know what's gotten into you, but for now, get out of my sight. I'll deal with you later."

Beth glared at Cherise before stomping from the showroom.

"I apologize for my niece's behaviour. The name's John Marethorpe, owner, and Blue's boss." He reached out his massive hand in greeting. "And you are?"

Her hand got swallowed up by the giant's mitt, but his handshake was gentle. "Cherise Hillyer. I thought... she said Blue got fired."

Big John shook his head. "No! Technically, he resigned, but I prefer to think he just took some time off to be with his family. His father was sick."

"Yes, I know." She frowned. "Was sick?"

"He just passed."

"Oh!" Cherise put a hand to her mouth, tears suddenly welling up in her eyes.

"His funeral is today if I'm not mistaken. I'm glad Blue got to spend a bit of time with him before he went." The big man surveyed her through narrowed lids. "You're a friend, then?"

Cherise just nodded and let her gaze drift down to the black countertop.

"You're the one he's been pining over, I'll bet."

Cherise blinked and looked up.

Big John laughed. "Don't look so surprised. Blue is pretty closed mouthed about his private affairs, but I suspected he had a broken heart and something tells me you're the cause of it."

"Beth said -"

"Never mind what Beth said. I'm the one who pushed them together and as far as I can tell it didn't pan out."

"Oh. But they were a couple once?"

Big John cocked his head to one side. "That, I'm not quite sure about. Blue's a real gentleman and doesn't kiss and tell. Beth on the other hand, has a penchant for telling lies." He pinned Cherise with his eyes. "I don't know what she said to you, exactly, but whatever it is, just put it out of your mind. She has some serious issues, but this time she's crossed the line. I don't mind admitting it, even if she is the closest thing I have to a daughter on this planet."

Cherise nodded. "Okay. I'll try."

"Now, I'd say you've got a little drive ahead if you're going to make it in time for the funeral."

Cherise nodded again and on a whim reached over the counter to give the big man a hug. "Thank you!"

CHERISE STOOD ON THE OUTSKIRTS, watching as each of the Shepherd boys threw a spade full of dirt into the hole containing the casket. She wanted to rush to Blue's side, but knew he needed this time to focus on his father, not on any personal drama. Instead, she kept her feet planted and drank in the sight of his strong back and shoulders under his suit jacket, his hair curling around the collar.

With an intake of air, she listened to the minister's words of internment with new ears. He quoted scripture that said they would meet again in paradise, a fact she now embraced with her whole heart. She closed her eyes to say a little prayer of her own.

I believe it, Lord! Thank you, Jesus, for how you work things out, even in the midst of death. Please comfort Blue and Zane and the rest of the family and forgive me for putting my desires above the pain that they must be feeling. Help me just be a good friend.

Someone touched her shoulder and her eyes flew open.

"I didn't know you were coming." It was Stella.

"Neither did I," Cherise admitted as they threw their arms around one another for a lengthy hug.

"Come on." Stella pulled on Cherise's arm. Many of the onlookers were moving away from the graveside. Zane and Blue still stood together, gazing into the cavernous hole.

Cherise shook her head. "I should wait here."

"Why?"

"It's probably not the right time."

"He's going to need you," Stella said. "It's been a tough year - for all of us."

"What if he isn't happy to see me?" Cherise countered.

"Believe me, he will be."

Without further protest, Cherise allowed herself to be maneuvered forward. When they reached the spot where Zane and Blue stood above the casket, Stella released her and put her arms around Zane's waist from behind.

Cherise held her breath. She was just a few feet away from Blue, but he still hadn't noticed her presence.

When he finally turned, shock registered on his face as he saw her for the first time. "Cherise."

"Hi." She lifted her hand in a wave.

"I... I didn't expect to see you here."

"I just found out about your dad this morning. I am so sorry." Her voice hitched.

Blue's hands were clenched into fists by his side. "Thanks," he barely managed to squeeze out, his jaw working overtime to control his emotions.

Stella cleared her throat nearby. "We're going to give you two some privacy. We'll meet you at the reception hall in a bit."

Zane and Blue hugged one another, slapping each other on the back before Stella and Zane walked away hand in hand. Cherise watched them go, but finally turned back to Blue. He looked to be schooling himself somewhat and was shoving a used tissue into his jacket pocket. She waited for him to make the next move.

Blue gazed heavenward and sighed. Then he looked back down. "Walk with me?" he asked.

Cherise nodded.

Silently, he reached for her hand and she took it. She liked the feel of his calluses and the warmth of his palm in hers.

They picked their way past several stone markers to another section of the cemetery. Blue stopped in front of a large granite headstone with two names on it and pointed. "My grandparents. And over there are some cousins and an uncle. Course, Mom and Dad are next to each other now."

"Lots of family history."

Blue nodded. "I expect I'll be buried here someday, too."

"Not for awhile, I hope."

"No, not for awhile." There was a moment of silence as they both considered what to say next.

"Blue, I -"

He cut her off. "I was a fool. I never should have let you go. I should have come after you. Chased you down like they do in the movies."

Cherise blinked, taking it in.

"Course, that isn't what you want, and I get that. But maybe if I'd tried harder to make you understand. Make you see that -"

It was her turn to stop him. "No. I was the fool, not trusting in us."

Blue glanced at her. "So, you do still care, then?"

She nodded. "I never stopped caring."

Blue let out a self depreciating laugh. "I was crazy jealous while you were in Mexico."

"But managed to find time for your boss's niece?" Cherise raised a brow.

Blue frowned. "Beth?" He shook his head. "No. I admit I considered it, but thankfully we never actually did anything." He looked at Cherise again. "And that's the God honest truth, no matter what you might see on social media."

"Social media?" Cherise furrowed her brow.

"It's a long story."

"Speaking of God…" Cherise began.

Blue interrupted her again, taking both her hands in his. "Look, I know we started off on the wrong foot and I don't care about your past history or even what you've been doing right up until this minute. That's all in the past. I want to start again. Fresh. Take a chance with you if you're willing to take a chance with me."

"I'd like that except, some things have changed with me." She looked down at the ground.

He dropped her hands. "You met someone."

Cherise smiled. "Kind of. His name is Jesus."

Blue's eyebrows shot up. "What's that?"

"I gave my life to Jesus. I became a Christian. I thought maybe Stella would have said something to you."

Blue shook his head and smiled. "I'm… speechless."

Cherise smoothed his tie. "Not what you expected, I'm sure. I'm a different person now. And for the record, I have not been with anyone else since you."

TRACY KRAUSS

"Oh." He let out a sigh. "I said it didn't matter, but that's a lie. I might kill the next man who even looks at you."

"That's a bit drastic."

Blue looked at her with a twinkle. "You think? I'm feeling rather possessive." He took her hands again. "I've made some changes in my life, too."

"Oh?" She gazed into his very blue eyes.

He nodded. "I accepted Christ, too."

Her eyes widened and she threw her arms around his neck. "I can't believe how God has answered my prayers."

"Me neither." Blue held her back enough to study her face and then slowly lowered his head for a kiss.

The passion that seemed to ignite each time they touched was instantly fanned into flame. Cherise pulled away first. "This isn't appropriate here. Now."

"You're right, of course." Blue stepped back and ran a hand through his hair.

Cherise giggled. "I can see this is going to be harder than I thought."

"What's that?"

"The whole celibacy thing - with you."

"Guess we'll learn to pray harder." He arched a brow. "Unless…"

"Unless what?"

"We could just get married."

Cherise gasped and put a hand to her mouth.

"Is that a yes or a no?"

"Neither!"

"Not the response I had hoped for," he said with a frown.

"You just proposed to me at your father's funeral. Don't you find that a tad ironic?"

"Ironic? Pathetic might be the better word," Blue said. "From your response, I take it you need a bit more time."

"Making life changing decisions at funerals hasn't worked out for us in the past," she reminded.

"Don't forget weddings," he added.

"And weddings," she conceded.

Blue took her hands in his again. "I admit it's not the best timing, but for me there's no point in waiting. I know that I love you, Cherise, and that I want to spend the rest of my life with you."

"And I love you," she admitted. "But where will we live? We come from different worlds."

"So let's make our own world, together," he said. "We don't have to decide right away. We can elope and travel the world together. I'll pick up odd jobs and we'll figure it out as we go."

Cherise laughed. "Anything but cleaning toilets."

"I don't mind cleaning toilets, as long as I get to be with you," Blue said quite soberly.

Cherise searched his face. "You're serious, aren't you?"

He nodded. "As serious as I can be."

Cherise let a smile slowly creep across her face. "Then my answer is yes. We'll see the world together and make our own place in it." Blue dived in for a quick kiss, but Cherise continued. "And you're forgetting that I come with cash, so no toilets!"

Their lips locked in another passionate kiss until Blue pulled away and asked, "Anywhere in particular you want to go first?"

"I know this nice little orphanage down in Mexico…"

MORE IN THE SERIES

There's more in this series!

Stella and Cherise have both found true love, but what about their quiet friend, Tempest? Will she finally find what she's been looking for or will her past keep getting in the way? Follow the continuing trials of passion and faith for all the characters you've come to love in *Tempest Tossed*, the third book in the *Three Strand Cord* Series — a story full of danger, intrigue and redemption.
https://www.tracykrauss.com/books/tempest-tossed/

～

Miss book one? Get the full story in *THREE STRAND CORD*, the book that started it all.
https://www.tracykrauss.com/books/three-strand-cord/

OFFER

Join Tracy's mailing list and get up to date info on all new releases, promos and giveaways when they happen. You'll also get a free book!

https://tracykrauss.com
- fiction on the edge without crossing the line -

If you enjoyed this novel, or any of Tracy's books, please consider writing a review online. Reviews help readers find books they'll love and are tremendously helpful for today's authors. Thank you in advance!

ABOUT THE AUTHOR

Tracy Krauss writes contemporary Christian romance with a twist of suspense and a touch of humour. Her books strike a chord with those looking for a hard hitting yet thought provoking read. Her work has won multiple awards and has been on Amazon's bestsellers' lists. She also writes stage plays tailored to a high school audience, and has contributed to several anthologies, devotional books, and one illustrated children's book. Tracy has a Bachelor's degree from the University of Saskatchewan and taught secondary school Art, Drama and English—all things she is passionate about. She is a member of ACFW, The Word Guild, and Inscribe Christian Writers' Fellowship, a Canada wide organization for writers of Christian faith. She and her husband have lived in five provinces and territories including many remote and unique places in Canada's far north. They have four grown children and now reside in beautiful Tumbler Ridge, BC where she continues to pursue all of her creative interests. Visit her website for more: https://tracykrauss.com

Non-Fiction

Life is a Highway: Advice and Reflections On Navigating the Road of Life

Thirty Days of Targeted Prayer

Divine Appointments: Daily Devotionals Based On God's Calendar

Children's book

The Sleepytown Express